If I Let You Go

By Charlotte Levin

If I Can't Have You
If I Let You Go

CHARLOTTE LEVIN

If I Let You Go

MANTLE

First published 2023 by Mantle
an imprint of Pan Macmillan
The Smithson, 6 Briset Street, London EC1M 5NR
EU representative: Macmillan Publishers Ireland Ltd, 1st Floor,
The Liffey Trust Centre, 117–126 Sheriff Street Upper,
Dublin 1, D01 YC43
Associated companies throughout the world
www.panmacmillan.com

ISBN 978-1-5290-8409-2

1 3 5 7 9 8 6 4 2

A CIP catalogue record for this book is available from the British Library.

Typeset by Palimpsest Book Production Ltd, Falkirk, Stirlingshire
Printed and bound by CPI Group (UK) Ltd, Croydon, CR0 4YY

FSC
www.fsc.org
MIX
Paper | Supporting
responsible forestry
FSC® C116313

For McFly, who was the best keyboard-warmer
and friend a writer could have

'But it is not enough merely to exist . . . I need freedom, sunshine, and a little flower for a companion'

—*The Butterfly*, HANS CHRISTIAN ANDERSEN

Three sheets of paper lie side by side.

Edges must be neat, lined up. The contrast between their off-white and the black mock-granite of the worktop exposes any misalignments.

She's owned the stationery for years. A present from yet another drifted friend. Never retrieved from the cupboard, never having noticed the delicate goldfinches printed in the right-hand corner. One perched on a branch, the other flying away.

The pen is heavy and cold. Initially nervous about him finding out that she's used it, her brain catches up. Of course, it doesn't matter now. These notes need to represent her properly, and nice ink is important. She'd hate to be remembered by the scrawls of a worn-out biro.

Shuffling further back into the tall stool, she blinks, slow, heavy, and proceeds to write. Though all three notes differ in their content, each one opens with the same words.

I am sorry.

Life

1

A Small Stuffed Scottie Dog

She is invisible.

A living ghost riding the number seventy-three bus through the streets of Salford. Crisp cotton blue top, like scrubs, ironed to perfection, the XL label cut out and not just because it itched. All humanized by the name badge *JANET*. And, as always, a memorial to lost inner spark, sparkly earrings – half-moons bought by Colin many half-moons ago.

The fierce sun is a welcome break from the days of perpetual rain, and she rests her overheated head against the cool of the window to watch the daily rushes. Summer sky poking between penthouse-topped high-rises and poverty-stricken high-rises and red-brick daisy-chain houses as she nears home. All accented with colourful litter, pecked at by grey hobbled pigeons.

Sitting up straight, she digs into her bag and removes one of the mini Bakewells brought in by Sam for Gemma's last day. She'd already eaten one with her post-shift tea but couldn't resist the offer to take another home. Peeling the foil from its base, she presses the short pastry into her mouth.

She likes Sam. Despite being unable to get to know them properly, she likes all the Sam's Cleaning Angels girls. Especially Nish. And she enjoys the hours, ending her workday not long after the majority of people are about to start theirs. Few jobs offer such instant satisfaction. Except perhaps a chocolatier. But even then, cocoa loses its pleasure after a while; there's only so many Ferrero Rochers one can eat in a day. And she's good at it, cleaning. The other girls know not to touch her trolley. Compared to theirs, it is meticulous. Microfibre cloths stacked neatly when not in use, potions lined up, nozzles facing the same direction. The truth is, it calms her. Cleanliness, neatness. Dirt erased; surfaces shined. All the things we can't do with our souls can be achieved elsewhere with a damp cloth and some Cillit Bang.

The bus slows to standing. Released air pressure from the opening doors, echoes. A lad hugging a rucksack and dressed in an oversized suit takes the seat next to her. A young hoop-earringed mother, barely an adult herself, wearing a season-defying puffer jacket, struggles to board with a buggy and toddler. 'Fucking hell, Kian, I've had enough.'

To avoid looking over, Janet balances the foil tray containing the last bite of the Bakewell on her knee, then searches the back of her head for her hairband. Pulling it free, her dry home-bleached locks protrude in the same position as if glued. After stretching the elastic over her hand, onto her wrist, she places the remaining tart in her mouth.

But she can't prevent another glance.

The young mother is staring into her phone. The child is distressed, crying.

While chewing, Janet pinches the black-threaded elastic between her thumb and index finger, lifts it taut like a catapult, and snaps it against the blue-threaded skin of her inner wrist. Wincing as it reddens and stings.

Aware that the suited boy has followed the sound and is

looking, she drops her head and brushes the crumbs from her trousers, then neatly folds the aluminium tray into a square and returns it to her bag.

But it's back.

The wave, the feeling. Crawling like ants beneath her top, over her skin, burrowing into her bones.

Willing her mouth free of the frangipane paste, she strokes her throat. Assisting the clagging tart to pass the newly formed lump.

'Kian . . . Kian . . . for fuck's sake, you won't get no sweets now, you cry-baby.'

He *is* a baby. He *is* a baby.

The heat has lit Janet's veins like a wick. Making her feel as if she's unable to breathe or swallow. Snapping the elastic again helps only momentarily.

The young mother grabs the child from behind and plonks him onto her knee. 'Jesus Christ, Kian,' she says, eyes glued to her phone's screen. But then, she does something equally hard to watch. She kisses his head.

'Excuse me.' Janet shuffles past the lad and extends her shaking finger to press the bell. The bus slows to a standstill and she moves unsteadily towards the door, then steps onto the unfamiliar pavement, three stops too early.

Hand on chest, she calms her heart. She's on Butterstile Lane in front of the small parade of shops that she usually stares into from the discomfort of the bus seat, watching folk go about their business, exhibiting their freedoms.

Central to these shops is OBJÉT. An establishment so out of place among the beauty salon, Chinese takeaway and newsagent's, it's as though the owners accidentally signed a lease thinking it was elsewhere.

The window display houses beautiful objects, unsurprisingly. Sumptuous, embroidered velvet cushions. Painted ceramic bowls she'd feel perturbed using for her Special K. A pair of wooden candlesticks which she isn't quite as keen on. All obscured by the tasteful *Closing Down* banner. It has only been open for six months. A stark reminder that shops, like people, should know their place.

According to her watch, it's almost 10 a.m. She needs to start walking to her dad's but instead she stands still for a moment, mouthing the calculations of how much time she could feasibly spend inside the shop.

Satisfied it's manageable, she pushes on the heavy glass door.

Inside, a woman rolls an ornament into soft pink tissue paper. Her glossy severe bob falling in front of her face as she lifts her head and forces a *Can I help you?* smile.

Admiring the woman's ruby lips, Janet touches her own, wishing she'd dare to attempt such a shade.

'Everything is fifty per cent off.'

The sound of sticky tape being pulled from a dispenser magnifies in the stillness of the space.

Janet flickers a smile. 'Thanks.' Then, remembering she's still in her uniform, strokes her earrings in an attempt to redirect the woman's focus. Her other hand remains on display, gripping the strap of her bag to ensure it's clear she isn't shoplifting. Not that she's stolen anything in her life. Except the time she accidentally bought a nest of small-to-large Tupperware from Debenhams without realizing they were supposed to have been sold separately. And to this day, she suffers twinges of guilt every time she scrapes in leftover Bolognese.

Investigating the shop, she craves its entire contents.

'Are you looking for anything particular?'

'No . . . well, a little present for my daughter.'

'Oh, lovely. Is it for a special occasion?'

Janet pivots. Turns her back on the woman. Suddenly not caring if she's thought a thief or not. 'Her birthday.'

'Oh, lovely, well, if you buy something, I'll throw in a card for free.'

Looking over her shoulder, to smile and thank the woman, Janet notices in the children's section a small stuffed Scottie dog, sporting a red collar from which swings a heart-shaped pendant. She's transported back to the park when Claire was a littlun. Skipping ahead in her tutu and Ariel T-shirt. Waving to every dog in sight, running towards them. *Don't touch, Claire, we have to ask the owners if the doggies like being stroked.* The explosion of excitement with each ungainly pat. Shoulders raised, frantic hands waving, feet padding the floor.

'How much is the dog?' asks Janet, pointing.

'You can have him for four pounds . . . He's cute, isn't he?'

'He is, yes.' She performs the maths in her head. Concluding she could still take the bus home from her dad's but walk to work on Monday. 'That's fine, I'll take him please.'

The woman glides from behind the counter, clothes not as pristine as expected. Her skirt distinctly creased.

'Sorry, I could have got it down myself,' says Janet. 'It's all I'm good for at this height . . . I wasn't sure if I—'

'Not a bother.' The woman is reaching up on tiptoes and

with summoning fingers captures the toy. Heels dropped, she tucks in her shirt, which had escaped during the stretch.

Back at the till, she pops the Scottie into a thick paper bag, begins padding him in with the pink tissue.

It's now 10.12 a.m.

'That's OK . . . I'm in a bit of a hurry, sorry.'

The tissue, already half inside, is pushed in fully and the bag sealed with a sticker printed with the shop's emblem. 'Are you paying cash or card?'

'Cash.'

'Do you want to pick your greeting card?'

'Oh . . . no, I don't need one,' she says. 'Thank you, though.'

'Are you sure? You can have any. They've got to go.'

To avoid any further verbal ping-pong, Janet walks over to the rack and extracts a white card that simply says, *I Love You.*

Transaction complete, she turns to leave. Hand on door, she smiles, pleased with both her purchase and rebellion.

'Bye,' says the woman. 'I hope she has a fantastic birthday.'

Janet stops. The words a bullet in her back.

It is as violent as ever. She hadn't managed to stop it at all. It was merely dormant, ready to explode.

This time she imagines lunging forward. Smashing her face into the glass with such force her ears ring with the crack of her teeth. Then pulling back, slow, calm, she observes the illusory blood-soaked, shattered cobweb.

'Thank you,' she says, and leaves.

2

A Window Overlooking a Car Park

For the remainder of the walk to her dad's, she takes the scenic route. Otherwise known as the cut-through by the leisure centre. A honeysuckle-scented dust track sandwiched between brambles, clustered with blackberries in bloom, awaiting the birth of their fruits. With the sun so intense, she pretends she's on holiday in the countryside. Until eventually emerging from the other end, where the sound of speeding traffic snaps her from the fantasy and car fumes tickle her throat. She decides from now on she'll always get off at that earlier stop. It's important to have something to look forward to.

'Hi Helen, it's Janet.' She dips to speak into the intercom.

The name Oakland House implies an idyllic country mansion, not a 1980s-built care home slap-bang in the middle of Salford. Her dad has been a resident for almost seven years. Moving in soon after her mother's death. His deterioration exacerbated, or perhaps more apparent, when mixed with grief. It was a struggle to make the decision alone, her brother Craig, useless and half a world away in New Zealand. The chasm of their relationship greater than the air miles.

Once buzzed in, she follows the colour-coded floral border to his room. She's always been partial to a border herself. At one point, their whole house was split horizontally by a four-inch burgundy fleur-de-lis. But even she knows there's no place for them in modern spaces and hasn't so much as contemplated one since 2012.

It's bluebells for the ground floor. Her mum's favourite flowers. However neat her beds of pansies, it was always the wild tufts of bluebells at the bottom of their garden that she loved the most. He'd be living with Janet had it not been vetoed by Colin. Probably for the best. It's unlikely she'd be able to give him adequate care. But this border, which she cannot help but trace with her fingers as it leads her down the corridor, was the only thing that made his move bearable. A sign of her mother's approval.

Registering music, she stops walking. 'Boogie Woogie Bugle Boy'. She'd forgotten about the entertainments now happening on the first Friday of each month. Turning, she follows the swing rhythm, and once at the communal lounge, she hovers outside the open door and observes.

There he is. In the corner, slouched in his favourite bat-winged chair. Even from this distance she can see the distinct white crust on his navy jumper. They don't seem to grasp how smart he likes to look. But at least he's smiling.

A skeleton wearing trousers, his legs jig to the music as he watches the performers. The Goldies Choir, according to the 'What's On' corkboard.

Roger sits on one side of him, Dorothy on the other. Her mottled hand inching towards his mottled hand. Never daring to touch. It's clear she believes herself to be his girlfriend, despite his obliviousness to this arrangement. And although Janet knows it doesn't matter, that he doesn't love Dorothy in any tangible way, she still feels somewhat aggrieved on behalf of her mother.

Jazz hands in action, the Goldies, dressed in black tracksuits with their logo in gold glitter on the front, bop from side to side as they sing. Most look like they belong in the home themselves. The presumed leader, a Barbara Cartland doppelgänger, is positioned front and centre, intermittently turning to waft her arms towards the rest of the troupe.

Watching her dad mouth the lyrics, enjoying himself, offers Janet a moment of joy. Especially as she presumes that he's thinking about her mum. How she'd always be jiving around the house. Putting out her hand for him to join her. 'Don't be bloody daft, Eileen,' he'd say in mock irritation, unable to disguise his pride, looking at her as if she was Rita Hayworth. 'You had the last dance you'll ever get out of me.'

They met at the Ritz in town. Dancing in the Dark night. When the lights would go out for the last dance, enabling couples to kiss. She was only twenty, and he was approaching thirty. The story goes that as they took to the floor for the first time, he said, 'Not bad for a wooden leg, eh?'

When she died, Janet didn't think he'd survive the loss. But that was misguided. Survival is easy. It's the living that's hard.

The song ends, followed by applause. Thinking it's all over, she steps inside the room, but Barbara Cartland declares they're about to start their final number.

Closing her eyes, Janet's shoulders sink with frustration. Time is trickling away, and she needs to talk to him. Today more than ever.

The intro is immediately recognizable. 'We'll Meet Again'.

All the old dears come to life. Her dad's smile widens. Most of them would have only been kids during the war, but somehow Vera Lynn induces instinctual camaraderie.

As her dad closes his eyes, belts out the song, Janet joins in quietly from the shadows. She loves a good singalong. Though Colin insists she sounds like an injured frog. Never knowing what that meant until next door's tabby caught one in their garden and the screaming . . . anyway, she doesn't sing much around the house.

It's funny how she knows the lyrics so well, but it's the first time she really hears them. That's what she does. Smiles through it all. And it's exhausting.

Helen passes with a tray of crumbs, presumably having once contained cakes or scones or some other delight. 'You all right, Janet, love?'

When she looks up, her vision is blurred, and she realizes she's crying. 'Oh yes, just . . . it's nice, isn't it? The singing.' Dropping her head again, she ensures her hair covers her face while rooting in her bag for a tissue. Helen momentarily places a hand on her shoulder, then continues towards the kitchen.

In her dad's room, she shadows him as he inches towards his chair. Banning her from helping, he's regressed to a stubborn toddler who can manage by himself. Breathing through her impatience, she glances towards the large wall clock displaying the hastening time.

'You enjoyed that, didn't you, Dad?'

'Enjoyed what?'

'The singing.'

'I didn't like it, no.' He feels for the well-worn arm, while she presses the button, raising the seat to meet his bony bottom. An act they've perfected.

'Yes, you did, Dad, I watched you,' she says, lowering the chair with him now ensconced. 'Is that porridge on your jumper?' Once he's reached a sitting position, she licks her finger and rubs at the crust.

'You can't sing, you know, Janet. Your mum and I were too nice to tell you when you'd put on your plays for us, but no . . . you're dreadful.'

She walks over to the window and pulls back the curtains to invite more sun, annoyed that it hasn't been done already, that the carers are so slapdash. 'I need to Glowhite these nets, Dad. They look the colour of my bras . . . and we need to brighten it up in here. I can't bear it.' He'd always talked about retiring by the sea. To his hometown of Pwllheli. Enjoying the views of the ocean and Snowdonia. And he's ended up with a window overlooking a car park.

She sits on the chair opposite his, clutching both her handbag and the paper one from the shop.

'Your mum said she'll do the net curtains when she gets back.' He turns on the TV, the *Hello Britain* theme tune blasting at a million decibels. Gently, she removes the remote from his hand, reduces the volume and activates the subtitles, catching the time on her watch. It's getting late. She wants to talk to him. Needs to talk to him.

'It's Claire's birthday, Dad. Her eighteenth. I bought this . . . look.' She peels away the sticker seal and delves into the tissue to remove the dog. 'It's cute, isn't it? Always mad about animals, Claire. From being a littlun.'

He takes it from her. She's uncomfortable about him

touching it, though she smiles and allows him to continue. He presses the fur against his dirty jumper, strokes its head. 'I have a dog. Bertie. Bertie . . . Bertie,' he calls out.

'He's gone for a walk.'

'Ah yes, your mum took him out. She should be back by now . . . Do you think she's OK?'

'She's fine, Dad.'

He grins at the toy and kisses it gently on the snout.

'Sorry, I . . . I don't want it to get dirty.' She slides it from his fingers. 'Sorry, I'll get you one too if I can.' She places it back into the bag, reseals it. 'You remember Claire, don't you, Dad?'

'Claire? Of course I do.'

Relief rides through her on a wave of comfort.

'Let's talk about her,' she says.

3

Little Mermaid Duvet

Time is slipping away, and she's poised by the exit of the bus, ready to jump off at her stop. Heart sinking as the train station scrolls by and her eyes catch the outside railings festooned with a mix of fresh flowers and vivid silk blooms. Only a couple of weeks prior, Colin had received a fine after being snapped parking on a double yellow line for the short time it took Janet to draw money from the cash machine and then for Colin to press her weekly allowance into her hand. Yet a teenager can get stabbed to death on a station platform and there are no working CCTV cameras.

Distressing floral tributes aside, she still can't help but fantasize about asking to be let off the bus, entering the train station, buying a ticket, and leaving. It's always just that, of course. A fantasy. She knows she must stay. Pay penance. The easier option of going to prison granted to someone else.

Finally, it's her stop. As soon as her feet hit the concrete, she near sprints down the road past St Mary's Primary School. Playground screams threaten to slice her, so she concentrates hard on blocking them out.

Turning the corner into the estate, then entering the cul-de-sac, their recently gravelled drive is dazzling and, thankfully, empty. But relief doesn't slow her, soothe her nerves. Her breaths remain sharp as she strides the last few yards, burning, sweating, like the oily column of meat in the window of the nearby takeaway, AbraKebabra. She focuses on her destination, avoiding catching the eyes of her opposite neighbour, Mary 'Gossip-Gob' Clarke, who's currently balancing on a stepladder, watering one of her ever-expanding hanging baskets.

Once at the door, her damp fingers slide over the metal as she inserts the key and enters the comparative cool of the dark, windowless hallway.

Bending forward to recover, her spirit sinks.

She never has liked this house. Even with the new gilt birdcage-patterned hall wallpaper and chemical-scented fresh paint, it's not right. Even with the wall of excessive mirrors she asked Colin to buy after watching a programme about creating the illusion of space – it feels oppressive. So different from their Victorian terrace in Eccles twenty years ago. With its tall ceilings and large bay windows. Leaking roof and dodgy boiler. This house was built in the eighties. The roof is secure. The boiler has a seven-year warranty which, rather than being a comfort, fills her with despair. It is warm and soulless and low-ceilinged. And then there's the trains. The constant trains, speeding down the tracks beyond the garden, shaking her foundations.

But Claire grew up here. All those memories wrapped in the magnolia walls. She won't ever leave. Not alive, anyway. That's the point of cul-de-sacs. You can't pass through.

Entering the lounge, she contemplates taking a quick peek at the Psychic Channel but accepts she doesn't have time. Anyway, she doubts it will be her favourite clairvoyant, Jason Quartz. He's not been on there for a while.

She drops her bags onto the sideboard, being careful not to knock her beloved collection of Royal Doulton lady figurines. After unravelling the dog from its tissue nest and placing it in her pocket, she carries the packaging through to the kitchen.

The back-door key is stiff in its lock, but once wiggled open she heads outside and down the side of the house. She never takes out the rubbish. Colin's good like that. While scanning for spying eyes she opens the refuse bin, removes some of the stinking sacks and drops in the now crumpled paper, then replaces the bin bags, ensuring nothing can be seen. Satisfied, she returns to the kitchen, and presses the door shut behind her.

After hurriedly washing her hands, she throws open the bread bin, grabs four slices of Kingsmill and slaps them on the cutting board. Retrieves butter, ham and mustard from the fridge, removes lids in record time and stabs a knife into the spreadable carton, before bounding upstairs to dry her sweat-knitted locks and darkened pits. The hairdryer flex pulled into the hall so she can listen out for the front door.

With all signs of rushing erased, she runs back down and places a slice of ham onto the bread just in time for the sound of tyres on the driveway.

She fills the kettle, removes a mug from the cupboard, pops in a teabag and returns to the sandwich, and as if a switch has flicked, in a calm, slow manner, spreads the butter against the white dough, preparing her smile. 'Hello. It's hot, isn't it?' she shouts.

He appears in the doorway of the kitchen. Short-sleeved shirt, damp, sticking to his body, the hair-free central section of his head buffed shiny by the sun. His right arm significantly browner than the left. It's funny how their twelve-year age gap seemed nothing when in her thirties. But fast-forward nearly twenty years, and she's frequently taken aback by how she's married to someone who will soon be entitled to claim his state pension. 'Is ham and mustard all right?'

He places his keys on the allocated hook on the wall. A reminder that hers are still in her pocket, so she removes them and does the same.

'Lovely, yes, thank you,' he says, rubbing his hand across the back of his neck then wiping his palm against his thigh, slightly staining the beige of his trousers. 'I had a fare to Didsbury, that's why I'm late.'

'Oh, what time is it? I hadn't noticed . . . Why don't you go in the other room, and I'll bring it to you.'

He's sitting in his chair when she enters, Clarks shoes at its side, feet now encased in his tartan slippers. An episode of *Columbo* plays on the TV. He's half watching and half eyeing his laptop, ogling cars on that Goodwood Revival site again.

Clocking her, he places the laptop on the floor, holds out his arms, and widens his little legs to create a more solid foundation for the tray. She moulds the beanbag underside into his thighs, then straightens, watches him tuck in.

'Oh, that's a good sandwich, that . . . Bloody hell, that's Faye Dunaway there, look, in *Columbo.* I never knew she did a *Columbo.* Did you?'

'I think so . . . I don't know.'

'Now that – that's what a beautiful woman looks like, Janet.'

Glimpsing the paste forming as he chews, slack-jawed, she turns in disgust and notices the OBJÉT receipt on the floor by the sideboard. Queasy at her carelessness, she goes over and swoops it up, screwing it into a ball.

'Oh, just one more thing,' says Colin.

She doesn't turn. 'Yes?'

'I was being Columbo, Janet.' He tuts.

'Oh, I see.' She gives him her best laugh, but what she really wants to do is remind him about Gemma's leaving drinks that evening. Even though she's already made her excuses because she knows what he'll say. But staring towards the crumpled paper in her hand, that earlier feeling of rebellion returns. 'I took some éclairs out of the freezer last night. I'll get you one.'

She places the pastry and steaming tea on his tray, waits for him to take a bite, become lost in the enjoyment of the cream and chocolate hitting his taste buds. Lengthening her spine, she makes herself as tall as she can. Which is tall. Four inches taller than he is, even when he's wearing his Simon Cowell chunky-heeled shoes. 'Colin, I . . . You know it's . . . Well, it's Gemma's leaving do tonight, remember? It was arranged a while ago. I . . . I feel like I should go.'

After taking his time finishing the mouthful, he reaches for the remote and turns down the TV. Carefully places the tray on the floor, then rotates in his chair to look directly at her. 'How would I remember? When it's the first I've heard of it.'

'It's . . . it's not, Colin, I asked you last week. You said you'd consider it.'

'I think I would have remembered that. Don't you?'

She does nothing, says nothing. Having learned this is the best thing to do.

'You know they only ask you to these things out of politeness, don't you? They're all young, Janet. They don't want some menopausal woman tagging along, cramping their style.'

She allows the wave to wash over her. Remains still. A rock that will erode so much, she may one day transform into a shiny pebble on a beach.

'They're starting early doors . . . so I could just show my face. If you dropped me off and picked me up, I'd be back in time for that documentary on the Falklands you want to watch.' Her hand slides inside her pocket, squeezes the toy for comfort.

He turns, restores the volume on the TV. 'OK.'

'Really?' Her palm reaches for her chest.

'If you want to go where you're not wanted, then that's up to you.'

Light with excitement, she bounds upstairs. She hasn't socialized since . . . well, so long her brain can't quite comprehend she's going.

Once changed into her dressing gown, she transfers the black dog into one of the pockets and chucks her work top into the linen basket. While hanging up her trousers ready for Monday, she considers what to wear. The jumper he'd bought her several Christmases ago, unworn, ticket hanging from its arm, immediately becomes the main contender.

While deliberating which trousers would look best, she goes out to the landing and stands there. Motionless. Kidding herself that she's attempting to resist. Until she steps forward and presses down on the handle, slow and quiet, so as not to be heard above Peter Falk's voice.

On opening the door, she sees Claire lying on her slight, midriff-exposed belly upon her Little Mermaid duvet, watching TV. Knees bent, toes pointing to the ceiling, feet wiggling like fins.

There are other duvet covers, but this is Janet's favourite. All the giggles at tucking-in time after Claire's transformation into Ariel. Though it clashes with the unicorn wallpaper and *High School Musical* poster above the white wrought-iron bedhead.

The bedding needs washing and ironing; the poster is faded. Janet crosses the room to the dressing table. Looks into the heart-shaped plastic mirror. Never Faye Dunaway, but now, something unrecognizable.

Claire's jewellery is kept neat. Mainly old beads Janet had given her, hung precisely on the branches of a miniature gold tree. Make-up, allowed for dressing-up purposes only, is stored tidily on a tray. The animal trinkets and ornaments, collected like an old lady, are precisely positioned.

Janet removes the dog from her pocket. 'I've bought you this for your birthday,' she whispers. After kissing the toy, she places it with care between the piggy bank and tiny ceramic kitten. Both dusty. It's all dusty. Changing her mind, not wanting it spoiled, she returns the dog to her dressing gown, then leaves for the airing cupboard on the landing to retrieve her cleaning caddy.

Back in the room she places the potions and cloths on the floor, then spritzes the mirror with luminous yellow fluid, causing the air to suffuse with the aroma of synthetic citrus. Duster in hand, she watches as the droplets cascade down the glass, unveiling Claire's reflection. *Why didn't you save me, Mummy?*

'Don't get in the shower yet, I need the toilet.' Colin is coming up the stairs.

'I'm not, the bathroom's free.' Her voice is forced light and breezy. Traces of chemical sting her eyes as she blots her face with the back of her hand. Willing him to go straight to the bathroom.

'What are you doing?' He's standing in the doorway, today's newspaper in hand. Head dropped to avoid facing the room.

She turns and starts to rub at the mirror. 'It was so dusty, Colin . . . I thought I'd give it a little clean, with it being her birthday. I haven't been in here such a long time, like you said . . . But—'

'Do you think it matters how clean it is?' His hand bangs against the door frame, making her jump. 'I'll have to lock it up again, if you insist on . . . this shrine, it's not healthy. What about me, Janet? I can't cope with it . . . I don't like seeing it.'

She turns back to him, face puckered with pain. 'It's her birthday. I just wanted to do something nice.'

He tightens his grip on the paper and, addressing the floor, says, 'You can't redeem yourself, you know. No amount of cleaning will erase what you did.' He turns and walks away. She remains still until she hears the bathroom door closing and returns to the mirror, wraps her finger within the cloth, and concentrates on removing a mark.

It's five thirty.

She's downstairs, hovering by the sofa. Inhaling the manufactured coconut scent of her hair treatment. The jumper is resting a little tight around the middle. Fine white knit is always unforgiving. But she likes how the sequined swallow on the front sparkles and catches the light. On the bottom half, she wears some old pale pink slacks and her faithful M&S silver ballet pumps. Across her body sits a little black beaded bag that doesn't really go, but at least she won't have the worry of it being stolen if she's dancing. Although, she suspects that stage of the evening won't happen until she's tucked up in bed.

After rubbing her lips together to disperse the fuchsia gloss that came free with a magazine, she says, 'I'm ready whenever you are.'

He mutes the TV. Turns, looks her up and down, then returns to watching the screen, instantly laughing at the silent footage of a woman falling into a ditch. 'I'm sorry, Janet, but I've been thinking, it's not right you going out tonight.'

Her breath catches, eyes prick. 'But I . . . I'm all ready now.'

'It's not right you going to the pub the night of Claire's birthday. Do you have any idea how selfish and uncaring that would make you look? No, I'm sorry, Janet. It's out of the question.'

'But . . . they don't even know it's her—'

'They don't even know?' He stands to face her and the room fills with the click of his knee joints. 'You've not even bothered to tell them?' Red creeps up his neck. 'Is that the jumper I bought you?'

'It is, yes.' She smiles. Hating herself for the attempt to placate. 'I've not had the chance to wear it yet.'

'I should have bought the next size up.'

She stares at him. Allows the wave to pass.

'Please, enough about it now, hey . . . I don't want you to go and that's that. Why don't you get back into your dressing gown, all nice and comfy, and I'll make you a cup of tea and that éclair you didn't have.'

Dropping her head, she closes her eyes and whispers, 'Colin, please . . . I'm begging you.'

'Jesus, Janet. All I want is a little respect for Claire. You know what I . . . No. No, I've got to get out of here.' His arm knocks hers as he pushes past.

She remains still, rigid, until she registers the familiar clinking sound coming from the kitchen and follows him in there. 'What are you doing?'

'I'm going to the depot.' He puts both sets of keys in his pocket, then goes to the back door and yanks that one from the lock.

'Colin, please don't. You know I don't like it. Stay, and we can watch that documentary.'

Stopping dead, he closes his eyes for a moment as if in contemplation. On reopening them, he walks over to her, reaches his hand around the back of her neck, and pulls her down to enable him to kiss her forehead. 'I know I keep saying it, but we'll book a table at that new Nico's place, I promise. You can wear the jumper then.'

Releasing her, he leaves the kitchen for the hall, Janet his shadow.

'Please, Colin. It frightens me.'

'Why don't you have a nice bath? Use that candle I bought you.'

The image of his hand on the front-door latch induces the crawl of claustrophobia.

He turns and sighs. 'I don't want to, but it's for the best. You can't be trusted to do the right thing.' With that he opens the door and leaves.

The sound of the turning Chubb lock rattles loud against the silence.

4

Like Normal People

She doesn't cry or scream. *If a tree falls in a forest.*

He'll be back soon. Acting as though nothing's happened. Barging through with a takeaway telling her to grab plates, that the documentary is about to start. And she'll be too weary to argue. Merely relieved she's no longer trapped.

But now, heat radiates throughout her body as if she's being burned at the stake. Running to the lounge, she opens the top windows, craving air. Palm smacking against the unopenable bottom pane.

Mary is standing on the pavement opposite, talking to that Roni woman from number thirty. Police officer husband, three kids, unsightly caravan in the driveway. Mary, alert to all twitches of net curtains, waves over. Janet forces a smile and returns the gesture, before sliding away from the lace like a bride removing her veil.

Armed with an éclair and tea, too drained to even go upstairs and change, she watches the Psychic Channel.

It's that Hazel, the clairvoyant she dislikes the most. All phony eye-rolls and henna hair. No sign of Jason Quartz. So she scrolls through the channels, stopping on *Gardeners' World*. Monty Don would be the perfect husband. Dogs and gardens.

Constant tips for her roses. What more could anyone want? Apart from living by the sea of course. She's certain he'd occasionally do the washing-up as well.

She'd hoped the programme would soothe. But the chocolate and cream rests heavy on her still-tense stomach. Once finished, she puts the empty plate on the side table and slips off her shoes, draws up her legs. Hand cupping her stomach as she did eighteen years prior. While plumping a cushion and placing it under her head, she notices Colin's shoes still next to the chair. The knowledge that he stormed out wearing his slippers gives her a moment of satisfaction before she does what she always does when she can't take any more, be any more – she switches off, android-like, and goes to sleep.

When she wakes, pulse speeding, the clock on the mantel reads ten past seven.

The contractions had begun around this time. On their old sagging sofa. Janet doubled over, calling out for Colin. And he, as always in moments of stress, only thinking to offer up a cup of tea.

Swivelling to sitting, she rubs the back of her neck, which is slippery with sweat. Her feet feel for her ballet pumps. 'Colin?' She would have heard him come in, surely.

She walks over to the sideboard and lifts the receiver of the dated, corded and rarely used phone which sits next to her porcelain ladies, ruining their aesthetic. Adrenaline-fuelled fingers dial his number. It rings once, twice, the third time voicemail. She slams it down.

*

Leaning against the island, she watches the water through the kettle's transparent centre. Boiling. Bubbling. She'd always wanted an island, so they added one two years ago with a whole new fitted kitchen from Wickes. But the space is too small really, and she often wants to shove the bastard thing out of the way.

Her exposed flesh enjoys the cool as it presses against the worktop. Still waiting, she stares inanely towards the back door. There's an unsightly black smudge on the PVC. Though even she cannot muster the energy to clean it off at that moment.

The kettle switches.

As do her thoughts.

She recalls earlier. The paper bag, the bins.

But what she doesn't recollect is re-locking the door.

Slowly, she walks towards it. Places her hand on the heavy metal handle, presses down. The sound of the seal unsticking. She pushes, extends her arm. The door moves with the motion.

It's open.

Releasing the handle, she steps back.

There's a garden party going on a few houses down. Talking, laughter. The dull thud of music. Is that what people do? Have friends around, go to parties, exist beyond work and their four walls. The gathering is momentarily drowned by a passing train. The entire kitchen trembles slightly, or maybe it's only her.

She uses her foot to further open the door. The lawn now visible, mowed by Colin on Wednesday.

And her roses. The only things that bring her joy. Each year, a visiting friend. Faithful, beautiful. Smelling of a fresh start, of life.

She stares at her freedom. Then reaches for the handle, and gently pulls the door shut.

Back in the lounge, she rings Colin again. Voicemail. But this time when she replaces the receiver, a match strikes inside her belly, setting light to resentments. Yanking open one of the sideboard drawers, she rifles through a laminated pocket of paperwork. The bank statements of Mr Colin A. Brown. The credit column frequented by her wages. A for Archibald. The middle name he doesn't like to publicize, thus creating enjoyable moments for Janet when it needs to be declared. Beneath them, a statement from her own account – Mrs Janet Amelia Brown. As always, only ever showing £1.86. Except when there's the irregular and fleeting flow of birthday or Christmas spends to keep her account alive. And buried under these and the utility bills is her paisley padded address book, which she removes and drops onto the sideboard, opens to the letter N, and dials the only entry. Cream rises towards her throat, as she's now willing Nish not to pick up. With relief, she doesn't.

Janet returns to the sofa. Sups her tea. Plays the part of someone happily watching the television. The gardening has ended. Mary Berry is now prodding the soggy bottom of a pecan pie.

It's nearly eight. Her waters broke around now. The shocking gush. Colin's petrified face, then framed with a wave of salt and pepper hair.

Forcing herself to be present, to watch the programme, she

lets out a deep breath and sinks into the sofa. But as soon as her back hits the velour cushion, the phone rings.

She freezes.

It's still going, shrill and intrusive. She puts down the mug, stands and slowly walks towards the sideboard, hoping the ringing will stop before she arrives. But it doesn't. 'Hello?'

'Hey . . . did you call me? Is everything OK? Are you coming out?' Nish is practically shouting, although the background music sounds faint. It's clear she's sucking on a cigarette.

'Yes, sorry. I . . . I was wondering how it was going, that's all. I'm really sorry I couldn't come, I—'

'When are you going to get a mobile like normal people? Anyway, I thought you were on your special meal with Colin . . . Excuse me, those three are done, but I'm still drinking this . . . Sorry, Janet, I'm a bit pissed. I don't know how because I've only had . . . actually yeah, I'm pissed. We're at the Chinese place in Eccles now.'

'Well, you have a lovely—'

'The karaoke place . . . you've got to come then if you're finished. We can do a duet, "I Got You Babe". We've got to—'

'No, no, I can't . . . I'm feeling stuffed after the meal, and anyway, Colin has had to nip to see a friend and he's accidentally taken my card, so I've got no money. I shouldn't have disturbed you . . . Go on, you go and have fun.' For such an honest person, lies slide from her tongue like satin.

'You don't need money, you silly cow. Get a cab . . . I'll pay this end.' She takes a loud drag on a cigarette. 'Janet,' she whispers. 'You know I love you . . . I do, Janet, I think you're brilliant, but I'm gonna be straight with you because I'm pissed . . . I think it's a bit shit that you haven't come to say goodbye to Gemma.'

Janet clamps her eyes shut. Immediately feels the desire to cry as she wraps the telephone cord tighter around her whitening hand. 'I know . . . I'm really sorry. You know what I'm like.'

'Well, get your arse down here then, for fuck's sake. I'll have a vodka and Coke waiting for you . . . I'm coming,' she shouts to someone. 'Look, I've got to go. I'm doing "Angels". Hurry the fuck up.'

'I can't, Nish, really I can't—'

The line goes dead.

5

Thelma Without Louise

Wide-eyed and frozen, like a Pompeii victim, she's perched on the top deck front seat of the number forty-three. Clutching her beaded bag, now laden with the useable contents of Claire's piggy bank.

She stands, needs to get off. Rectify her terrible mistake.

But the bus is pulling away from the stop, driving off, jolting her back down.

It's done now.

Trying to relax, she reasons with herself. There's no punishment that he hasn't inflicted before. What's the worst he could do? Lock up Claire's room? It amazes her that he thinks she doesn't know where he keeps the key.

Leaning towards her distorted image in the window, she's conscious that her make-up must have smudged by now. It went unchecked before leaving the house. Nish's call had illuminated the absurdity of the situation. And during *Bake Off's* strawberry tart technical, she felt wild. Wild with anger. And before she knew it, she was in Claire's room ransacking her unspent pocket money.

Removing a tissue from the bag, she erases migrating mascara. An explanation for the sniggering girls she'd encountered at the bus stop in their tight dresses and those platform shoes that Janet always feels looks somewhat orthopaedic. Without a proper mirror it's impossible to identify the intricacies of her face. But it will have to do.

As the journey continues, she alternates between peaks of excitement and fear, disbelief, at what she's done. Leaning towards the latter as the distance from home stretches behind. These repetitive thoughts are thankfully broken by the thud of passengers coming up the stairs.

Via the window's reflection she can see it's a young couple holding on to polystyrene boxes filled with potent-smelling fish and vinegary chips. She'd love to turn and pinch one, a much-needed savoury antidote to the cream curdling inside her stomach.

'OK, road trip films – go,' mumbles the girl, gob filled.

'Erm . . . *Thelma and Louise.*'

Janet's mouth kinks upwards at the corner. For right now she is Thelma. Without Louise. Older, plainer, bigger. Instead of that wondrous vintage Thunderbird, a bus that smells of urine and chip shops. But for this moment, she is Thelma.

The karaoke bar is above a Chinese restaurant called the Happy Dumpling.

Although Janet has never been before, she's listened to endless stories of fun evenings spent at this favourite haunt of the girls.

Positioned down a cobbled alleyway full of overflowing bins, scattered with smokers and snoggers, she looks up to the first-floor windows flashing blue and green. Colin invades her thoughts. Him arriving home. Raging beyond anything she could imagine. Regretting not letting her have a mobile phone.

Inhaling deeply, she pushes open the door, wondering if it's too late to order some prawn balls.

Breathless from climbing the steep flight of stairs, she loiters in the doorway, observes the space. It resembles a school disco. A huge room inhabited by clusters of awkward people at various stages on the intoxication scale. Some attempting to appear cool, sipping on their drinks while indulging in stiff off-beat semi-static dance movements. Their bodies sliced with criss-crossing colourful lasers. Beamed from either side of a booth in which sits a bearded DJ in a Hawaiian shirt.

'Oh my god.' A screaming barefoot Nish is hurtling her way over. Extended arms the only body part unrestricted by her orange dress. The launched hug is tight and heartfelt, but Janet feels so lumpen attached to tiny Nish, who's repeating variations of 'I can't believe you're here.' Janet smiles, unable to express that however much Nish can't believe it, she is infinitely more disbelieving.

Nish is the nearest thing she has to a friend. All others gone before, pushed away, pulled away. She's aware that the rest of the girls consider her flaky. That she doesn't want to interact, join in the fun. Once overhearing Gemma gripe that she 'thinks she's above everyone', which was particularly hurtful. But Nish doesn't seem to care about such inaccurate observations.

The rest of the girls wave over. Gemma ducks down and talks into Maria's ear. It's funny that she's called Maria, her being the spit of Natalie Wood. And whenever Janet sees her beautiful face, she's compelled to internally sing 'Maria' from *West Side Story*.

'Drink . . . what are you having?' says Nish.

With shaky fingers, Janet sweeps hair off her face. Reactivating the coconut scent. 'Oh, erm . . . a Coke, please.'

Nish impersonates the incorrect-answer sound effect from *Family Fortunes*. 'Rum or vodka in it? Your choice because you aren't getting no pure Coke.'

'No, honestly . . . I'm not drinking.'

Nish walks off, skinny arm held aloft, dismissing Janet's abstinence.

'Bacardi then,' shouts Janet.

Now alone, she steps further into the room. A fixed smile, natural as nylon.

A middle-aged man in a suit, shirt half untucked, tie skewed, is jumping around in front of her performing the worst rendition of 'That's Life' she's heard since Uncle Matty's efforts at her wedding, moments before he was removed for mooning.

Eager to escape the area, she sucks in all the air she can and heads over to the girls.

'Sorry I'm so late.'

Gemma kisses her cheek. 'Just glad you made it.' Gemma is a Goth. Fascinating piercings puncture her face, even her cheek. Janet's also seen evidence of a nipple ring beneath her work top but would never mention it.

Sam is decidedly drunk and leans forward, eyelids drooping, breasts – which Janet has heard on good authority were purchased in Turkey – bulging over her dress. 'We're down for the next one. All of us. You too . . . you've got to . . .

"You Make Me Feel Like a Natural Woman".' The title slurs together as though it's one long word.

'Oh, no . . . I'm not going to sing, I—'

'Here, woman, get your sexy lipstick around that.' Janet takes the drink from Nish and sniffs it for potency before sipping. It's the first taste of alcohol she's had since bringing in the New Year at home with Colin. And that was one watered-down Baileys with ice. The alcohol's burn encases her throat. But the sensation of it sliding through her veins calms her tense body, until she's hit with an image of Colin shouting her name through the house. She takes another gulp.

Empty glasses clutter the table in front of the sofa where she sits, consuming her third Bacardi and Coke, soothed yet giddy, watching the girls' screeching rendition of 'Single Ladies'. Among her woolly-headed musings, Colin is a mere abstract thought. A distant husband. The glass finds her lips once more. He was so wrong. Just wrong. She knows what she's done, deserves, but he was wrong.

'Come on, Janet,' shouts Nish, summoning her with exaggerated arm gestures.

'I'm not single.' She holds up her ringed finger, does the hand movement.

The suited guy from earlier and a girl in a buttock-skimming skirt are dancing. Jiving, in fact. Which, aside from being unsuitable for the music, highlights their immense lack of rhythm. The girl is far too good for him. Legs Janet dreams of having, and only looks about eighteen.

Eighteen.

Claire will never be able to dance, even with a . . . The glass slips through her hand. Lands on the table, thankfully unbroken. As she places it upright, the spilt sticky liquid drips over the edge and blots her trousers. Without caring, she turns her watch, checks the time.

She was in labour now. Panting, breathing through. Colin, holding her hand, stroking her sodden hair from her face, while she suppressed the desire to bite down onto his fingers, press all the pain into his skin.

She downs the remnants of the drink.

She's now sitting on the wall near the small courtyard car park, after having been dragged outside by Nish for company while she smokes. Nish is so drunk, her slight bottom keeps sliding off the bricks, and her cigarette went out a couple of minutes ago, though Janet hasn't said anything because it's a horrible habit. Janet sips on another drink while her friend tangles herself up in knots about the drummer guy who ghosted her.

'I'll order a cab for us in a bit. Not yet though, you need to sing first . . . Argh, Janet, I know he feels the connection too, he's just scared. But I can't do it, I can't . . . He's shit, he's a shit . . . Hey, have you got any spare prawn crackers?' The last part is shouted over to the chef putting empty boxes in the alleyway. He ignores her plea.

'He sounds an idiot, Nish. You can do so much better.' The cool air is sobering. 'Oh God, I shouldn't have come out tonight.'

Nish sticks the dud cigarette in her mouth, enabling her to grip both of Janet's arms and shake her. 'Shut up,' she mumbles. 'You're having fun . . . let yourself have fun.'

Janet imagines the state she must look now. Make-up smeared, once-buoyant hair glued flat across her forehead with sweat. The lip gloss a distant memory. 'I am having fun. That's what I mean.' She almost tells her. That it's awful. That it's Claire's birthday and she can't endure it anymore. Her life. But she's saved by Nish's ringing phone. 'Oh hello, can I order a cab from the Happy Dumpling, Eccles, to Swinton, then on to Chomlea Manor, please.' Face contorted, she pulls the phone from her ear and looks at the screen. 'Cheeky bastard. He hung up.'

'It was an incoming call, you daft cow.'

The music is loud, the room now spinning. Nish has pushed her towards the kiosk. 'Go on, choose. We've all done it, and you'll not come out again for ages.'

'I can't . . . no way.' But despite these objections, she flicks through the laminated pages of the songbook. Only to appease. She's not really going to sing, she can't . . . just can't. Then she sees it.

'You Don't Own Me'.

She picks up the little Colin-dick pencil and scribbles the corresponding number onto the paper scrap, then thrusts it towards the DJ's beard.

While waiting her turn, the concept has become horrific. Some bloke is currently murdering 'Bohemian Rhapsody', and she's the only person in the room that doesn't want it to end.

Sam is slumped asleep. A plastic tiara placed on her head by Maria, who's cross-legged, suppressing a wee induced from laughing with Gemma and Nish as they take photographs of their snoozing boss.

Chuckling at their antics, the fun being had, it's not only

the Queen song that Janet doesn't want to come to an end. Going home will be like that film *Awakenings* when Robert De Niro returns to his catatonic state.

'Janet.' The music has stopped and the DJ is shouting her name from the kiosk. She shakes her head and waves her hand to refuse, but he's not looking. 'Janet . . . Janet.'

She pushes herself up, unsteadily walks over to tell him she's changed her mind. Except the girls have started chanting her name and the DJ can't hear what she's saying and the microphone is now in her hand.

Somehow, she's standing central, like a self-conscious teen forced on stage by pushy parents. Zig-zagged by lasers. Mic gripped with both hands, like a bridal bouquet.

There's a whoop from the room, followed by laughter. Dipping her head towards the mic she says, 'I'll sound like an injured frog, though.' Reverb screeches, makes her wince.

The intro begins.

It's been so long since she's heard this song that despite the screen displaying the lyrics for assistance, she's unsure if she can remember how it goes. But she's started singing. Quiet, shaky. Each line resonating, mirroring the frustration she carries through each of her identical days. As the song progresses, the kinks in her voice iron out, her shoulders press back. She is taller, lighter. The words louder, clearer. Does she still sound like an injured frog? Maybe, probably, but who cares. She'll sing this every day, she vows. It will follow her around. Be her theme tune. It will be OK. She will be OK.

'Bohemian Rhapsody' man is watching her, grinning. She returns a smile, blinks. Is she attractive?

Closing her eyes, her hand beats flat against her chest. She's telling the room, Colin, that she's free. That's what she wants. To be free. And she imagines the message floating through the air and reaching him, wherever he is, and screaming into his ears.

The music finishes to slow, disjointed claps. The girls cheer. Janet's back in the room as if counted out of hypnosis. Simultaneously buzzing and embarrassed. But as she walks towards the DJ to return the microphone, she catches the time on her watch. It's nearly half ten. Colin's right. She is selfish, vile.

At the booth, the mini-skirted girl is looking through the book. Janet manoeuvres her out of the way with her hips, ignoring the tuts, complaints. 'I'm sorry, I really need to do another one . . . sorry.' Frantic, she flips through the lists of songs – L, M, N, O, P – and there it is: 'Part of Your World' from *The Little Mermaid*. She writes down the number and hands it to the DJ.

Back central, she stands. The girls wave over, clap. Others talk among themselves. A lone male voice shouts, 'Gerroff.'

She brings the mic to her mouth. 'In three minutes, it will be eighteen years since I gave birth to my beautiful daughter. She died eleven years ago . . . Claire . . . her name was Claire . . . and I'd like to sing this for her . . . it was her favourite song.' She's aware of heads dropping, eyes averting.

The intro starts.

Janet stares ahead. And there she is. Claire. Twirling in her Ariel T-shirt and tutu.

Salt tastes on Janet's lips. Blinking hard, she erases the image. 'Sorry, I . . . it was a mistake. I'm sorry.' Gently, she places the microphone on the floor. And as she runs towards the door, descends the stairs, the slightly off version of 'Part of Your World' swims behind.

Outside, she gasps for air. Runs towards the wall and sits, bending forward. Tears drip onto the cobbles, followed by the evening's alcohol mixed with chocolate éclair. Her cheeks ache with the pained expression she cannot remove. Wiping her mouth free of acid, she closes her eyes to stop the world from turning. But that's the problem; it does. It keeps on turning.

She takes a deep breath, opens her eyes, and tries to focus. And as her vision clears, she realizes that the car parked directly opposite is Colin's.

6

Glowing Remnants

'Janet . . .' Nish is running towards her, wobbling now she's wearing heels. Once reaching the wall, she lights a cigarette, then rubs Janet's back with her free hand. 'Shit, are you OK?'

'I'm fine . . . just drank too much, that's all. You get back in and enjoy yourself.' Her eyelids lower at the forgotten comfort of human contact.

'I'm not leaving you, you silly cow. I'll call us a cab.' Janet feels Nish's palm leave her back to fumble in her bag. 'I'm so sorry about Claire. I don't know what to—'

'No, you go on in. Colin's here, see. He's come to collect me.' She nods over to the car, attempting to interpret his level of rage through the window. But all that's visible are the white rosary beads from his rear-view mirror.

'Oh brilliant, can I cadge a lift then?'

She turns to Nish, smacked sober. Ready to perform. 'I'll have to check if there's room . . . Colin had a load of stuff in the car earlier, ready for the skip.'

Standing from the wall, she's surprisingly steady. Wide-eyed, with exaggerated calm, she leaves Nish and crosses the cobbles towards the car. As she approaches, the passenger window lowers.

She bends forward, speaks into the vehicle. Addressing the

side of his face as he stares straight ahead, hands gripping the wheel.

'I'm sorry,' she says.

No response, acknowledgement. She turns towards Nish who's now sitting on the wall, smoking, waiting. Returning her gaze to the car, Janet dips again. 'Nish has asked for a lift . . . She lives nearby so it's awkward.'

Nothing.

She glares into him. Glad at what she's done. Glad. Then straightens. 'That's fine, Nish,' she shouts.

She hasn't been inside the car for a couple of weeks. It smells like it's been cleaned and there's a new Magic Tree interlaced with the rosaries. Strawberry, she thinks, but is unsure. Either way it's sickly.

Nish is too drunk to notice the contradiction to her tip story. The interior is immaculate with no evidence of cleared-out rubbish. But even if it had been questioned, Janet would improvise another falsehood with ease. Thinking on her feet, that's what she does. She doesn't consider them lies, more survival.

'Thanks for this, Colin, I'm on Chomlea . . . I know you know where that is, being a cabbie. We know all about you, don't you worry.' She laughs, then hiccups.

Janet catches sight of Colin, his front teeth scraping down on his bottom lip. 'I tell the girls all the lovely things you do for me. How hard you work.'

'She does . . . us singles are well jealous of you two.'

Janet laughs nervously, continues looking in his direction. Gauging. Always gauging. 'I . . . I just mention how you take me for nice meals and things.'

'How long have you lived on Chomlea?' asks Colin.

Janet gulps down her surprise at his interaction. Even if he wasn't furious, he doesn't believe in talking while driving. She roots inside her bag for a Polo mint to both appear unflustered and to remove the stale, vomited Bacardi aftertaste.

'Only ten years.' She giggles. 'Sorry, two . . . two years. Anyway, Colin, your wife has kept something very quiet.'

Panicked, Janet flicks her head to Colin, who is looking at Nish in the rear-view mirror with a forced smile. 'Oh yes?' he says.

'She can't half belt a song out. Like bloody Mariah, she is.'

Pulling down the sun visor, Janet attempts to communicate with Nish via the reflection. 'No, I . . . Shhhh, don't be silly.'

'Yeah, OK, Mariah . . . She was like whoaaaaa giving it all this . . .' Nish performs a strange shoulder movement, which Janet hopes is an inaccurate impersonation of what she actually did. 'Though the next song, she . . . Well, your wife's amazing, Colin. How she, you know . . . Life's so . . .' Her thought dwindles, to the relief of everyone, but for entirely different reasons.

Wishing she still felt as inebriated as her friend, Janet crunches down on the mint as a release. 'You need a strong coffee inside you, missy. Then a pint of water and into bed.'

Nish slaps her knees. 'Yes, Mum . . . Oh shit, sorry . . . sorry, Janet.'

Janet smiles and shakes her head minutely, then snaps up the visor.

Parked up outside Nish's house, Colin insists they wait to make sure she's safe inside. He's good like that. But after her last wave and disappearance, they remain static, staring beyond the windscreen as though at a drive-in movie. The car, dark, humid. Their silence loud against the still air. Glow from the nearest streetlight slicing a wedge between them.

'I'm sorry,' she says. 'But you shouldn't have tried to lock me in.'

His voice is calm, robotic. 'It's her birthday and you were doing your stupid dancing. She'd have not long been born now.'

'I know. That's why I had to go.'

He turns to her. She doesn't dare look but can feel his anger burn into the side of her face. 'It's your fault,' he says. 'Just know that it's your fault. But if you don't care about her birthday, well . . . I'm glad you finally want to move on. Now I know I definitely did the right thing.'

She doesn't understand what he means by this. Yet her warm body prickles cold beneath her clothes.

Before turning into the driveway, he switches off his headlights so as not to wake the neighbours with the glare. He's considerate like that, is Colin.

With the engine cut, he gets out first. Doesn't wait for her like he usually would, or hurry her along so he can activate the central locking. The crunch of his slippers across the gravel ceases as he disappears into the house. The front door left open for her to follow.

Brain already dehydrated, beating against her skull, she emerges. After pressing the car door closed, she stands for a moment, squints. A burnt aroma hangs heavy in the air, and she imagines those earlier partying neighbours now drunkenly throwing frozen burgers onto a barbecue.

Inside, she hangs her bag on the banister newel before entering the lounge.

Colin is already in his chair. An old film plays on TV. Watching the screen from afar, she realizes it's *Kes*. It's near the end and she can't bear to look, it's far too upsetting, so she goes to make a cup of tea.

In the kitchen, she notices the back door is open. Surely he can't have left the house without shutting it. Or had she left it open herself and he was unaware?

These thoughts are distracted by the swarm of moths hovering at the entrance. Disgusted, she steps forward to bat them away. But they're not insects at all, they're tiny floating fragments of ash. The film score loudens in the background. The delicate grey fairies dance to the haunting woodwind.

She steps through them and into the garden.

And blinking, slow, silent, her soul is sucked from her body.

Hypnotized, she watches the glowing remnants. Various recognizable shapes. The mermaid's tail draped over the rim of the fire pit. Turquoise popping against the black char.

Still, mute, she observes the incinerated debris.

Until her screams fill the cul-de-sac.

7

Her Roses (The Only Thing She Will Miss)

'Janet . . . Janet . . . shush, everyone will hear you.'

Warm hands search beneath her armpits, attempting to lift her from the ground, from her knees. Bent forward, she squeezes the burnt offering of duvet. He manages to pull her to standing, groaning at the weight beneath his arms, as if carrying the dead body that she wishes she were.

Manoeuvring her around to face the house, he tries to walk her back inside. 'Come on, Janet, please. I did it for you . . . for both of us.' The tremor in his voice undermines the conviction of his words. 'She's eighteen now, we couldn't keep living like that.'

She is forming steps, but her legs belong to another. The crying has stopped. Face hot, smeared with fluids, she licks her top lip as he shuffles her through the kitchen.

'Come on, shhhh . . . it's OK. I'll get you a nice, sweet tea.'

As they pass the cutlery drawer, she imagines removing the sharpest knife, the one with the rust marks she can't seem to erase despite all her efforts, and plunging it deep into her stomach.

In the lounge, she sits rigid on the sofa. A piece of black-rimmed mermaid duvet on her lap as if someone has kindly tucked her up, made her warm. But she's cold, ice cold. She looks at the TV and *Kes* has been found dead. She laughs.

'Come on, come on . . . drink this.' Colin is handing her a steaming mug of tea, his hands trembling more than hers. He bends towards her, strokes her hair, as if it were someone else who had perpetrated the worst act, inflicted more hurt than she thought possible. 'Sip it. Come on, sweetheart, sip.' He manually weaves her fingers through the handle as if she's a doll, not real – she isn't real anymore. She watches as he goes to his chair, sits. Drops his head into his hands, rocks forward. 'You just made me so angry . . . and it's not right, love, it's not right having a shrine like that. It's not normal.'

Hand slackening, she allows the mug to drop to the floor. Tea scalds her feet as it falls and pools over the beige carpet which she vacuums daily until she cannot see a speck. Now she's unperturbed as brown liquid bleeds into the pile.

When she stands, he copies. Moves over to blot the stain with the duvet she's released.

In slow motion, she glides towards the door. His pointless excuses floating behind. 'It'll be so much better, you'll see. We'll make the room all nice . . . I'll decorate and we can have visitors, my mum can come and stay.'

She stops. Turns to look down at him on his hands and knees, scrubbing. Her wet nostrils flaring as she stares at him, dead-eyed. 'Can my dad move in?'

He pauses as if taken aback at her sudden ability to speak, and swipes a wrist across his forehead. The forehead she craves to cave in using Elaine, the blue-dressed dancing figurine to her side.

'No . . . No, of course not, love.' He returns to rubbing at the mark. 'Your dad's not well enough.'

He may still be talking but she's not listening. Leaving the room, she's only aware of the film's closing credits music mixed with the emery-board tune of polyester scraping against polyester. Both growing fainter and fainter as she enters the kitchen.

Once back outside, she's decided. Her sentence is over.

Having thought about this moment day in, day out, it's finally going to happen.

She stops and glances beyond the cremation towards her roses.

The only thing she will miss.

The woman sits at the small kitchen table. Her husband in the chair opposite. Their view of each other masked by the cut-glass vase, propping the stems of her precious roses. Vibrant and plush. Despite their life being cut short by his un-green fingers.

Next to the flowers stands a Valentine's Day card – FOR MY DARLING WIFE. Oversized, appliqué. Lone. No FOR MY DARLING HUSBAND equivalent by its side.

Their daughter sleeps upstairs. And the woman hopes she'll shout down, ask for a story. But she's settled.

'Tuck in,' he says, nodding towards the peppered steak he's made for her, rare in every way. She collects up her knife and fork, hovers them over the plate.

As they eat, the stainless steel clinks against china, against silence. The plates were a wedding gift. Only used for special occasions. There have been fewer and fewer of these with each passing year.

'Delicious.' She has to give something. Each syllable elongates to fill the space.

Wives across the world would probably be grateful for such a dinner. As would she, had it not been the case that less than eight hours prior she'd finally plucked up the courage to tell him she wants to leave.

8

Manchester Royal Infirmary

Elastic voices. Slowed, distorted. Sibling memories of playing 45-rpm records at 33 speed.

Is this what it's like? Death? Pleasant and warm. Uncertainty about where limbs are positioned. Is her arm above her head or down by her side? Legs straight or sprawled?

No . . . no, this isn't pleasant at all. Reality is catching up. What's happened. Not heaven, but hell. 'I need to see her.' The words barely make their way out of her spit-glued mouth.

'Janet . . . Janet . . . Hi, Janet.' Her name projects from blurry blue. 'Hey, sleepyhead, are you going to wake up properly this time?'

Gritty-eye blinks gather both clarity and pain. Met with the sting of citrus cleaning fluid hanging in the air. 'Where is she? I have to see her.'

'Where's who, love? Your husband's gone to get a cup of tea.' A smiling blonde looms. Scrawny. In a Sam's Angels uniform. Her name badge says . . . MARION. Is this Gemma's replacement? No, what's she talking about, this isn't work. She knows where she is. 'I need to see her.'

An elderly stranger in the opposite bed peels a tangerine. The woman's dishevelled cotton-spun hair prompts Janet to lift her own lead-heavy hand and tentatively touch her bandaged head.

Marion pulls a machine towards the bed and wraps a cuff around Janet's arm. 'You've been sleeping for hours . . . how are you feeling? You're in the Manchester Royal Infirmary. Do you remember, Janet, love? Blood pressure is still up a little . . . Give me your finger, sweetheart.' Marion clips on the oximeter then notes down the readings. 'You're such a lucky lady . . . it must have been terrifying. The doctor will be doing his rounds soon.'

The nurse isn't listening to her. Or is she not speaking?

Old Woman is pushing segments of fruit into her puckered mouth. Whimpers rise from the bed to Janet's left, but she doesn't turn to look, doesn't want to see.

'Don't you fret.' Marion pours water from the jug into a plastic beaker and encourages her to drink. 'You've got a head wound and concussion . . . and some other scrapes and bruises. You've been in a crash, do you remember, Janet?'

'I can't be here . . . I need to—'

'Why don't I see where your husband has got to . . . He'll be upset he wasn't with you when you woke up.' She clicks her pen and pops it back into her breast pocket.

'Nurse, nurse . . . they're trying to kill me.' Old Woman's shouts force Marion to stride over to her bed and pull the curtains around them both like the end of a play.

The plastic pillow protector crunches loudly next to Janet's ears. All sounds amplified as she grows aware of her throbbing head, the ache nestled into her entire body. Arms smarting beneath her bandages. The tinnitus of sirens and creaking of scraping metal.

Pushing herself up to sitting, she winces through the pain. Marion's as delusional as Old Woman. Why doesn't she realize she has to leave? Throwing off the layers of sheets and blankets, she slowly swings her legs over the edge of the bed, feet searching for the floor.

Then she notices her slippers. A piece of home, right there. Confirmation that she'll never escape him. Submitting, she slides into them. Puts on her dressing gown which is draped over the visitor's chair.

The Victorian corridor stretches to a pinpoint. Floors, angled. There are people. So many people. And police. Huddles of police, radios crackling. As she shuffles along, the wall skims her shoulders, fingers intermittently touching the cold white paint.

She knows where the Children's Hospital is, but doesn't understand why nobody's taking her there. *Hold on, baby. Mummy will be there soon.*

Ahead, a man cleans the floor. Face dropped in his own thoughts. Pressing the mop into the bucket, he lifts it out and back and forth, back and forth, swirls the dirty cotton strings across the brightening path. Disinfectant fumes carry towards her, inducing nausea. Her free hand hugs her mouth as she walks, then slides across her cheek to dry her face before fishing inside her dressing gown pocket for a tissue.

Then she stops.

Soft fur tickles her fingers.

Slowly, she pulls out the culprit and stares down. A little black Scottie dog.

And so, she's back in the present.

Head, light. Deer in headlights. Turning, she leans against the wall and looks upwards, beyond the glass roof and the pallid Manchester sky. To Claire.

9

Thirty-One Injured, Five Dead

It was a train crash.

Although she knows that now, cavernous blanks remain where memories should be. Along with perplexity as to why she was on a train in the first place. But they've all been telling her – the nurses, Colin, Dr Rashid who's since been and gone. Throughout, she gently nods, accepts.

'Thirty-one injured, five dead,' says Marion, applying fresh tape to one of Janet's bandaged arms.

'Oh goodness, that's terrible.'

Marion pats her grazed hand. 'You're one of the lucky ones, hun.' Then she turns towards the adjacent bed, to attend to its groaning occupant.

It's hard to comprehend. Janet feels no more involved in the event than she does when Colin insists on reading out the blurb for an imminent television programme. His hand has now replaced the nurse's. 'So, you've no idea where you were going? Why you were on the train?'

She shakes her head. The action generating more pain. 'You tell me. Was I going out somewhere?'

His chin drops to his chest, voice lowering to a whisper. 'No . . . I don't know.'

'How can you not know?' She tries to dip her head to read

his hidden expression, but blood pumps to her wound and she sharply sucks in air.

'Nurse,' he calls out. 'Is she due more painkillers? She seems in terrible pain.'

'I'm fine . . . but I'd like to watch the news now, please. I need to see it.'

His grip tightens. 'No . . . no, I don't think that would be a good idea. I don't want you getting upset.'

Marion turns back towards them. 'I think it'll be fine . . . it might help her remember. And no, she's not due her meds for a while yet.'

'Sure . . . OK.' With a fixed smile, he leans back in his chair. 'You know best, nurse.' The tension between him and Marion is palpable. He'd already kicked up a fuss about Janet being allowed to wander off during her . . . confusion.

'Colin's always saying how wonderful our NHS nurses are, Marion.' The reality being, at one point he had crushes on a couple of the actresses from *Holby City*.

Following a long-winded phone call to activate the TV, Colin grudgingly puts on the news channel.

Thirty injured, six dead, the banner now states.

'I'm going to turn it off if it stresses you.' His voice is louder than usual, and he flicks a glance towards Marion.

'*The busy eleven twenty-seven Manchester Piccadilly to Walkden passenger train was travelling around 70 mph when it derailed near the . . .*' The damaged train fills the screen. A toy, swiped from its track by a tantrum-throwing child. The camera pans out to show small Lego-like figures, rescue workers, dotted throughout the picture. '. . . *thought to have been caused by a landslip following weeks of torrential rain in the area.'*

Though the horrific visuals are disturbing, she still feels a mere observer. Detached. 'Oh, how awful, Colin. Those poor people.' The exact same thing she would have said had she been a regular viewer watching it from the comfort of her sofa.

Squeezing her eyes, she attempts to force memories. Fill in the gaps. *It's Claire's birthday . . . She leaves work . . . gets off the bus . . . buys the little Scottie dog.* Her hand slides beneath the sheet to stroke the toy in her pocket. *Visits her dad . . . goes home . . . makes a sandwich . . .* then the reel unravels, distorts, snaps. Exchanged for other minuscule fleeting images. Impossible to grasp, like sand through spread fingers. *A close-up of the train track . . . sleepers . . . fire . . .* It's normal with a concussion apparently, according to Dr Rashid. Being unable to remember an incident or the events leading up to it. Befuddlement. Though she'd been assured that her memory should return within hours or a few days. Only rarely, weeks. 'Please try not to worry, Mrs Brown,' he'd said. 'It's quite common.' His manner, calm, face so kindly. Yet still, it's as worrying a condition as anyone could have.

'Has it said anywhere that the train caught fire?' She turns to Colin.

'What?'

'The train . . . did it catch fire? It doesn't look like it did, but I keep—'

'I think you've seen enough now. There's an *Escape to the Country* about to start.' He goes to stroke her hair. Stopping before touching the bandage. His expression sincere, full of concern. But as she looks at him, she's stabbed with a disconcerting hatred. 'Just a bit longer, please,' she says with a smile.

On the screen is a selfie of a lad taken on what looks like the top of a mountain. '*Matthew Proctor, aged seventeen, was on his way home from a night out with friends.*'

'Right, that's it. I can see you're getting upset.' Colin attempts to grab the remote, but she retracts her hand. 'Leave it,' she says with a bravery born from being among other people. Noting his reddening face, she returns her gaze to the TV which is now showing another photograph. This time of a woman and a little girl around Claire's age.

'*One of the injured is Elizabeth Pilkington, eight-year-old daughter of footballer turned TV chef Robbie Pilkington and his wife Mia. We understand that Elizabeth is being treated at Manchester Children's Hospital but the severity of her injuries is currently unknown. Zofia Nowak, Elizabeth's au pair, was one of the fatally injured. Both were returning from a night at the theatre.*' The child's dimpled grinning face is framed with chocolate-brown plaits. Exactly how Claire used to wear hers, though she was much fairer. And Zofia, so youthful and pretty. The snap was apparently taken moments before they left for the evening. Janet's stomach knots, witnessing how happy the young woman looked, unaware that she'd soon be dead.

'I feel sick, Colin . . . I'm going to be sick.'

His chair scrapes against the vinyl floor as he rises, calls out, 'Nurse . . . nurse,' in a panicked voice.

Janet grabs the grey cardboard dish from the bedside cabinet, pulls it in front of her and throws up. As she lifts her pounding head, breath-heavy, wiping her chin, Colin is now merely a bending, heaving shadow behind the curtain.

'It's OK, I'll put *Escape to the Country* on now,' she says.

Once cleaned up by Marion, and given her next dose of pain-killers followed by a few sips of sweet tea, she's feeling altogether better. Colin is back by her side, hugging his own brew in a polystyrene cup. 'I can't do vomit, you know that.'

'I know . . . I know you can't, don't worry,' she says. But she recalls the months spent suffering with morning sickness. How he'd hold her hair, rub her back.

For the next couple of hours, she listens to his silent scribbling into a crossword grid. It's been years since he's asked for her help with clues. Resting her eyes, she slips in and out of swift dozes. And as her body almost fully submits, he says, 'Do you even remember it was her birthday yesterday? I think I'm going to go to the cemetery after here.' She doesn't answer, doesn't move. Feigning deep sleep, until the pretence becomes reality.

It's lunchtime. Her choice: a brown lumpy liquid otherwise known as beef bourguignon. But the upside of having to eat gruel is that Colin has been asked to leave.

Tension peels away now she's alone. But the bourguignon's taste lives up to its appearance. Although at least she didn't have to make it. One perk to being in hospital. Along with everyone's kindness and telling her how brave she is. Caring about her. She wonders if there's a way to extend her stay.

Realizing that's a terrible thing to think, she leans over, opens the bedside cabinet, and reaches for the washbag that

Colin had brought in. Sliding it out, she notices her watch on top of her neatly folded pink trousers and the unworn sequined jumper Colin had given as a present a few Christmases ago. How typical of a man to bring a hospital patient such ridiculous clothes.

Once upright and regretting the motion, head pounding brutally, she's aware of Old Woman staring over. Addressing her with a smile, she roots inside the washbag for a hairband and places the elastic on her wrist alongside the hospital bracelet, then flicks it against her skin. Though she experiences relief, she's forgotten what had instigated the need in the first place.

Old Woman has started shouting again and Marion is striding over. 'What's all this then, Florence? You want the television on?'

As Florence is being pacified, Janet switches on her own TV to distance herself from the fracas.

Things have settled. She's eating rhubarb crumble while watching the lunchtime news, waiting for any further coverage. And after sitting through an item about a woman charged with murdering her husband, but exonerated because of his years of abuse, they finally report on the crash.

She places down her spoon to focus. Then lifts it again, deciding that eating helps. There's the same picture of Elizabeth Pilkington and her poor au pair. Dead eyes emanating from the screen.

As she attempts to increase the volume, she accidentally switches over the channel. Eventually locating the correct button, she returns to the news, but the report has already moved on. It now appears to be amateur footage. Dark and grainy, as though filmed on a phone.

She squints, tries to concentrate. But Florence is shouting nonsense again, making it near impossible. Janet leans forward. Obscured by rain and the lack of light, someone can just be made out staggering towards the camera. There are muffled voices but the words spoken are indecipherable.

The lens angle skews. The person filming has dropped their arm.

The indistinguishable mutterings start to clarify.

Fragmented, distressed, familiar.

'Help, please . . . I did everything I could . . . I pulled her out and gave her mouth to mouth to bring her back . . . Please, she's just a child . . .'

10

The Juxtaposition of Joy and Emptiness

'Can you believe it's time for your vitals again? Honestly, where do the days go?' Marion drags the machine over to the bed, moving aside the metal bracket holding the TV. Although the screen is no longer entirely visible, Janet can hear that the report has now changed to highlights of a football match.

Marion dips her head towards Janet's. 'Ignore Florence. She was the sweetest lady on earth when she came in on Wednesday, but . . .' She contorts her mouth to one side as though enabling the information to tumble out. 'She's developed a UTI, bless her . . . makes the elderly temporarily batty.'

Janet smiles, both wondering if that was appropriate to share and if perhaps she too was temporarily batty. 'Did you see that footage on the news just now, Marion?'

'Perfect.' The air releases from the arm wrap. 'No, love. What was it?'

'I'm . . . I'm not sure.'

'Don't you be worrying if you're a bit confused today, my love. As Dr Rashid said, it's normal.' She taps the top of the machine. 'You're doing great. Hopefully, it won't be too long until you're home.'

'Do you think?' She experiences a peculiar disappointment

at hearing this, and finds herself touching her head, screwing up her eyes, and saying, 'My head still really hurts, though.'

For the next few hours, she flicks through channels, searching for that footage. She can't find it anywhere, but the same picture of Elizabeth has popped up intermittently. This time, on *North West Tonight*. Her angelic face, bright-eyed and very much alive. Unlike the blank, flat look of her au pair. Jason Quartz highlighted this phenomenon on the Psychic Channel. How it's evident from photographs that someone has passed over. Once he'd said it, she found it even harder to look at pictures of Claire. Even the happy snap of her on the beach, grinning, building an impressive sandcastle. Her eyes always give it away. The juxtaposition of joy and emptiness too much to bear.

The thought of Colin at the cemetery catches her breath. She never goes because it's so upsetting. The shame of this is firmly felt, but it's just too hard imagining her under that dull grey stone. Janet had at least wanted it to incorporate a mermaid. Have something Claire would like. But they could only afford the basic options. Though she comforts herself with the fact Claire's not there anyway. She's still with her in spirit. At home. In her room. Where she belongs.

'Excuse me,' Janet calls to the passing young nurse. 'Hi . . .' She's not seen this one before so searches for their name badge. '. . . Lauren, I'm feeling much better and would like to visit the prayer room, if that's OK . . . for my daughter's birthday.'

'Oh, right . . . well, I'm not sure—'

'She's dead, you see . . . and it was yesterday.'

*

The hospital is still disorientating.

There's a difference between sitting or lying, and negotiating bustling, identical corridors. It's busier than she's ever known. Compared to when attending appointments over the years with her parents.

Mumblings on the ward had said it was in a *State of Emergency*. She'd not understood what that meant, until now.

Hit by the change of temperature, she's overtaken with shivers as she continues through the main foyer among the other dressing-gowned zombies, dragging drips towards the entrance, presumably for an ill-advised cigarette.

A policeman is walking towards her. Tall and ominous, radio crackling. She stops for a moment, closes her eyes, concentrates hard on not being swept back in time. Feeling for her hairband, she flicks it hard against her wrist.

'Hi, love . . . love . . . you've dropped this.' Eyes opened, she's relieved to see only a pale, greasy-haired man in pyjamas holding out the belt from her robe.

'Oh . . . Thank you,' she says, pulling it through his hand. Hurriedly, she ties it around her, conscious that she'd been so exposed, that people would have seen her braless shape through the cotton of the gown. The concept induces queasiness, so she follows the herd to get some air.

Outside is cloudless and warm.

The quiet stillness contrasts with inside, despite the presence of folk milling around. Their state of undress in public seems peculiar. 'Only types like her do that,' her mother would say about Mrs Miller the next-door neighbour, who'd collect milk from the doorstep wearing only a nightdress, and a cigarette suspended from her mouth. Ordinarily, Janet would never contemplate such a thing, yet here she is, not caring, eyes softly squinting towards the sun. Though on realizing that among the patients is a group of reporters, her self-consciousness immediately returns, and she makes her way back inside with as much haste as her battered body allows.

The regular entrance is currently blocked by someone struggling with a wheelchair, so she has no choice but to use the revolving door instead. She always finds them perturbing. Claustrophobic. Freedom dependent on other people. Holding her breath, she shuffles along with the rotation, eager to arrive at the other side.

A young woman steps into the opposing compartment. Flame-haired, like Ariel. Smartly dressed. Head down, finger prodding at her phone.

Janet stares at this stranger, this somehow familiar stranger, for as long as the mechanism allows. The recognition frustrating. Like the time she'd waved at a woman in the Trafford Centre before realizing it was Anneka Rice.

The prayer suite is as aesthetically cold and basic as she recalls. Lacking the ostentation of the various churches she visits for answers. Each with their heavenly ambience and kaleidoscopic light.

Curved wooden dividers create separate areas for different religions. Centre of the space, swirled around a pillar, is a wrought-iron tree from which dangle multicoloured glass leaves interspersed with paper versions carrying handwritten messages to loved ones, dead, alive, barely alive. A space split between different faiths, but at its core, desperation.

She walks over to a table, picks up a leaf and chewed biro, and writes a message of her own.

> *Hello, sweetheart. I hope wherever you are you had fun yesterday, laughing and singing and dancing. I couldn't bear it down here without you. Love you forever, Mum xxx*

Back at the tree she kisses the leaf before placing it on the highest branch she can reach, to make it easier for the message to find Claire. And as she rewraps her gaping dressing gown to prepare to leave, she notices a priest standing by the table. A sort of casual priest if that's a thing. His black trousers are in fact jeans. What might be considered informal religious wear. Not dissimilar to the outfit Colin wore for the vicars and tarts party they attended many years ago at Sheila and Terry's, their neighbours back in Eccles. When they had to leave early because things were moving over to the hot tub.

She snaps the band against her wrist for thinking about such salaciousness in a prayer centre. Then realizing he's seen her, she plays with the elastic as if it had happened by accident. But this doesn't seem to appease him, as he's now walking in her direction. 'Hello. Just to make you aware there's an area to pray in private, or for us to talk if that's something you'd like to do?'

'Oh . . . I'm OK, Father . . . I'd better be getting back to the ward.' It's strange how whenever she speaks to a priest and uses the word 'Father' her accent automatically becomes a bit Irish.

He smiles and nods. 'That's absolutely fine, I just wanted to make you aware. I shall leave you—'

'It was my daughter's birthday yesterday. She'd have been

eighteen. She died . . . well, it's eleven years ago now . . . They brought her here, to the hospital. And I was in the train crash, and . . .' As she speaks, she realizes what she's saying sounds almost fatalistic.

'Come,' he says, walking away, beckoning her to follow.

It feels a terrible idea now. He's sitting opposite her, legs crossed, face full of forced empathy. Her knees are clamped together and her head lowered. The silence lingers so long, to such an unbearable pitch, that she can't stand it anymore and says, 'I really should be getting back, Father. My husband will be visiting soon, and he'll be ever so worried.'

'Of course . . . only, you seemed to want to talk about your daughter. I'm so very sorry for your loss.' He reaches over and touches her shoulder, turning her to stone. The tableau an awkward religious statue. But she wants to voice so much. Wishes they were in a confessional. That she was anonymous and brave. That she could say, *Forgive me, Father, for I have sinned.* And he'd Hail Mary it better so she'd pull back the curtain lighter, cleansed of her guilt-infested wound.

She pushes herself up from the chair and says, 'Thank you . . . I'm fine, though. That was very helpful, Father . . . thank you.'

He stands also, face riddled with puzzlement.

As they walk back towards the wooden wall, she realizes what she should have asked. 'Father, how do you know if God has forgiven you? If you've paid your penance?'

'Well, I don't know entirely what you mean, but God forgives all our sins. He will show you if you let Him.'

She smiles politely. Wishing for once one of them would give her a straight answer.

Before leaving, she goes over to the table and takes another leaf. On it she scribbles:

Please God, give me a sign that I am forgiven.

Back at the tree, she goes to hang it on one of the branches, then stops, scrunches it tightly in her hand and puts it in her pocket. She's got no right to ask for such a thing.

The Children's Hospital is in another building. Colin will arrive soon, the nurses will be concerned, but being in the prayer centre again has driven her to pick further at the scab. It's a terrible idea, she knows that. Yet there's a magnet pulling her, and she's merely a metal shaving.

The breeze that's now whipping the air floats her hair above the bandage. Her body aches as she struggles on. Goodness knows what her blood pressure reading would be on Marion's machine.

She crosses the small gardens. A neat and pretty haven full of colourful flowers, bees and non-medical scents. A snippet of heaven to distract people from hell.

It's funny how she remembers it so well after all these years. This specific route taken only once when she was half unconscious. Yet it's cauterized onto her brain. And unlike her, it appears unchanged.

Nearing the building, she's breathless, but her injuries render her unable to bend forward, gather herself. Instead she pauses, closes her eyes, and rubs at her chest, lungs grappling for oxygen.

And when she opens them, it all makes sense. The reason for the draw, the irresistible pull. It wasn't only the need to relive that night. She's supposed to be here. Right at this moment. Because ten feet away, oblivious to Janet's presence, is the mother. Elizabeth's mother. Mia Pilkington. Not appearing as she does in the pages of *Hello!* magazine, but still recognizable. Wealthily dressed in cotton and cashmere. But most noticeable is the raw, pained expression that transcends social status. An expression with which Janet is all too familiar.

There's only the two of them. Mother and mother.

She so wants to approach her, put out a hand. Touch her shoulder like the priest. But less awkward. *Please God, save this woman from what I have endured.*

Mia drops her head, covers her face with her hands. Janet lowers hers too in respect, sympathy. As time stretches, she can feel Mia's energy, a connection. Until Janet is brought back to the now by the sound of the opening electric doors.

She knows she shouldn't follow. No good will come of that. Only immeasurable upset. But once again she's lured forward, and soon the glass is sliding apart, summoning her inside.

The reception is awash with cartoon murals. Blue-toned paintings transform the dreaded area into a spaceship. Jolly monsters, brightly coloured curvy seats. She's unsure if it was like this before. But remembers the smell. She'll never forget the smell.

She's alone. Mia has disappeared and she's standing amid the pretend happy fun. Still, useless. Still useless.

'Hello, are you OK?' a woman in a white uniform calls from behind the desk. 'Can I help you?'

Janet smiles. Chest constricted. 'Sorry, I . . . No, I'm fine . . . I'm just a bit lost, that's all.'

*

It's hard to sprint when you're barely even able to walk. Yet she must. The headache that had hummed in the background has now burst to the forefront. Though uncertain of exactly how long she's been, she knows it's too long. Passing through the foyer, she imagines Colin instigating an embarrassing argument with Marion.

Now nearing the ward, her shoulders drop, breathing slows. Once outside, she's about to reluctantly press the buzzer when she notices a middle-aged couple about to leave. They hold the door open, and she smiles while ducking beneath the man's arm.

Head down, she shuffles past reception. Marion is on the phone and Lauren is walking on ahead. Both oblivious to her arrival and hopefully her long absence. Squeezing her eyes, she prays Colin isn't already there, while conjuring unfeasible excuses as to where she's been. And turning into the side room, she's so relieved not to catch sight of his bald head that she fails to register someone far worse.

11

Munch's *Scream*

'Mrs Janet Brown? Police Constable Walker, British Transport Police.' He stands, meeting her at eye level.

They have a different energy, the police. Being up close to them brings with it a similar surrealness to stepping onto a film set. Though his demeanour is different to the family liaison officer they'd sent about Claire. He's a man for a start. Lacks the head-tilting sympathy.

'Yes, that's right.' Continuing towards the bed, the familiar vile sensation crawls through her body. Hand on mattress, she turns, offers him an eye-avoidant smile. *Always smile at the police so they know you're a good citizen*, her mum would say. But his presence is triggering.

Once, when watching a programme about PTSD with Colin, she was screaming inside, *That's me, that's me.* Expressing it out loud would have been redundant. He doesn't believe in mental health issues or therapy.

'I'm afraid I can't tell you much. My memories of it are all shot.' Pulling aside the bedding, she slides beneath the thick cotton as gracefully as possible, to avoid exposing herself through the gaps of her gown, like a pound-shop Sharon Stone.

Once sufficiently hidden, she dares to look at him directly. He's younger than she'd initially thought. A mere baby.

Square-chinned and long-eyelashed. The chair taking on the appearance of a child's seat beneath his athletic frame. Removing a notepad from his pocket, he says, 'I'm very sorry to hear that, Mrs Brown. If I could take a few details from you, I'll leave you to rest.'

And it happens. Impossible to supress. Being transported back in time to a specific moment. When the family liaison officer had edged her chair closer to the hospital bed, cupping Janet's hand. Colin pacing behind, a re-enactment of Munch's *Scream*.

'Mrs Brown? Your full name?' Officer Walker's voice is soft, confused.

'Sorry, I was just . . . It's Mrs Janet Amelia Brown.' Clamping her eyes shut, she eradicates the memory. Snaps the elastic band against her concealed wrist. 'Will it take long, officer? Only I really don't feel very well.'

'No, sorry, of course . . . I need your full address, though, if I may?'

After providing him with the required details, she adds an unsolicited fabricated explanation as to why she doesn't have a mobile phone. 'The world needs to slow down, don't you think? We were fine before. Without them.'

The transference of scribblings into his pad is so quick, she wonders if he's merely doodling.

'And where did you board the train?'

'I don't know, I'm afraid. Though I should imagine Swinton.'

As though properly noticing her existence for the first time, he squints. 'That must feel very strange for you. Not being able to remember things.'

'Yes . . . yes, it's very strange.'

He stands, and she's unseen once more. 'OK, well, you'll receive a questionnaire from us at some point. Hopefully by the time it arrives you'll have remembered more details.' A voice crackles through his radio. Ignoring it, pad returned to his pocket, he bends to adjust the legs of his trousers, pushing the rigid central crease towards his shiny shoes.

'Is that it?'

'That's it, Mrs Brown. The investigative team will now work to piece the incident together using statements of witnesses such as yourself and any CCTV footage we can gather. I hope you're feeling much better soon.' He dips his head towards his walkie-talkie. 'Yep, I'm making my way down now.'

When alone, she's once again carried back to that moment. To the tightening squeeze of the policewoman's hand. To Colin, breaking apart their grip. Barging his body between them. 'No, I'm going to tell her. I want to tell her.'

12

Fish Pie and Broccoli

She's had a settled night.

Dream-seeped sleep filled with the seaside, pistachio ice cream and Claire frolicking in the froth of gently lapping waves. Much-needed respite from attempting to piece together fragments of memory and ruminating over the strange footage, Elizabeth and Mia. Even Florence had remained quiet, apart from the snoring. The antibiotics must have kicked in.

Janet waits for Dr Rashid as he does his rounds. Sitting in the chair like the Queen posing for an official portrait. Disappointed that her body, although aching, is less sore. Her headache has considerably dulled.

Despite having been poised for his arrival, the curtain whooshing open still makes her jump. 'Ah, Mrs Brown . . . how are you feeling today?'

'I still have a headache,' she says, fingertips hovering near the bandage.

'I see.' He collects up the clipboard, lifts a page and reads. 'Has it improved at all?' Dropping the paper, he frowns at her, as if in consideration.

Reluctantly, she nods.

'And what did you have for dinner last night?'

Thinking how especially lovely of him it is to bother making conversation when he's so busy, she says, 'Fish pie and broccoli.' With emphasis on the word broccoli to highlight how she tries to be healthy.

He returns the board to its slot. 'Ah, well, I'm very glad to see that you're laying down new memories. That's what we need to ensure.'

She smiles, thankful to have pleased him.

'And I'm happy that your head wound seems to be healing nicely and your vitals are all good. No, I can't see any reason for you to stay in another night. I'm sure you'll feel much better once back in the comfort of your own home.'

'Oh, that's excellent news. Thank you, doctor.' The smile remains. Although now masking her desire to cry.

After she's made the most of her morning, eating cold toast and marmalade and sipping sweet tea as if enjoying the last hours before checking out of a swanky hotel, Colin arrives, carrying a rolled-up copy of *Take a Break* magazine. He knocks it against his other hand like he's threatening to beat someone with a baseball bat. His eyelids, though always contrasting pink against the aquamarine of his irises, appear to have been lined in carmine and swollen into shininess.

'Oh, thank you,' she says. 'But I'm being discharged. I'm not sure I should be, though. Don't you think it's too soon?'

She wills his overbearing possessiveness to ignite a protest, but he says, 'They wouldn't let you if they didn't think you were well enough.'

'No . . . no, I suppose you're right. Have you been taking your Piriton? Pollen levels are high today, apparently.'

'I forgot.' With finger and thumb he rubs at his eyes. 'Look,

I'm going to go back and clean up a bit, or you'll only start doing it . . . and we don't want that.' Before she can form a response, he's heading out towards the reception desk. When he returns, he says, 'They'll take you to the collection lounge around three and I'll come and get you.' He rests the magazine on her lap. 'I'm so glad you're coming back home, Janet.'

It's almost three and she's said her goodbyes. Telling Marion and the nurses she'll drop in a tin of Roses when feeling better. Knowing it's unlikely Colin would accommodate that. Florence is also due out tomorrow, which makes her happy.

At half her usual speed, she throws away any accumulated rubbish and makes the bed even though she knows it'll be stripped. The holdall in which Colin had brought her belongings is placed on top of the neatened covers. It's the old brown one with peeling vinyl. The one she avoids, shoved to the back of the wardrobe, but can't bring herself to throw away. And she wonders if he'd chosen it for cruel effect.

From the cupboard she retrieves her washbag, watch and the ridiculous clothes he'd brought in for her to wear. Though the decision has already been made to remain in her dressing gown. She can't leave hospital in a sequined jumper. It's not Stringfellows.

Shoving the items inside the bag, she notices something. Stops.

Unfolding the jumper reveals filthy smudges and rust marks. A whole section of sequins is missing from the swallow, others hanging low on loose threads. There's an obvious tear in the sleeve. And most prominent, the reek of smoke.

Holding up the trousers, she takes in the similar dark smears. The crusted mud on their seat, the ripped knee.

Dizzy, dry-mouthed, she reaches behind for the arm of the chair, lowers herself into the seat. Realization descending. Confusion as to why she'd be wearing these clothes at all.

But as she sits, fabric gripped within her tense hands, her brain finally accepts the reality. That she really has been in another crash.

13

Middle-Aged Man in a Cardigan

Colin has gone to collect the car while she waits outside in a wheelchair.

It's likely he'll be a while. Utilizing extreme caution as he emerges from the parking space at one mile an hour. Paranoid about the possibility of a scratch. He's been like this ever since getting the Avensis.

The journalists are still hovering, though their numbers have dwindled. The comforting strokes of warm breeze act as a tranquilizer, and she's less conscious of being in her dressing gown now her faithful M&S cardie is slung around her shoulders, flapping behind like a superhero's cape.

A man in a football top, beer belly fit for the maternity ward, waddles towards the adjacent pay station, sifting through coins cupped in his hand. She's not overtly looking but is aware of him side-eyeing her while inserting the money. What a sight she must look. Thankfully Colin has just parked up as near as he can, and she's relieved when he gets out and walks towards her as fast as his little legs will allow.

All is quiet except Smooth Radio playing on low. Along with the occasional monotonous tick-ticking of the indicators, and whenever they stop at traffic lights Colin's asking if she's going to be sick. The no-talking rule, purported to be born out of safety, though really part of her punishment, is often a blessing.

As Randy Crawford sings 'One Day I'll Fly Away', she pulls down the sun visor and checks herself in the mirror. The scratches and bruises look even worse in daylight. Using her tongue to puff out her cheek, she inspects a newly emerged purpling mark. Feeling quite sorry for herself, she snaps the visor back up, knocking a new Magic Tree dangling from the rear-view mirror.

And something strange happens.

A sensation.

Heightened by the burst of sickly strawberry scent. The most real déjà vu she's ever experienced. Of her doing the exact same thing while wearing the sequined jumper.

Light-headed, she winds down the window.

But as they halt at a set of lights he says, 'I've told you a hundred times, you must keep them closed when the air conditioning's on.'

The traffic is rush-hour heavy. Wincing at the closeness to the car in front, her codeine-induced serenity prevents any thoughts of smashing her head through the windscreen. As they drive on, subdued, her eyelids drooping with the car's motion like a baby rocked in a pram, she mumbles, 'How come I was wearing those clothes? Had we been somewhere?'

He doesn't respond, of course. The no-talking rule. Instead, he continues up the dual carriageway before turning into Tesco Express and parks up, switches off the engine. 'Not us, you,' he says, staring into the rear-view mirror, at what she doesn't know. 'It was a leaving do for one of the girls. In Eccles.' The sentence is punctuated by the crank of the handbrake.

'I went to a leaving do?'

'That's right,' he says. 'You didn't want to, but I said it would do you good. And I collected you and Nish.'

'Then what?'

He turns to her. 'We met here, you know.'

'Of course I know.'

'We never mention it, though, do we? We come here all the time, but we never mention it. I mean, I know it's not Paris, but it's like it doesn't even register with you.'

He couldn't be more wrong.

It was a Shell garage back then and she was thirty-three. She'd just been dumped by her long-term boyfriend, Ned. Or not exactly dumped, more that she discovered him snogging the barmaid from the Dog and Duck in the pub car park.

Fleeing the scene in her Mini, the slow puncture that Ned had promised he'd sort at the weekend soon became too flat to continue to drive.

Colin wasn't so much knight in shining armour as middle-aged man in a cardigan. 'Come on, pet, It's all done now, see. It'll get you home, but you'll need to take it in somewhere in the morning.' He'd sorted the tyre after finding her slumped, crying, on the forecourt, unable to unscrew the valve. 'This guy of yours sounds an utter prat. You need someone who appreciates you, treats you well. Or what's the point?' Those were his words. His words.

So yes, it does register. Every time they turn in to the place, she wishes she'd gone to the Esso garage instead.

'Well, we can't mention it every time we get some milk, can

we, love?' she says. 'Anyway, go on . . . you picked up me and Nish, and then what?'

His demeanour alters. Shoulders slumped, head down, he speaks quietly towards the steering wheel. 'We had a row . . . and you walked out. That's it.' Sitting upright again, he turns, looks directly into her eyes. 'I couldn't bear it . . . you know that, don't you, Janet. If you left.'

A woman wearing tartan pyjama bottoms tucked into Ugg boots and carrying a large bottle of Coke and a packet of cigarettes nears the car. Colin smiles at her as she climbs into the adjacent Audi, and remains silent as the woman buckles up, checks her hair. When she finally reverses out of the space, he says, 'You were, weren't you? Leaving me.'

'I can't remember anything, but no . . . I wouldn't . . . I said I'd stay and . . . Colin?'

With his forehead resting on the wheel, he's making the weirdest of noises. For a moment she thinks he's laughing. But he's weeping. With intensity she's not witnessed since Claire.

'I thought I'd lost you . . . and I . . .' He looks up again. Wet face blotched red, eyes desperate. The swollen lids he'd had when visiting earlier clearly weren't due to pollen. 'No one else would still love you, Janet . . . forgive you like I did.'

His sticky, damp hand slides on top of hers, squeezes. In her mind she lifts her other, burrows under her bandage and digs her nails into the wound. 'I know, Colin . . . I know they wouldn't.' She forces a smile, wipes away his tears with her thumb.

'Could you pass me a tissue from the glove compartment, please?'

She releases the latch and frees the white tufts from the box.

'I'm going to get a paper. Do you want anything?'

She shakes her head. 'Can I pop in to see Dad for a couple of seconds before we go home?'

'You want your dad to see you with a bandage around your head? Worry the hell out of him?'

'No . . . I didn't think, I—'

'You never do, do you.' He dries his eyes with the tissue, blows his nose, and places the dirty remains into her extended palm. In turn, she disposes of it in her handbag so as not to mess up the car.

The woman weaves red ribbons through her daughter's hair.

On the dressing table lies a copy of Disney Princess *magazine, opened on a picture of Ariel for reference.*

As the mother plaits and knots, the girl sits, wonkily applying red lipstick, legs swinging beneath the foil fabric fin, its crackle amplified with each motion. As she admires her reflection in the heart-shaped mirror, her tiny palm pats her chest, covered by a bralette, hand-bejewelled by the mother with plastic gems and shells. 'I think I'm going to be the best one there, Mummy.'

When they descend the stairs together, slow, elegant, enacting their own entrance in a Disney movie, the father, lift-giver, waits at the bottom, keys in hand. 'You're not wearing all that make-up. Go and take it off,' he says.

'It's fine . . . she's Ariel. She's got red lips,' says the woman, grip tightening around her daughter's fingers.

'I don't care, it's far too much. She's a little girl.'

The daughter stares up at the woman, scarlet bottom lip protruding with pre-cry trembles.

'It's just fancy dress, love.' The woman's voice is calm, in contrast to her insides.

He turns from them both, walks towards the door as if relenting. Then he inserts the key and locks the Chubb. 'Fine, then. If she doesn't want to go.'

14

Do You Know This Woman?

As they roll into the cul-de-sac, Mary stops trimming her hedge and uses her hand as a sun shield while squinting towards the car. Janet avoids her stares, pretending she's oblivious.

Once parked up, Colin gets out, places the folded newspaper under his arm. He walks around to the passenger side and opens the door. How caring he must look to prying eyes. Though Janet can barely contain a smirk at Mary's desperation to know what's happened.

Entering the house is already strange. It's the first night she's had away in eleven years. And as her slippers hit the prickles of doormat, it's as though a pin has pierced her stomach and deflated her.

He removes her cardigan as she clumsily twirls to assist. The closest they've been to dancing since 2007. 'You get yourself up to bed, I've put the electric blanket on.'

'Thank you,' she says, even though it's over seventy degrees and she's menopausal.

Facing the stairs, she doubts her ability to make it to the bedroom. But she's desperate for a wee and doesn't want a repeat of the Greggs incident. She's never been able to go back there, and Colin misses his weekly sausage roll.

When she's halfway up, he says, 'And Janet . . .'

She turns, looks down towards him, crosses one leg over the other.

'Remember how the doctor said you must try to avoid stress? Well, you know how Claire's room upsets you, so I've locked it.'

'Oh . . . OK.' Head dropped, eyes sadly lowered, she delivers the reaction he wants.

After an awful night's sleep, she's relieved it's the morning. As well as his snoring and bed-hogging, her injuries made it impossible to get comfortable. And as she lay there, unable to even toss and turn, her brain was awash with a myriad of thoughts, never letting up.

As Colin dresses, it's obvious he doesn't want to leave her and do his shift. Thankfully, it's too short notice not to go in. He's already on thin ice after a row with the owner, Steve, about refusing long fares, which concluded with him agreeing to do one to Leeds on Thursday. Not to mention the verbal warning he received for being rude to Mel on reception.

Before leaving, he presents her with stewed tea and anaemic toast with jam. Making her yearn for the less inedible hospital breakfast. 'I'll be fine . . . you get going,' she says. 'I'll just sleep, I'm sure.'

As soon as she hears the slam of the front door, her anxiety evaporates. Throwing off the covers she gets up and looks out the window, peeking through a crack in the nets to ensure he's gone.

Dressing gown now on, her mindless stroking of the dog in her pocket is hampered by a stiff spike of screwed-up paper leaf. Removing it, she goes to throw it in the bin, but stops, slides it back in next to the toy, and heads to Claire's room.

The door handle doesn't budge. He wasn't bluffing.

Opening the airing cupboard fills the hall with the scent of fabric conditioner. Blindly, she pats the wooden slats of the top shelf, feeling her way behind the old, folded sheets. He always hides the key there when he's had enough, locks it up. It not only amazes her that he's never cottoned on she knows, but that he can reach to put it there in the first place. Once located and the cold metal touches her fingertips, a shot of pain strikes through her eye to the back of her skull. She drops her hand and clasps it over her socket. Maybe he's right. It would upset her, cause stress. Exhaling through the throbs, she closes the cupboard, deciding to take this opportunity to wean herself off the continual need.

Instead, she slowly makes her way downstairs and goes to the lounge. Sitting in his chair, she powers up his laptop, password Ferrari_man. When they first started dating, she'd asked him if he was a leg or breast man. 'I'm a Ferrari man,' he said.

She searches for the train crash and ingests all the information she can find. There's nothing that hasn't been gleaned from the news. The mobile phone footage is nowhere, and she considers if perhaps she'd imagined it. A symptom of her head injury.

A picture of Elizabeth comes up. A different one. This time with both parents. She lingers on it for a moment, prays for them.

After clearing the history and returning the laptop to its exact spot, she goes over to the sideboard and takes out her address book. But as she flicks through to Nish's number, she pauses. It's there again. That unsettling déjà vu.

Hands shaking, she tries to dismiss the sensation, and dials. After several rings, she's about to replace the receiver when she hears, 'Hello?' Nish's tone is uncharacteristically restrained and polite.

'It's me. Janet.'

A huge sigh breathes down her ear. 'Oh, thank fuck. I thought that was Colin, saying . . . Are you OK?'

The comfort of hearing Nish's voice makes her smile. 'You know, then? Yes, yes . . . a bumped head, that's all, and a bit battered. I don't remember anything about it.'

'I rang to see how your hangover was, and it turned out – really fucking bad. I'm so relieved you're OK, I can't tell you. Colin said you weren't allowed visitors at the hospital, so I thought you were really fucked up . . . in intensive care or something.'

'Sorry . . . yes, he did say but I wasn't really up for talking in there. I'm home now, though.'

'And what do you mean you can't remember?'

'No, it's so strange. I can't remember it . . . it's completely blank.'

'Like full-on Jason Bourne?'

'Who? Anyway, I was just letting you know that I'm OK. But I won't be coming in for a few days – well, I'm not sure how long to be honest . . . Will you let Sam know? I don't feel up to talking to her, to anyone really at the moment.'

'Of course . . . bloody hell, Janet. Six died, you know? And did you hear Robbie Pilkington's kid was in it too?'

'Yes . . . yes, I know.' The cord of her dressing gown is wrapped so tightly around her hand, white knuckles peek through. 'You didn't see some footage on the news at all, did you?'

'Of the crash? Yes, I've been watching—'

'No, not the . . . it doesn't matter.'

'I can't believe it. We had such a good night as well.'

'Did we? Look, I promise I'll speak to you soon, but I—'

'What I don't understand though, is why you were even on the train. Colin was driving you home. He dropped me off and—'

'I . . . I don't know, Nish. I've no idea where I was going. That's what I mean.'

She's been dozing in bed for a couple of hours, overheated. Disorientated by the white noise of TV and the screams of next door's trampolining children. During this sleeping limbo she identifies the jarring sound of a doorbell, and covers her face with her bandaged arm, presuming it's on *Homes Under the Hammer*.

But it dings once more. Infiltrating the house. When her brain catches on that it's her doorbell, she scrambles for the nightie strewn on the adjacent pillow.

Putting on her dressing gown, she peeks through a gap in the curtains but can't see anyone, so reluctantly heads downstairs.

The caller rings again, adding an impatient rat-a-tat-tat with the knocker. 'I'm coming,' she shouts, her headache now also awoken.

As she opens the door, the sun stabs her tired eyes.

It's Mary Clarke. Standing before her in a boob tube bodice sundress exposing white marks over her shoulders. Ghosts of previously worn straps. She's gripping a newspaper between her fingers. The front page, a photograph of the crash, distorted by a fold.

'What can I do for you, Mary?' Janet pulls herself upright. Bandage clearly visible. Unflinching. Until she's thrown by the neighbour's expression. An excited, wide-eyed grin.

'Were you in that train crash, Janet?'

Here it is. She's never called her Janet before. Never even bothered speaking to her before. Not since Claire, anyway. In films, communities come together. Neighbours rally round, leave casserole pots on the doorstep. Here, there was nothing but speculation, judgement.

'I was, Mary, yes.' Annoyed at herself for so readily offering up information, she refrains from elaborating.

'Can I come in?' As though it were a parallel universe where it's acceptable to barge into people's homes uninvited, Mary pushes through the doorway, throwing, 'Have you seen this?' behind her as she strides towards the lounge.

Janet follows the unwanted guest. 'You can't just . . . I'm really not feeling very well. I was in bed. Sleeping.'

Mary stands in the middle of the sitting room, opening and folding over the paper with exaggerated arm movements.

'Mary . . . Sorry, but you can't just walk in and . . . What are you doing?'

'I kept saying to Nigel when they showed that footage—'

'Footage?'

'"I recognize that person," I said.' She stabs at a page with her finger. '"Oh, who is it, Nige," I kept saying, "it's driving me mad."' She looks up for a moment, takes in the room, nostrils flaring as she appears to be analysing the decor, then resumes. 'And I sat down for a read with a cup of tea, and I saw this, and I thought, of course . . . of course. That's who it is. It's Janet from number twenty-seven.'

Janet snatches the paper from Mary, stares at the picture. The awful picture. It's a still from the footage she'd watched in the hospital. Not imagined at all. And explains the pre-occupation she's had with it. There's the same blurred graininess, but it's been lightened for clarity. The flesh packed into the jumper, not blurred enough. But it's true. It is her.

She drops onto the sofa, pages now draped over her knees, and stares into space as Mary paces the room, barking into her phone. 'Nige, it's me . . . No, shut up, I can't talk, but it's Janet . . . on that footage . . . yes . . . that was driving me mad . . . Janet . . . from number twenty-seven. Janet . . . from opposite. Janet . . . no, Janet. How many have you had? Nigel, you can't even talk properly . . . It's the middle of the day. No, not one more pint . . . I'm telling you, get home right now.' She prods at the handset, then turns to Janet and smiles. 'He says hello.'

'Well, thanks for showing me, Mary.' Her voice is dazed, flat. 'Yes, I was in the crash and yes, this is me, so you've got your answers . . . but I need to rest now. Doctor's orders and all that.'

Mary glides to her side. 'Have you read it though? Have you read what it says?'

'Yes, Mary. I've seen it. I've seen everything about the crash and I'm going to have to ask you to leave now, please.'

'No . . . not about the crash.' She shakes her head as if exasperated. 'About you.'

'What?' Janet lifts the paper from her legs, begins to read.

DO YOU KNOW THIS WOMAN?

'How fantastic that you saved that little girl . . . I do enjoy her father on that programme. I made his vegetarian lasagne once and I'm not even a fan of courgettes, but Nigel said it was the best he's had. You should . . .'

Mary's voice fades, the room transforms into a carousel.

Our journalist Molly Sullivan captured footage showing a woman emerging from the scene seeking help for eight-year-old Elizabeth Pilkington, daughter of celebrity chef Robbie Pilkington and model Mia Pilkington. The woman pulled the child from the wreckage and resuscitated her with CPR. Elizabeth is now in a stable condition in the Manchester Children's Hospital.

'They want to find you, look. There's a number to call if anyone knows—'

'My eyes haven't been injured, Mary. I can read.'

Elizabeth's parents want to find this brave passenger. 'Whoever helped Elizabeth and alerted the rescuers is a hero. We will forever be indebted and beyond grateful,' said Mr Pilkington.

'You're a bloody hero, Janet. To think it was my friend all along.'

'A hero . . .'

'Don't worry, I'll call them. You're not well enough.'

'What?' A knee-jerk panic propels her to standing. Imagining Colin's reaction. 'No, no . . . looking at it closely, Mary, I don't think it is me after all.' She hands the newspaper back. Despite the forced rigidity of her arm, she cannot restrain its shakes.

'What are you talking about?' Mary frantically reopens the pages. 'It's you, look . . . you.'

'I don't think it is . . . I don't remember it, so please don't call them.'

'Well, it doesn't matter if you remember it or not, it's there.'

The room shifts beneath Janet's slippers, heat surges through her body. 'Look, I . . . I need to go back to bed. Really . . . I don't feel well.'

The excuse has morphed into reality, and Mary looks perturbed by the sweat seeping from Janet's top lip. 'OK, well . . . I'll come back in a while, so you can look again. Because it is you.'

Janet feels for the sofa with the backs of her legs and sits. 'Do you mind letting yourself out?'

'Of course . . . you get some rest.' A polite smile fixes upon Mary's face. 'You look like death.' The crumple of folding paper fills the otherwise silent room.

'Thank you. Though actually, would you mind if I keep the paper? To read about the crash.'

After hoicking up the shirred elastic top of her sundress, Mary gently places the newspaper on the couch. 'Oh . . . well, OK. I suppose it's only forty pence.'

*

As soon as the slam of the front door ricochets through the house, Janet repeatedly reads the article. Slow, deliberate. Mumbling each word quietly as her knees move up down, up down, expelling accumulated energy, like steam from a pressure cooker. With each read, one word lingers. Fizzes on her tongue.

Hero.

Sliding her hand inside her dressing gown pocket, she strokes the dog, fingers swirling around its soft fur, then feels for the paper leaf.

She pulls it out, screwed and tatty. Flattens it onto her palm.

And she remains there for some time. Staring at her scribbled handwriting.

Please God, give me a sign that I am forgiven.

The facade of Mary and Nigel's isn't that spotless now she's close up. Considering the time spent outside preening and spying. The uPVC window frames need a good bleaching, and the brass knob is a patchwork of fingerprints.

The doorbell's sound is low and feeble, so she presses her fingertip hard against it multiple times. The repetitive tune circulates through the house, a faint version raining back down onto her via an open upstairs window.

A blurred Mary approaches, pixelated by mottled glass. 'I'm coming,' she shouts, an angry lilt to her voice.

She seems surprised to see Janet as the unveiled caller. 'Oh, hello . . . have you realized it's you, then?'

Janet holds out the paper, giving it one last smooth down

before it exchanges hands. 'Yes, you were right. It is me. I looked again, and it definitely is. If you want to call up, then that's up to you.'

'Well, I won't if you don't want me—'

'No, you must . . . I mean, it's not for me to tell you what to do. It probably would be the right thing though, I suppose. You do know who it is, after all.'

Mary is stumped for something to say, which Janet imagines is a first. Until she finally manages a small, 'Oh, OK . . . well then, I'll do it right now, if you—'

'It's only right, Mary. Anyway, I must . . .' She gestures behind with her thumb.

'Of course.' And as Janet turns and walks away, she can hear, 'If there's anything I can do, Janet, let me know and I'll come over.'

She doesn't acknowledge the gesture. Merely strides forward towards her open door. Not once did Mary make such an offer when Claire died. Not once.

15

Tomorrow's Chip Paper

The next couple of hours pass with bursts of either sitting, in a desperate attempt to remain calm, or pacing the lounge – fireplace to sideboard, sideboard to fireplace. Breaking only for cups of tea – eating not an option, as her churning stomach would surely rebel.

During one of these laps, she remains at the sideboard and removes her address book, flipping the pages to H. A number used so often for her dad, she should really know it off by heart. 'Hello, can you put me through to the Children's Hospital, please . . . Oh right, could you give me the number then, please?'

Concentrating on the jotted digits, she dials again. Launching into her poshest telephone voice when someone picks up. 'Hello . . . hi, I was calling up about a patient. Elizabeth Pilkington. I was wondering how she's doing . . . No, no, not family, but I saved her and . . . Oh, yes of course, yes . . . yes . . . I understand.' She replaces the receiver, riddled with indignant disappointment. Feelings that dissipate when the sound of key in lock reverberates through the house, and she freezes as if partaking in a lone game of musical statues.

'Janet.' It sounds as though he's shouting up the stairs.

'I'm in here,' she calls back. Her perky tone an affectation.

Appearing in the doorway, he's out of breath, face drained of colour. A rolled-up newspaper clutched in his fist. 'Janet, there's . . . Oh my god, Janet, there's something—'

'I know. I know, Colin.' She frees herself from the awkward stance and sighs.

'How? Did they—?'

'Mary . . .' Her arm swings towards the window. 'Barging in here like bloody Poirot.'

Stiff and dazed, he enters the room. Not making it to his chair, but dropping onto the sofa, staring outwards. He never sits there. Everything is skewed, peculiar. 'Stop pacing, for goodness' sake, woman.'

She complies. Unaware she'd even started doing so again.

'It's true then? You saved this little girl?'

'Yes, I suppose it is . . . I still can't actually remember.' A smile spreads over her face like spilt ink on blotting paper.

'But how, Janet? How did you save her, when you couldn't save—'

'I can't believe it.' She giggles. 'I saved her . . . I saved that gorgeous little girl.'

'How . . . what did you do?'

'And she's going to be OK. Because of me.' She turns to look at him, face illuminated. 'What? Well . . . I, I don't know that bit yet, do I, Colin? Though by the sounds of the footage and the article, I pulled her out, gave her mouth to mouth . . . That's what it says . . . I saw it, you see. In the hospital. The footage. I didn't understand at the time, because everything was so muddled . . . but that's because it was me. It was me.'

She drops into his chair. Cured of all injuries. Aches and head pain disappeared. Like a seesaw in action Colin stands and, as though having taken the baton in a relay race, begins pacing. Elbows forming triangles as he clasps his hands behind his head. 'Wow . . . You know she's Robbie Pilkington's child, don't you? I've seen him around Worsley, in his new Porsche 911 Turbo S. God, it's beautiful.'

Janet reaches behind for a cushion and places it on her knee, squeezing all her excited energy into the foam. 'I know, I was with you when you saw him.' The back of her hand presses against her mouth to suppress her happiness. Then she takes it away. She doesn't want to suppress it. 'I can't believe it.'

Colin stops, turns to her. 'What about where you were going? Do you remember that now?'

'Jesus, Colin.' She looks at him. He cannot help but dim her light. 'I don't know, do I? Probably back to the girls in Eccles . . . I don't know, it's all irrelevant. What matters is that I was meant to be on that train. For Elizabeth.'

His widening eyes indicate she's gone too far, so she lowers her voice and stands. 'Let's have a cup of tea, eh, love. You've been at work all day and it's a bit of a shock, this. Things like this don't happen to people like us. You'll need something inside you.'

He collects up the paper and still with an air of bemusement, sits in his chair. 'I . . . I suppose a sandwich might help.'

'Yes, see.' She tucks a rogue tuft of hair back under her bandage. 'I've got those nice turkey slices you like.'

The TV comes to life. On the way towards the door, she neatens the reeds in a diffuser, basking in her new high.

'It's fine anyway. It's not like they know it's you.'

She stops still. Sensing him turning towards her, she does the same to meet him.

'No, Janet . . . tell me they don't know it's you.'

'It was Mary.'

'I don't want—'

'I know, I know you don't . . . and neither do I, but she was adamant she was going to ring them. I begged her not to, but I didn't feel well enough to argue.'

He stands, appearing to gather his thoughts. Fist balled tight. 'I'm going over there. I'm not having some stupid cow interfering.'

Rushing over to him she strokes her hands down his arms, then unfurls his fingers, relaxing each digit, one by one, while calmly saying, 'No, don't be daft. Remember what the doctor said. Don't you think that would stress me? Arguing with the neighbours? It's done now. If it hadn't been her, it would have been someone else. And I know for a fact Nigel goes to the Martial Arts Club in Swinton.'

As he releases a long breath, she follows suit.

Back in his chair, he reaches for the remote and flicks through the channels.

'I'll get you that sandwich then, shall I?'

His scrolling stops on an old episode of *Dragons' Den*. 'Anyway, I'm sure it'll all be tomorrow's chip paper.'

'Of course it will be. It'll all blow over in a day or so.'

But as she walks to the kitchen, hand inside her pocket, bypassing the dog to touch the leaf, she smiles.

There's nothing 'tomorrow's chip paper' about a message from God.

16

Titian Hair

The next morning, rousing from a sleep deeper than she can remember, her first thought isn't her injuries or the crash. Nor the usual gnawing dread of the empty robotic day ahead. It isn't even Claire. Thankfully, those intense horrified realizations on opening her eyes stopped some years ago. Today, the only thing that dominates her mind is – she saved a child.

And with this comes the alien sensation of waking happy.

Eventually her musings transfer to Elizabeth's recovery. Wishing she were still in hospital so she could attempt to visit her. *I'm Janet*, she'd say. *The lady who saved you.*

Tingles build inside her stomach, travelling through her arms as she spreads them like branches and yawns.

Colin is clanking around the kitchen, presumably making his own breakfast. Further mark of a special occasion. She should stay in bed, revel in laziness for once. But after a further ten minutes of forced relaxation, she gets up, pulls on her dressing gown and heads downstairs.

'Why don't I do that?' She slides the spatula from his hand, gently placing herself between him and the smouldering pan. 'We both know I'm the queen of the crispy edges.'

She can feel him close against her back, his hands sliding

around her waist. Rigid, she ignores the gesture. 'It's all about the temperature of the oil.'

He buries his head into her neck, while she takes a spoon from the drawer and coats the yolk with the hot liquid.

'I am trying to be proud of you, Janet,' he says.

She nods, relieved to feel him slip away, followed by the scrape of the stool against the lino. 'Only, it's hard. That you managed to save a girl when . . .' He doesn't finish the words, but she hears them all the same, and her intake of breath is audible over the spitting fat.

After he's left for work and she's alone with the greasy pan and delicate eggshells, the giddy internal fires burn brightly and will not be doused. She should tell Nish. Perhaps she already knows. The article is there for all to see. And her dad. She can't wait to tell her dad.

The house isn't up to its usual cleanliness standards, and she must resist remedying that. But the stench of fry-up means she at least needs to clear up the kitchen, get rid of the greasy staleness. Starting by opening the back door, letting in clean, hopeful air.

It's a beautiful day. Periwinkle sky and the smell of cut grass, only faintly tainted by distant car fumes. She can't help but step out, welcoming the warm breeze on her face.

It seems Colin has finally started work on the garden. Ash litters the fire pit. She'd have appreciated it more if instead he'd done some cleaning while she was in hospital, but at least it looks like he's not touched the wilderness at the far end. He'd let it get that way on purpose to stop Claire going near the buckled fencing bordering the railway embankment. Rather than arranging for it to be fixed, he allowed brambles to take over. Like their marriage, a problem left to worsen and now too big to tackle. Brambles, resentments, they're all the same. But she appreciates it now. A secret forest sheltering a vixen and her little cubs when they're not loitering around the tracks. Coming and going as they please. She doesn't mention how often she sees them to Colin. He'd probably do something to deter them. He has no concept of leaving things be. Like Claire's room. He doesn't grasp the importance for her things to remain exactly as they are. But thankfully, he's all talk. The garden's been like this for so many years now, she can't imagine it ever being sorted.

Her roses have drooped. Their coral tears cried to the ground.

She probably shouldn't be moving around so much but can't resist dropping down the step and walking the stretch of lawn for a snatch of their scent to further lift her spirits.

Running her fingers over the velvet petals, she bends her head, slowly, so as not to shake her brain, then closes her eyes, inhales. Lost in a peaceful moment.

Then everything alters.

The sound of an approaching train steals away her calm, carrying her elsewhere. To rust-coated tracks. Close up. An intricate photograph of the tarnished metal. Cold against the warm of her blood-dampened skin.

The train is nearing.

Now passing.

Nailed to the ground, her body rocks with light-headed sways. And she remains in this state, as though paralysed in sleep, until she's finally snapped into the present by the shrill of the doorbell.

*

Heart racing, she strides back up the garden.

It will be the postman, or a request to take in yet another delivery for next door. But she doesn't feel she could even manage to communicate with a postman.

As she steps inside, the bell rings again, further shredding her nerves. 'Hello,' she calls out, entering the hall. 'Can you please leave it on the doorstep.' The unpleasant tune fills the house once more. 'I'm coming,' she shouts. It dawns on her that it could be Mary. *Oh God, please don't be Mary.*

With a deep breath and plastered smile, she presses down on the latch and pulls the door inwards, ensuring her undressed state remains hidden. Only her bandaged head and a single eye exposed.

'Hello?' A stranger stands before her. A familiar stranger. Suit inappropriate for the heat. Titian hair. The woman from the revolving door.

17

The Royal Doulton Lady in the Lilac Dress

'I've found you.'

Janet inches open the door, studies the smiling woman and her dark, blank, impenetrable eyes. On closer inspection, a fine layer of white cat hairs cling to the suit. Mud tips the toes of her pointed shoes.

'I'm sorry, I don't under—'

'Are you aware you're bleeding?' The woman nods towards Janet's hand.

'What?' She glances down. 'Oh . . . oh my goodness.' A thread of blood is trickling down her finger, veering towards her palm. She automatically sucks at it like a baby on a pacifier. Only removing it to say, 'It must have been the roses . . . Sorry, can I help you?'

'Course, sorry. My name's Molly. Molly Sullivan. I was the person who you . . . well, who you collapsed on at the crash scene.'

Withdrawing her finger from her lips, despite being all Mrs Miller in her dressing gown, Janet says, 'Oh . . . Oh, hello. Please, come in.' The decision to do so is instinctual. They're connected. Anyone involved with the crash is immediately considered bonded to her in some way. She holds the door open, trying not to fret about the mud as Molly steps inside. 'So . . . I was right then. I did know you.'

'Sorry?'

'I saw you in the hospital and knew your face, but I didn't know why . . . The lounge is the first on the right.'

The front door is pressed shut, but Molly remains in the hall, staring back towards it. 'Sorry, Janet, I've got someone with me, the photographer, David, though he—'

'Photographer? I don't understand?' She tightens her dressing gown belt. 'What's going on?'

Molly places a hooked finger beneath her nose, as though thinking of what to say next or how to form its delivery. 'Nothing's going on . . . well, not unless you want it to, which I hope you do.'

'Can you cut the riddles, please?' The connection she was so certain of a moment ago is severed.

Molly smiles softly. 'OK, well, I was the person who helped you, but I'm also a reporter.' She opens her jacket to show a laminated pass clipped to the top of her skirt. Janet notices the bottom button of her shirt is missing. 'I work at the Manchester office, and I'm the one that filmed the footage and subsequently the stills which helped find you. We ran an article and—'

'Yes, I know.'

'OK. Well, we've been looking for you . . . because it appears you helped save a girl called Elizabeth – the daughter of—'

'I know, I know I did. At least I . . . But why are you here? In my house?'

The doorbell rings.

She maintains eye contact with Molly then breaks off and goes to open the door. A man with a hound-dog face, flakes of pastry speckling his shirt, and a large camera in his hand is standing on the step. He flicks a smile at Janet then extends his neck to view into the hallway, 'Am I coming in or what?'

'Go and wait in the car for a bit, will you, Dave?'

He saunters back towards a Peugeot parked up on the pavement, almost touching her pansy border. Janet closes the door once more and faces Molly, who says, 'That's Dave, the photographer,' and turns, seemingly following Janet's previous instruction by heading for the lounge.

'Look, I'm going to have to ask you to leave. You can't come here under false pretences. I'm not even dressed.'

'You've got a lovely home, Mrs Brown. Very . . . neat.' Molly picks up Victoria, the Royal Doulton lady in the lilac dress, swivelling her, viewing the bone china from all angles. 'My gran used to have one of these.'

'Could you put her back, please? She's been discontinued.'

'She died a couple of years ago. I've no idea where it is now.'

'Well, I'm . . . I'm very sorry to hear that.' Janet wonders how long would be appropriate to wait before she can ask again for her to leave the figurine alone. But thankfully, Molly puts Victoria back down of her own accord, albeit in the wrong position.

Noticing her dressing gown is sliding open, Janet turns around to tighten the belt, taking the opportunity to blurt out what she needs to say. 'Look, I . . . I don't want to talk to the press. Not without discussing it with my husband first . . . and I can't remember what happened anyway, so I've really not got anything to tell you.'

When Janet is back facing the room, Molly is looking through the window. 'He never stops eating, that man,' she says, quiet, as though to herself. Pulling away from the net curtains, she turns to Janet. 'I completely understand, Mrs Brown. But the thing is, a neighbour called up and identified you, and I've no doubt there'll be others. It's out there now, who you are . . . and, well, the story's going to run with or without your consent. In the paper, on social media.' Janet stares, says nothing, forcing Molly to complete her point. 'So . . . well, what I'm saying is, you may as well speak to me. Get some money for it. Get the words you want printed. Otherwise, people can make up any old lies . . . I couldn't use your toilet, could I?'

Janet wants to tell her no, to bugger off. 'Up the stairs, first door on the left.'

To the background noise of court shoes climbing treads, Molly's muddied toes an additional unwelcome thought, she goes to the sideboard, repositions Victoria, then calls Colin. It rings out. Each subsequent redial ending with the same robotic voicemail message.

Quitting at the sound of the toilet's flush, she rushes to the window with the impossible hope of him having just arrived home. But there's only Dave, chomping down on something emerging from a white paper bag. And now Mary. Bloody Mary wandering over, wearing uncharacteristically bright lipstick and a floaty top.

At the thud of Molly descending the stairs, Janet heads to the hall just as the doorbell rings.

'So, have you had a think?' Molly is poised on the bottom step.

'I've told you, I'll have to speak to my husband. And anyway, I can't have myself or the house photographed in this state. I haven't even hoovered.'

'OK. OK, that's no problem. What time?'

'I don't know . . . he'll be back about two.'

'Great, well, how about we come back at two thirty?'

The bell rings again, and Janet relents with a small nod.

Opening the door reveals a beaming Mary, who's acknowledged by Molly with a dry, 'Hi,' as she brushes past.

Both women watch in silence as Molly gets into the car next to Dave, who's busy ridding his shirt of crumbs.

When the Peugeot has completed its three-point turn and exits the cul-de-sac, Mary swivels back to Janet. 'Oh, this is so exciti—'

'I can't talk now, Mary,' she says, and closes the door.

18

Done Up Like a Dog's Dinner

She's had her name in a newspaper before. As Claire's mother in the obituary, and the time she was a witness to the raging drunk man who overturned a trolley in Lidl and rampaged through the store with a rounders bat stolen from the central aisle.

But this is entirely different. It's huge, national. Not a freebie stuck through doors in Salford, half of which were probably destined for use as cat litter-tray liners.

Everyone will see what she's done. The good she's done.

She wouldn't entertain any 'new age' nonsense before Claire died. But afterwards, when she encountered signs – feathers, Claire's favourite songs playing on the radio, she became more open to such things. It was then she started to watch the Psychic Channel. Well, primarily Jason Quartz. Unlike the others who smack of phoniness, he has a true gift. Referring to the dead as 'energies' that are still with us, but in a different form. Which is exactly what she feels in Claire's room. That she's still there. Tucked up under her mermaid duvet.

And so, by that logic, if the dead carry energies, then so do the living. And for eleven years, Janet has imagined hers to be dark, murky, heavy. But sitting on the sofa, waiting for Colin, she already feels lighter. Lake-water clear. Resolved that she will prepare for the newspaper interview. With an uncharacteristic inner confidence that it *will* go ahead. That she'll not allow him to take it from her. Not this. Whatever pretence of reluctance she'll perform.

Opting to wear something smart and unfussy, she picks out the grey trousers bought in the Next sale at the same time as the pink ones. Being woollen, they're slightly too wintery but nicely classic. And no one will be able to tell that she's too hot. For her top, she's chosen the white blouse with an embroidered butterfly on the breast pocket. A favourite charity shop purchase.

In her underwear, she irons the blouse and places it on a hanger. Noticing yet another wrinkle, she goes over it again. Then again. After four attempts, she accepts it will have to do.

She brushes her hair as sleek as she can while having a bandage wrapped around her head. Trying to ignore all thoughts that she looks like Björn Borg, she applies a pop of pink lipstick.

Before going downstairs, she nips into the toilet to open a new Lily of the Valley Glade Solid Gel.

In the lounge, she plumps the cushions, debating if she should swap the filling with her bedroom ones, because they're ever so deflated.

After all the dusting and titivating, head pounding and fatigued, she knows she's overdone it. But stopping isn't an option, so she fetches the Dyson. She can't risk the nation thinking her sloppy. You only get one chance for your home to appear in a national newspaper. Even if it ends up only showing the arm of the sofa.

She vacuums the arm of the sofa.

*

Hearing wheels across gravel, she deactivates the Dyson. The key clicks in the lock. 'Hello, love . . . I'm in here,' she shouts.

Colin is soon standing in the doorway, his neutral facial expression switching to puzzlement. 'What's going on?' He flings his newspaper onto the sideboard, clipping red-dressed Estelle in her delicate face. Janet pretends not to have noticed. 'What are you all done up like a dog's dinner for? You're supposed to be resting.'

She presses her wrist against her mouth to blot the lipstick. 'I'm not . . . I had to get dressed because . . . now, please don't go off the deep end, because I had no choice, they were going to do it anyway. She said she would run it regardless, and—'

'Slow down . . . what the hell are you on about, woman?' He crosses the room to his chair, drops onto the seat, and proceeds to undo his laces. 'You're feeling better then?'

It's vital she just says it before losing her nerve. 'The paper's coming to do an interview in half an hour.'

There's no acknowledgement. He says nothing, does nothing. Then the cogs set in motion and he turns towards her, forehead concertinaed, his rogue head-vein worming its way towards the skin's surface.

'I had no choice, Colin. They were running it anyway and I said, "No . . . definitely not," but she made it very clear that they'd make it all up if not. And we can't have that. Them making up lies about me . . . about you. Because they will. You tell me they will, you always say what a bunch of—'

'Shut up, Janet. Just shut up.'

Mouth clamped, she remains still, rigid.

'They're coming here? To do an interview?'

She nods, adding, 'But we'll be paid. And as she said, why should we let them write any old—'

'Me as well?' The corner of his mouth twitches.

'Yes . . . yes, of course you as well.'

'How much?'

'Well, I don't know that . . . I did try and call you numerous times, Colin, but—'

'Janet.' His arm protrudes, palm faced in her direction.

Head dropping, she can feel the opportunity slipping away. The vow of standing firm going the same way as all her other broken vows. Silence fills the space. She dare not look at him. Merely closes her eyes and waits for the wave to pass.

'I'd better go and put on my new jumper then,' he says.

While peeking through the net curtains, Dave's Peugeot rolls up and parks across the driveway, blocking the Avensis. Colin comes behind to look, and to her astonishment doesn't comment. His heart beats rapid against her back, breath smelling strongly of Listerine. When she turns, their faces brush, and he smiles in a way that reminds her of who he used to be. 'I'll go and let them in,' she says.

In the hall, she pats down her hair, gathers herself. Then with a fixed look of delight, opens the door.

'Any joy?' Molly's tone is no fuss, her expression flat.

Janet nods.

'Great, well, we won't be long, Mrs Brown. I'll get a few quotes from you, then Dave will grab a shot and we'll be off.'

Janet senses the change. Like the difference between a salesman before you've bought the car compared to once you've handed over the money.

'Is it OK if we come in?'

'Yes, of course . . . sorry, I'm still not quite with it.' She steps back, holding open the door as they walk through, clasping the wooden edge so tightly her fingers feel bruised. 'It's the room on the right . . . Oh, you've been here before, ignore me.'

She follows behind. Trying not to feel like she's relinquished control. Colin is standing in the lounge, central; arms straight like a painted toy soldier, wearing his previously unworn burgundy jumper, which, like her trousers, is far too wintery. 'This is my husband, Colin. He wasn't on the train. This is Molly, and this is . . .'

She can't remember the photographer's name, but he steps forth and presents his hand to Colin. 'Dave.'

Apparently having forgotten the basic concept of a handshake, Colin performs a peculiar stroking movement. To distract from this embarrassment, Janet says, 'Can I get you both a cup of coffee? Or tea? I have Earl Grey.'

Dave shakes his head and Molly says, 'No, I'm good thanks. I've got a Coke in my bag.'

Janet internally shudders at the possibility of sticky cola spurting over her carpet. But this leads to a far more unsettling image. The frantic scrubbing of a brown stain. Back and forth, back and forth. And as her eyes are slowly drawn downwards, she notices a patch of stiffened pile.

'Are you OK, Mrs Brown?'

'Yes . . . yes, sorry, Molly. Please, you must call me Janet. Right, how do we do this?'

Janet and Colin are sitting on the sofa like conjoined twins. Bodies twisted at awkward angles to face Molly, who sits next to them in a far more relaxed manner.

Catching her reflection in the framed print of Constable's

The Hay Wain hung above the sideboard, Janet winces, suddenly conscious of how ridiculous she must look.

Thankfully, she's distracted by Molly saying, 'Is that your daughter? I'm so sorry.'

There's only one photograph of Claire on display. It sits, centre of the mantelpiece, housed in a diamanté-studded frame with a red gem heart at the top.

'It is, yes . . . Claire. How do you . . .' Her words trail away, realizing the naivety in asking this of a journalist. People who hack grieving mothers' phones. Of course she already knows.

Colin stands, goes to get the frame, and holds it out towards Molly. 'She's a real mix of us in this one. It was taken at a beach in Pwllheli . . . she loved our holidays there.'

'I'm so sorry.' Molly takes the picture, reluctantly released by Colin. 'She was only seven when she died, wasn't she?'

Colin gently retrieves the frame and walks it back over to the fireplace. 'That's right. It would have been her eighteenth birthday on the day of the crash.'

Molly's eyes widen. 'What? So . . . but that's incredible. So, to get this straight, on the night of what would have been your daughter's eighteenth birthday, you saved the life of someone else's child?'

Hearing it summed up like that reinforces the clarity of God's message. His forgiveness. Janet sits taller, infused with confidence. 'Yes, that's right.'

'Well, Mrs Brown . . . Janet . . . that's some story.' Molly breaks a smile and fishes her phone from her bag, headphone wires tangling. The movement exudes potent perfume. Its sickly vanilla base wrestles with the nearby citrus reed diffuser.

'Right, I'm going to record now if that's OK?' She presses her phone, activating a small beep.

'Sorry,' says Colin. 'We'll be paid for this, yes? How much are we talking?'

'Oh, sorry . . . yes.' She turns off the record button. 'Fifty pounds.'

'Fifty quid? That's ridiculous. You've just said yourself what a story this is. No, I'm sorry—'

'Colin . . . please.' Janet squeezes his hand.

'Hundred quid or she doesn't say a word.'

Molly flicks a glance towards Dave, before looking up at the ceiling and blowing out her cheeks as if thinking. 'Well, I suppose it'll have to be then. Sure . . . sure, all right.' She turns to face Janet. 'So, I'm going to record now, OK?'

Janet nods. Colin pats her hand.

'Shall we start with that day. Had you done something to commemorate Claire's birthday?'

'No, we . . . I find it too upsetting to visit her grave. It's very difficult for me. Seeing her like that. I'd hoped over the years that we'd have at last been able to save up to get her a better headstone. Something she'd like that wasn't so . . . cold. But no, I hadn't been to the cemetery or anything.'

Molly's icy face softens. 'OK, so why don't we start with that night? Where were you going? At what point did you notice Elizabeth?'

'Unfortunately, like I said earlier, I don't remember any of it because of my head injury. I don't know where I was going.' The empathy is short-lived and Molly's face screws up like paper. 'The doctor said it's common. That it'll probably return soon, but . . . well, does it matter where I was going?'

Colin squeezes her hand. 'It does, but never mind for now.'

'Not at all,' says Molly. 'Did she not tell you where she was going, Colin?'

He scratches the side of his nose. 'No . . . no, she didn't.'

'Oh . . . OK. Only, readers like to get a full picture, but that's fine. Go on.'

Janet's throat tickles, escalating into an irritating cough. 'Sorry, can I get a glass of water.'

'Of course.' Molly's tone tightens through a smile. 'Colin, you couldn't get her a glass of water, could you? Then we can carry on as time's a bit limited.'

Janet can't bring herself to look at him. But her hand is released, and a flash of burgundy crosses behind Molly.

'So, you don't know where you were going but do you remember being on the train?' Molly's concentration is broken by the sound of Dave listening to something on his phone. 'Dave, mate, I'm recording here. Sorry, Janet. Let's try that again, shall we? So, you remember being on the train.'

'Yes, well, not exactly. Just that I know I was.'

'OK, great . . . and were you sitting near Elizabeth Pilkington?'

'I don't know . . . maybe. I don't know . . . sorry, I—'

'OK, that's fine . . . please don't fret, you're doing great, Janet.' Molly's cold hand rests on top of hers, then is lifted almost immediately. 'Are you able to tell me anything about the actual crash?'

'No, but I keep getting these strange flashbacks. Of rusty metal . . . and blood and . . . and there's burning.'

Colin re-enters, passes the water to Janet, then sits, patting her back like a baby as she sips.

'What about the moment of impact? Was that when you banged your head?'

Janet squeezes her eyes. 'They're only images . . . thoughts, maybe.'

Molly bends forward, intense eyes latching on to Janet's.

'Only snippets of things, I'm afraid.' Colin takes her hand again, his skin warm and clammy, the opposite to Molly's. 'Look, I really can't recall much, but I do know that seeing the little girl lying there, I couldn't let her die . . . I just couldn't.'

Molly stops the recording. 'And thank God you didn't.' She smiles. 'That's it. You did great.'

Colin raises his hand. 'Do you need to ask me anything?'

'No, thanks. You're fine.'

Red-faced, he nods.

Molly stands, puts her bag on her shoulder. 'Mate, you're up.'

Dave springs to life, camera poised in his podgy hands. Janet stiffens, adopts a fixed grimace. The explosion of flashes makes her blink repeatedly. 'Try and keep your eyes open, love.' She concentrates on adhering to the request. Maniacally so. While simultaneously developing an Elvis Presley lip twitch. She dares not even imagine what Colin's doing.

'That'll do,' says Dave, returning to his bag on the floor, packing away the camera.

Janet stands, and for the first time in what seems like hours, notices her headache. 'Well, thank you so much. I've never done anything like this before.'

'Well, I suppose you've never been a hero before and saved a child.' Molly places a hand on Janet's arm.

'No.' Janet smiles despite the words ripping her apart.

'And to think I had no idea it was also your daughter's

birthday. Such a fantastic story. If it all gets signed off OK, it should run tomorrow.'

The effort required to remain composed is immense as she follows them out to the hallway, her insides a bubbling concoction of excitement and apprehension. But as her fingers touch the door latch, Molly says, 'Oh, Janet . . . just one thing. You don't have a headshot picture of Claire we could have, do you?'

'Of Claire?'

'If you don't mind, I'd like to mention how it was her birthday as well. So, a picture would be great.'

Janet drops her head, unsure, then imagines Claire's beautiful face for the nation to see. For them to know she existed. 'OK . . . yes, that's fine.' She turns to Colin who's now standing at the bottom of the stairs, blocking her way. 'I need to get into Claire's room.'

'No, I'll go—'

'Actually,' says Molly, handing her a card. 'If you could email a digital one over, that would be ideal.'

As she watches them exit the cul-de-sac, Mary is sweeping her driveway, one eye hitched in her direction, body language threatening to come over. Janet goes back in and closes the door.

The house is now tranquil in the absence of guests. She and Colin stand in the hallway. Static. Avoiding each other's gaze.

'Right . . . well, that's it then, I guess. You're going to be in the paper.'

'I know.' Then their eyes do lock, and her breath catches. His expression changes, softens as though he's about to say something. Tell her he's proud. That she did something good.

'What's for dinner?' he says.

19

Read All About It

The effect of her returned sleep deprivation is different this morning. Most of the night had been spent ceiling-gazing. The Artex swirls, a screen projecting the overused film transition – the spinning newspaper. *Read all about it, read all about it. Train Crash Hero – Woman Saves Famous Chef's Child.* On the cover, a picture of her. Not Colin. And without the stupid bandage. Next to her, Claire's beautiful face.

And now, as she fries Colin's breakfast, oil spitting and pricking her arm, she's remarkably energized and doesn't feel exhausted at all. Visualizing Maggie's, the newsagent's up the road. The bales of papers ready to be sold. How people will buy a copy. The residents at Oakland House. Builders passing through. Folk from the housing estate opposite, picking one up with a pint of milk. They'll go home, have a brew, a read. 'Hey,' they'll say. 'That woman from round here saved a child. What a thing she's done. How terrible she lost her own. What a beautiful little girl she was. Claire.'

Positivity flows through her, escaping via a faint rendition of 'You Don't Own Me' floating from her lips. She hasn't heard the song for years and has no idea why it's entered her head. But as she stands over the crackling fat, spatula poised, the lyrics resonate.

'Are you singing?' Colin enters, putting on his watch.

'Oh . . . was I? I didn't realize. Do you want it in here or the lounge?'

Before he can answer, the phone rings, and with a huff he's gone again.

She cocks an ear, pauses the egg-pushing, but can still only detect the faintest murmur.

He returns, face flushed. 'That was the *Tribune*, wanting an interview. As if you'd be talking to some local paper. In fact, that's it now. If anyone else calls, make it clear you're not interested. I don't want this turning into a circus.' He pulls out the island stool and sits while she slides the contents of the pan onto his plate.

'OK,' she says. Although she'd happily talk about this to every paper, every person, she's grateful for her lot. 'I need to go and see Dad this morning. He'll wonder what's happened to me.'

Colin shoves a forkful of egg into his mouth. Rubbery white hangs over his lip, unable to make it inside before he responds. 'Well, he won't have a clue whether you go or not, will he?'

The pan hisses under the tap. 'All the same, if I could . . .' She stops. Remembers what she's done. How the world will see her from today. Pressing back her shoulders, she says, 'Well, I'm going to pop down, anyway. Say a quick hello.' She doesn't dare turn around. Merely squirts Fairy into the sink and stares as the bubbles form on the green-tinged water.

Chews squelch from behind until he says, 'It wasn't your best, love. You know I hate a snotty egg-top. I'll drop you off before work. Wait outside. A quick hello shouldn't take you long.'

The phone rings again. 'Ignore it,' he says.

*

As they drive past Maggie's, she turns to Colin, attempting to identify hints of altered expression. There aren't any, and she wonders if he's forgotten that his wife is in a national tabloid. 'Should we stop and get a paper?' Her voice is as casual as her desperation allows. There's no response. The no-talking rule. Until they stop at traffic lights, and staring straight ahead he says, 'I'll get one later, bring it home.'

Her dad looks content in his chair. Tray table over his legs, on which sits a fraying plastic beaker. He's grinning at the TV, *Hello Britain*. The presenters, Nick and Jessica, are laughing at something or other. They're always laughing. No one has that much of a sunny disposition.

'Hey, Dad, it's me.' She kisses his cheek. 'Sorry it's been a couple of days; I've been a bit poorly.'

As he turns, head only, his smile drops. 'Oh . . . oh dear, we need to get you some Germolene.' His age-warped hand reaches for her head, and taps at her bandage, making her wince. 'Such a clumsy girl, you are.'

Perching next to him on the little old pouffe, its velvet buffed shiny from years of her heavy bottom, she's now transformed into the tiny girl he's imagining.

Her eyes flick to the wall clock. Fifteen minutes, she's allowed. 'Hey, Dad, guess what?'

He points at the TV. There's a segment about school funding cuts, showing a group of screaming primary-age children cavorting around a playground. 'This is how you fall over, see.'

'Dad . . . Dad . . . look at me a minute.' Gently, she places her hand on his silk crêpe jowl and turns him towards her. 'Guess what I did this weekend?'

His brow furrows. She knows the origins of that expression. 'It's me, Dad, Janet. Your daughter Janet.' Gently, she rubs the delicate skin of his hand. 'Eh, guess what, Dad. I saved a little girl's life.'

'Claire?'

An arrow in her chest. 'No . . . no, not Claire. Her name's Elizabeth.'

After looking at her blankly, he returns back to the screen. 'Stop running around and get back inside.'

Time has slipped away. Peeking out of the window, she can see the fumes cloud from the Avensis's exhaust. 'I'm going to have to go, Dad. It's a quick visit today, I'm afraid.' Before leaving, she cleans his filthy tray. 'Which carer gave you your breakfast?' An answer is unlikely, but expressing her disapproval helps. Turning to throw the crumb-speckled wipe in the bin, she hears the name 'Pilkington' on the TV, and lunges towards the remote to increase the volume.

Nick and Jessica are wearing serious expressions. '*. . . home from hospital, which is excellent news. We hope you're back to your ballet classes very soon, Elizabeth. And lots of love to Robbie and Mia . . .*' The camera angle changes. '*And now, the woman who has up to forty spontaneous orgasms a day.*' Janet urgently presses the volume down, down, down, until no sound emits at all.

Retracing the bluebells of the corridor, buoyed by this new information about Elizabeth, she doesn't even care that she's now been twenty minutes. Elizabeth is OK. He cannot burst this bubble, dampen her spark.

When she turns the corner, Roger is sitting by the exit, as he often does when waiting for his daughter to take him out. An open newspaper balances on his lap. Helen stands next to him, reading over his shoulder. Their eyes widen at her presence. 'Janet . . . Janet, this is you,' says Roger.

Her cheeks warm pleasantly and she cannot contain the smile spreading over her face. 'Yes, that's right. It's me.' Her voice has acquired an affectation. Reminiscent of a bashful Victorian lady pursued by a suitor. She stretches her neck, glimpsing the photograph of Claire.

'Well done, you,' says Helen. 'That's amazing. What a hero you are. We all saw it at breakfast and, well, it broke our hearts about Claire's headstone, so Dorothy's already started a whip-round for one. Not sure how much we'll raise between us, but it's at least a start.'

A lump constricts Janet's throat. 'Oh, that's . . . I don't know what to say, Helen. That's lovely.' And it's as though a hundred-watt bulb has been switched on in her soul. People are talking about Claire. Acknowledging her existence. And as she says her goodbyes, exits, she can barely breathe through her elation. Because it's finally happened. Things have changed.

Sitting on the mermaid duvet, gently rocking her daughter's arm, the woman whispers, 'Sweetheart, wake up. We're going to Grannie and Grandpa's.'

The child rouses, swiping away the hair covering her face like creeping vines. 'Why, Mummy? I don't want to.'

'We have to, sweetheart.' Maintaining the forced, smooth calm of her voice, she eases her daughter out of bed, helps her dress, put on her shoes. 'Collect what favourite toys you want to take with you. We'll be staying a while.'

The girl's agitation, confusion, increases with each action. As they go downstairs. As they take hold of their luggage waiting in the hall. The mother's brown vinyl holdall. The daughter's small case in the shape of a ladybird. As they step out into the first smatterings of rain, run to the car. As the woman straps her daughter in securely.

'Is Daddy coming?'

'No, but you'll get to see Daddy soon.'

20

Bricks

As a teenager, she towered over her classmates. 'What's the weather like up there, Janet?' Always being positioned as Goal Defence in netball as all she had to do was extend her arms, zombie-like, to prevent opponents scoring. And as she was forever being asked to assist her dad with any heavy lifting rather than her brother, it soon became a family joke that she was, as Uncle Charlie put it, 'Built like a brick shithouse.'

'Leave her alone, Charlie,' her mum would say.

Though Janet took it as a compliment. Brick shithouses were strong, solid. That's how she always felt growing up, both inside and out.

Fast-forward forty years and she's been demolished. Is mere debris.

But, since knowing she saved Elizabeth, it's as though she's picked up a brick from the heap of rubble, smeared it with mortar and pressed it, hard, into the floor. Immoveable and secure. With each nice comment, each word of praise, more bricks are added.

And when they turn into the driveway, and she clocks the baby-pink paper bag on the doorstep overflowing with a wild-flower bouquet, and she checks the small, scented envelope while he watches with the engine running – *For a true angel.*

We're all so proud of you. Get well soon. Sam and the Angels – another brick is firmly cemented.

'From the girls at work,' she calls over to him. 'Says they're really—'

The car window slowly closes, shutting her both up and out.

Enjoying time alone, she sits in the garden. She'd happily stay there all day. Cup of tea in hand. Listening to the birds and sniffing the air like a cat. Unable to stop her childlike giddiness about the paper. Wondering what the article is like, hoping Dave hadn't captured her twitching lip. Debating if it's worth suffering Mary to see if she has a copy.

Sinking into the mesh chair, eyelids fluttering with heaviness, she allows herself to fully relax. Swathed in sun, her tensions ease. Consciousness drifting, further and further away, until in a state of near sleep. Still aware of her surroundings. Leaves rustling in the soft breeze. Faraway voices. Car ignitions. The distant rumble of a train.

And it happens again.

The images, or thoughts. Impossible to differentiate. Arriving on a wave of sickly dread.

Her head lying upon orange rust, drowning in rain. The screech of grinding metal. Dancing flames. Blood-dripping temple.

Bolting upright, she presses a palm against her chest and shakily reaches for the tea. Each sip gradually slowing her heartbeat, bringing her back. And as she concentrates on inhaling deeply, calming herself, it's clear that however happy she is about saving Elizabeth, the fact she's been traumatized by the crash cannot be escaped.

*

Back inside the house, still unsettled, she calls Colin for comfort . . . not comfort, assurance. Hating that she wants to call him at all. When he doesn't pick up she remembers he's doing the long-distance fare to Leeds. But almost as soon as she puts down the phone, it rings. 'Sorry, I forgot you were . . . Oh, sorry, yes, Janet Brown speaking.' She straightens, face stern to assist with her assertiveness. 'I'm afraid I'm not inter— Did you say *Hello Britain*?' A ripple of excitement washes over her, then remembering Colin's instruction, it leaks away. 'Sorry, I'm not interested.' She scrunches up her eyes. 'No, I'm afraid I'm not interested in doing any more interviews . . . Well, OK, I'll take the number, but I can't change my mind, I'm afraid.' She roots in the sideboard drawer for her address book and a pen. As the details are dictated, she scribbles them on the back inside cover. 'OK . . . well, thank you,' she says, and puts down the receiver. Freezing in position. Digesting what's just happened. Quashing the intense pang of regret at what she's done.

Snapping to, she puts the address book back in the drawer, to the back of her mind. But despite her best efforts, *Hello Britain* buzzes around her brain like a house fly.

At the sofa, she sits, switches on the TV. Searches Catch Up for that morning's episode. Uncertain at what point in the programme they spoke about Elizabeth, she lets it play from the beginning, muttering to herself, 'It's for the best, Janet. You'd probably make a fool of yourself anyway.' And during the process of accepting the situation, deciding that a cup of tea and an orange Club might help, the doorbell chimes.

She closes her eyes. Praying for it not to be Mary. Then launches herself up to answer the door.

It is indeed her. Article in hand. 'Have you seen this?' Her smile is broad and genuine, as she tucks her in-need-of-a-root-touch-up hair behind her ears.

'No . . . no, I haven't yet.' Janet's desire to remain aloof is overridden by curiosity. 'Can I have a look?' When sliding it from Mary, she catches sight of Nish's pink Fiat 500 turning into the cul-de-sac. Both women watch as she parks up, honks the horn.

Nish emerges from the car, exuberant, carrying what appears to be a box of chocolates and a newspaper, which she holds aloft.

'Don't worry, Mary, my workmate seems to have brought one.' She hands Mary's copy back.

'Oh . . . oh well, OK.'

'Oh my god, Janet.' Nish is at the door now, waving the tabloid like a flag.

'Well, I'll leave you be then.' As Mary turns to go, she says to Nish, 'I'm so proud of our friend.'

'Thorntons, my favourite. Thank you.'

Nish gives her the chocolates and walks down the hallway ahead of Janet, as though she's a regular visitor, screeching, 'Oh my god, you're in the frigging paper.' Once she's been ushered by Janet into the lounge, the high-pitched frenzy gives way to a more sedate, 'Bloody hell, I knew it would be immaculate, but do you even live here?' Nish negotiates the room as if perusing a bric-a-brac shop. 'I can't believe you're a bloody hero, and in the paper. You're a hero, Janet. In the bloody paper.'

'Stop being daft. Can I have a look?' Taking the paper, she opens it up to the correct page. Her initial reaction is to cringe at her photograph. Ridiculous in the bandage. Smiling like a ventriloquist's dummy. And why did she ever think that blouse was flattering? But then she sees Claire. Colin had sent them a beautiful school photo that she hadn't been able to look at for years. Fingers tracing over her face, she says, 'It's Claire.'

'I know, she's the spit of you.'

'Do you think?'

Nish nods. 'I do. She's got your twinkling eyes.'

Janet sniffs, smiles. 'Shall I get us some tea? And orange Clubs? Oh no, we've got the Thorntons. I can read the article later. Though I know what I said, I suppose. Colin went to get one for me first thing, but they'd sold out.'

Nish dips her head towards the framed picture of Janet and Colin's wedding day. 'Look at you,' she says. 'Was that a perm?'

'Rollers.' Janet remains in the middle of the room, smiling, awkward, like a child having a friend home after school for the first time. 'Well, sit down then. I'll get the teas.'

Nish drops to the sofa, eyes fixed on the television. 'Jessica's like a sexy au pair, isn't she?'

In the kitchen, Janet pops teabags into the cups, amazed at how unperturbed she is at having a visitor. Merely excited. Not worrying if Colin might have skipped going to Yorkshire, returning early. Almost wanting him to. And as she pours in the water, 'You Don't Own Me' emerging from her lips once more, she's in such a pleasant state that she's shaken when Nish screams, 'Come here right now.'

The rush to the lounge makes her head throb.

'How do you rewind this?' Nish is holding out the remote control.

'Bloody hell, you nearly gave me a heart attack. I'm not supposed to have stress, you know.' Her palm rests upon her chest, drumming home the point.

Nish stands, her spindly fingers stroking Janet's arm. 'Shit, sorry . . . but show me how to rewind and sit the fuck down, because you're going to need to.'

Janet does as she's told, slowly lowering herself to the sofa. 'What is it? What's going on? It's that button there. You can't see it properly . . . It's worn off a bit.'

Ignoring her, tongue out in concentration, Nish rewinds, then presses pause at what appears to be the part of the show that Janet's already seen at her dad's. 'Oh, bloody hell, is that it? I got worried then. I know, I've seen it. Isn't it fantastic? She's out of hospital.'

'Janet . . .' Nish drops onto the sofa next to her, shakes her head. 'Just watch, will you. It's not that.'

She activates the presenters. Nick turns to the camera. '*As you know, we've been following the progress of Elizabeth, the daughter of our chef, Robbie. You may have seen that they've now found the wonderful lady who helped save Elizabeth. An incredibly brave woman named Janet Brown, who was herself injured in the crash. From all of us at* Hello Britain, *we just want to say thank you, Janet. What a hero you are.*' The unflattering still from the footage comes on screen. '*And we're delighted to report that thanks to Janet and our fantastic NHS, Elizabeth is now out of hospital and doing really well, which is excellent news . . .*'

It freezes again. Jessica's face in an unfortunate position, teeth exposed like a rabbit.

Janet fixates on the screen, as if she too has been paused.

'Oh my god, Janet, Nick Jansen mentioned you on TV. Thanked you. Nick Jansen.'

As if now switched back on, but playing in slow motion, Janet turns towards her friend. 'They called this morning . . . *Hello Britain* . . . Asked me on the show. But I can't.'

'I'm sorry, what?' Nish exaggerates screwing up her face. 'They've called you to ask you on the show and you what? Erm, there's no way you're not going on that show. *Hello Britain*? *Hello Britain* wants you on the show . . . of course you're bloody doing it. They put you in a hotel and everything. I know, because my cousin's boyfriend was on there with his phobia of beards.'

'His what?' Janet shakes her head. 'Look, I just can't, OK. It's not fair on Colin, all this . . . I'm only happy Elizabeth is OK.'

'What are you talking about?'

Consumed with Nick's words, Janet repeats them over and over in her head. *Incredibly brave woman. What a hero.* Each time, endorphins release like a puff from one of her air fresheners.

'Janet, are you going funny on me?'

Dampening her happiness, her rational mind takes over. 'No, I'm not, Nish. But I don't want to be on TV. Now, I'm going to finish those teas.'

The liquid swirls clockwise as she frantically stirs.

'You deserve good things to happen, you know, Janet.' Nish has followed her and is standing in the doorway. 'Janet . . . Janet . . . stop being weird and look at me.'

'I think I may have double sugared by mistake. Have a sip.'

'And I don't want to sound like some Instagram wanker, but you have to grab good shit when it happens, because God knows it rarely does to people like us, and life stays the same. So I really think you should call them. Now, while I'm here.'

Janet turns, drops the teaspoon in the sink and lowers her head.

'Oh shit, are you crying? Oh God, I'm sorry. I'm such a stupid—'

'No, it's, well . . . I don't want things to stay the same, Nish. I really don't.'

21

In for a Penny

Standing behind the kitchen island, components of a tuna melt lying before her, she begins to build a sandwich. The best weapon in her armoury.

Dipping into the grated cheddar or scooping the fish flakes and scoffing them as she ordinarily would isn't possible, as her somersaulting stomach would protest.

There's the familiar alert of tyres on gravel.

She turns on the grill. Transforms into a bistro pub chef to the noise of his entering.

He's now standing in the doorway. Face drained, eyes heavy. 'Well, that was a nightmare. There was an accident on the M62.'

Transferring the sandwich onto the wire rack, she slides it under the heat. 'Oh no . . . well, I've got a tuna melt on the go.' She attempts to conceal her rising anxiety, desperate to show itself in her voice. She hadn't factored in a terrible fare. But then she notices his lack of newspaper, which he has under his arm every day, except the day his wife is within the pages, and her anger bubbles like the cheese beneath the flames.

'That's my favourite,' he says. Not in a happy, appreciative way, but full of suspicion. Sometimes she swears he can climb inside her brain, suck out every thought. 'I know,' she says, forcing a smile. 'I thought we could celebrate.'

He hangs his keys on the hook. 'Oh yes?'

She turns from him, pulls out the grill plate with jittering fingers, lifts the bread and sprinkles even more cheddar, as though that will help. 'Well, you'll never guess what happened today.' She waits for him to ask, but he doesn't. 'So, the phone rings . . .' She pushes the rack back inside the grill. 'And it was *Hello Britain*.'

'*Hello Britain*?'

'That's right, and they asked us to go on the show.' Removing a plate from the cupboard, she winces and adds, 'I said no, of course . . . like you said. But they wanted to give us a night in a swanky hotel . . . and dinner . . . and I tried to call you, but you didn't pick up . . . and because I know how much you love that programme, and Jessica . . . and dinners . . . I thought I'd better snap up the opportunity because . . . well, tomorrow's chip paper and all that.' She takes a spatula from a utensil hook, slides the melt onto the plate and turns to present it to him with a smile.

He is staring at her. Doesn't speak.

'And Nish popped round to bring us some chocolates.' In for a penny. 'She was here when they called and after I'd originally said no, she was like, "Oh but you must, Janet, it will be nice for Colin to have a break too." It would be, wouldn't it, love. You've been working so hard.'

'Nish was here?' He presses the toast with the tip of his finger, leaving an oval indent. 'That's nice. And you've said yes to this then, have you?'

'I did, yes.'

The atmosphere hangs so heavy, she turns, squeezes Fairy Liquid into the sink and whisks the water with her fingers.

'None of this changes anything, you know.'

She pulls the tea towel from the oven handle and dries her hands. 'Do you want ketchup or brown sauce?'

There's the sound of his fingernails tapping against the Formica. 'Janet . . . Janet, are you listening to me? All this fuss, it doesn't change anything. You can't rewrite history with this girl, you know that, right? It doesn't change—'

'It does, though.' She turns, throwing the towel down on the island. 'It does, Colin. And God agrees.'

'What's God got to—'

'Colin.' She sweeps hair from her eyes. 'Look, I've said yes now. I'm going to London, and I'm going to go on the show. You can come with me or not.'

He chews on the melt, staring at her. 'Is that right? And what if I don't let you?'

Calmly, she walks to the fridge, removes the ketchup, places it next to his plate. Then does the same with the brown sauce she retrieves from the cupboard. 'Then I'd have to tell everyone why I wasn't going, wouldn't I?' She turns back around, picks up a dishcloth and wipes crumbs from the worktop into her palm. 'Oh, and don't worry about the paper, Nish kindly brought me one. And I . . . I look very nice, considering.' She shakes her hand over the food caddy and throws the bread knife into the bubbles. Turning to leave the room, she's unable to look at him, though imagines him agog. At the doorway, she stops and says, 'And a thank you once in a while wouldn't go amiss.'

22

Four Pieces of Blu-Tack

The suitcase smells of cedarwood. The moth problem of 2017 was shocking. All their woollens ravaged. Including Colin's favourite John Player Special V-neck which was irreplaceable.

Once upon a time, the luggage was used for weekends away and annual trips to their favourite location, Pwllheli. It was where her father was born, and the majority of Janet's childhood holidays were spent there visiting grandparents.

Then with her own little family, they'd rent a nearby apartment with sea views. Sometimes with her mum and dad, but usually not. And weather permitting, they'd enjoy a fortnight of heaven. Fish and chips, sandcastles, sunbathing. After a dip in the sea, she and Claire would flop onto the warm towel floating on the sand. Experience that special kind of relaxation only ever felt on holidays. She loved watching her little girl enjoying herself. Carefree. The sun gradually gilding her perfect skin. Hair blonding, saltwater-matted. All the while Colin would remain in his deckchair reading the latest Ken Follett. Then afterwards, they'd stop at the best little cafe called Annie's, whose pistachio ice cream has made any subsequent ice cream seem substandard.

But for the past eleven years, the luggage has only been used to store clothes unsuitable for the present season. Until now.

It had somehow transformed into being his idea. 'I've always wanted to go to the London Transport Museum,' he'd said. 'We're due a break, so I think we should go to this thing. I'll be interviewed too, won't I?'

She nodded, made noises such as, 'Well OK then, let's do it.' Joining in with the rewriting of history.

Colin talked to the production team to arrange the travel. First class, no less. Initially, he was furious they'd booked for them to go by train. But when he was letting loose on the phone, Janet put her hand on his arm, shook her head. Because the strange thing was, the thought wasn't scary. Not as much as the concept of driving with Colin for four hours in the Avensis. She supposes one of the positives of blocked memories is that whatever can't be recalled is probably best unremembered. And when it was confirmed that they'd be staying at the Daventry near Marylebone, all Colin's previous grievances were forgotten, and he couldn't hide his enthusiasm.

Now, only a few days later, he's at the precinct picking up his resoled Simon Cowell shoes from Timpsons, even though she'd assured him they wouldn't be seen on screen. And she's in the bedroom, finally bandage-free – apart from her left arm, which is more for the protection of a large tender bruise – and eagerly folding her favourite summer dress, with its long swishing skirt that makes her feel free and feminine. For the TV appearance, she's packing the suit she'd worn to her cousin's third wedding. Pale blue, mock silk.

She considers the matching fascinator but concludes it's too much, so rehangs it on the edge of the dressing table mirror. Its feathers ruffled by the draught from the open window, which she peeks through. Mary is talking to that Roni from number thirty again, while simultaneously supervising Nigel as he Kärchers the front drive. Without much thought, Janet goes downstairs, out the front door, and crosses towards them.

After mouthing a 'Hi' to Roni, she focuses on Mary. 'I couldn't ask you to keep an eye on the house, could I? Colin and I are leaving early in the morning for a night away.' Waiting for the question certain to follow, she suppresses the smile that's been floating around her lips.

'OK, yes, no problem. Off anywhere nice? Nigel, you got my leg then.' He moves the spray out of the way, but the women continue to be gently coated in a mist.

'Oh, just to London. We're going to be on *Hello Britain*.'

'*Hello Britain*?' interjects Roni, pushing her giant acrylic talons through her hair.

Janet drops her head for a moment to feign humility, clocking that all three of them are wearing slippers, then looks back up towards Roni. 'Yes, you know – well, you probably don't know, but I saved—'

'Yes, Mary was filling me in about it all. Well done you.' She stands taller, face riddled with new interest. 'And they've asked you on *Hello Britain*?'

Janet can only imagine the gossip that's taken place. 'Oh, it's embarrassing really. I only did what anyone would have done.' She slows her speech to prevent it tumbling out, powered by the effervescent energy inside, like a child talking about presents received on Christmas morning. 'But Elizabeth's dad is a chef on the show. That's the girl I saved.'

'We know that,' says Mary.

'Of course.' Janet allows her smile to break now it's imbued with insincerity. 'And thank you. For keeping an eye on the house. Anyway, I'd better get back to packing.'

As she's about to leave, Roni pipes up. 'Janet, hang on, you wouldn't be interested in opening my new cupcake shop on The Height, would you? Next Thursday morning? At eleven? Right next door to Mr Chicken.'

Tingles regather, bursting through Janet's mouth as a genuine grin. 'Oh, well, yes. I'd be delighted. I'll see you there then, shall I?' With that she turns, walks back towards her front door, a whole row of bricks laid.

Once upstairs she watches them again from the bedroom. Mary ramping up the orders to Nigel. Undoubtedly full of envy about what's just happened, what's about to happen. Part of her feels bad for taking enjoyment from this. But the rest of her revels in its existence. Knowing everything will be different after the show. She just knows it will. The chrysalis forming from which she will emerge.

And as she folds her knickers into the neatest of rolls, precisely how she'd originally removed them from their M&S packet, she imagines life afterwards. How she'll be called upon for radio interviews, TV appearances. Invited to parties, events. Awards even. The Pride of Britain Awards. Rolling up in a limousine, blinded by flashing bulbs, deafened by cheering crowds. She'll be dressed head to toe in designer clothes. Karen Millen. As she waves to the people, she'll smile, teeth whitened. Hair bigger, better. Make-up done to perfection. Arm sliding into the crook of her plus one. Not Colin. Because after her interview with *Hello Britain*, she'll be standing in the foyer about to leave the studio when she'll lock eyes with Jason Quartz. And from that moment, he'll pursue her, turning up at her work, but not in a weird way. And so, as she walks elegantly down the red carpet, rubbing shoulders with the real

Simon Cowell, she'll be linking arms with Jason. *I'm so proud*, he'll whisper into her ear as they stand for a photograph. *And I love you so much.*

'I'm back and I've got us both a sausage roll,' shouts up Colin, the clatter of the front-door keys echoing up the stairs.

When the alarm goes off at 5.30 a.m. she's already wide awake. Not just awake, but alive. 'I'll get us a quick breakfast,' she says to a stirring Colin.

On the landing, she pauses. Twinged with desire to enter Claire's room. But she continues downstairs, allowing a smile to rise as she passes the cases in the hall, poised, handles raised.

She makes the brews and toast. For him, peanut butter. For her, Marmite. Carrying this elation is so alien she's unable to steady her hands. A feeling that new possibilities lie ahead. That perhaps she'll get brave enough to leave. No, whatever happens she could never leave here. Leave Claire. But still, although he may never forgive her, and she may never forgive herself, God has made His stance very clear. And He overrides them both.

They haven't got long now. Colin booked one of his fellow cabbies, Marvin, to arrive at six forty, prompt. Lateness triggers his psoriasis.

He's going round the house switching off all the sockets. Apart from the plug timer for the lamp in the lounge, delighted he could finally put it to use. She's in the kitchen, making up a Tupperware of biscuits and a flask for the journey – 'Have you seen the prices they charge, Janet?' – which she presses into the bottom of a Bag for Life. Her mouth dry with anticipation, she puts on the kettle for one last cup of tea. The casualness she's been faking all morning slips into a grin.

'There's a cuppa there for you. I'm going to get my jacket, it's a bit chillier than I thought. What time is it?'

'We've got twenty minutes, but I'm going to stand outside with the cases in ten.'

Upstairs, she runs through an imagined list of all things potentially forgotten. When confident everything is packed, she heads to the toilet.

Pausing at Claire's room, she runs her fingers across the gloss door. Assailed by a pang to go inside, say goodbye. A sudden fear of leaving her alone.

'I'm going to wait on the drive then,' shouts up Colin.

'OK, I'll be down soon. I'm just going to the loo.'

Cheek pressed against the door, she whispers, 'Mummy will be away for a day or so, sweetheart. She's going to be on TV. Isn't that great? Though you'll already know that. I'll be back very soon. I've got your dog with me.' She blows a kiss, then lifts the neck of her top over her face, buries her emotions. Re-emerging, she takes two deep breaths then heads downstairs.

On the third step, she stops.

The air from outside floats up the stairwell. Colin's left the door open while he waits. Forcing herself to move again, the toe of her ballet pump extends, hovers. Then retracts.

She's now striding back up towards the landing.

Hands fumble against the top slats of the airing cupboard for the key. She's been so good, strict with herself. But the idea of going without saying goodbye properly is intolerable.

She needs to touch some things, that's all. Or grab a T-shirt. Yes, taking one of her T-shirts would help.

Key in hand, she moves over to the room. He'll be screaming for her any second, but she'll only be a moment.

The lock unclicks.

Slowly, quietly, she presses down the handle.

Pushes open the door.

The bed is stripped of the duvet. Four pieces of Blu-Tack mark the corners of an invisible poster. The dressing table is bare, apart from a set of shell beads hanging from one of the heart-shaped drawer knobs. Lone socks and random articles of clothing are strewn like litter in a park after a heatwave.

She stares. Motionless. Attempting to absorb the harrowing version of what the room should be.

Dizzy, she holds on to the door frame for support. Bends forward as if winded, closes her eyes. Willing it to be a hallucination. An after-effect of her head injury. But when she reopens them, all is the same.

Her mouth forms to scream Colin's name, but she stops herself. Presses her hand, hard, against her lips, before releasing the pressure to retch into her palm.

An image drips onto her brain like hot wax.

Then another.

And another.

Each one more painful than the last. Karaoke. The drive home. Floating ash in the kitchen. The pit. The fire pit burning the remaining world of her beautiful girl.

Screwing her eyes shut again, other disjointed snippets follow. Pushing a shopping trolley. The sound of blood dripping onto its metal. Other confusing images. No . . . no, that's not right. It's not right.

Eyes back open, misted red, she surges towards Claire's closet. Her clothes, the remaining essence of her, gone. Aside from a sundress hanging from one strap on a pink wooden hanger, and the scattered pieces on the floor.

She frees the dress, carries it over to the bed, and sits silently screaming into the gingham fabric, inhaling the scraps of Claire's presence.

'For Christ's sake, woman, get a bloody move on. Marvin will be here any minute.' His voice barges through the house, punching her in the stomach.

Mummy . . . don't be upset.

'Mummy's fine, sweetheart,' she whispers into the soft folds. 'It's going to be OK.'

Standing, sedate, she presses her eyes dry, dabs her nose.

'Janet . . . Janet, he's here. Come on.'

Calmly, she stands, starts to leave. En route bending to collect a single sock – blue, speckled with yellow spots – which she presses into her pocket. After closing the door behind her, slow, robotic, she returns the key to the airing cupboard.

Head straight, chin raised, she walks down the stairs.

'Oh, there you are . . . He's here, get a move on. Are you OK? You look peaky. Got the runs again?'

'I'm fine,' she says, with a smile that doesn't reach her eyes.

Outside, Marvin is shoving the cases into the boot. 'Aye, well done there, Janet. I saw the paper and everything.'

She maintains the same smile. 'Thanks, Marvin.'

She and Colin sit on opposite sides of the back seat. The child-sized space between them. And as they leave the cul-de-sac behind, she can't tell him what she now knows. Not as she rides in silence for the entire journey to the station, aside from fake laughing along with the men about how much 'bloody women' need to pack for a night away. Not as she turns her face towards the window, imagining smashing it against the glass so violently she can almost taste the blood slipping down her nose into her mouth. Not as they board the seven fifteen train to London Euston, and Colin holds her hand, offering comfort for her bravery as they pull away, her wanting to take his fist in her mouth, bite it raw to the bone.

She still can't say.

Because along with the knowledge of what her pig of a husband did to his own dead daughter's belongings came with it the other memories.

She didn't save Elizabeth.

She wasn't on the train.

23

Bit of a Shit Ferris Wheel

The train has arrived at Euston. Colin holds out his hand to help Janet squeeze past the table, emerge from her seat. 'You've jumped back on the horse now.' He chuckles. 'Imagine you being a jockey, Janet.' The dribble running towards his chin is swiped away with the back of his hand. 'Did you manage to nod off too?'

'I did, yes.' But she hadn't. The entire journey was spent wide-eyed, catatonic. She's aware of the concept of fight or flight, but what if neither is possible? What happens then?

Freed from the constraints of the seating area, she's left standing among the other passengers, gathering their belongings, chatting. As normal people do. Not her. She is stiff, blank, like a hollow tree. Watching as Colin manoeuvres himself down the aisle, hand touching the corner of each seat he passes, reminding her of an orangutan swinging from vines.

A horsey-attired woman still seated nearby smiles over while stroking down the hair of her little boy. Janet wonders if her distress is obvious. Though perhaps the woman is just being friendly. Or worse – recognizes her from the newspaper, from online, from the pictures on TV. As the hero that she now knows she is not.

Janet responds with a semblance of a smile. The blood that had been rushing to her head swiftly falls back down again, pooling in her weakened legs. Certain they'll disintegrate beneath her, she sits once more, attempts to soften her breathing by closing her eyes, picturing her roses, her sweet-smelling roses. But all thoughts are as soiled as the ground from which they grow.

'Are you OK? You look bloody awful.'

She opens her eyes to Colin, chest out, shoulders up and back. A stance reserved for when he's about to attend a party, or a hospital appointment. The extended handle of a case resting in each hand, as though he's walking dogs.

'I'm fine,' she says. 'Being on the train has hit me, I suppose.'

Her anxiety heightens as they enter the vastness of the station. Bodies everywhere. The incoherent murmur of voices. She struggles to function even in the Trafford Centre. He enjoys her neediness in such circumstances. Not to be left. Lost.

'I've got to go to the toilet. Can you wait for me right here? Don't go anywhere,' she manages to say, looking up at the large board hanging above. Stress making all information impossible to comprehend. 'So, they're to the left?'

'What? You can't even read signs now? Ladies' . . . straight ahead.'

She can read signs. She can.

Once locked inside the toilet cubicle, the hubbub of hand dryers and jabbering beyond the door, she gasps for air as if emerging from underwater. Before sitting, she removes a wet wipe from the pack in her bag, cleans the seat, then discards it in the sanitary bin. Satisfied all is sufficiently sterile, she lifts her skirt, lowers her knickers and sits, thighs against the cold damp. And hugging her handbag, rocking into it as if it were a lifebuoy, finally she allows herself to cry.

The wallowing doesn't, can't, last long. She digs inside the leather folds of her bag, feeling blindly through its contents. The first out of the lucky dip is a hand pack of tissues. After extracting one, she dries her eyes and blows her nose. She wouldn't dream of using the loo roll after a TV programme informed her that on average there are one hundred and fifty times more bacteria on that than on the seat.

Watching her tear-drenched, snot-ridden tissue float down the pan, she delves back into the bag, and from the side pocket retrieves both the dog and the paper leaf.

The latter she opens, staring at the scrawled message. How can it still not be a sign? How can it not? She presses the soft fur of the dog against the inflamed skin of her cheek.

'What am I going to do, Claire?' she whispers.

Whatever you need to do, Mummy.

After a smartly dressed driver, Al, ushers them into the silver Mercedes sent by the studio, they commence their drive through the busy London streets.

Colin has transformed into an exuberant ten-year-old. Pointing to landmarks, buildings: 'There's the British Museum, Janet. I wish we had time to go and see the Rosetta Stone . . . Can you believe Leicester Square used to be residential? It's now like bloody Piccadilly Circus . . . I thought it would be a bit of a shit Ferris wheel, but it's actually rather amazing, isn't it?' All the while, he's oblivious to her current state. Her widened eyes. Dilated pupils, which she catches intermittently in the rear-view mirror. Her rigid posture.

Just tell him, Janet. Tell him.

The truth loops her brain, but never leaves her lips.

And while Al entertains with chat about Egyptian mummy collections, she feels for the door handle. The smooth plastic against her fingers. One pull and she could throw herself out. Then she realizes even that option doesn't exist with these new-fangled safety locks.

'. . . that's what I said to them, didn't I, Janet?'

Unaware of the conversation she's been dragged into, she nods. 'Yes . . . that's what you said.'

According to Al, they're approaching the drop-off area which is adjacent to a high-rise building, seemingly perched on pillars, like a concrete tiered wedding cake.

'Hey, Janet, are you getting excited?' asks Colin, his top lip catching on his teeth, causing it to disappear. A sure sign of nerves. The last time this happened he was taking back a used garden hose, adamant it was faulty when he'd in fact accidentally picked up the ten-metre length rather than the twenty-five. Luckily, he doesn't await a response, unbelievably still unaware that the cheerful disposition she'd exuded that morning is now something entirely different.

They lean against the high-gloss white desk, fill in their passes. Her hands shaking so profusely, her signature is illegible.

The youthful receptionist passes them on to an unfriendly-looking security guard to have their photos taken. Colin with his hospital-appointment stance and lipless grin. Janet staring, blank. An imposter's mugshot. Then a young man called Will, with a vibrant white smile and thick-rimmed glasses, makes his greetings before instructing them that their photo passes now attached to lanyards should be hung around their necks. This third wheel asks questions that he doesn't really desire the answers to, such as 'How was your journey?' and 'Is it a lot warmer here than up north?' All delivered with a buoyancy that electrocutes her severed nerves.

Tell them, Janet. Just tell them.

She's in the lift now. Deeper into the mire. Smoothly elevating with Colin, Will and someone she vaguely recognizes from one of those reality shows.

Once again invisible. No one noticing the fear manifesting in the sweat oozing from her upper lip, forehead, armpits. Nausea rises, settles in her throat. They don't find anything strange in her quietness. Merely talk around her, about her. Colin giving a history lesson to Will about what used to be where the building stands. They even laugh.

But she remains isolated, unread.

The lift doors ding open, and the men step onto the carpeted corridor of the sixth floor. She could stay inside. Go downstairs. Run. Or she could tell them the truth.

But she is walking, walking, walking, down the white-walled corridors. Sandwiched between black-and-white prints of smiling celebrities.

'This is you,' says Will. They're standing outside Dressing Room 7. Beneath the number is a piece of card with *Janet and Colin Brown* written in marker pen, slotted into an aluminium sign. It's not particularly neat. Whoever wrote it has shocking spatial judgement. The *w* and *n* squashed together to form a strange symbol. 'That's us,' says Colin to Will, very much as though he feels he's arrived.

As a youngster, she yearned to be a famous actress. *Don't be daft, you need to get yourself a proper job. You can't eat dreams, Janet*, her dad would say. But this didn't stop her fantasizing about one day winning an Oscar. Rehearsing speeches in her bedroom, while holding up her Sindy as the trophy. Her own face made up thick, far beyond her years, wearing an old evening dress which had once belonged to her grandma. Canary yellow with chiffon arms. Even then she knew 'don't be daft' was code for 'not people like us'. So instead of pursuing acting, she completed her typing exams. And even those skills she never utilized.

The dressing room isn't quite the depiction of her fantasies. No large bulbs around the mirror, only a fluorescent tube across its top. No make-up laid out, no rail of glamorous clothes with a screen for her to change behind. But the royal blue carpet tiles with matching chairs, the empty rail for them to hang their coats and change of clothes, the minute en suite with loud extractor fan, is the nearest she's ever got.

Janet sits, staring at the bare off-white wall opposite. Colin has been in the toilet for ten minutes. Will has gone to fetch their teas.

When Colin finally emerges, he heads to the mirror, rubs at his crow's feet and chins. 'I hope they can do something with my psoriasis. It's really flared up.'

'I can't do it, Colin.'

'Not you, I meant the make-up people.'

'No, I . . . I can't go on the show. I'm really sorry but I'm not up to it . . . The doctor said I mustn't get stressed, and I feel too nervous. You're going to have to tell Will.' The words spew in a hurried slur.

He turns from his reflection to look at her, the crease between his eyebrows deepening. 'What are you talking about? We've come two hundred miles.'

'I know . . . I know we have, but—'

'I wasn't sure if you wanted semi-skimmed or full-fat milk, so I've brought both.' Will is pushing through the door with his back, tray in hand.

'We're full-fatters here, Will lad,' says Colin. 'Listen, Janet's having a bit of a wobbler. Very nervous.' He mouths the last part. Like her mum used to do when saying the word 'sex'.

Will slides the tray onto the side, then goes over to Janet, drops to his haunches as if speaking to a small child. Elbow balancing on her knee, she rests her uninjured temple against her fist.

Tell them, Janet. Just tell them.

'If I had a pound for every guest who feels like this . . . I promise you, Janet, it's completely normal to be nervous. Everyone is—'

'See, love? You need to keep remembering how brave you've been. You've survived a train crash and saved a girl. This is a piece of piss in comparison. Now, how long before we're on, Will?'

24

Water, Vodka, Bleach

The walk down the corridor is dreamlike.

Will and Colin are in front, laughing again. Occasionally turning their heads to ask if she's OK. Sound muted. Moving lips she cannot read. Her only response a nod and a robotic smile.

Damp blots her pits, obvious against the pale rayon silk. Ordinarily, she'd be mortified. Now, it's the least of her worries. Each step is unsteady. As though the floor is moving beneath her feet, reminiscent of the fun house when the fair would come to Buile Hill Park every year as a kid. But this isn't fun. Or fair.

She'd thrown up just before Will called for them, and the acid lingers on her tongue, in her gullet. Colin didn't knock on the en suite door to ask if she was OK. Didn't acknowledge the retching and crying he had surely heard. But it was in there that she decided what to do.

It will all come back to her during the interview.

She's watched enough Psychic Channel to know how to fake such things. As they ask their questions, she'll rub her head, purport to be feeling peculiar. Which she does. And with a shocked face, she'll declare the return of her memory. That it's all been a huge mistake. That she didn't save Elizabeth. And she'll grab Colin's hand. He'll like that. And she'll cry. Because she'll want to cry. Already wants to cry. And they'll have to be kind because of that. Kindness must be shown on live TV. *It's not your fault, Janet*, they'll say. *It's not your fault.*

They turn a corner to be faced with another long corridor. Almost stretched to a vanishing point, tipped in red. As they advance, the red transforms into the words *On Air*. Lit from inside a rectangular box above a set of double doors. She pauses to contain her nausea. Then continues.

They're at the end now, slowing to a halt. The sign is even more vibrant once up close. Will holds on to the door handle as if about to pull it open, but instead offers instructions on what to do once on the other side. The majority flies through one ear, out the other, until he says, 'So you wait on the floor, Colin, and I'll take Janet round to the side so she can make her entrance . . . and don't worry, Janet, you'll be able to look over to Colin throughout for support.'

Colin's face almost matches the sign. His eyes protrude from their sockets.

'But I thought he'd be on there with me?' she says, unnerved by the unexpected change.

'Oh, sorry guys, Alison should have made it clear . . . No, it's just the woman of the hour, I'm afraid.'

Woman of the hour. Minute. Second. However long it will be before the story ends.

All is dark as they enter. The suction of the door's seal releases the smell of rubber. There's a hit of heat, like when getting off the plane in Mallorca.

Vision adjusting, she gradually makes out figures, walking, holding cameras, standing around. Will guides her through with a gentle touch to the small of her back.

They head towards the light, as though entering heaven. Or

hell. Stark, bright. At its centre, the familiar set. The huge yellow, curved modular sofa, with matching chevron rug. The glass coffee table, on which sit the strategically placed *Hello Britain* mugs. She's stepped into the TV.

Nick is sitting, looking over to Jessica on the other side of the set, who's talking to a woman in front of a selection of food processors. All displayed on plinths as though it were a sculpture exhibition. Jessica bends forward with a fit of the giggles. A domino causing Nick to laugh also and rub his eyes free of apparent tears. What Janet had witnessed daily on screen is even less real in person.

Aware Colin is no longer by her side, she feels lost. Like a child separated from its parent in a shopping centre. She hates that she can find comfort in his proximity.

Will summons her behind the set wall. Once there, it highlights the fakery. The raw wood framework, weighted at the bottom, fragile and precarious. Like her.

'Are you OK?' asks Will.

She nods, smiles through his whispered instructions as he clips a microphone to her lapel and inserts the attached black box into the back of her skirt. The movement releasing a burst of acid into her mouth.

And after a couple more minutes, following a gentle push from Will, she steps into the light.

Having crossed over to the other side, she's guided to the sofa by a young woman who stands before her like a dog trainer instructing her to sit. Janet's grateful for not receiving an edible reward, as her skirt is pulling across her stomach, pressing on its contents which are desperate to escape, one way or another.

Nick beams a veneered smile. She returns a subdued version, then reaches for the mug which she hopes contains something to lubricate her mouth. Not caring what. Water, vodka, bleach.

Jessica is now joining Nick on the sofa, also offering the whitest of grins. Then as though a switch has flicked, their expressions transform into utter seriousness.

Nick turns towards the camera. It's happening.

Janet wipes the dribble of musty warm water cascading down her chin.

'Now, if you're a regular of the show, you'll have followed the recovery of Elizabeth, the daughter of our chef, Robbie, and his wife Mia. Elizabeth was involved in the recent Manchester train crash, which tragically killed six people including the driver and Elizabeth's au pair, Zofia, and left many more injured.'

Jessica takes over. 'Yes, and among the passengers was our next guest, who, despite suffering her own injuries and eventually collapsing at the scene, managed to pull Elizabeth from the wreckage, and gave her mouth to mouth before seeking help. And following a nationwide search, we now know this lady to be Janet Brown, whom we're delighted to have here with us today. Welcome, Janet. So lovely to have you on the show and we're glad you're feeling much better.'

'Thank you.' Her voice is so quiet despite the microphone.

Jessica leans forward and touches Janet's hand. 'Don't worry, you'll be fine.'

Void of saliva, Janet reaches once again for the lukewarm water, sips.

Nick takes his turn. 'And I should add – what also makes this story incredible is that the very night you saved Elizabeth's life would have been the eighteenth birthday of your daughter, who tragically died eleven years ago, is that right?'

'That's right.' She manages to look directly at the presenters. Her senses awakened by the opportunity to talk about Claire. 'She died when she was seven.'

Jessica shakes her head and applies her most sympathetic look. 'I'm so sorry, Janet, I can't imagine. So, going back to that night – am I right that you don't actually remember much about it because of your head injury?'

Janet glances towards the darkness. Colin is standing next to a cameraman, his arms folded, face rigid. 'That's right. Though the doctor said it should only be temporary.'

And so, she prepares. Proceeds with the plan.

Lifting her hand to her head, she rubs her temple in a circular motion. Exactly as rehearsed in the toilet. 'Actually, I . . . I think being here has made me remember more.'

Jessica audibly inhales, leans forward, eyes earnest. 'Oh goodness, really? You've remembered more about the crash?'

Only one memory is truly evoked by that word.

Janet looks out once more towards Colin, unmoved in his stance, expectant. And she fast-forwards to their return home. Life going back to how it was.

'Janet? Are you OK? Is it coming back to you?'

She turns to Jessica. 'Sorry, yes . . . Well, it's . . . it's still all quite hazy . . .'

When the spinning stops, the woman stares beyond the steering wheel, towards the shattered windscreen. Rain beats the car like a drum and finds its way through the cracks onto her legs. The downpour drowning the hiss of steam seeping from the bonnet.

'Sweetheart, are you OK?' Her lips stick with blood.

Only silence returns.

Body twisting with difficulty, she looks towards the back seat. The girl is quiet, still. Blanched. Aside from the poppy, bloomed on her forehead.

There's the sound of feet on tarmac. Voices. 'An ambulance is on its way.'

She's outside the vehicle now. The tinkle of glass dropping to the ground. Her body, sodden in an instant. After lunging towards the door, she wrenches it open. 'It's OK, sweetheart, you're going to be OK. Mummy won't let anything happen to you.' The girl is limp. Wrist absent of a pulse. The tiny wrist she's kissed so many times. She must bring her out. Bring her out so she can bring her back.

She unclips the belt, removes her from the car like a cradled baby, and lays her on the ground.

'An ambulance is on its way.'

Is that all they can say, do?

She'll give all her breath; transfer her life.

After wiping the blood and rain from her face, she pinches her daughter's doll-like nose, her mouth engulfing the soft, cold lips, and exhales. Once, twice. Then pushes, pushes down on her chest. Worrying she'll hurt her.

Sirens pierce the air.

As she pushes, pushes, the paramedics run towards them, causing her to release all the screams that she'd contained. 'Help, please . . . I did everything I could . . . I pulled her out and gave her mouth to mouth to bring her back . . . Please, she's just a child . . .'

Looking up to God for assistance, the woman catches sight of a soaked man standing by the van that had jousted into their car. He's shaking, crying, and her immediate thought is to collect up the fallen exhaust and bludgeon his head. Rub jagged glass into his face.

The paramedic pulls her away as they work on her daughter. They try to treat the woman, stem her blood. As though she'd care if she bled out.

Her head grows lighter and lighter until her legs crumple and her world fades to black.

25

Sharp Ice-Blonde Fringed Bob

'. . . Then I laid her down and she was unconscious. And after wiping the blood and rain from my face, I held her nose and gave her mouth to mouth, and CPR. Worried when pushing down on her chest that I'd hurt her. But it worked. I couldn't believe it . . . she started breathing again. It was a miracle. I could see her little lungs moving and I checked her pulse and it had worked, and . . . and she was alive.'

There's a moment of silence.

As if emerging from a trance, she looks around the studio. The sea of faces staring back. Quiet, still. All now viewing her differently. Or seeing her for the first time.

It's been said now. Can't be undone.

The fantasy. The lie.

Entering the ether, snaking its way into the homes of millions.

'Oh goodness, Janet. How incredible. And then you sought help?'

Janet looks back towards Colin, rubbing his nose, visibly touched. 'Yes, that's right . . . but then I collapsed.' Her mouth is so dry she's unsure of her clarity. The urgency for water is overwhelming, though her shaking hands would make it impossible to lift the cup.

'And that's the footage we've all seen. Of you seeking help. What a brave lady you are.' Nick looks beyond her, bursts a smile. 'And we've got someone here who wants to thank you personally.'

Following his gaze, Janet turns her head to see Robbie Pilkington walking towards the sofa, carrying a huge bouquet which almost masks his face.

Each step, each stem, hammering on her conscience.

He's bending towards her now, kissing each cheek. Taller than she'd presumed, more handsome. Musky aftershave strong under the warmth of the lights. 'Thank you.' His words, heartfelt, infiltrate her ear, then her bloodstream, pumping guilt around her body. 'And this is from Elizabeth.' He passes her a flimsy homemade card. On its front, a drawing of a rotund woman with daffodil yellow hair, *Thank You* rainbowed over her head.

Children's cards and drawings are so precious. She used to display Claire's all over the house. 'I love it, thank you,' she manages, pressing it close to her chest.

'And this is from Mia.' As he hands her a silver envelope, he bends towards her, whispers, 'Open that one later.'

'So, Robbie,' pipes up Nick. 'Is there anything you'd like to say to Janet?'

'Honestly, Nick mate . . .' He takes Janet's hand. 'Mia and I . . . and Elizabeth – we can't ever thank you enough.' He presses a wrist over his eyes, clearly unable to continue.

'Ah, Robbie . . .' Jessica stands, goes over to give him a hug, cluttering Janet's personal space. 'And we couldn't have such a brave lady on the show without sending you off for a makeover with our wonderful team. We need to make sure you look all glam for your champagne dinner tonight.'

The dog trainer lady, while remaining off camera, gestures for Janet to stand. Following instruction, the room spins and her nausea returns. The 'team' have appeared like genies. Animated into life. Discussing plans for her improvements. Covertly mocking her current appearance.

Jessica touches her arm and says, 'Don't look so worried, Janet. You deserve this. Enjoy every moment.'

In the make-up room, Janet stares in fascination at the woman sitting opposite.

Feline blended umber tones, enhancing the cornflower blue of her eyes. Cheekbones sharpened by opalescent liquid. Lips soft and plump and glistening. The type of hair Janet has always envied, but never dared try. Sharp ice-blonde fringed bob. Her dress is sexy. A trendy Aztec print, peeping through the brightness of a yellow cape, which matches her wedges.

Janet leans towards the mirror, pressing her lips together, unable to comprehend that this woman is her.

Chloe, the make-up artist, steps back, analysing her work. Giving Janet a welcome respite from the coffee-mixed-with-spearmint-gum breath she'd been enduring. A concoction that Glade won't be releasing in a hurry. In the reflection, Janet notices how untidy Chloe's own make-up is. All mussy hair and smeared eyes.

'So, do you like the new Janet?'

The immediate answer her brain generates is no. The new Janet has done a terrible thing. But she responds with, 'I do . . . it doesn't even look like me. Thank you.'

Chloe smiles, emerging tears glinting under the lights. 'I've got a little boy,' she says. 'And, well . . . everything you've been through . . . you deserve this.'

Janet stares again at the result of her metamorphosis. Mulls the words everyone keeps repeating. *You deserve this.*

'Yes,' she says. 'I suppose I do.'

26

Her Roses (The Only Thing She Will Miss): Part II

Once back outside, she's decided. Her sentence is over.

Having thought about this moment day in, day out, it's finally going to happen.

She stops and glances beyond the cremation towards her roses.

The only thing she will miss.

Walking the stretch of garden, she's overcome with a warm numbness. Nothing to do with the remaining alcohol sloshing through her veins, but a peace not experienced for so long.

At the roses, she cups a bloom and pulls it forward, inhales the fresh perfume. Something so simple, yet her only source of happiness. Releasing the flower, she takes a last look towards Claire's room. Her empty room. Then continues towards the brambles.

Head down, she enters the spiked mass. Pushes her way through, arms as shields. Scratching, pricking, tearing at her jumper, her skin. Though consciously aware of each stab, signals to her brain are severed. As if loaded with anaesthetic, she feels no pain.

Swallowed by the dense tangle, the sound of each movement crackling like fire, her senses are confused. It's so dark, it's impossible to know where she is, where she's going. But she hears a rustle that she knows she didn't make, and stops.

A pair of green eyes glow through the blackness. Below, another four. And after a moment she can vaguely make out the shape of the vixen. Cubs tight by their mother's body, ensuring no harm comes their way.

'Janet.' A muted shout from Colin filters through to her ears. 'Janet,' he calls again. She remains still. Waits for the third. When it doesn't arrive, she pushes forward, deeper and deeper, until her hand touches the cold metal of the fence.

As hoped, it's still buckled and broken. Pools of electric lighting from beyond brighten the surroundings enough for her to see. Although Claire could have easily got through the gap, she's a different matter. Though how incredible the power of want, need. Determined, she pushes, contorts her body, until finally she's atop the embankment.

It's like a portal to another world. Her Narnia. Except instead of snow and Aslan, there are sleepers interspersed with ballast, sides linked by a cat's cradle of cables attached to steel poles, faintly lit by the Tesco sign across the way.

After pausing for a moment, allowing her vision to adjust, she prepares to negotiate the steep bank.

It's difficult. Each step unsteady, resulting in additional slips and slides.

Halfway down, she loses her footing completely, dropping to her backside, unable to stop the downward momentum. Guttural noises punctuating the skid. When she finally comes to a standstill, not far from the bottom, she eases herself to standing. Wipes her grazed hands against the thighs of her now ripped trousers and shuffles the last few feet.

The tracks are much wider than they were moments ago. From above, they were almost toy-like. Now they're solid, real.

She sits on the edge where the hardened soil and dead grass meet the stones. A dirty version of their newly gravelled driveway.

The bulk of the towering houses are screened by trees and bushes. Only some roofs and top windows remain visible. A few still lit yellow. People awake, alive.

It's started to spit again. An entire day's break from constant rain coming to an end.

Swivelling her wrist to view her watch, it reads almost eleven. She's uncertain exactly when the last train runs, but when tucked up in bed, she usually feels a shudder through the house around this time.

So, she'll sit and wait.

The rain is heavy now. Droplets large and forceful.

She'd hate to die of hypothermia. That would be terrible. They once said on *Casualty* that at the end, when the person is so cold their organs shut down, they actually feel incredibly hot, and the victims are often found with their clothes ripped from them. Naked. It's important that doesn't happen.

She rubs the exposed skin of her shins, then each arm. Though soon stops as her pain signals are awakening, the scratches beginning to smart.

This other world has a magic of its own. The moon highlights the rusting metal of the track. A spotlight for her last stage appearance. Picking out objects that scatter the outer edges. A boot, a shopping trolley, a decapitated doll, head adjacent to its body.

For her eighth birthday she received a doll just like it. Head still in position, of course. She'd begged her mother for months after seeing it in the Kays catalogue, which she would frequently flick through for entertainment, drooling over the toys.

The doll, Lucy, never left her side. She would feed it, change its nappies, take it for long walks, chastise her parents for talking too loudly when she was sleeping. *You'll be a wonderful mother*, they'd say. As would her parents' friends who'd come round for parties. Filling the room with the smell of Martini and cigarette smoke. Janet would stay up, parading Lucy, telling them she had colic. *What a wonderful mummy you are*, they'd say.

That doll is intact in the attic. Carefully placed in a box. Its clothes neatly folded inside a vanity case. Yet Claire . . .

She wonders what Colin's doing. If he's still looking for her or has given up. Then she thinks about her dad. But she can't. She can't think of that. He'll join her soon enough.

Closing her eyes, she bends her legs towards her chest, stretching her ruined jumper over her kneecaps, and drops her head onto the swallow, plucked of its sequins. She stays there for some time, foetus-like, until the muffled rumbling of the train can be heard in the distance.

Soaked, shivering, she opens her eyes, catches her breath.

OK . . . OK. It's fine. It's time.

Grappling with how best to do it, where to place herself, she stands, turns her back to the tracks and faces the bank.

Are you coming to join me, Mummy?

'I . . . I think so, sweetheart.' She's surprised how unsure she is despite her previous certainty. She wants to see her so much. It's all she wants.

Backwards, she walks.

One step, two step.

Edging towards the sleepers.

And the noise grows louder, and the train gets closer, and the ground vibrates, and she breathes in, prepares, and the noise grows louder, and the train gets closer, and it's here now . . . but she can't. She can't do it. Can't take that final step.

The train passes.

Its force propelling her forward.

Face down, temple knocking against the hard clay.

Rain thrashes her back. Mud from the bank trickles towards her like melting chocolate. Stinging her scratches.

And she listens, dazed. The opportunity to die trailing off, and off, and off, until the sound transforms into a distant screeching cacophony.

Pushing herself up, her vision blurs. Ice-pick stabs in her left eye force her to clamp it shut. She's a coward. Can't even kill herself properly. 'I'm sorry, baby . . . I tried. I'm so sorry.'

Struggling to her feet, she stands, hunched, arms swinging ape-like, and staggers back towards the track.

This time, she steps onto them fully, stands in their centre, rotating one hundred and eighty degrees, arms held out to her sides. 'Come and get me . . . please come and get me,' she shouts. And she waits, soaked to her rattled bones, for another train to come along and finish the job.

She's been walking for some time now. On and on, far away towards the continual faint noise. Towards darkness. Each step more painful and difficult to make than the last. Stumbling so frequently she crosses back over the metal and continues instead on the soft saturated ground, alongside the track.

The scenery swings like a pendulum. Each image, object, doubled. Maybe she did step back. Maybe she is dead. But she keeps walking, walking, in whatever state this is. The rain that creeps through the crack of her lips now tastes of iron. A swipe of her mouth smears her hand devil red.

There are other noises. Sirens. Multiple high-frequency yelps and wails. And she stops. She's outside the vehicle. 'It's OK, sweetheart, you're going to be OK. Mummy won't let anything happen to you.' The sounds increase. Louden. More sirens. There's an odour in the air, scratching her throat. Burning rubber. She knows this smell, she thinks, as she slips, cracks her knee against the ground.

Back to standing, the tang of blood lingers in her mouth. Her wet, soiled fingers touch her head, sticking against a wound. 'Are you OK, sweetheart?' She stops. Sways on the spot. One eye transfixed.

It's the train. She can just make it out. Flashlights. Twenty, thirty, forty feet away. Distance not a concept her brain can decipher. She moves towards the scene. The dismantled, distorted, smoking scene.

She's there now, amid the devastation. People searching twisted metal. She's not cold anymore. Having stepped into a furnace. Everyone is busy. No one can see her. Maybe she did step back. Maybe she is dead.

There's Claire. Where she'd gently laid her down. To transfer her life. The rain covering them both. Must pinch her little nose first. But the paramedics are here now. 'Help, please . . . I did everything I could . . . I pulled her out and gave her mouth to mouth to bring her back . . . Please, she's just a child . . .' There's a young woman, filming. But she needs to do something. That's not right. Filming when they need to help. Is that all they can do? Her vision splits completely, the pain in her head intensifies. The woman is saying things, but she doesn't know what. Her ability to stand, lost. A man hovers over her as she drops to her knees. He's asking her name. But she can't remember it. Then finally it's here. The nothingness she'd been desperate for all along.

The After-Lie

27

Birds in an Aviary

The Daventry Hotel is a monumental building.

Colin links arms with her as they walk beneath the extended curved glass of the canopied entrance, like a bride and groom. A million miles from their ceremony at Swinton Town Hall.

A bowler-hatted doorman pulls on the heavy brass handle, welcoming them with a polite nod and hello. On the other side a rather attractive concierge – she's always liked a man in uniform – takes their cases before leading them through the foyer, across the silky marble floor.

Heat penetrates the sunray-shaped window, beating down onto the back of her neck. Fragments of light, lasering around the airy space, bounce from the church-like curved stone, down to the carved wooden panels.

'Bit better than the Premier Inn, eh?' Colin is like a cat watching a fly, his head darting in all directions.

It is better than the Premier Inn. It's better than almost anywhere she's been before. Anywhere manmade, that is. Nothing compares to the ocean. The epitome of freedom.

The concierge – Peter, according to his name badge – leads them on what seems to be a never-ending journey down corridors and into lifts, while Colin bombards him with architectural-based questions. Until finally Peter stops outside a door with the number 306 displayed in buffed brass.

The room is plush, fancy.

Immediately, she's drawn towards the huge window, framed with luxurious weighted striped curtains, which looks out onto the most incredible courtyard. At its centre, gigantic palm trees reach high towards the roof of the spectacular glass atrium, creating the sensation of being abroad, or even in another world. Inside, people are sitting at tables, laughing, smiling. A colourful array of birds in an aviary.

The soft furnishings are crisp and impeccable. A look she dreams of achieving at home. Although, she's never quite understood this modern way of mixing fabric patterns. She prefers things to match. Even the Radox she buys depends on the current colour of her towels and dried flower display.

Managing for a moment to block out the wrongdoing that has brought her here, she flops onto the cloud-soft bed. The profusion of cushions standing to attention fall like skittles. She attempts to return them to their positions. 'I was on TV today, Peter. *Hello Britain*. I was in the train crash in Manchester recently, and I saved a little girl who was the daughter of their chef, so they're treating us to all this.' She needs to say it out loud. Once again taste the lie on her lips. Decipher how it makes her feel.

Colin shakes his head as though she's embarrassing herself. But immune, she continues. 'It was ever so exciting . . . they did my hair.'

'How do we call for room service?' Colin cuts across her towards the phone, taking Peter along with him. Standing beside the concierge while receiving the instructions, he looks especially small and old. Peter on the other hand has a hint of Jason Quartz about him. The hooded eyes. And when he turns around and looks at her, to bid farewell, they carry a glint that sets her cheeks aflame.

'Thank you so much, Peter,' she says, in a voice as unfamiliar as her new look.

Reality seeps in once they've been left to their own devices.

While Colin silently investigates the wardrobe, she escapes to the bathroom to have some space, gather herself. Holding on to the sides of the large Victorian-style sink, she exhales slowly. *It will be OK. It will be OK.*

When lifting her head, for a split-second she thinks someone else is in the room with her, then remembers she looks like this now, and traces her fingertips over her lips, pushes her hair behind her ears.

They've decided to stay local and take a stroll to Baker Street.

Before leaving, while waiting for Colin to go to the toilet she'd needed something to numb the anxiety, so had raided the mini bar, downing two miniature vodkas which worked their magic far too swiftly and acutely. And now, as they walk around Marylebone, and she's enduring his interminable tour-guiding, appearing sober is proving a challenge. 'Hang on, I've got a blister,' she says, swapping the wedges for her old ballet pumps crammed in her silver tote bag. Now more grounded, she focuses on straightening her steps, her gait.

Although Manchester has some incredible architecture, and she's always in awe of the Town Hall and Central Library on the few occasions they venture into town, the buildings in London are bigger, grander, whiter. Or perhaps the width of the road is creating an optical illusion. Or the vodka. But either way, it's a different world. A Richard Curtis movie. Black cabs, tourists, the Union Jack protruding at angles from buildings and on mugs and tea towels and a cushion which she wants to buy but Colin won't let her. 'You're not Liam Gallagher, Janet.'

Now having reached Baker Street, they stop outside the Sherlock Holmes Museum and read the blue plaque. 'You know there's no actual 221b, don't you?' says Colin.

She doesn't respond to that because she knows he knows she doesn't know.

Inside is a replica of Holmes's lodgings. A cosy Victorian parlour complete with faux roaring fire and the dinginess born of a time before electricity.

She likes it. Imagining it as her new abode. Alone, cosy. Perhaps a cat stretched out before the flames.

While Colin inspects the room, he can't help but spew information. Things such as, 'He first wrote the address 221b in *A Study in Scarlet*,' and, 'Do you know, Conan Doyle never actually wrote "elementary, my dear Watson" anywhere in the books?'

She can't let this one slide. 'He did, though.'

'He didn't, Janet. He says both things separately. "Elementary" in "The Adventure of the Crooked Man" and "my dear Watson" in "The Adventure of the Cardboard Box", but never together. They added it in the films.' All this is spoken with a newly acquired pompous gentleman's voice.

For a while she's enjoying herself. Successfully burying the guilt. Until Colin says, 'You know my nickname was Sherlock when I was younger?'

'You never told me that. Why though? Wasn't he tall?'

He turns and looks at her. 'Yes, thank you, Janet. They called me Sherlock because nothing – nothing – gets past me.'

Fear mixed with alcohol makes it impossible to know if she's imagining his eyes boring into her. Witnessing her blackened soul. But the once-comforting room has turned dark and dank and claustrophobic. 'Sorry,' she says. 'I feel a bit queasy. I'll wait for you outside.'

28

Little Sherlock

They too are now birds within the aviary.

The atrium restaurant is even grander once inside. The distance between their crisp white linen-draped table and the peak of the glass dome is vertigo-inducing. The excellent acoustics utilized by the pianist tinkling a mellow rendition of 'Summertime'.

She imagines, as married couples go, they appear happy to onlookers. Smiling towards the piano, sipping champagne. The half-empty bottle sitting in an ice bucket on a stand like a third person at the table. Bubbles crackle on her tongue, then warm her gullet. 'That's nice,' she says, despite it not tasting as good as the Aldi prosecco.

The alcohol is loosening her restrained emotions. Horror at what's occurred floating to the surface. Not only her wrong-doings, but also his. Although she plans to keep that knowledge to herself. Not wanting to open cans of worms, interrogations. Not from anyone, but especially not Colin. Little Sherlock.

She sips on her drink to dislodge the resentment stuck in her chest, and opens the leather-bound menu. Clasping the edges to squeeze away the shakes in her fingers. He copies the action, and they both study in silence, until he says, 'Are you OK? You seem nervous.' He stares at her through his cheap off-the-peg readers.

'Yes . . . yes, I'm fine. A bit tired, that's all.' Further scanning the choices, she avoids his eyes. 'Are you OK? I thought you seemed a bit on edge too.'

'Do I? No . . . no, not at all.' He turns a page of the menu. 'Nope, I'm all good, thank you.'

Though his performance is unconvincing, in case he really is feeling particularly pleased with himself, she decides to break the news. 'No steak, I'm afraid.'

'What? Oh, you're joking.' Tilting back his head, he directs his vision through the narrow lenses as his eyes flit over the pages. 'What's wrong with proper food?'

She squirms at his uncouthness, but the menu doesn't appeal to her either. Foie gras, veal, lobster – the more money, the more cruelty.

'And this can definitely be charged to the show?' he says, still perusing.

'Yes, you heard Will.' She wishes he hadn't mentioned that. Reminded her.

'Right, well, I'll have the lobster, then.' He snaps the booklet shut and lays it back on the table.

'You don't even like seafood, apart from tuna.' Her voice is low, tight.

Leaning forward, he half whispers, 'It's forty-five pounds. When will we ever get the chance to have forty-five-pound lobster for free?'

'But you know it upsets me that they boil them alive.'

'Well, what are you having?'

She takes another look. 'The lamb, I think.'

He leans further forward. 'Well, they didn't stroke it to death, Janet.'

Returning her own menu to the table, she reaches for the bottle of champagne and fills her glass, ignoring his glare.

'It's gone right to your head.' He leans back in his chair.

She forces a smile, enjoying her secret of the vodkas. 'I've only had one glass.'

'I'm not talking about the champagne.'

After a waiter with an unidentifiable accent takes their order, they return to the silent pretence of enjoying the pianist. Smiling through the varied repertoire as though at the theatre and unable to speak. All is as calm and forced-pleasant as can be, until, during the rendition of 'Baby One More Time', without even a glance in her direction, Colin says, 'So you remember it all then?'

She flicks her eyes towards him while turning to reach for her glass. 'Yes, it just came back when I was on there . . . it must have been the adrenaline or something. But let's not talk about that now, eh? It's still all too stressful, and we're watching the piano.' She returns to doing so, the added armour of champagne sliding smoothly down her throat.

'It's strange how it suddenly came back like that.'

In her peripheral vision, she can tell he's still facing outwards, his agitated foot moving up, down, up, down, unrelated to the music.

'It's not, though. That's what Dr Rashid said would—'

'Hello, we have the lobster in artichoke foam.' They both turn to the waiter now placing a white ceramic oblong in front of Colin. 'And the seared lamb.' Janet's plate makes a tiny thud. They're asked if they require anything else. She'd love some ketchup but shakes her head and smiles.

Once they're alone again, Colin stares towards his food. 'What the hell is that?' His hand forms a fist which he positions in front of his mouth.

'The lobster . . . what you asked for.'

He forces a little burp then conjures a noise as if he's trying not to vomit. 'It's like someone spat all over the plate.'

'That's foam, Colin. You've seen them do it on *MasterChef*.'

He makes the noise again. 'No, sorry, it's disgusting. Why would anyone want to make food look like spit?'

'You've got to eat it . . . It was boiled alive.'

With raised arm he attempts to attract a passing waitress, who remains oblivious to his needs. Janet lifts his plate and pushes hers towards him. 'You can't get them to take it back now. You can't. I'll have to eat it . . . you have mine.'

Dishes now swapped, he picks up his knife and fork. 'Well, you should have told me what foam was if you know so much about it. How was I supposed to know it meant spit?'

'It doesn't mean . . .' She presses her fingers over her mouth and closes her eyes to compose herself. Collecting up her cutlery she deflates the foam with the knife, now also unable to see it as anything but bodily fluids, then uses the special lobster fork they'd rested on the plate to dig the flesh from the poor creature's red claws. All the while knowing it had been alive so very recently and had died because of her. A familiar thought.

'Gorgeous,' he says. 'Very tender.' She glimpses masticated flesh through his parted teeth, for which she's grateful because it equally puts her off the lamb.

He takes a swig of his drink. 'So, you must remember where you were going now, then? What else?' His speech is precise, calm, but his eyes avoid hers, and his finger runs back and forth beneath his nose, eliminating the sweat developing above his lip.

'You seem worried, Colin. Is there something you'd rather I didn't remember?'

He turns away, lifts his hand to summon another waiter who comes directly over. 'Can I get another bottle of champagne, please?'

'No, no, please don't worry . . .' Janet smiles to the young man, despite the brewing of anxious tears. 'Just a bottle of sparkling water will be fine.'

'No, we'll have a bottle of champagne, please.' Colin smiles too. His overrides hers and the waiter nods towards him, with an 'Of course, sir,' and leaves to carry out the request.

'You'll have to pay for that, you know . . . they won't let us take the piss.'

'But you're an amazing hero, remember. It's the least they can do.'

Unable to bear looking at him, she scans the atrium. People laughing, having fun. The pianist now playing 'When I Fall in Love', which makes the couple on the table opposite search for each other's hands. With nowhere to go, hide, she picks up her knife and fork once again and continues eating. Sensing him watching her for a while, until he removes his meat-juice-spattered napkin and drops it onto the tablecloth. 'You're still you, you know, Janet. You won't have a make-up artist and hairdresser with you all the time. You're still just you under there. Do you think in a few weeks anyone will give a shit that you saved some girl?'

She cracks at a claw. 'But it was meant to happen—'

'Don't let it go to your head, or it will be embarrassing. It doesn't change anything, make it OK.'

She looks up at him, sharply. 'It does though . . . it does, Colin. God sent me a message.'

'What's this God nonsense again? He's sending you messages now?' He lets out a laugh. 'What did God say about the . . .'

His mouth is moving but she can no longer hear what he's saying, as once again the realization descends. That what she said about God isn't the case anymore. Because it didn't even happen. But it still must all mean something. It must. She's drunk too much. The room is moving. She needs a coffee . . . to ask for a coffee. The fork slips from her hand, dropping on the plate with a clang before bouncing off onto the floor. A waitress runs over and collects it up, a magician, immediately swapping it for a gleaming alternative. Janet forces a grin, contains her threatening tears as she takes it from the girl with a 'Thank you'.

'You're one of those people, aren't you, Janet? Always the victim.' He takes the bottle and pours himself the dregs.

Of all the disparaging remarks he's hurled her way, this really stokes her fire. Lifting her glass, she tips the remaining liquid into her mouth, petrol onto the flames, then looks him directly in the eyes. 'You burned your own dead daughter's belongings. What sort of person does that make you?' She maintains the stare for as long as she dares, then carefully, precisely, presses food onto the prongs of her clean fork.

His puce face moves side to side. 'No, it wasn't like that . . . it wasn't like that. It wasn't healthy. You—'

'I wasn't coming back, you know.' The words shoot from her mouth and harpoon him in the chest. The shock on his face makes it impossible for her to stop. 'I waited around on the streets, sick, disgusted with you . . . wondering how I could ever look at you again. Thinking, what can I do? And so, my only option being to go back to Eccles, I walked to the station . . . but I was penniless, didn't have my bag . . . and, well, this lovely man, a soldier, in his uniform, asked if I was OK because I was so upset. "I just need to get on a train," I told him. And he dug into his pockets and paid for me. Then walked me to the platform, making sure I was OK and boarded the last train safely. So there . . . now you know. I wasn't coming back.'

29

A Different Child

She's used to this treatment. The silence. As though she's dead. One of those ghosts who don't realize they've passed over, foolishly attempting to communicate with the living.

As they walk the hotel corridors, she knows Colin well enough to sense his dilemma. How desperate he is to exact punishment by abandoning her in a scary, strange city, but knowing that would set her free in an exciting, strange city.

They arrive at their room, entering without a word uttered. Once inside, the only sound being the slurping suck of Colin's swigs on the remaining champagne, which instead of offering up to her, he slams on the console table, its neck emitting sparks of fizz.

Clumsily swaying, he undresses apart from his socks, and slides under the duvet, the white of his shoulder merging with the Egyptian cotton. Balding head barely hitting the voluptuous pillow before the snores commence.

She stares at him for a moment, her lip involuntarily curling, then goes and sits by the window and switches on the TV. As she flicks through the channels, he mumbles, turns over, so she lowers the volume and moves the chair nearer the screen.

She's tempted to finish the champagne, but he'd only add that to her list of crimes. Instead, she tiptoes over to the mini bar and quietly removes a can of Britvic orange which she opens against her bust like a gun silencer, then tips in another miniature vodka.

Back in the chair she reverts to her teenage years. Secretly swigging on booze, smirking at her rebellion. The only thing missing, a cheeky cigarette nicked from her dad's pocket. And with the addition of her new look, she's more akin to youthful Janet than the one she's become.

Deluding herself that she's no desire to watch back her TV performance, she puts on the Psychic Channel instead. It isn't Jason Quartz, unfortunately, it's Hazel O'Brien again. Janet watches the show, Colin's snores escalating. She tries so hard to concentrate on the clairvoyant's possessed eye-rolling, but can't continue and caves, searching Catch Up for *Hello Britain.*

It's a shock, seeing herself. Voice so common and shrill. It's the strangest thing, witnessing oneself as others do. The suit looks creased despite all its ironing. The dampened armpits, presumed successfully concealed with clamped elbows, are glaring.

She rewinds. Presses play. Analyses her movements.

With each nervous sip of water on screen, she gulps on her spiked orange juice.

Allowing the programme to continue, she endures the interview.

It didn't feel so at the time, but the lie is fluent. A frozen stream now thawed, flowing once again.

Closing her eyes, she holds the can against her face, listens. Pushing the aluminium deeper into her cheek, hoping it will somehow absorb the horror of it all.

She rewinds. Presses play.

This time, she views it in its entirety. Unflinching. Transfixed at the car crash. Metaphorical and literal. At Robbie who she'd watched on screen for years, now hugging her, presenting her with the precious card from Elizabeth. The beautiful flowers, which she realizes have been left in the dressing room.

Unable to bear it anymore, she switches off the TV. Allows her brain to absorb all she's seen. Then with precision, she walks to the side of the bed and, bending as silently as possible while focusing on Colin's open mouth, retrieves her bag.

She's sitting on the toilet with the lid down. The cards resting on her thighs. First, she looks again at Elizabeth's offering. Smiling at how she's depicted her mouth with its exact shape. Although probably by accident.

Acidic orange crawls its way back up her oesophagus as she opens Mia's envelope.

The card is beautiful. Tasteful. A watercolour of a pink rose on the front. A rose. As though Mia knows her so well. Surely a sign.

Dear Janet,

It doesn't feel enough to write a thank you card, but we couldn't get to the show today because it didn't feel right to bring Elizabeth. Like you, she doesn't remember much about the crash, but I couldn't risk her becoming distressed.

I don't really know what to write to be honest. Except to say thank you a million times over. You gave me my little girl. And knowing you no longer have yours both breaks my heart and makes it burst with love for you without us even having met.

Elizabeth and I would love to thank you in person.

Perhaps you could come to ours for lunch one day? Robbie could make food, nothing formal. I know you're local which is fantastic. Or we could drop by yours if that's easier. I don't want to intrude, but I'd rather not meet out somewhere as we'll get hounded. Anyway, no pressure, but it would be so lovely if you got in touch. I'll leave my number below.

Mia x

Shaking hands make it difficult to put the card back in the envelope. As soon as it's hidden, she removes it again, re-reads the part that's caused her eyes to sting, her stomach to constrict.

You gave me my little girl. And knowing you no longer have yours both breaks my heart and makes it burst with love for you without us even having met.

Everything she'd said on the show was the truth. Only a different child, crash. A better outcome. But where was the TV then? The papers? The flowers, the neighbours? Where was the outpouring of love when *her* little girl had gone?

Wiping her wrist over her intoxicated face, she notices something caught within the fold of the envelope. The leaf.

Please God, give me a sign that I am forgiven.

She stares at the words. Mouthing them over and over, each line punctuated with Colin's muted snores. Taking out the card, she reads Mia's message one more time, lays it out open on the floor next to the toilet, and leaves for the bedroom to get the hotel phone.

*

It's difficult to count the rings against the blood pumping in her ears. She's about to give up, end the call, when a breathless voice says, 'Hello?'

'Oh . . . oh, hello.' There's a slight slur to her voice that she can't control. 'Is that Mia?'

'Yes, who's calling?' It's the murmurs of someone half asleep, and Janet swivels her watch around to discover it's ten thirty. She screws up her eyes, mouths 'Shit.'

'Sorry, I've just realized the time . . . It's Janet . . . Janet Brown.'

'Oh . . . hi Janet, it's . . . well, nice to hear from you.'

Janet notes the pause.

'Again, I . . . I'm so sorry for calling at this time . . . The day has whizzed by—'

'It's fine. I'm really pleased you called.' Mia appears to be copying her slur, then Janet recognizes it's an accent. A drawling American accent.

'Well, I . . . I just wanted to thank you for the lovely card.'

'No . . . goodness no, please don't thank me, I can't . . . we can't thank you enough.'

'And I was wondering if you were around at the weekend? To meet, I mean.'

There's another pause. This one lingers. Followed by the rustle of bedding. 'Erm . . . OK sure, why not? I think we're free this weekend—'

'I mean, don't worry if you're not.' Elizabeth's card catches her eye, and she imagines the girl's tiny hand moving back and forth, scribbling in her yellow hair.

'No . . . yes, that sounds perfect. Why don't you and your husband come over to ours? We'll have a bit of lunch in the garden? Give me your details and I'll call later in the week, make proper arrangements. I'm in bed now . . . an early bird, I'm afraid.'

Squeezing her eyes shut, Janet replies as calmly, as soberly, as guiltlessly as possible. 'Well, if you're sure. That would be lovely.'

'Where is she? I want to see her.' The woman throws off the blankets, arm restricted by the plastic tube fed into her vein, and swings her legs around until her feet meet the cold vinyl.

'I'm Constable Fay Towers.' The officer touches her hand. 'I'm a family liaison officer and . . .' She pauses to glance towards the husband who's pacing, hands on head, mouth contorted like a pained animal. The woman feels the touch turn to a squeeze. 'And I'm afraid I have some very bad news. I'm so—'

'No, I'm going to tell her. I want to tell her.' The husband surges forward, intercepting the space between the women. 'She's dead, OK? She's dead. You took her and now she's dead.'

He's being asked to quieten down, manoeuvred away. But it doesn't matter because the woman knows he's wrong.

The officer employs the serenest of tones, instructs her to get back into bed. 'I can't imagine how terrible . . .' But what she's saying is irrelevant. The woman yanks the tube from the canula and stands, walks, runs out of the ward.

'Nurse,' calls the husband. Other voices follow behind.

She's through the doors now, into the corridor. Hit by the icy air circulating up towards the Victorian vaulted ceiling. She knows where it is, the Children's Hospital. She's been there for her daughter's persistent ear infections. That's where she'll be. Waiting for her.

Hold on, baby. Mummy will be there soon.

30

Cinderella Back in Her Uniform

It's a complex thing, carrying a tortured conscience after committing a terrible deed while simultaneously grappling with the desire for its life-affirming effects to continue. For the few days since they've returned home, she's been both desperate for Mia to make contact and praying she doesn't.

Now it's Friday, there's a certainty the call will never materialize. And as she purposefully rides the round-the-houses number twenty-nine to work, with the aim of easing herself back in, it's with both immense relief and the familiar dull ache of disappointment.

Finally reaching her stop, she steps off the bus. Cinderella, back in her uniform and comfy shoes. Although now with added make-up, having used the palettes gifted to her by Chloe. An inferior attempt at recreating 'New Janet'.

Sniffing the air, she ambles down the route along the bridge. Enjoying the proximity of water, even if it is only the Quays. Her thoughts drift towards the staffroom. Initially, she enjoys the daydream. The girls gushing. Similar to when she was pregnant and the whole world became nicer. Imagining them saying things like, *Aren't you brave, Janet*, and *It must have been so hard after what happened with Claire*. Wondering if they'll have brought in cake for the occasion. But now, standing in front of the huge, mirror-windowed building, feeling so small in comparison, she's bitten by reality. Nausea rising as the acute awareness clamps down.

She'll have to lie to their faces.

Look directly in their eyes and lie.

'Here she is . . . Oh hey, and there's me thinking Marilyn Monroe was dead.' Sam turns to an awkwardly smiling unknown girl in glasses, barely out of school. 'Emma, this is Janet who we haven't stopped talking about. The hero. Janet, this is Emma. The new Gemma. Erm, hello . . . just realized they only bloody rhyme.' Sam drops teabags into four cups. Her mint-green nails contrast with the over-washed red rawness of her hands.

'Welcome back, Janet.' Maria plonks her limp toast onto a paper plate and gets up, walks towards her, seemingly for a hug, but instead sets off a party popper. Emma screams.

In the following shocked silence, strings of multicoloured tissue float down over Janet's head and face. Remaining rigid, she presses her hand against her chest to steady her racing heart, while Sam charges towards her and starts picking off the strands with the tips of her nails, saying, 'Are you bloody stupid, Maria? She's just been in a train crash, for Christ's sake. You'll give her bloody PDSA . . . Janet, love, are you OK?'

'PTSD . . . I'm fine, fine.' Forcing a smile, Janet strokes her hair to dislodge any popper residue before finally moving from the spot and placing her bag onto one of the plastic chairs.

'Sorry, Janet, it was only because I had some left from Terry's birthday.'

'It's fine Maria, honestly. Thank you, I appreciate it . . .

Hello, Emma, nice to meet you.' The words snag on her dry tongue.

'I feel as though we should sing "For She's a Jolly Good Fellow" or something,' says Maria, back at the table and shoving the peanut-butter-coated toast into her mouth.

'No, don't you dare,' says Janet, while thinking what a nice thing it must be to be on the receiving end of that song.

'What? You've given her a heart attack, and now you want to kill her off with your singing?' Sam is coming towards them again, this time carrying mugs of tea which she places on the table, then pulls out a chair and gently forces Janet to sit. 'Now, get that down you.'

Cup poised at her lips, Janet stares into the steamy liquid and blows. Utilizing the opportunity to regulate her breathing. 'Where's Nish?'

'She's gone to the coffee machine for a cappuccino. She's a right fancy pants, that one. So, come on . . .' Sam sits in the chair opposite and bites on a granola bar. 'Tell us all about it.'

'I don't know what to—'

'We've not stopped talking about you, you know.' A flurry of oats tumble from Sam's mouth. 'Even the poncy office lot. Everyone's so proud.'

'What was Nick like? Is he as fit in real life?' asks Maria, words dulled by the dough bulging her cheeks.

'No . . . well he is, I suppose, but he's not really my type. I'm not a fan of these new big bright teeth they all have. But Robbie Pilkington seems lovely. I'm supposed to be going to their house for lunch.' She can't help but sit taller when she says this, to accommodate the butterflies releasing in her stomach.

Sam flicks Janet's arm with the back of her hand. 'Give over . . . you're going to lunch round Robbie and Mia Pilkington's? Did you hear that, girls?'

'Nothing formal, just in the garden . . . you know.'

'Hark at her, "nothing formal".' Sam impersonates Janet's voice, which would have been upsetting had she not witnessed the even worse version on TV.

'They want to thank me, I suppose.' She's in her stride now. No lies have been uttered, which enables words to flow freely. Though thinking she should quit while ahead, she stops and slurps her tea.

Sam dabs at the crumbs stuck to the inside of the foil-lined wrapper. 'We're so glad you're OK, aren't we? You're our Sam's Angels angel.' It's clear she's used that line a lot since the news broke.

The girls mumble in agreement. Even Emma, who she's known for an entire five minutes. And guilt spreads up through her like rising damp. 'Right . . . what's the plan? I hope my trolley's still neat.' But despite her attempts to steer the conversation away from events, she can't shake the encroaching reality, claustrophobia, because they won't stop.

'Is Jessica as pretty in real life?' Emma miraculously speaks.

'I'd so do Nick,' says Maria.

'Less of the filth, please. Oh, come here you . . .' Sam gets up, stands behind Janet's chair and embraces her. 'We've got cake for later.'

'Get off her, she's mine.' Nish is standing in the doorway holding a paper cup. After a pause she rushes over, puts the coffee on the table and lunges herself at Janet, forcing Sam to release her arms. 'We all watched you. They let us stay behind and we all watched it in one of the marketing rooms. Oh my god, I can't believe it, Janet . . . I can't believe this has all happened.'

The last words stab Janet in the chest. Feeling herself paling as though blood is seeping from the wound. 'Thanks for the flowers and fuss, everyone. But I'd just like to get back to normal now.' She wants to mean this, but knows she doesn't.

Sam has left with the girls to start the clean, after suggesting that Janet and Nish stay behind for a catch-up. But now they're alone, Janet doesn't want a catch-up. Cannot face the pressure of one-to-one scrutiny.

'Jesus, Janet, it was like an episode of *EastEnders* or something, remembering it all on air like that . . . I tell you what, we couldn't breathe. Honestly, I—'

'Yes, it was a surprise to me too.' Gripping her mug, she restrains her hands. Lifts it to her mouth to hide her face.

Nish stands, walks over to the door and pushes it to. 'Sorry, Janet, but I've got to ask you something.'

As though the oxygen has been shut out, Janet's breaths quicken. 'Oh heck, look at the time, Nish. We'd better get on . . . the toilets on three are always the worst and it's nearly—'

'Sod that.' Nish sits again, scraping her chair even closer. 'Look, we're friends, aren't we?'

Swallowing hard, Janet nods. 'Yes . . . yes, of course. But I can't stay later today—'

'And you know, if there was anything that was difficult to tell someone, you could tell me, right? That you can trust me.'

The room swivels on its axis. Janet blinks, beams a smile

which transforms into a nervous laugh. 'Of course . . . yes. You're a good friend, Nish.' She stands, picks up her mug and takes it to the sink. 'Now, stop being silly. Sam's going to—'

'Where were you going?'

Janet pauses. Turns on the tap, twisting it to full stream.

'I mean, why were you going anywhere? Colin was driving you home.'

Dropping her head, speckles of water bounce from the stainless steel onto her face. She lowers her eyelids, prepares. 'We had a row, that's all . . . I was pissed, wasn't I? You saw my dancing.' She laughs again. Incongruous with the tone of the conversation. 'So, I went off in a stupid huff.' Her hands scald under the hot tap as she rubs the rim of the cup. The pain a welcome distraction. An alternative to snapping the elastic band. 'I don't even know where I was going. I suppose back to the karaoke.' She shuts off the water, turns to witness the effects of her story.

Nish is there to immediately catch her eyes. 'OK . . . OK,' she says.

'Right . . . good. Now, let's go and sort out those loos.' Her pulsating fingers feel sore against the tea towel as she wipes them dry.

Nish joins her at the sink, tips away the remainder of cappuccino before throwing the cup in the bin. 'Only . . . well, you never go anywhere. Then you get on a train late at night.' She flicks a look at the remnant of bruise to the left of Janet's eye. 'It must have been a bad argument. He didn't—'

'No . . . God no.' Janet's seen enough badly acted TV shows to know how people behave when confronted with this. How this is the moment to come clean. To tell sweet, understanding

Nish everything. The years she's suffered. The hole into which she's fallen.

'It was just an argument, Nish. Colin wouldn't do anything to hurt me.'

31

For She's a Jolly Good Fellow

Haunted by Nish's suspicious face, even taking the route via the leisure centre cut-through isn't enjoyable. Instead of inducing serenity, she imagines wading into the brambles, inviting the thorns to once again scratch until she bleeds. She makes do with a snap of the elastic band.

By the time she reaches Oakland House, the culminating worries have climaxed with a pulsing headache. The skull-penetrating buzz of the pressed intercom adding to the pain.

Helen is striding towards the glass.

Having usually been let in remotely, Janet's arms prickle with unease.

The electronic door gradually opens. As soon as there's air between them, she says, 'What's up? Is Dad OK?'

Helen's nod is solemn. 'He's fine. Can you come this way though, please?' She turns without waiting for a response, walks ahead. Janet following a few steps behind, silenced by the newly formed lump in her throat. They don't turn down the bluebell corridor. But left, towards the office and communal lounge.

Whichever room she's being guided to, the steps are difficult. Her feet, the ignition for the rush of heat sweeping over her body.

It's the police.

They know.

She wasn't home, so they've come here.

The twenty-second journey seems endless, but unfortunately isn't. They're standing outside the double doors of the lounge.

'Helen, what's going on?' Her voice is feeble, sheepish.

'I think it's best if you come inside.' Helen pushes the right-hand panel. It opens with a sucking noise, then all is quiet as she holds it ajar, beckons.

Janet enters, confronts her fate.

Silence transforms into applause. Whistling. Explosions of the same poppers that had terrified her earlier. A glittery *HERO* banner hanging over the serving hatch. And even more touching than she'd imagined, 'For She's a Jolly Good Fellow' sung with frail gusto.

Hand on chest, her mouth opens, eyes alight. Endorphins rising beyond her control.

'Your face,' says Helen, laughing. 'What on earth did you think I was going to do with you?'

Janet smiles, shakes her head. Aware of the tickle of wetness on her cheeks. Then returns to viewing her personal concert. They're all here. The familiar faces she's watched deteriorate over time. Central, her dad, clapping heartily. At what, she doubts he knows. But chooses to believe he does. That he's proud. 'Oh goodness . . . thank you . . . thank you everyone. But you really shouldn't have. I'm no hero,' she says, as though stating this somehow dissipates the wrongness.

Dorothy is walking towards her with a cup of tea and a plate containing a bouncy white bacon sandwich. 'This is for our hero,' she says, putting them down on the nearest table.

Roger shuffles behind. 'You were in the paper, Janet. And now you've been on the television.'

'I . . . I know, Roger . . . yes.'

Dorothy edges closer, wiping Janet's cheek with her arthritic fingers. 'You look lovely . . . not just the make-up. I can see how happy saving that little girl has made you.'

'Oh, it has, Dorothy.' And she means it. Until she remembers, and her mouth twitches.

'What sort of train was it?' asks Roger.

'I . . . I don't know, sorry.'

'Did you think she was dead?'

'Roger, don't be so rude.' Dorothy turns around, playfully slaps his wrist.

'You can't say anything these days.'

And as Janet stands amid the bickering, pressing the salt-savoury into her mouth, she stops resisting her enjoyment of all this attention. Accepts the warmth gleaned from her stolen pride.

'You know how we were doing a collection for a headstone?' Helen's voice glides over Janet's shoulder, and she turns, a mouthful of sandwich lodging in her chest.

'Yes,' she says, voice an octave deeper than usual. 'But honestly—'

'Well, my son Jack, who you met a few months ago at Curry and Quiz . . . he set up this thing instead.' She's holding a tablet, prodding the screen. 'I can't bloody see anything these days,' she says, putting on the glasses that hang around her neck on a tarnished gold-coloured chain.

'What thing? You're so kind, I'd love to change Claire's headstone, but—'

'And can you believe, it's doubled overnight? I'm not sure what stone you were after, love. They're so expensive, I know. Anyway, he posted on the local Salford page, but since you were on *Hello Britain*, it's shot right up. Look.'

She's faced with a picture of herself. Paper plate in hand, piled with korma and pilau. Beneath the photograph is a passage both explaining the reason for the fund and a description, interpretation, of her as a person. *Hard-working . . . pillar of the community . . . daughter's passing . . . hero . . . saved a child . . . headstone.* These words standing out between others she cannot fully absorb. To the left of the text is a list of donors, either names she doesn't recognize or *Anonymous*, and their generous offerings. £3, £5, £10, one for £50. All headed by a long green bar with the goal of £1,500. The current total, £580.

Janet slides her plate onto the table, willing the bacon to stay down.

'Can you believe it, Janet? All those people watching you on the TV, wanting to donate. Who knows how much it'll go up? Jack says they sometimes grow beyond anyone's dreams. But I'm sure you'll get the stone for Claire. I don't really know about all these things myself. I'm useless.'

Eventually, Janet manages to shake her head. 'No, I . . . no, Helen. I mustn't have that, it's too much. Do you think you could ask Jack to take it down? Please.'

'Oh, don't be so ridiculous. His girlfriend's going to share it on her Twitter and Instagram accounts. It is called Instagram, isn't it? I only do Facebook, myself. She's a . . . what do they call it now? Influencer. Are you OK, love?'

The room lacks oxygen. Helen's face blurs. 'I'm sorry, Helen,

I . . . I've overdone it a bit today. Thank you so much for all this . . . but I think I need to go home now.'

Outside, heart racing but with the relief of freedom, she rushes towards the bus stop. Sucking in the air as if smoking a cigarette. Nicotine exchanged for the fumes from the A666. Trying to calm down, she reasons with herself. Does not having saved Elizabeth change the fact Claire deserves the correct stone? That is why they're raising the money.

A bus soon arrives. It's the number thirty-six, but she doesn't care about the extra walk at the other end. Only that she needs to be further away from Oakland House. Hoping distance will make it feel less real.

As the door folds inwards with the sound of compressed air, she pushes herself up onto the large step while counting her change. 'Hospital Road, please.' It's that driver she can't stand. Grumpy as anything. Accumulated spit crusting at the corners of his mouth.

The coins are now neatly piled in her hand and she's about to drop the small tower towards the plastic dish when he says, 'You're that woman, aren't you? The one that saved Robbie Pilkington's girl.'

After a shocked pause, she nods. Unable to look at him directly and not only because of the saliva. 'That's right.'

'Well, hop on, love . . . no need to pay.'

The bus has stopped outside the big church on Bolton Road. One she's never been inside. Only ever driven past with Colin. She always reads the ever-changing signs attached to the railings. The neon paper printed with black lettering reminds her of bargain basement shops. This one simply reads, *Jesus Loves You*. Although she's certain He would prefer more elegant signage, the good thing about our Lord and Saviour is He doesn't judge. She hopes.

But today's screaming yellow appears to have worked. Because she's been drawn off the bus and is now standing before the entrance. Climbing the worn steps, she follows the path winding towards the chunky wooden door, split down the middle. One side open, the other closed.

Despite the perpetual pull towards places of worship since losing Claire, she's not religious. Growing up, visits to churches only occurred for weddings, christenings or jumble sales. But even then, she'd be in awe on entering. Experiencing a sensation she'd describe to her mum as 'God's rays'. Something special exists inside these magical ornate spaces. And this one is no exception.

Maroon velvet curtains hang heavy either side of the altar. Beyond which is a magnificent stained-glass triptych projecting beams of primary shades. Four extraordinarily tall candles stand like pillars. She loves candles. Though she's never seen ones like these before. Not in B&M, anyway.

A vicar emerges from another large door to the left. Black-gowned and spectacled. Taking a seat on one of the pews, she desperately hopes he'll come over and talk. Hands on knees, head dropped, she waits. Intermittently shuffling her bottom, finding it difficult to get comfortable against the hard oak.

Soon she feels a presence. The vicar's, not God's. He sits further down on the same pew. 'Vicar,' she whispers. 'Can I ask you something?'

'Of course,' he says, moving closer. When he smiles, only one cheek rises, as though he's affected by a paralysis.

She pulls on her earring, now unsure how to express what she wants to say. Or even what it is she's trying to express. 'The thing is . . . my daughter died. Eleven years ago, now. Not that it will ever be better. And it was my fault, you see . . . Oh, I didn't murder her or anything . . . Jesus, no.' Her hand slaps against her mouth. 'Oh God, I'm so sorry . . . shit, not God.' She closes her eyes and shakes her head. 'I'm so sorry, vicar. I don't even swear in real life.'

'Please don't apologize.' The right side of his face lifts, then drops again to deliver, 'I am sorry about your daughter.'

'And a priest at the hospital recently – I was in the train crash, you see, and he said God forgives us and I have to look for the signs . . . and there was a sign . . . a big sign. Huge. But it turned out not to be the sign it looked like and now I've done something terrible. Again. I've not killed anyone or anything, don't worry. No . . . I don't even like eating lobsters. Though I did eat one recently, but that wasn't my fault. The thing is, I don't understand why it all happened if it wasn't for a purpose.'

His bewilderment shows via only one eyebrow. She looks straight into his eyes, feeling her own fill with tears. His hand covers hers. 'Trust in the Lord with all your heart, and do not lean on your own understanding. Proverbs three, verse five.'

She smiles, despite the disappointment of it being yet another riddle when all she wants is a straight answer. To understand the meaning of it all. Maybe religion is too intellectual for her. But then again, her school friend Liza Perkins ran off to be a nun and she couldn't even do her five times tables.

*

Once home and through the door, she bends down to collect the post. Unable to deal with bills at that moment she drops the envelopes on the sideboard, goes and sits in Colin's chair and starts up the laptop.

Finding the fundraiser, she's relieved the bar hasn't extended further. This all needs to end now. Become yesterday's chip paper.

She erases the history then snaps the lid shut. And as she returns it to its original position, moving it a centimetre here and a centimetre there to get it exact, the phone rings.

Neatening her hair as if that will help, she walks over to the sideboard and picks up the receiver. Her nervous movements lacking coordination. 'Hello,' she says, jittery hands straightening the unopened post.

'Hello . . . is that Janet?'

The cold plastic of the phone slides below her ear.

Because peeking between the gas bill and a bank statement is the severe, black-franked logo of Greater Manchester Police.

'Is that not Janet Brown?'

'Yes, sorry . . . Janet Brown speaking.' She flips over the envelope. Buries it beneath the others, so it can no longer be seen.

'Oh good, I thought I'd dialled the wrong number for a moment there. Hi Janet . . . it's Mia.'

32

A Resin Driveway

She's certain the man loitering by the Pilkingtons' electronic gates has photographed her through the car window. 'I think I've been papped, Colin.'

'As if they'd want a photo of you.' He dips his head to inspect the man. 'The paparazzi don't go around with Sainsbury's bags full of groceries. Look at that baguette.'

She so wishes Colin wasn't there. That she could have something for herself. Even if she doesn't deserve to have it. After ruminating for days about ways this visit could be concealed from him, she conceded all attempts would be futile. When she finally told him, he responded with, 'I'd better get to see the Porsche.'

The house is elevated.

The long, steep driveway causes the Avensis to over-rev as Colin's clutch control goes haywire. The car stalls. 'Why would they build a house up here? You'd never get a fire engine to it.'

She glances towards him. What mind would think such a thing? He's the same colour as the lobster she was forced to eat. Sweat gathering on his upper lip, twinkling in the sun bouncing off the rear-view mirror.

Approaching the top, the building doesn't look residential.

It's akin to the brutalist architecture of the old Swinton Lancastrian Hall and Library. Apart from it being mainly painted white and most of the walls exchanged for fine, black-framed glass. She's seen these types of homes before. Not in real life, but as the rich couple's abode in every TV thriller.

Once parked up, ensuring not to obscure the three-car garage, the house appears even larger. Ominous, in fact. The upper level protrudes over the raw brick lower half. A scaled-down version of the Manchester Hilton, always appearing as though it's about to topple.

Emerging from the car, carrying a bottle of Aldi prosecco, she uses her free hand to smooth down the makeover dress. Hopeful it won't be recognizable without the cape. Initial concerns about walking on the gravel in the wedges are alleviated on realizing the stones are glued in place.

Colin dabs at his head with a tissue. 'Marvin's just got one of these resin drives.'

She shushes him as though he's said something deeply personal, then allows him to take control, push the brushed-steel bell attached to the huge door that looks as though it would be a right bugger to slam shut in a rush. As they wait in silence, she can't help but feel the whole entrance would benefit from some lovely hanging baskets.

As the door opens, there's an explosion of hellos. Mia's hair is pushed back, wet, and she's wearing a pastel paisley chiffon kaftan, see-through, exposing a tiny white triangle bikini. Lured into unfamiliar air kissing, Janet makes a strange chicken's head movement, while Colin, appearing not to know where to look, opts for the sky, viewing it with a sun-shielding hand.

'Oh goodness, look at me . . . I am so sorry. It was boiling hot, and I couldn't resist having a dip and didn't realize the time.' Mia's voice stretches and lilts like a meditation, and regardless of the zero effort she's put into her appearance, nothing could lessen her raw, free-spirited beauty.

'I brought this.' Janet presents the wine to Mia, who accepts it with a straight-toothed smile. 'And these for Elizabeth . . . if she's allowed.' She extracts a jar of multi-flavoured jelly beans from her bag.

'Oh my, you're going to be her new BFF. She's not normally allowed candy, but who can say no to jelly beans . . . Oh goodness, what am I doing? Come in, come in. I'm so excited to finally meet you.' She pulls the oversized door back further, her delicate wrist wrapped in fine gold chains, gesturing for them both to step into another world.

The discomfort has now transferred to the hallway. Or rather, foyer.

'May I?' Mia widens her arms for a hug, and Janet, wood-stiff, slots into them. 'I can totally feel your energy already, Janet. You're a beautiful soul.'

Colin coughs. 'I like your driveway,' he says.

'Oh, thank you.' Mia delivers her gratitude with an elegant hand on heart, perfectly arched eyebrows lifted, as if told she's the most beautiful woman in the world. A compliment she's undoubtedly received. Colin blushes. A tiddler caught in her chiffon net.

Finally, she turns and walks them further into the house, her bare feet padding against the shiny white tiles. 'Come see Robbie.'

Following, Janet's head rotates in all directions. 'You've got a beautiful house, Mia.'

'That's so kind. Oh my god, it's been a labour of love.'

It is stunning. But also one of those homes that Janet doesn't understand. Massive, minimalist, cold. The staircase is made up of suspended wooden slats, sandwiched between glass panelling. Beside it, a metal-framed chair, positioned like a set for a photo shoot. No signs of Elizabeth. No bike with its pink bell and peeling glittery stickers resting against the wall. No frog-patterned wellies poised for outings. She's never understood why people would want to live this way. Open plan, eliminating cosiness. All those bare windows. What's wrong with a nice pair of curtains and nets? And carpet. She'll never fathom this trend of favouring department store flooring over a nice bit of pile beneath your feet.

'Here he is, he's been so looking forward to seeing you again.' For the first time, Mia's grin appears disingenuous. Now in the kitchen, or kitchen area, or whatever this space is, Robbie is standing by the sink, even more handsome than before.

'Come here, you.' He's now holding her, his head on her shoulder, emanating warmth. His voice cracks. 'Thank you, thank you, thank you.'

She pats his back. Understanding his pain at what could have been, while mentally fending off her encroaching conscience, dousing her in shame. 'Elizabeth is OK – that's all that matters.' Stating this fact may help. It is all that matters. It is.

'Leave the poor woman alone,' says Mia, while her husband extracts himself from Janet, wet-faced and sniffing. 'Honestly, I thought you Brits were all uptight and didn't like showing emotions and it was us Yanks who were the blubberers.'

'That's not true . . . it's not true, is it, Janet? Oh God, how rude of me to launch myself at your wife there without even a handshake.' He moves over to Colin who is separate from them all, arms stiff by his sides like a child on best behaviour. 'Colin, so pleased to meet you. Do forgive me for dearly loving your wife.'

'Ah, take my wife, please do.' The joke, unfunny even if Colin had delivered it correctly, hangs in the air wrapped in confusion. Janet drops her head, hoping he won't try and rectify it, overcompensate. But all he says is, 'So is that a resin driveway?'

Janet is sipping on a glass of the prosecco, having ignored Colin's disapproving look when making her request. He's pretending to drink the freshly squeezed carrot, ginger and turmeric juice Mia talked him into trying. Robbie is topping up his whisky with carbonated water miraculously flowing from a tap.

The kitchen is breathtaking. Mocks the idea that the lump of cabinet at home could be considered an island, when before her stands a huge white gloss rectangle topped with a slab of genuine granite. At its centre, a flat black square resembling a TV screen, but presumably one of those posh induction hobs. Their only commonality is displayed fruit. Hers is placed in a nice ceramic dish bought from a charity shop. Theirs in an angular contraption made from copper wire, with gaps so large it wouldn't contain a satsuma.

Though fascinated at being in the house of Robbie Pilkington, the only famous person she's ever met apart from that incident with Anneka Rice, the objective of the visit remains prominent in her mind. As Mia pulps another juice, and Robbie explains to Colin why the resin driveway is better for his cars, which he'll show him after lunch, all she can think about is Elizabeth. 'Where's Elizabeth?' her thoughts verbalize.

The juicer stops. As does the men's conversation. She wonders how loud she'd spoken. If her internal desperation had shown itself.

'Catching up with some homework. She'll be down soon.' Mia picks up her phone from the side, taps away, then puts it back down. 'I've texted her,' she says, forcing another carrot through the machine.

Half an hour later and there's still no sign of Elizabeth.

Robbie has mixed a colourful salad and reveals his plans to griddle tuna. Miniature white dishes are filled with unfamiliar foodstuffs that Janet's frankly a little nervous of tasting in case she hates them. They're carrying the mini banquet outside now. Janet offers to help. 'Don't you dare,' says Mia. 'This is for you to enjoy.'

The outside area mirrors the inside. There's a large L-shaped sofa, though this one at least has cushions. Mia takes a seat. 'Janet, Colin, come on . . . scoot on over here.' They obey. Janet sitting closest to Mia. Colin a few sections away. Despite the cushions, it's still uncomfortable as the waterproof coating has removed any softness.

Robbie has started to pull back the bi-fold doors that appear to make up the entire side of the house. Once finished, it's as though they're both inside and out, which is rather confusing to the brain. 'I'll get going with the tuna,' he says, moseying back towards the kitchen, his shiny, toned legs bandy beneath the cotton of his cargo shorts.

'Colin's a big fan of tuna,' she responds to Robbie's back. Far too quietly for him to hear.

'It must be great to have in this weather.' Colin nods towards the swimming pool. Its glaring white surround pops against the chlorinated blue of the gently rippling water.

'Oh goodness, Col . . . can I call you Col?' He nods, though Janet knows he hates the abbreviation. Makes him think of a colonel. 'It's an absolute godsend. I can't believe how few homes have them in England. And air conditioning. My goodness, how do you all cope?'

'We got a very decent fan from B&Q last year, I must say,' says Colin.

Mia stands, walks towards the water's edge. 'No, a pool is one of those things that once you have, you can't then not have. Like a coffee machine or a chef husband.' Mia laughs as she bends to retrieve a lone, floating leaf. Janet imagines passing her, descending the steps, submerging herself underwater and remaining there until the pressure in her chest forces bubbles from her nose and mouth.

'Janet used to swim for the county,' says Colin. 'She trained to be a lifeguard . . . destined to save people, it seems.' Janet's head swishes in his direction. Wanting to climb inside his mouth, silence him. But she looks away, dismisses what he's said with a shaking head, a smile.

Mia's mouth has dropped in an over-exaggerated gape. 'Shut the door. You were?'

'It's not . . . I was a teenager. But this is where I get the . . .' She gestures towards her shoulders, the mime extending outwards as if they are twice their actual width. 'But I don't swim anymore.'

'Is that how you managed to do CPR on Lizzie so well? Without even hurting her little chest?' Mia walks back over to the sofa, flicking her fingers free of the remaining droplets.

Janet nods. 'Yes . . . yes, it was.'

'Well, maybe you could teach Elizabeth to swim. She's so nervous about swimming. Manages a bit of doggy paddle but that's about it.' She places her straightened hand to the side of her mouth, pretending it's created a shield of privacy. 'I mean, we tell her she's doing great but—'

'No, I . . . No, sorry . . . I'm not good enough anymore.'

'Course you are, love. She's got no confidence, you know, Mia,' says Colin.

Janet takes a gulp of wine.

'Obviously, we'd pay you . . .' Mia continues.

'Don't be ridiculous, she wouldn't dream of taking money.'

'No, no, of course I wouldn't. I'll have a think about it,' says Janet. 'I don't like seeing myself in a costume these days.'

Mia rests her hand on Janet's knee. 'Hell, I know exactly what you mean . . . Oh, here she is. Come on over, honey, and meet Janet.' Mia looks towards the house. Janet follows her gaze.

She's finally here.

Elizabeth.

In a Bardot-style dress. The vertical blue and white stripes making her appear tall for her age. Hair loose, curly, a white plastic clip on one side. Quite different to the photograph. There's a bandage on her wrist. Bruises and scabs still apparent. One clearly visible on her temple, which automatically makes Janet touch hers.

'I'm done,' she shouts over the suck of her flip-flops as she walks.

'Good girl, Lizzie Lobs, Mrs Marshal will be very impressed that you've managed to do that,' shouts Mia. 'Come on, don't be shy.'

The child heads straight towards the safety of her mother, without acknowledging Janet or Colin. Once on the sofa she flings her arms around Mia's neck and pulls her down. 'I'm starving,' she says, elongating the 'r'.

Mia fakes being choked as the child tugs harder. 'Say hello to Janet . . . she's come to see you.'

'Hi.' Elizabeth flicks up a hand for a split-second, then turns back to Mia and asks, 'What's for food?' Her accent a fusion of English and American. Like those precocious stage school kids that often ruin a good TV show.

'We're trying to convince Janet to give you swimming lessons,' says Mia. 'Wouldn't that be cool?'

'I already can swim,' says Elizabeth, with jutting bottom lip, and a shove to her mother's arm.

Mia laughs. 'I know, I know, baba. You totally can.'

Janet spikes an olive with a cocktail stick and presses it into her mouth. It's covered in an unpleasant pungent herby oil, and she smiles through her chews.

They've finished the tuna. Succulent steaks, not the tinned flakes they're used to having. So tasty with the homemade 'slaw', as Mia called it.

Janet gently dabs her lips with a serviette, wishing there were seconds. 'That was delicious,' she says. 'I didn't want it to end.' Disappointingly, there's no announcement of it not having to.

For the duration of lunch, she's managed to restrain thoughts of her sin. But they're still there. Dancing in the periphery. Like the time she developed black floaters and the optician said they'd never go away, but her brain would acclimatize. Though she's grateful for not having told an outright lie to these nice people who believe they owe her so much. These people who have so much. So very much. Is she even taking anything away from them? And she refers herself back to that hug with Robbie. Elizabeth is OK. That's all that matters. It is.

Elizabeth is playing in her wooden Wendy house. Not a basic square one like they were saving up to buy Claire. It's Americanized. Bigger. All painted wooden slats, jutting porch and a white picket fence. She's changed into an orange and pink geometric-pattern swimming costume, with a ruffle on the waist. Though she's not ventured into the pool. Watching her from afar, it's not how Janet had imagined it. Not the instant bond she'd hoped for.

The men are standing by an outside bar. Tuning into their discussion she can hear it's all about cars and horsepower. Mia is telling Janet how she plans to complete more courses so she can reach Master-level Reiki. 'I'm currently at level one. I don't like to publicize it, because you know how awful the press are in this country, but I'm a spiritual person, you know.' Janet nods, attempting to appear engaged, but her eyes drift once again towards Elizabeth. 'Modelling is so empty, you see . . . and there is so much more to everything than we could ever know.' She widens her arms to their full extent as a visual aid to highlight this point. 'The whole crash thing . . . well, I took it as that final push, you know? A sign.'

It's unclear to Janet how a crash that killed six people

including their poor au pair, and nearly her own daughter, could be interpreted as a sign to do a course, but once again, she nods. 'You believe in signs, then?'

Mia puts her manicured hands on either side of her face in phony shock. 'Do you not believe in signs, Janet?'

'Well, I . . . I didn't, but I do now . . . recently. Very much so.'

'I knew it.' Mia pats her knee. 'You must let me do Reiki on you at some point. I promise you will feel amazing after.'

'Oh . . . yes, that would be lovely, thank you.' Janet's unsure exactly what Reiki is but hopes it's a facial.

Mia must have caught her glancing towards the Wendy house again because she says, 'Sorry about Elizabeth, Janet. She's been quieter since the crash. I expect it's normal, but I'm taking her to see someone. A child trauma specialist. She's excellent apparently. Dr Paul from the show recommended her. I feel I have to do something. Goodness knows what's going on inside her little head. She doesn't seem to share anything.'

The crash. Every mention of it jars. 'Children are resilient,' says Janet. Though she has no idea what happens to children who survive accidents.

'I know, I know . . .' Mia pulls one of the stiff cushions onto her lap and presses it into her stomach. 'Zofia dying . . . it's really hit her as well as her own trauma. Well, all of us actually. Sorry, Zofia is . . . was . . . her au pair. She was with her in the crash and . . . well, she didn't make it.' Her eyes glisten and her nose pinks. She pauses, gathers herself, then after fighting back tears, adopts a smile. 'Zofia had promised Lizzie a trip to the theatre as an early birthday present. We'd paid for a night in a swanky hotel for them as a treat, but . . . well, Lizzie didn't like being away from me, so they were coming back and . . . She didn't even have to take Lizzie . . . She was only twenty-seven, and I . . . I have this horrible guilt. Sorry, sorry, you must be so traumatized yourself, I—'

'No, no . . . that's just terrible, Mia, but you mustn't feel guilty. How could you have known? You mustn't feel guilty.' Her hand circles Mia's back, like when she'd wind Claire as a baby. And her entire infrastructure of internal justification crumbles.

Mia looks up at her, eyes now overflowing. 'We spoke to her parents, and oh God, it was . . . Can you imagine what they're going through . . .' As she trails off, a look of mortification spreads over her face. 'Oh goodness, Janet, I am so sorry. I—'

'No, no, it's fine.' Janet's face burns with the reality. Those poor parents. She knows. She knows exactly what they're going through and here she is invading. 'That must be really hard for you.' She drops her head, the prosecco hitting along with everything else. 'I think we should be heading back now . . . It's been lovely. Thank you so much.' Her hand rests upon Mia's who's shaking her head, her other fist gently hitting between her brows. 'Oh please, Janet, don't leave now. I feel so awful—'

'No . . . no, don't you be silly.'

'I'm such a klutz sometimes. Of all the people I'd hate to upset.'

'I don't want to hear another word about it.' And she truly didn't. Mia mustn't feel bad. She's the bad one. She is. But she still can't let go. 'If you ever need a babysitter, I'm not far away.' Mia smiles but doesn't thank her or say yes. Embarrassed, Janet nods towards Robbie and says, 'You struck gold with that one.'

He's now clearing away the dishes, shadowed by an unhelpful Colin, their conversation still centred around cars. 'Do you want to have a look at the Porsche? You can take it for a spin around the block if you want.' Colin's face lights up like a young boy whose friend has suggested playing on their new Scalextric.

Mia rolls her eyes, smiles. 'Coffee, Janet?'

Sitting alone, Janet watches Elizabeth from afar.

Through the open shutters and doors of the Wendy house, she can be seen serving up tea and plastic cake to a line-up of various toys. Janet stands, takes a few steps towards her, then stops and diverts to the pool. Desperate to communicate, fearful of rejection. Staring into the water, she observes her reflection, large and looming. Proof that she really is there.

Slowly, she turns and walks to the mini mansion. Ducks through the child-sized doorway into the scaled-down interior, like Alice in Wonderland. 'Hey, Elizabeth. Can I join you?' Despite the lack of response, she maintains her grin. 'This looks great.'

Elizabeth ignores her presence, pours imaginary liquid from a tiny china pot into tiny china cups. 'It's been lovely seeing you today.' Janet's tone changes. Low and genuine.

Elizabeth looks up at her, puts down the teaspoon she's holding, and after a long pause says, 'I'm sorry that I don't remember you saving me.'

Janet concentrates on not altering her expression. Wills her cheeks not to signal red. 'Well, you were very poorly . . . unconscious. As long as you're OK. That's all that matters.'

Elizabeth restarts the pouring. This time it's for Janet. When handed the thimble-like cup, she's stabbed with a forgotten happiness. And for that moment she knows that she should be there. That the signs were right. This is right. But as she pretends to sip, eyes fixed on the playing child, the cup starts to tremble in her fingers. An awful thought has descended.

She didn't save Elizabeth. She didn't pull her from the carriage.

And all she can think is, does that mean someone else did?

33

About to Fall

As they drive home, the tuna and slaw rest heavy in her gut. Stomach aswirl with competing emotions, exposing themselves via jittery legs and unruly hands. Colin is oblivious and, to her astonishment, talking.

'The smell, Janet . . . it had that smell of luxury leather, you know. And oh my god, I can't even tell you what it was like to drive. Well, I can – a dream. It was a dream. We only went around the block – he was a bit nervous, you know – and I kept saying, "Robbie, mate" – I felt I could say that – I said, "Robbie, mate, I've been driving since you were in nappies." I never thought I'd say this, Janet, but it feels very disappointing to be driving the Avensis.'

Elbow against the door, chin resting upon her hand, she stares beyond the window. Going over and over the concept of someone being out there. The real hero. Watching. Waiting. She's thankful she doesn't have a mobile phone. Knowing how it works in those TV dramas. The main character receiving sinister anonymous texts. *I know what you did.*

'You're very quiet.'

'What? No, I'm listening, that's all.'

'I mean, look at all this cheap plastic crap.' His hand leaves the steering wheel to punish the dashboard with a slap.

'It's been a big day.' She pulls down the mirror and checks the hot, pink triangle of freckled flesh on her chest. Strokes her beetroot cheeks and the burnt bridge of her nose. Is everything different now? It feels different. Even Colin seems to want more from life. The Avensis diminished to the point where he won't shut up while driving.

'He wouldn't let me take out the Bentley. Which is fair enough, I suppose. But not really, because he could see how careful I was with the Porsche.'

'He's a nice man, though. They're both nice. And Elizabeth . . . she's precious.' They are nice. But what's become apparent is that she's not.

Flicking up the visor, she attempts to suppress all feelings of trepidation by recalling Elizabeth's tea set. How sweet it was, with its polka dots. Claire had a similar set but made from plastic and decorated with dancing elephants. The two girls would have been great friends, she's certain.

The silent-driving rule seems to be back in force, enabling her to continue meandering among these more pleasant thoughts, until he says, 'And what about their garden? It was perfect, wasn't it?'

She smiles, nods. Replaying in her mind how, when Elizabeth handed her the tiny cup, she could feel it. The bond she'd hoped for. Friendship.

'It's inspired me, Janet. You don't need to be a millionaire to have a snazzy garden.'

'We've got roses. They don't have roses.'

'No, it's spurred me on to get cracking with ours. I've been talking about it for far too long. Enough now. I'm determined to get it done before the summer's up. First off,

I'm going to get rid of all that bloody wilderness at the bottom.'

The pleasant tingles created by her ruminations transform into vicious prickles. Her mouth drains of saliva. 'What do you mean?' She awaits the response which doesn't arrive. The rules are now reinstated. He reaches down and switches on the radio. Elvis. 'Suspicious Minds'.

They turn into the cul-de-sac.

Yet again, Mary is sweeping her driveway. And the insane idea enters Janet's head that she's been doing it all day, awaiting their return.

Back in the real world, her soul deflates. The weather has cooled, grey clouds hovering. Even the sun doesn't want to be here.

During the stillness of the switched-off engine, he turns to her and, as though there hasn't been a ten-minute gap, says, 'The brambles and the wilderness at the bottom. It's all got to go. That looks sore, love. You should have put on some lotion . . . you know you pink up like a pig.'

The insult drifts over her like liquid smoke. It's his other words that are a cause for concern. She's propelled back to the night of the crash. Clothes tearing as she scrambled through that very wilderness towards the tracks. The sequins missing from her jumper.

Once he's outside the car, she closes her eyes and gasps for oxygen. Reopening them to find a face glaring through the window.

'Can I have a quick word, Janet?' It's Mary. Hand shielding her eyes to facilitate a better nosy of the car's interior.

Janet pushes open the door, catching Mary on the leg in the process, and gets out. It appears Colin has already made his escape.

'You look very nice, Janet. They did a good job on you at the show.'

'Thank you.' Janet's smile drops on registering the back-handed nature of the compliment.

'It was so . . . interesting. How you remembered it all like that suddenly.'

'Is there something I can help you with, Mary? Because I really need to—'

'That journalist was round here earlier.' She leans against the car, bra peeking beyond the stretched V-neck of her yellow T-shirt.

Janet smiles again, attempting to conceal the blood she can feel flooding her cheeks. 'Journalist?' She immediately realizes this is a ridiculous tack. It's not like she's friends with the whole of Fleet Street.

'The journalist that did your interview. I thought your memory was supposed to be better.'

Janet now also leans against the car. Casually disguising the sudden weakness in her legs. 'Oh, right . . . Yes, sorry. We've been outside, by a pool . . . I've got a bit of sunstroke, I think. But yes, it must be about some forms she wanted me to fill in . . . for the payment. Thanks for letting me know.'

Mary nods, pushes herself away from the vehicle, straightening her neckline. 'Oh, I see. Well, she asked me when you'd be back, and I said I didn't know. That you rarely go anywhere.'

'No problem, I'll give her a call tomorrow. We've been to

lunch at Robbie and Mia Pilkingtons', but thanks for letting me know.'

Mary's left eye exhibits a noticeable twitch of envy.

A moment Janet would have relished, had she not become light-headed. Not felt the heavy sky closing in. About to fall.

34

Electric Hedge Trimmer

She's making Colin's breakfast. Cracking an egg into smouldering oil.

'It's £657 now. Have you started looking at headstones?' He's sitting at the island slurping his tea. The laptop taking up the space required for the imminent plate.

'No, not yet,' she says, eyes widening at the burgeoning total.

Initially, she'd hoped she could somehow keep the fundraiser from him. Add it to the armoury of lies. But once it was all over the internet, she had no choice.

'Well, at this rate, we'll be able to get a corker. Right.' He slaps the laptop lid down. 'I'm going to make a start today.'

'What do you mean?' She stares down at the frying pan, hand tightening around the spatula pushing the egg and the accompanying sausages.

'The brambles, I'm going to make a start on them today. It'll take a few attempts, but I can't leave it any longer.'

'But . . . isn't it silly to start it now? Why don't you leave it until next spring?' Her mouth dries as she rubs at the back of her neck, overcome with a heat not caused by cooking.

'What are you talking about, woman? You moaned for years about it being a mess and now that I am doing it, you tell me to wait. I'll never understand you lot . . . I'm thinking we can put some trellis against the fence when it's done, and you can pick some climbers from the garden centre.'

'Yes . . . OK.' Her eyes close in surrender. Opening them again to the fry-up preparation reaching its stressful climax.

'Janet, you haven't done this yet.'

'What?' She finishes plating up and turns to discover him reading the police form. With pretend calm, she slides away the laptop and exchanges it for the breakfast. 'No, I . . . I keep forgetting.' Avoiding his glance, she turns and drops the pan into the sink, filling the kitchen with spit and sizzle.

'Well, come on, get it done now. I know you, it'll play on your mind otherwise.'

He does know her. But on this occasion, Sherlock couldn't be more wrong.

'We all hate forms,' he says. 'But you'll feel better once it's done.'

Face full of sincerity, he hands it to her, along with the pen resting on his newspaper. 'Let me know if there are any questions you don't understand.'

Taking the stool next to him, she concentrates on not allowing the pages, herself, to waver. His chews grate as she tries to read. Her mind is blank. Unable to entirely remember what she'd said on the show, despite the times she's watched it back. 'Would you like another cup of tea? I haven't had one yet. I'll need it to wake me up first.' That's not a lie. She'd spent the night staring at the ceiling. Instead of sheep, counting the possible reasons for Molly's visit. None of them good.

During prolonged tea-making, it dawns on her that she doesn't have to actually fill in the form. She can just put a stamp on the sealed envelope, show him. Relieved, she turns, sips on her tea as he shovels the last forkful of beans into his mouth. 'Right,' he says, necking the dregs of his brew. 'I'm going to the shed. Check what tools I've got.' He rubs splashed tomato sauce from his chin. 'Call me in when the cricket starts, will you?'

'Of course.' She smiles, returns to the stool, feeling the tension of the last ten minutes dissipate.

'I'll read it through when you're done,' he says. 'Make sure you've not embarrassed yourself with your spelling.'

Once alone, she presses her palms against her eye sockets to suppress desperate tears. Rushing to the sink, she fills a glass of water, gulps it down, allowing dribbles to cool her chin and neck. After wiping her mouth, she inhales deeply and returns to the form.

First, she tackles the easy questions.

Name, date of birth, address.

At which station did you board the train?

What was your destination?

Soon they become difficult. In need of lies. Lies she can't even conjure.

Which carriage, counting from the front of the train, did you occupy? If not known, please estimate.

Where in the carriage did you sit?

Do you know how many passengers were in the carriage? Are you able to name any of the passengers?

Please provide any information regarding your experience during the incident which may be relevant to the investigation.

Investigation.

The last word lingers, squeezes her guts.

But she shakes her head, saved by another thought. It's fine.

It's going to be fine. How stupid she's been. She doesn't have to lie to the police, because it doesn't have to be posted. She'll throw it into a bin somewhere on her way to work tomorrow. It's doubtful they'll chase, and if they do, she can claim it's been lost.

Stress levels lowered once more, her body temperature drops, breaths calm, and she continues to fill in the invented answers.

'The cricket's about to start.' She's standing at the back door, shouting towards the direction of the shed. The response, a muffled noise.

As she puts on the kettle, he enters the kitchen. Filthy hands, shirt smeared with dust. 'I'm going to have to go to B&Q. I can't believe my shears have disappeared. Have you seen them? Not that I think they'd do the job anyway.'

She shakes her head. 'I didn't know we had any . . . What about the cricket?'

'I'll have to watch the highlights later. Are you done?' He nods towards the form.

She turns from him and heads to the fridge. 'Yep,' she says, pulling out the milk.

Silence lingers as she makes the tea to the slicing sound of lifted pages. 'You woke her with CPR? Woke?'

'Well, you know . . . brought her round.' She stirs in the sugar, takes a sip while staring out of the window. Oblivious to his expression, too scared to look.

'Shall I change that to "resuscitate"? You sound completely dumb.'

'Yes, please. I couldn't think of the word.' She musters a smile, maintains it while turning around.

But the smile drops.

He's sliding the form into the envelope.

'What are you doing?'

His face contorts like she's an idiot. 'What do you mean, what am I doing? I'll post it on the way to B&Q.'

'No, I . . . I need to find a stamp. I'm not sure where they are . . . I think we've run out.' She extends her hand for its retrieval.

'It's a Freepost envelope and the box is right there.' He gestures towards outside. 'What's up with you?'

'Nothing, nothing . . . OK, well, if you want to. Thank you.' Unsure of what to do with herself, nausea tickling her throat, she turns and pours the freshly made tea down the sink.

Upstairs, she puts away clean washing to the raucous noise of Colin's new electric hedge trimmer.

On his return there was no mention of posting the letter, but also no evidence of its existence. And as she pairs socks and places them in the drawer, all she can think about is her lies waiting in the darkness of the post box, ready to compound her wrongdoing.

Unable to settle, as the continuous hum of work in progress confirms Colin is out of the way, she takes the opportunity to grab the key to Claire's room from the airing cupboard.

Her stomach lurches as she enters. It was a mistake. Feeling sick as she's once again confronted with the scene. The awful, heart-ripping scene.

Stiff with hatred, she walks over to the window, pulls the nets slightly to the side, and watches him, shirtless and baggy-backed. Wading with his blade through the brambles like a warrior.

The urge to open the window, scream to the whole cul-de-sac about what he did, is stopped dead by the phone ringing.

She snatches another look towards Colin, ensuring he's not heard, then locks up the room, returns the key with fumbling haste and runs downstairs.

Fearing the caller may be Molly, she automatically straightens her hair, smooths down her top. Prepares her sternness. 'Hello,' she says in a faux-calm voice. Breathlessness seeping into the receiver.

'Hey, Janet.' The soft drawl hits her like a tranquilizer dart.

'Oh . . . hello, Mia.'

'I hope you don't mind me calling—'

'No, not at all. It's lovely to hear from you.'

'Only Lizzie hasn't stopped talking about you and keeps asking when you're coming back to visit.' Janet's face erupts with a smile. 'And, well . . . Robbie's working away for a week, and I wondered if you fancied coming over for dinner one evening? I was thinking a girls' night, pizza . . . that kind of thing?'

Janet's mind is back in the room. The motorized sound, once again like chalk on a blackboard. 'Oh, well I . . . I'd love that.' Her hand drops. The earpiece rests against her mouth as she squeezes her eyes closed. When she lifts it back, so distracted with excitement, she only deciphers 'Wednesday' and 'She'll be delighted.'

Once the call has ended, she clasps her hands in prayer. Though for once she's not asking something of God but thanking Him. The phone rings again, and she lifts it immediately. Voice light and childlike, she says, 'What did we forget?'

'Hi, Mrs Brown, this is Molly . . . Molly Sullivan.'

35

Crème Cafe

Agreeing to meet Molly after work was a mistake.

Sheer panic had made her accept the invitation. The noise of the hedge trimmer had stopped, and Colin was clanking through the kitchen. Without asking the reason for the request, or deciphering Molly's tone, she said yes, purely to end the call.

And now, shift over, she sits with the others in the staffroom. Tea undrunk. Too nauseous to keep it down. Apologizing to Sam for absentmindedly leaving her trolley in the third-floor toilets and forgetting to hoover the conference room. 'It's so unlike you, Janet.'

When it's time to leave, and they all shuffle towards the door, Nish holds Janet back by her arm.

'Nish, what are you doing?'

The question is ignored, the door closed.

Nish is now rooting inside her rucksack. Extracting items, putting them on the table. A box of tampons, her gym kit, a packet of Marmite crisps. Janet's never tried Marmite flavour, and wonders what they're like. 'Nish . . . what the hell are you doing? I've got to meet someone.'

'Hang on a minute.' Finally, Nish stops, looks at her. A small rectangular box in hand. 'Who are you meeting?'

'Who am I . . . ? You're not Colin, you know.' Immediately

regretting bringing him up in that context, she smiles. 'Look, I . . . I'm not being funny, but I've really got to go.'

Nish stares at her to the point of discomfort. Then extends her arm, hands over the box. 'It's only cheap . . . a pay as you go, and I've put twenty quid on there for you.'

It's a phone. An old-style Nokia. 'I . . . I don't understand.'

Nish's eyes remain on their target. 'Look, I . . . well, I realized after we spoke the other day that although we're friends, I don't really know you. Not really. Or what your home life is like or . . . or what you may go through. But I do know that you don't have a phone. And that's unusual.' Janet hangs her head, stares towards the gift. 'All I'm saying is that a woman should have a phone. I've saved your number and I've inputted mine into yours . . . and you can call me – you must call me, if . . . if you ever need to. OK? Day or night.' A silence lingers. 'Promise me.'

Janet nods. Unable to lift her head. Wondering where the hell she'll have to hide the thing. Under the bed, perhaps. 'Nish . . .' Janet finally musters. Voice breaking at the level of kindness and care she's not felt for so long. Knowing she should tell her there's no need. That she's making a fuss about nothing. That it's her choice not to have a phone. 'Thank you,' she says. 'I promise.'

Despite walking past the Crème Cafe every workday, she never contemplates entering. Not dressed in her scruffy work gear next to all the trendy media types. Though the real reason, of course, is she neither has the time nor the spends.

But today she is sitting inside in her scruffy work gear. On a bench not dissimilar to those in her old school dining hall.

Uneasy hand lifting a glass of tepid tap water to her lips. She'd told the barista that she'll get a coffee once her friend arrives. Except she can't afford a coffee, and Molly is no friend.

A tinkling bell alerts the entire cafe to the opening door. Acid lurches up towards her throat. But it's a couple, linking arms, enjoying each other's company. She looks beyond them through the glass wall for an approaching Molly. There's still no sign.

A pair of mothers are standing chatting on the pavement. A child's coat draped over one of their arms. Janet imagines the conversation. How hard it is having children, how tiring. Interspersed with stories depicting its wonderfulness. Two toddlers chase, weaving between their mothers' bodies in a figure of eight. And Janet is thinking they should stop talking, watch their babies, when the glass slides free of her hand. Clunks to the table.

There's someone she recognizes beyond the women. Doesn't want to recognize. Standing there. Still. Ghostlike. Staring in her direction.

Water drips onto her lap, but she can't move. Closing her eyes, she prays it's her imagination. And when she looks again, it must have been, because they've disappeared.

A barista is re-erecting her glass, mopping the liquid with swathes of kitchen roll. 'I'm sorry,' says Janet, rubbing her temple, avoiding the scab. 'I'm so sorry.'

The bell over the door rings again.

This time, it is Molly.

Now gliding between the benches, in the same pale blue shirt and navy suit. 'Oh dear. Had a bit of an accident?' She takes a seat on the opposite bench. 'Could I get a double espresso, please?' she says to the squatting barista, gathering the sodden paper towels. 'Janet?'

Janet shakes her head. Not knowing if her heart is thumping because of her imaginings or Molly's presence. 'I've only got a moment . . . I'm visiting my father, he's not well.' Immediately knowing this is a terrible thing to say, tempting fate, she adds, 'He's a lot better, but I still need to visit.'

Once the barista leaves, Molly cracks a fake smile. 'I'm glad to hear he's on the mend.' Removing her jacket and draping it on the bench releases her sickly-sweet perfume. Paris, perhaps. Or more aptly, Poison. Whatever it is, it's curdling Janet's stomach. 'God, I need this coffee. I've been stuck at a clothes factory in Bury doing a story on poor working conditions . . . Honestly, they're lucky to have a job these days.'

'What can I do for you, Molly?' Janet raises her chin, pushes back her shoulders.

The barista arrives with the coffee and Molly makes a contactless payment. 'Can I have the receipt, please? Thank you.' Her smile drops as soon as his back is turned. 'I was hoping we could have another chat. Now you appear to have remembered it all.' She loads the miniature cup with one, two, three demerara sugar cubes.

'What do you mean? I've done your interview.' Janet's mouth drains of saliva and she wishes she'd asked for another water.

'We paid you good money, and then you—'

'A hundred pounds.'

Molly raises her stencilled brows, takes a sip of her coffee, licks the residue from her lips. 'We paid you a good rate for not very much in the end, and then you went on TV and told the lot for a new hairdo.'

Janet moves her hands to her knees. Hiding them beneath the table so as not to give away her anxiety. 'I couldn't remember it all when I spoke to you . . . you knew that. I didn't even want to speak to you.'

'You didn't? And yet you accepted the money.'

'I don't know what to . . . what do you want from me? I did your interview.' Her voice cracks.

Molly reaches over, pats her arm. 'Hey, Janet . . . can I call you Janet? My intention isn't to upset you. But I think it's only fair that in light of you remembering, you now give me a proper interview.' Met with nothing, she retrieves her hand and takes another sip of the drink. 'You drive a hard bargain, Janet, I'll give you that . . . OK, I'll pay you another hundred. I don't think you can say fairer than that.'

Janet coughs. Makes an attempt at composure. 'That's very kind of you, Molly, and I'm sorry that I didn't remember until after – though I'm not sure how I could help that – but I'm really not interested. Thank you ever so much, though.' Retrieving her bag from the floor, she places it on her lap. The universal signal of an impending exit. 'I really must go and see my dad now.'

Molly nods. 'Of course.'

Janet slides from the table, lifts her bag onto her shoulder. Actions calmer, slower, than the turmoil inside.

Molly remains seated, seemingly intent on finishing her coffee. 'I just thought it would be a good way for you to clarify the anomalies.'

'Anomalies?' Janet's voice is weaker than intended. 'What anomalies?'

Molly tips back her head, drips the dregs into her mouth.

Takes her time. 'You know . . . like you said you saw her lying there. But on the show—'

'I, I hadn't remembered properly . . . how many times do I have to . . . I couldn't remember properly.'

'So, what are you saying? You made some things up?'

'No.' The volume is so loud, the cooing couple turn to look. She lowers her tone to an almost whisper. 'No, of course not. I was confused, that's all. It came back clearer . . . The doctor said—'

'Hey.' Molly reaches out, lightly touches her arm. 'Look, I'm not accusing you of lying or anything. Why would anyone lie about that?'

'Exactly.' Janet straightens her back.

'OK . . . OK, Janet.' Molly smiles, stands. The bench scrapes loud against the tiled floor. 'Well, it's been nice to see you again. If you change your mind . . .' She offers out a straightened hand.

'I won't . . . but thank you.' Janet meets it with her clammy palm, shakes. 'I just want to get on with my life now.' Molly's grip is so tight, Janet's wedding ring digs into the skin of the adjacent finger.

Their connection unlocks. It's done now. Over.

Turning to leave, internally congratulating herself on holding her own, she gets as far as the next table when Molly says, 'Have the police contacted you about the CCTV yet?'

Janet stops, faces her again. 'CCTV? No . . . no, what—'

'Apparently, they've got a fair bit of footage they're going through.'

Her palpitations reactivate. Desperate to know what the footage is, where it's from. Questions she cannot, will not, ask. A waft of the intrusive poisonous scent makes her want to vomit. 'That's great,' she says. 'I hope they get to the bottom of it . . . so it doesn't happen again.'

Once outside, free of her bona fide enemy, Janet rubs at her constricted throat, hands shaking.

Nearby, the mothers are still gabbing, while the toddlers are edging towards the road. Closer and closer. 'Can you watch them rather than talking, please,' Janet shouts. The women's mouths gape. Hands reach for the shoulders of their offspring. Janet wipes her cheeks. 'Sorry, sorry, I . . . They were near the . . .' She drops her head and walks away from the tuts and grumbles. Vision distorted with tears.

36

Two Golden Tickets

For once she wishes Colin had prevented her from going somewhere.

Since meeting up with Molly, she's felt physically sick. Two nights unslept, food barely touched. Each knock at the door, each automated PPI call, imagined to be the police. *We've looked at the CCTV footage, Mrs Brown . . . We've received your form, Mrs Brown . . . You're a liar, aren't you, Mrs Brown.* As much as she longs to see Elizabeth, the concept of spending time snared within the web is unbearable. The only saviour would have been Colin's usual refusal of her freedom. But no, so keen is he to drive the Porsche again that his unwelcome response was, 'Make sure you get us both invited next time, I'll get him to buckle about the Bentley.'

And now she's being ushered through the front door with urgency by a prancing, breathless Mia. Walking to the lounge area. Standing there, deep within the spiral, as Elizabeth and Mia dance around her to blaring music, like she's the offering in a pagan ritual.

'I'll get you a drink in a minute,' shouts Mia, followed by exaggerated panting. 'I promised her I'd dance to this one.'

Janet waves her hand as if to say, *Don't you worry.*

Elizabeth stops, pulls her mother down towards her, whispers in her ear. The intimacy, ease, perforates Janet's heart. Mia nods and straightens. 'She wants you to join us.'

Janet shakes her head. 'No . . . no, I'm a terrible dancer.' But Elizabeth is grabbing her hand. The sensation of tiny fingers wrapped around hers, shocks electric through her body. Initially freezing, she submits. Bends her elbows, knees, clicks her fingers.

'You go, girl,' says Mia, stretching out her linen T-shirt to release heat.

Elizabeth is giggling. 'You have to flick your hair to this bit.' Janet copies the movement, seconds behind the beat. The scene plays out in slow motion. Laughter, singing, dancing. Lingering in time. Janet on the outskirts. Desperately wanting to be within. Knowing she has no right to be there at all.

The homemade pizzas were delicious. She had pineapple and pancetta on a sourdough base. A fancy Hawaiian. She doubts she'll ever be able to eat her usual anaemic frozen ones again.

'Daddy gets annoyed at pineapple on pizza,' says Elizabeth, shoving the last piece of margherita into her overstretched mouth, lipsticked with tomato.

'Well, we'll have to keep it secret then.' Janet playfully taps her nose.

'Secrets are bad. Aren't they, Mummy?'

'Yes, sweetheart.'

Janet fixes a smile. 'Oh, yes, of course they—'

'Oh goodness, before I forget . . .' Mia stands, licks her fingers and pats her non-existent belly, despite having only eaten a sliver of dough. 'Are you and Colin free on the fifteenth of July?'

Thankful for Mia's interruption, Janet turns from Elizabeth. 'I'm not sure . . . I—'

'Only, Robbie and I would love it if you could come to our annual charity ball.' She's at the white cubed bookshelves now, holding up two golden tickets. Reminiscent of the ones in *Charlie and the Chocolate Factory*. 'This year is in aid of the Royal Manchester Children's Hospital. It felt the obvious choice. It's at the cathedral. Robbie's the compère as always, and there'll be food and an auction and drinks. It's real fun . . . all the *Corrie* lot will be there . . . and footballers. It's an excuse to dress up.'

'I don't know, I—'

'Oh, come on now, you'll have a great time.'

She needs to say no. Distance herself from the treacherous situation. Molly's words ring in her head, the police questionnaire taunts. But as if possessed, unable to stop, she says, 'OK, yes . . . we'd be delighted.'

Elizabeth has asked Janet to see her room.

Upstairs is carpeted clotted cream. More homely and to her taste, apart from the black doorways and skirting. She imagines dust shows up like nobody's business.

The child runs ahead, stopping at the third door to hang on to a large, brushed-steel handle. 'This is mine,' she says, then disappears through the dark entrance.

Despite its pinkness, it's unlike any little girl's room she's seen before. The same black woodwork runs through from the hall, picked out by a bold monochrome striped rug. The bed – a double, or king (it's hard to tell in a room of this size) – is unmade. The duvet scrunched like a ball of candyfloss.

Although the ceiling is starred with spotlights, Elizabeth turns on a huge central sphere made from white feathers. Once that's shining, she dims the others. 'This is prettier,' she says.

But the illuminations aren't over. At the bed, yet another switch is flicked and the word LIZZIE erupts on the wall in neon. 'Do you like it?'

Janet doesn't respond for a moment. Repressing an unwanted, unwarranted bubbling emotion. 'I do . . . you're a very lucky girl.' As she speaks, her eyes are drawn to the dressing table. White, surrounded by large bulbs. Her dream. Claire's dream.

She walks towards it, overtaken by Elizabeth, who adds their glare to the room. 'These are best for putting on your make-up.'

She thinks of Claire's plastic heart-mirrored dresser. How excited she'd been to receive it that Christmas. *It's like a princess one, Mummy.*

Janet's gaze is drawn to her own reflection. The mix of the person before and after. A decent haircut styled badly. New make-up applied incorrectly.

'Will you braid my hair?' Lizzie jumps up onto the black leather rotating chair. Then opens a large drawer exposing brushes, hairbands and clips.

'Yes, of course . . . how would you like it?'

'One main one, but not too flat here.' She pats the top of her head. 'And I want it coming down the side like this . . . and I like these silver ties.' Taking the bands, Janet puts them on her wrist for safekeeping. Gathering the silky curls into her hands, she allows the tickling tresses to cascade back through her fingers as though playing the harp.

Lizzie scrolls through her phone like a businesswoman at a

salon, sighing as Janet talks. 'I wish I had hair like this, Lizzie.' With the pink Mason Pearson brush, she slides the soft bristles through the shafts. From top to bottom. Top to bottom. The motion soothing and monotonous. Inhaling the soap scent of a child's skin. Hair. Strands crossing strands crossing strands. And when she looks up, she's staring into the heart-shaped mirror at Claire's reflection. Rosy cheeks rounded with a smile. 'It's going to look lovely, Claire.'

'Elizabeth, silly.' The child giggles.

Janet steps backwards. 'Sorry . . . sorry, Lizzie. It's going to look lovely.'

'Your hair is funny, Janet.'

'That's not a very nice thing to say, is it?'

'But it was long and pretty at the crash. Now it's all funny.' She throws back her head, grin exposing her short teeth.

Janet steps forward again, hastily interweaving the final section. 'I . . . I didn't think you remembered me at the crash?'

'I don't.' Elizabeth pats the top of her head and says, 'It's not quite right here.'

'Sorry . . . no, it's not, is it.' Janet smooths the brush over the crown. 'I had a makeover, remember, Lizzie. My hair was a bit longer before.' She wraps one of the bands around the thin tail end of the plait. Then with hands lowered behind the chair, out of sight, she pulls the other band away from her skin, taut, and snaps it back.

Masking the smart with a smile, she awaits relief that does not arrive.

Having witnessed her cold child, identification tag on ankle, the woman, now dead herself, has insisted on going to the hospital prayer room.

It's chilly, basic. At its centre, a wrought-iron tree. Hanging from its branches, leaves of multicoloured glass and paper. The latter scrawled with messages.

She shuffles to the table, emotionless, composed. Takes a leaf of her own, its consistency more robust than her, and writes.

Once finished, she goes to the tree, hangs it on the top branch. A man enters, causing all the desperate words to ripple. The man is pained, but does not hurt as much as she does. No one hurts as much as she does.

Palms together, eyes closed, she prays. Solidifies her written request.

Please God, punish me.

37

Sean Kearney

It's the day of the shop opening.

She'd tried to get out of it. Knocking at Roni's to cancel. But Mary was there, and she couldn't bear to give her the satisfaction, so pretended she needed a couple of fairy cake paper cases instead.

She's changing into her *Hello Britain* outfit in a cubicle of the toilets on the third floor at work. Nish is waiting for her, sitting on the countertop. 'I can't believe you do things like open shops now.'

'Neither can I.' Squeezing the wedges onto her hot swollen feet, the bruised discomfort is immediate.

'What the fuck,' shouts Nish. 'Get out and look at this.'

'Oi, stop swearing so loudly. We're not even supposed to be in here, you know.' Accepting she's unable to cope with the added torture of the wedges, she guides her toes back into her scruffy work shoes.

'Oh, do shut up, Mrs Victorian, and come and look at this.'

With everything shoved into her bag, she emerges, witnessing herself in the opposite mirror. Even more dishevelled than she'd imagined. 'Oh Jesus, look at the state of me.' Edging nearer to her reflection, she unpeels the hair that humidity has plastered to her skin. Takes a paper towel and dabs away the perspiration coating her face like a fine mist.

There's a thud as Nish jumps down and comes to her side. 'Look, Gill Doyle, with the whole Gill Next Door thing . . .' Janet turns to her, face blank. 'Oh God, Janet, you're like one of those people in films who've been locked in a bunker for years. Gill Doyle is a huge influencer from Manchester, and look . . .' She extends her arm, pushes the phone towards Janet's face.

It's Twitter. She knows that at least. 'Oh, right . . . well, yes, Helen mentioned her son's girlfriend was one of those.'

Nish jerks the screen forward. 'Look, though.'

This beautiful soul ♥ saved the daughter of Robbie and Mia Pilkington in the Manchester train crash on the anniversary of her own daughter's death. Please help buy her the headstone she wants for her child #bekind #lovewins #notallheroeswearcapes

Below is the link to the fundraiser. Below that, 34k hearts and 6k rotating arrow symbols, lots of comments.

What an amazing lady, donated.
An angel on earth ♥
Things like this reinstate my faith in human nature. Donated.
I know this woman. She cleans at my offices.

'Oh, I don't think we know him, do we? . . . But anyway, it wasn't the anniversary of her death. It was her birthday.' She throws the towel in the adjacent bin.

'Oh my god, Janet, missing the point or what. Look at how many likes and retweets. You're trending.' They stand shoulder to shoulder while Nish scrolls. Janet presses a hand against her face, attempting to cool her flaming hot cheeks.

'Enough now,' she says. 'I've got to go. It's very kind of her but I . . . I just want it to all stop now.'

Nish ignores the plea. Taps the screen to open the GoFundMe page.

Janet closes her eyes, praying that it has now at least ended. She had wanted some money towards Claire's stone at first but not now. She just *needs* it to stop.

Her eyes open to the sharp sound of Nish's inhalation. 'Oh my god,' she says, pressing the phone against her chest.

'What? What is it? Please don't tell me it's reached the target. I don't want—'

She breaks off to the squeak of the opening door. A middle-aged woman in a too-tight suit enters and heads into one of the cubicles. Janet and Nish remain silent. The stream of the woman's pee fills the space.

Without a word, Nish slowly swivels the screen towards Janet, who in turn recoils back against the sink. Trying not to emote. To conceal the sickness, the cold shiver sweeping over her body.

As feared, the target has been met. But the total isn't £1,500.

It's £5,356.

She can barely walk to Roni's shop. The total figure cauterized on her brain, stretching her conscience so tight her chest constricts. Each breath, each step, difficult to execute.

'I'll return the excess,' she'd declared. But Nish burst that one comforting bubble with a swift prick. 'It doesn't work like that. It keeps going until it's over. You're quids in, Janet.'

And now here she is on her way to further perpetuate the charade.

A method actor preparing to walk on stage, inhabiting a character. Janet Brown, hero.

Roni's extravagant preparations are unmissable as she approaches. Pink balloons line the doorway, bobbing in the breeze. Red carpet peeks through the legs of those waiting, covering the filthy gum-speckled slabs. Roped barriers stand on either side, like it's the Oscars. Fitting.

A group of kids in hoodies stand in front of the chip shop, Northern Sole, holding polystyrene cartons. Legs wide over static bikes. As she passes, the smell alerts her taste buds. Despite all this new-found prominence, she still doesn't have the means to do what she wants; get a portion of fish, chips and mushy peas, with both curry sauce and gravy. Doing so would mean she'd have to walk to work in the morning. This reminder of who she really is destabilizes her controlled facade. And all enticing thoughts of food transform into stomach-curdling repulsion.

Roni waves over. Hair bigger than usual. The white of her dress glowing against the grey surrounds. As Janet lifts an unconfident hand to return the gesture, a soft drizzle of rain speckles her arm. She looks upwards, hopeful. Praying the dark threatening clouds will open with a vengeance. Force rushed proceedings. But for now, it's a gentle spit, spit, spit.

She's nearly there. Pasting her best smile.

Then she stops. Grin dropping. There's a flash of Titian hair between two men.

But the woman turns, and is in her fifties, hard-faced, caked in make-up. Not remotely like Molly.

Janet closes her eyes, gathers herself. She can't continue to live like this but can't get off the ride.

Roni strides towards her. Heels so high she teeters forward, her eyes dipped towards Janet's scuffed work shoes. 'Hiya, we're going to have to do it quickly, if that's OK. It's about to piss down.' She seems agitated, not enjoying her big day.

'Sorry, I had to wear these shoes because I think I've broken my toe.' The lie isn't even necessary. It's as though she's unable to act with integrity. Is unalterably bad.

'Honestly, Janet, the till won't open, the Wi-Fi isn't working, and one of the assistants hasn't turned up – your rank shoes are the least of my worries.' She turns, resuming the top-heavy waddle towards the door. Janet follows, affecting a slight limp.

Approaching the shop, the guests part ways, chattering. 'That's the one that saved that girl . . . Didn't her daughter die? So brave of her . . . I thought Roni was getting someone from *Corrie*?' And the irrepressible swell of misplaced pride arises in Janet once more. Bricks laid on her wall, cemented by attention.

Standing on the entrance steps, she inhales the aroma of baked goods sweetening the polluted air, while Roni springs into action. 'Hello, everyone. Thank you so much for coming to the opening of Roni's Cake Emporium. Since I was a little girl . . .'

As the speech drones on, Janet's initial enjoyment morphs into self-consciousness. So unused to being looked at, she stares down towards her awful shoes, wishing she'd persevered with the wedges. Attempting to reduce her discomfort, she refocuses on a magpie over the road which instigates the need to salute, followed by the pretence of scratching her face. After which she turns her head, glances back down the road towards the chip shop, her appetite returning.

It's then that she sees him.

Like she'd imagined outside the cafe.

Just standing there. Watching. She blinks. Her brain, the enemy. Playing tricks again. Except this time, on each reopening of her eyes, he's still there.

'. . . and so, I'm thankful to that appendectomy for giving me the strength to make my dream come true. And now I'm going to hand over to our local hero and my lovely neighbour, Janet Brown, to cut the ribbon.'

As Janet takes the scissors in shaking hands, the rain finally arrives.

Expressionless, she separates the blades. Cold wet beating on her face, amid the low-grade screams and calls to hurry inside.

'Cut the ribbon, Janet, come on,' says Roni, fake smiling, hair ruined.

'Sorry . . .' Her voice is weak, breaking. 'I . . . I declare Roni's Cake World—'

'Emporium.'

'Emporium . . . open.' Janet hacks through the ribbon. The act requiring several attempts.

Claps erupt, followed by people barging past, clamouring to enter the shop. Articles of clothing, bags, held above their heads.

However, Janet remains outside. Soaking up the water. Instructing herself to look again. Witness his disappearance. The proof that what she saw is merely a symptom of her damaged mind.

But she doesn't. Because she can hear soles beating against the water-skimmed pavement. Feel the air, contaminated with his presence.

Sean Kearney. The man who stood trembling in the rain that night.

The man who killed Claire.

38

Fish, Chips and Peas, with Curry Sauce and Gravy

It's the closest she's been to him since court. Now inches away, she scrutinizes his face. Eyes hooded, sorrowful. Hair thinning at the temples. Skin criss-crossed with lines. He's had the privilege to age. To live his life. Even if some was spent behind bars. Not enough.

Eventually able to separate her lips, her speech is barely audible. 'What are you doing here? What do you want?'

'I just want to talk to you.' His hands reach into the pockets of his beige cotton jacket, greyed with wetness.

'Are you coming in for a cupcake, Janet?' The voice of Roni interrupts from behind.

'No, sorry,' she responds without turning. 'I feel rather sick.'

Roni tuts, her presence subsequently evaporating. Leaving only the sound of balloon knocking against balloon.

The rain intensifies. Suddenly torrential. Hurting her cold skull as her mind flashes back and forth between the present and that night. Interchangeable images. Both agonizing. Ripping at her insides.

'I only want to talk with you,' he says. 'Please . . . can you hear me out?'

There's a delay. The film paused. Until she shakes her head, the movement small, before growing resolute. 'I want you to go, please. I'm not interested in anything you've got to say.' She turns, chest caving as if winded, and begins to pound the pavement. Each gasp for air fills her mouth with droplets. The need to move away from him, immense. Her skin crawling as though having encountered maggots.

As she passes the chip shop, the lads drop their cartons outside the bin. 'Hurry the fuck up,' one shouts, as they mount their bikes.

Behind, his feet smack the puddled concrete. She doesn't turn, will not turn. Instead, she picks up speed. But all she can hear is, 'Please, Mrs Brown. I beg you . . . I only want to tell you I'm sorry.'

Inside, she's adamant she doesn't want to hear it. Doesn't need to hear it. But for some reason she's stopped and is lifting her hands to her head, her head to the sky. Willing herself to be smothered by rain.

'Please, Mrs Brown. I'm begging you. I just want to say I'm sorry. I knew it was you as soon as they showed that footage.'

She lowers her head. Slow, steely-eyed, she turns. His voice remains soft, as if coaxing an elusive stray cat. 'Not because of the image, but because of what you said. Those words, I'll never forget them . . . they haunt me every night I close my eyes. And then after everything, you saved that girl. You were so brave and—'

'I was.' The words spit. 'I was so brave, Mr Kearney; you have no idea.' She takes a step backwards. 'But that was a different thing . . . I was in the train crash.'

His look of confusion slides smoothly into tear-filled desperation. 'I know . . . I know you've been through so much, Mrs Brown, and that's why . . . I just wanted the opportunity—'

'You have to leave me alone. Or I'll call the police.' She tries to remain firm, but his tears become sobs as he drops to his haunches. 'Get up . . . don't do that.'

'I'm sorry . . . I am so, so, sorry . . . I know I can never make it right . . . Doing the time doesn't make it right . . . I can't bear it. Knowing I killed a little girl. It haunts me every day.' His face twists. Pained in a way with which she identifies. A shot animal slowly succumbing to death.

Her brain grapples with what he's saying. So used to accepting the blame. That she killed Claire. Which she did. She did. 'You have to get up. Mr Kearney . . . Mr Kearney, you have to get up.' She puts out her hand, gestures for him to take hold. His fingers clamp around hers, and she winces as if touched by those maggots. With effort, she pulls him up to standing. 'What do you want from me, Mr Kearney? Forgiveness?'

He drops his head. 'I . . . I don't know. I can't expect you to forgive me—'

'You killed my daughter. My beautiful, kind, special little girl who had her whole life ahead of her. And you killed her – for what? Because you were late meeting your girlfriend? No . . . no, sorry. I can't forgive that.'

He looks up, and she permits him to lock eyes with her for the first time. 'I know. I know,' he says. 'I saw that you were in the crash and I . . . and it came out where you worked and that you were doing this and I . . . I just needed you to know that I'm sorry.'

'Well, I know now. But I'm afraid, Mr Kearney, you're just going to have to forgive yourself.'

Once far enough away from him, and she's confirmed he's diminished in the distance, she stops and cries. Not out of sadness and anger and hatred and loss. But out of relief.

Gathering herself, the rain swilling away the residue of tears and mucus, she can't face going straight home, or even visiting her dad. She'd already told Colin the event could last a while, so she keeps walking. And walking. All the way to Monton. To the posh chip shop that she's never been in before, and orders a large portion of fish, chips and peas, with curry sauce and gravy.

Eating under the cover of the brick monument by the cemetery, air perfumed with wet grass and stale urine, she observes the people running for shelter. Friends entering the pub opposite, couples with shopping bags darting to their cars. And despite being engulfed within a terrible lie, accidentally stealing almost six thousand pounds from kind strangers, and potentially being rumbled at any moment, she feels the most herself, the most normal, that she's felt in a long time.

39

They Were Discontinued

As soon as she turns into the cul-de-sac, she can feel the energy radiating from the house.

The Avensis is parked in the driveway earlier than expected. Its presence is different, threatening.

Having ground to a halt, she urges herself to continue. Glancing towards Mary's. For once wishing her neighbour was cutting the hedge or sweeping the pavement. Unknowingly providing the comfort of another human.

To prolong the short journey, she reduces the distance between steps. But too soon her shoes become unstable against the gravel, and the TV is flickering through the window.

'Hello,' she shouts, gently pressing the latch shut. A western shootout bellows into the hallway. But with it, no response. She removes and hangs the wet cape, pushes back her still damp hair. 'Sorry, the opening went on longer than expected. There was quite the turnout.' So much breeze is applied to her tone that it reaches an unnaturally high pitch.

Still, there's nothing.

She walks towards the lounge, the actress immersed in her other role. Sweet smiles and soft features.

From the doorway, the only part of him visible is his hand,

fingers digging into the chair's arm. The room is unlit. Dingy from blackened skies.

'Oh no . . . I forgot the cupcakes Roni gave me.' Still, no response. Although reluctant, ingrained with the need to get him on side, she attempts, 'The fundraiser's gone over five thousand now.'

'I know, Janet.' He doesn't move, as though engrossed in the film.

'Oh. I don't want to keep the remainder, though. But we can at least get Claire a—'

'I don't mean about the money.' His speech is deliberate, monotone. 'Although that is a lot.' He slaps the arm of the chair. 'I mean . . . I know. I know what you've been doing. What you've done.'

Pistols shoot. A saloon bar brawl breaks out, loud against the ensuing silence. Dizzy, she covers her eyes with her fingers before allowing them to slide over her face, nails scraping. She steps further into the room. 'Colin, I swear at first I . . .' A deep crunch sounds beneath her foot. Looking down, she's met with white shards, interspersed with coloured fragments, glaring against the beige of the carpet. Her ladies. Her beautiful ladies.

'Who is he? Do you love him?'

She attempts to decipher the questions. 'What?'

'Don't try and deny it. I saw you together.'

The realization descends. He doesn't know at all. He doesn't know. The relief so strong she's forced to lean against the sideboard, now bare except for the telephone.

He stands, faces her. Taller than usual. Elevated with fury. 'I drove past you.' His shout ricochets off the walls, punctuated by another gunshot. 'I'll finish early, see how Janet's getting on at the shop, I thought. Give her a lift because of the rain – and I saw you . . . you fat filthy cow. Holding his hand.'

Her brain urges her to explain. To put him right. But what emerges from her mouth is a laugh. A bubbling, hysterical laugh which she's unable to suppress.

'What the hell is so funny? Nothing about this is funny.'

As the giggles intensify, so does his rage. Body and face so taut he could shatter to the floor like her ladies. He's never hit her. But she wonders if this is the moment.

Striving to stop herself, bring the delirium to an end, she wipes beneath her eyes and presses her hands against her hot cheeks. Once gathered, able to speak, she says, 'It was Sean Kearney, Colin. Sean Kearney.'

He mouths the name to summon the meaning, then the cogs align and he mutters, 'Sean Kearney?'

For a split-second she's uncertain if he still thinks they're having an affair. That she'd lie down with the man who killed their child. 'He's been following me apparently, after seeing me in the paper . . . wanting to say he's sorry.'

Seemingly dazed, Colin feels for the back of his chair, lowers himself into the seat. 'Sean Kearney.' He shrinks down further, smaller than ever. Like a child, body folding in on itself.

'I feel better for talking to him, Colin. His saying sorry shouldn't help, but it has. He was suffering.'

'We're suffering.'

'I know. I know we are . . . but at least we know that he is too.'

Crouching down, she starts to collect up her precious ladies. Freya's head, cupped in her hand. Staring, separate. Palms full, she stands, drops the mess onto the sideboard. Wincing as they clatter against the mahogany veneer.

Colin unfurls himself, rushes over to the debris, raking a mound of ceramic splinters with his hands like the beginnings of a sandcastle. 'I'm so sorry . . . I—'

'They were discontinued, Colin.'

Sean Kearney killed Claire. He did. But here she is, still bearing the punishment.

Fighting the desire to help Colin, absolve him of what he's done, she walks away. Leaving him to pick up the pieces.

40

Hear the Sea

The following day when she arrives home from work, she refuses to allow her usual deflation on entering the dull hallway.

In the kitchen she drops her bag on the island stool and makes a cup of tea. After slapping two slices of bread onto a plate, she grabs butter, ham and mustard from the fridge, and with haste builds a sandwich. Each ingredient thicker than usual. More delicious. And once it's completed, cut neatly into triangles, she eats it.

When finished, sucking her fingers free of grease, she drops the plate and knife into the empty sink, clattering against the stainless steel. The food is left out. The island speckled with crumbs.

He'll not be long.

Upstairs, she goes to the airing cupboard and retrieves the key to Claire's room.

Once the lock has clicked and the door is pushed open, she stares into the ever-disturbing space.

Powered by rage, she runs down the stairs, opens the back door and strides down the lawn, past the fire pit, without even acknowledging her roses. And at the bottom of the garden, standing in front of the partly destroyed brambles, the alive entwined with the dead, she pulls back her arm like a javelin thrower, and lobs the key as far as she can. Watching as it flies past the mass of knitted branches, and lands soundlessly somewhere beyond the fence.

After a long inhalation, she turns and marches back towards the house. This time, pausing to sniff her roses.

Back upstairs, she re-enters Claire's room. Slowly blinking before daring for the first time to fully digest the reality. Lingering on the details. Mentally ticking off an inventory of items no longer there. Registering the things that still are.

She bends to retrieve some socks and clothing from the floor, like they'd been dropped while carrying a load to the washing machine. Pressing the bundle against her face, she absorbs any remaining particles of Claire. When she can bear to separate herself, she places them on the bed.

At the dressing table, she gently releases the necklace which hangs from one of the heart-shaped knobs. It was purchased at a market in Pwllheli. White shells interspersed with mock pearls. She'd given it to Claire among a huge knot of others for dressing up. The shells were her favourite because Janet told her if she was very quiet when wearing them, she'd be able to hear the sea.

She puts it on. Strokes one of the shells resting cold against her collarbone. Listens for the ocean.

Returning to the bed, she neatly folds the items. The mismatched socks pressed flat on top of each other. The vests and T-shirts transformed into the smallest squares. Then she places them all back in the homemade closet built within an alcove. Empty hangers swing. She unhooks one and slips on the dress that had fallen. If the creases don't drop, she'll iron it later.

After collecting her cleaning caddy from the airing cupboard, she disinfects the sides, polishes the mirror. Fetches the Dyson and runs it over the carpet, ensuring she gets deep into the corners.

When finished, she goes to the main bedroom and from the top wardrobe pulls down a plastic vacuum-packed bag, hard and misshapen. Once dragged to Claire's room, she opens the valve and watches the spare duvet spring to life.

Returning the caddy, she removes her favourite bedding set. The one with pretty yellow embroidered daisies, bought with vouchers given as a birthday present from the Angels a few years ago. And back in the room, she makes up the bed.

Following a wrestling match with the pull-down steps and ceiling hatch, she's now in the loft. Armed with Colin's high-powered torch, she aims the beam across insulation sandwiched between joists. He once joked that she couldn't go up there because she's so heavy she'd drop through the ceiling. And although she knows this was said purely out of nastiness, there's now a genuine concern that if she puts a foot wrong, it might be the case.

It was too hard to watch him hide Claire's toys and games up here. And she's never looked since. Most of the baby stuff had gone to charity as soon as Claire had outgrown them. Probably now disintegrating in landfill. How was she to know they'd become priceless to her? All those programmes encouraging people to declutter, but who knows what will be treasured further down the line.

The torch's beam illuminates a variety of boxes and cases. As well as Claire's things and Janet's own doll, Lucy, there are ornaments saved from the sale of her mum and dad's house that Colin wouldn't allow to be on display, and a general hoard that neither her nor Colin wished to part with.

A plastic container catches her eye. Through the pearly white Perspex she identifies the blur of photographs. A potential Pandora's box. Carefully, she negotiates the beams and bravely removes the lid. Latent dust causes her to sneeze, disturbing further particles.

She sifts through the memories. Holidays in Pwllheli. Claire on the beach eating an ice cream. What child chooses pistachio as her favourite? Claire with her grandparents . . . First day at school . . . As a donkey in the nativity play . . . A home-made card. *Happy Mothers day to the best mumy in the world*, scrawled in wobbly felt tip, above a drawing of Janet in a spotted dress holding a cat. They never had a cat. Colin wouldn't allow one. And she has no recollection of ever owning a spotted dress.

She absorbs the images avoided for so long. Heart in a tourniquet, cheeks itching with wet. Then, emptying an old Woolworths bag of bits and bobs, she fills it with a selection of photos and the card.

She's sitting on Claire's bed. Her bed now.

The Blu-Tack that had been left on the adjacent wall has been covered with most of the photographs. Along with the Mother's Day card and the one from Elizabeth. The remaining pictures decorate the dressing table mirror, in front of which stand Janet's perfumes, creams and make-up. And the wild rose and vanilla candle she'd been bought by Colin, wick never lit, a box of matches by its side. The closet now contains her clothes and shoes.

The room is bright. Filled with colour and love. What is now Colin's room is so gloomy. She hadn't realized how dark it had been all this time.

When she hears the familiar sound of tyres on gravel, she suppresses her Pavlovian response. Instead, she stands and goes over to the dressing table, stares at her reflection, tucks her hair behind her ears, straightens her top.

You can be brave, Mummy. You can.

Calmly, she walks out onto the landing. Watching from above as he removes his jacket, places it on the peg. 'I'm home,' he shouts towards the kitchen, then notices her looming figure. 'What are you doing up there?' He extends his neck to see beyond her. 'You're in that room, aren't you? How did you find the—'

'I've left the stuff down there for you to make yourself a sandwich.'

His face warps with puzzlement. 'Aren't you feeling well?'

'I feel great. The best I've felt in a long time.'

'What the hell is going on?' He huffs his way upstairs, eyes widening as he sees into Claire's room.

'This is my room now, Colin. This is where I sleep.'

He turns to the airing cupboard. Stands on his tiptoes, hand searching the top shelf.

'It's not there. The key's gone.'

'You're not moving in there, Janet. You're my wife.'

'The ham is really nice. It's Finest rather than basic range.'

His hands lift to his head. That elbows-out exasperated stance he makes when control slips away. 'You've gone mad. We should talk to the doctors again . . . about your injury.'

'I'm not mad. I'm saner than I've been for years.' She goes back inside the room, collects up the candle and matches, and returns to the landing. 'Right, I'm going to have a bath.' Ignoring his protest, she heads towards the bathroom, heat from his fury burning into her back. Then she stops, faces him. 'If you touch anything in that room I will out you, Colin. I will tell the world what you do. What you did.' Heart smacking against her chest, she turns back around, only imagining his speechless expression. 'Don't forget I'm the woman who rescued Elizabeth Pilkington. They'll believe me.'

41

Beneath the Water's Surface

The next day Colin has a surprisingly pleasant disposition. Mentions nothing about the bedrooms. Only that he's experienced the best night's sleep he's had in years, and his intention to continue with the brambles.

While washing the breakfast dishes, she observes him through the window as he wades towards the entangled mess. His gardening wear, the same as his regular clothes, only older. She's concerned he'll collapse in this heat. Especially not wearing a hat and never drinking water. And for those brief moments, life seems almost normal, serene. As though everything is OK. Could be OK.

Then the phone rings.

Mia's voice is pitched high with incoherent sobs. Janet's first thought is that she's been found out, and holding on to the edge of the noticeably empty sideboard, swallowing down panic, she exhibits pretend calm. 'Mia, I can't hear you, love . . . slow down.'

Following a string of staccato breaths, Mia says, 'Sorry . . . sorry . . . it's my finger . . . I've gone and sliced it . . . real bad.'

Inwardly overcome with relief, Janet switches to caring mode. 'Oh no, love.'

'I've done everything . . . I'm holding it over my head, but it won't stop bleeding and oh God, Janet . . . I feel faint and . . . I need stitches, I think . . . Lizzie, stop it . . . just stop it, you have to come, OK.' Janet deciphers her own name being shouted by Lizzie during their fraught off-stage conversation. 'Sorry, Janet . . . Lizzie's freaking out because she's scared of hospitals now . . . I don't suppose Colin's free to take us, is he?'

'Oh, I'm sure that'll be fine. He's in the—'

'I'll pay, of course . . . but you know, I don't think I can drive and Robbie's not back until tonight . . . My neighbours are out . . . My friend said she'll come from Alderley Edge, but that would take forever and the car firm we—'

'Mia, it's fine.'

'Oh, thank you . . . Lizzie, can't you see Mummy's not well?'

Janet detects her name again. Lizzie is crying. 'I can stay here with Janet, Mummy.' But Mia is ignoring her daughter's request.

'Please, don't you worry, I'll go and ask him now. Do you want me to stay with Lizzie while you go?'

There's an overlong pause. 'I . . . OK . . . Sure . . . I suppose that may be best then . . . if that's OK with you?'

'Of course . . . Of course. Stay there, I'll go and ask Colin.'

Resting the receiver on the sideboard, she's concerned about his reaction. Ruminating over what excuse she'll make for him if he refuses. But as agreed, she runs outside, hopeful that her urgency will induce him to say yes. 'Colin,' she shouts breathlessly. 'Mia's had some kind of accident with a knife . . . She needs taking to A&E while I sit with Elizabeth.'

He turns to her, trimmer held like a swordsman. Initially appearing amazed she'd dare ask him for anything, he says, 'Well, I'll have to lock this in the shed first, Nigel had his Kärcher nicked this week while they were at Morrisons.'

She performs a split-second shake of her head, blinks, long and slow. 'OK, but I think she's quite bad.'

He's never been able to speed. Even during emergencies, the warning radar signs never flash red for Colin. It was the same when she was in labour. Pootling down the dual carriageway to the hospital, cars overtaking. 'I hope Mia's not bled out by the time we get there, Colin.'

Finally, they pass through the electric gates, head up the driveway. The house still feeling an eternity away. As soon as the wheels hit the resin, Mia exits the front door, hand wrapped in a bloodied tea towel. Eyelids swollen, their whites blending with reddened rims.

'Oh, sweetheart,' says Janet, climbing out of the car. 'Make sure you get Colin's number off him and he'll pick you up when you're finished.'

'I was making brunch . . . There's half a salad there with some homemade flatbreads and falafels. Some may have blood on them so obviously throw those, there's some more shop-bought ones in the fridge . . . Oh, and don't let her go in the pool.'

With appeasing nods, Janet gently coaxes Mia towards the car, ensuring she ducks her head while getting inside, like the police do when taking a suspect in for questioning.

Mia shouts over to Lizzie, who's hugging the edge of the front door, barefoot in a yellow bikini. Eyes in a similar state to her mother's. 'Lizzie, Mummy won't be long. You be good for Janet.'

As the Avensis drives away, she joins Lizzie. 'Mummy's going to be fine, she'll be back soon. The doctor will give her a couple of tiny stitches, that's all.'

Lizzie looks up at her, crimson face glistening. Janet eases her into a hug, until the closeness to the child, a child, the sensation of a small wet face against her shoulder, becomes unbearable. Pulling away, she says, 'Hey, come on now. Let's get some flaff fells. What are flaff fells anyway, Lizzie? Do you know?'

It's strange being in the house alone. Or minus adults. Ridiculous, she knows, but its vastness makes her feel a child herself. Like Lizzie in her mini mansion.

The island's granite is blood-speckled. On a plate sits a pile of fresh-smelling flatbreads, next to them a bowl of flaff fells, also bloodied. Retrieving the packaged ones from the fridge, she realizes what they are. Recognizing them from the deli section in supermarkets. Though reading the packet properly, she's embarrassed about having been pronouncing it all wrong. She pops one into her mouth, and it's delicious. A morsel of chickpea escapes, resting upon her chest. 'Right, are you going to help me get some lunch for you? Does Mummy wrap these in the bread with salad?'

Thankfully, Lizzie's crying has been exchanged for chattering. Torso draped over a stool. Legs kicking up behind. 'No, silly.' She laughs. 'You do a mezze with everything on a plate.'

Refusing to ask exactly what a mezze is, Janet says, 'OK, I was just checking.'

Lizzie slinks away from the seat and starts skipping towards the garden, the bi-fold doors opened fully.

'Hey, where are you going, I thought you were helping me?'

'I'm busy,' she shouts back, without even a turn.

'OK, but don't go near the pool.' Janet mindlessly inserts another falafel into her mouth.

The patio is a sun trap. She melts with relaxation, rays massaging her head as they eat. Pretending she has every right to be there. Not existing in a minefield. Waiting for the explosion.

The food is good. She'd never ordered mezze in restaurants because she always thought it meant small portions. But as their over-stacked plates suggest, it turns out it can also mean massive ones.

Lizzie sits cross-legged on one of the loungers, hands dripping with hummus, crumbs stuck to the perimeter of her lips. Janet is on the adjacent one, legs outstretched, plate resting upon her belly. Thankful that she's wearing her light and cool fine poly-linen trousers and top. She smiles at her young companion as she witters on about a girl at ballet class who can't do pliés. '. . . and I told Olivia that her bottom was sticking out like a duck's.' She giggles and stands up, impersonating the unfortunate stance of her peer.

'Oh, poor Olivia. Maybe you should have fibbed and said she was almost there.'

'No, Janet, lying is bad.'

'Not always.' Janet drops her head towards the plate. Defusing her guilt with yet another falafel.

Lizzie stares towards the sky as if thinking very hard. 'Hmmm,' she says, then, as though the notion has vanished, she adopts her best ballerina posture. 'I can plié properly, see.' Her plié also looks suspiciously like a duck.

'Yes . . . very good. Now finish your food, please.'

Lizzie returns to her plate, forearms leaning on the lounger, bum in air. Energy wriggling through her gangly body. 'Janet . . .' The name is elongated with undertones of a whine.

'Yes.' Janet follows the vocal pattern.

'Can I go in the pool? Can *we* go in the pool?'

The piece of flatbread thickens to a dough in Janet's throat. When it's finally sliding down her gullet, she says, 'No . . . no, Mummy said you mustn't.'

'Zofia used to let me.'

'Well, I'm not Zofia.'

Lizzie's face pinks. 'No, you're not Zofia,' she says, tearing at a piece of flatbread.

'I'm sorry. I'm sorry, Lizzie, but Mummy said you mustn't go in the pool . . . and I don't have a costume. Hey . . .' She places her plate on the floor, widens her eyes in forced excitement. 'Why don't we see if there's any ice cream in the freezer?' She fixes the perky expression until Lizzie finally relents.

Back outside, Janet is sucking on a coconut lolly, while Lizzie spoons mango sorbet into her mouth and flicks through a copy of *Vogue*. 'Janet . . . do you think she's pretty?' Her finger presses on the face of a moody model.

'I do, very . . . although perhaps a tad miserable.' Lizzie doesn't appear to care about the answer to her question, as five more pages have already been turned.

Her finger stabs again. 'Do you think she's pretty? She looks like Zofia.' Janet leans over, swivelling the magazine with her lolly-free hand. This model is barely out of her teens. Beautiful. Chiselled. Freckled. The wind blowing her long honey hair artistically across her face. Ice-blue eyes glaring from the page.

'Yes . . . yes, she's incredibly pretty.' And it's back. It can't be escaped. The crash. The reality. Zofia, so young and full of life, dead. Janet, an imposter. The coconut ice falls from the stick, onto the concrete slab.

Lizzie laughs. 'You're such a silly, Janet.'

'Sorry, I . . . I'll get something to clear it up.'

Striding inside she goes straight to the sink, turns on the tap and splashes her face. Water drips from her skin as she attempts to cool a sudden radiating heat. Hands pressing down against the cold granite, as she stares at the monster reflected in the gloss white splashback.

She's outside again, kitchen roll in hand, mopping at the melted mess. Lizzie has discarded the magazine and is bending over the end of the lounger, pulling all her hair into a scrunchy.

Catching sight of her watch, Janet's amazed how the time has flown, and wonders how long the wait in A&E will likely be. Concluding it would be one of the quieter periods, she says, 'Are you OK while I go and clear up the kitchen before Mummy gets home?'

Lizzie flicks her head up, face reddened from rushing blood. 'Janet . . . can you be my new au pair?'

Janet suppresses both a giggle and tears. 'No . . . no, I don't think so, sweetie. I'd love to visit you though, whenever your mummy allows . . . Now, have you finished with all this?' She collects up the plates, balancing them against her arms like a waiter.

*

She's having to wash up the old-fashioned way. Initially unable to locate the dishwasher, concealed somewhere among the flush handle-less cupboards, she discovered it by accident after thumping one in peak frustration, causing it to open like the entrance to a secret passage. But once found, the digital display and lack of knobs were impossible to decipher, so she's now humming to herself as she swirls a strange bamboo sponge over the plates, using some eco liquid which lacks the bubbles of Fairy. For a kitchen of this size, the sink is piddling, and for some reason instead of a draining rack there are only grooves carved into the granite.

Pausing both the song and washing-up, she turns off the tap. Convinced she'd heard Lizzie calling.

She drops the sponge back into the water and walks over towards the patio, drying her foam-coated hands on her trousers. 'Did you call me, Lizzie?'

Standing on the threshold of inside and out, she scans the area. The loungers are empty apart from the copy of *Vogue*, pages flapping in the breeze like wings of a dead bird. The door of the mini mansion is closed, and there's no sign of her through its windows.

Stomach sinking, she stretches to look towards the pool. Thank God that too is empty. 'Lizzie?' she shouts again. 'Are you there?'

All is still, quiet.

Concluding she must be in the house, snuck past the kitchen without her realizing, she turns to go back inside. But after only a couple of steps, a squeal erupts from behind.

She spins back around to find a giggling Lizzie, darting out from behind the Wendy house. 'You couldn't find me, you couldn't find me,' she sings, jumping up and down on the spot. And Janet's about to tell her how she shouldn't frighten people like that, mustn't hide when she's being called, when Lizzie sprints across the patio with forced laughter and jumps into the swimming pool.

'Get out of there right now,' shouts Janet, running towards the splashes. Standing by the pool's edge she kicks off her sandals. 'Get out of there right now, Elizabeth.'

But Lizzie doesn't chat back or giggle. Because she doesn't emerge. And all that can be seen is a shadow beneath the water's surface.

42

The Cycle is Complete

Janet carries a sobbing Lizzie through the treacly water, and up the steps of the pool.

Once out, heavy-legged and waterlogged, she places her onto the paving, which blots dark grey. Dropping to the ground next to her, she pulls her close. 'Shhhh, come on, it's OK. You're fine now.' The child sobs into Janet's soaked chest as they rock back and forth, back and forth. 'My baby, my baby, I got you out . . . It's OK. You're OK.' Lizzie's sobs escalate into a wail, and Janet pushes her away, forces their eyes to lock. 'Shhhh Lizzie, you're OK, calm down . . . come on.' She attempts to erase tears and chlorine from the child's face, her own wet fingers rendering the act useless. Lizzie's teeth begin to chatter. 'Hang on, sweetheart.' With effort, clothes weighty with water, Janet manages to stand. Once upright, she pulls her puckered top away from her skin, pushes her hair off her face, then makes her way towards the house. Feet slapping against the tiles, a damp patch beneath each step, she runs through the lounge area, up the stairs to Lizzie's room, and grabs a couple of large towels from the en suite.

Back on the patio, Lizzie is sitting on a lounger. The sun so hot her bikini is already patched dry, lighter. Her hair, fluffy.

She stands at the sight of Janet and starts to step side to side, agitated. 'Janet . . . please don't tell Mummy.' Tears arrive again. Her face contorted, strands of spit stretched between her top and bottom lips.

Janet looms over the poor little thing, strokes her hair. 'Lizzie, I have to tell Mummy. Look at the state of me. I can't lie to her.'

Lizzie shrugs the petting hand away. Steps back, mouth pursed, eyes narrowed, and turns, marching towards the mini mansion. 'You have lied to Mummy. You have.'

It's hard to tell if it's the sodden clothes or the words that have chilled Janet's skin. Erupted her arms with goosebumps. 'What do you mean?' she whispers, before following the child, calling after her, 'Lizzie, what do you mean?'

She dips her head, manoeuvres her body into the tight space. 'Lizzie . . . what do you mean?'

Lizzie is laying out the cups and saucers, neatly. The dolls gathered to partake in tea, sit in a row. Finally squeezed inside, Janet asks again. 'Lizzie, what did you mean I've lied to Mummy?'

All tears have stopped now. Exchanged for head-bobbing while singing an indecipherable tune. 'Here you go, Barbie . . . a chai latte, your favourite.'

'Lizzie, answer me.'

Teacup in hand, Lizzie pauses. Turns her head towards Janet and blows away the hair sticking to her cheek. 'Zofia saved me. She pulled me out. Not you.' She animates again. 'Come on, Barbie, drink up . . . you've got yoga soon.'

For a ridiculous split-second, Janet is relieved. It was Zofia. No one will come forward. Out her. But her mind's trick soon expires. The space drains of oxygen. The walls encroach, ceiling depresses. And as Lizzie moves the spout from cup to cup, Janet's hand searches for the wooden door frame, something solid, real, to grip on to. 'No . . . no, it was me. I saved you, Lizzie.'

'No, you didn't.' Her eyes don't move from the teapot. 'Oh no, Barbie, I've run out. I'll have to make some more.'

Janet remains still. Knowing there's nowhere for her to go other than further down the rabbit hole.

'Lizzie, listen. I won't tell Mummy what you did. She'd be so angry if she knew. You were struggling, drowning. She'll be furious, devastated . . . She'll never let you in the pool ever again. Any pool. We mustn't tell her.'

Lizzie looks at her properly now. Puts down the teapot. 'You promise?'

Janet's fingers dig into the wood. 'I do. I promise, of course I do. I wouldn't want her to be so angry at you, and Daddy too. He'd be furious. And you love the pool, don't you? I wouldn't want you to never be able to go in it again . . . of course I wouldn't. But, oh no . . . I suppose there is a problem.' She drops her head.

Lizzie crawls over to her. 'What? What is it? You promised.'

Janet looks into her innocent doleful eyes. Hating every cell of who she's become. 'Well, you'd have to keep my secret too. That's very important. That's how secrets work. They're a pact.' She extends her pinkie for her to accept.

Lizzie bites her lip. 'Mummy says we shouldn't have secrets.'

'Well, Mummy said you mustn't go in the pool, but you did and almost drowned. But I saved you.' She's certain her heartbeat can be heard echoing through the timber. 'But don't worry. I understand if you'd rather we told Mummy—'

'No, Janet,' says Lizzie. 'Don't tell Mummy.' And slowly she hooks her tiny finger onto Janet's, whose concentration is placed on not crying, collapsing into the child's arms.

'Right, well, I don't think Mummy will be long.' Her voice is thin, fake in its composure. 'We need to get rid of any evidence . . . where's the tumble dryer?'

As they walk across the patio, hand in hand, pact cemented, a telephone's ring emanates from the house.

They lock eyes for a moment, silent against the shrill noise. 'It may be Mummy,' says Janet. 'Do you usually answer the phone or shall I?' Lizzie looks set to cry again. 'You go and change and dry your hair, I'll get it.'

Lizzie runs towards the stairs, while Janet follows the ring in search of the landline. Finally, she spots a sleek white handset resting upon a Perspex table. After inhaling deeply, she lifts the cold plastic to her damp ear. 'Hello.'

'Oh, hi . . . who's that?'

'It's a friend of the family, Janet.'

There's a pause. A droplet falls from her nose to the floor.

'Oh, Janet, hi. It's Robbie. Mia and Lizzie weren't answering their phones and—'

'Robbie, hello. Sorry, I didn't recognize your voice. I'm picking up because Mia's cut her finger . . .' She turns her watch to check the time, but the face is watermarked, ruined. 'So, I'm minding Lizzie while she's at A&E.'

'Oh shit.'

'No, no, don't you be worrying, she'll be fine. She just needs a stitch or two, that's all.' Janet's head drops towards her soaked body. Each wasted second, vital. 'I'll get her to call you as soon as she's back, shall I? I'd better go, Lizzie's about to show me a dance routine.'

The operation is regimented. The sun complicit, drying out the patio and loungers. Lizzie is now wearing a dress, newly washed hair in a scrunchy. Messy but dry. Janet has been escorted to the utility room, a space twice the size of her entire kitchen, and shown the new-fangled Miele dryer. Digital like the dishwasher, devoid of any knobs.

Wrapped in a towel, she removes all her clothing, underwear included. Vulnerable, heart racing, she throws them into the machine and tries to decode the damn thing. 'Do you know how to use this?'

Lizzie shakes her head, so Janet returns to the screen and takes a deep breath to properly engage her brain. Unable to do so, she resorts to random pressing. Beep, beep, long beep. 'Lizzie, can you try your mum, please. See how she's doing? And does she use dryer sheets? They may help with the chlorine smell.'

Lizzie points to a cupboard, before running off. Returning moments later with the phone, she makes the call. Janet expects, hopes, it will go to voicemail, and for Mia to still be in the hospital.

'Hi, Mummy . . . where are you?'

Janet's stomach overturns like a tombola. Throwing a dryer sheet into the drum, she mouths to Lizzie, 'Ask how long she'll be.'

Lizzie repeats the words out loud like a dire child actor, then says, 'Thank you, Mummy. I shall see you soon.' With the call finished, she looks over at Janet, eyes wide, and once again teetering on tears. 'She's outside waiting for Colin.'

Janet returns her focus to the dryer. Scrolls through settings. Pressing OK to the only instruction that means anything, she sets the time at twenty minutes and presses START. The machine surges into action. They both stare towards the tumbling clothes.

'Your hair,' shouts Lizzie.

Hair freshly blow-dried, she joins Lizzie again in the utility room. Thirteen minutes have passed according to the dryer display. It's difficult to ignore the little girl's anxious jig from foot to foot. An anxiety that she's induced. 'You go and look out for them arriving, sweetheart. Mummy will be here soon.'

Once alone, Janet continues the surveillance. With a renewed glaring awareness of what she's doing. In a near stranger's house, wrapped only in a towel. Covering her back in the most unscrupulous manner. Coercing an innocent child. Not her proudest moment.

The clothes rise and drop, rise and drop. Flip in slow motion. And she stands there, transfixed. Willing the numbers to rise.

Fifteen minutes. Sixteen minutes. Seventeen minutes.

At eighteen minutes, thirty-one seconds, Lizzie reappears, hands squeezing her waist as though her tummy is aching. 'They're back, Janet . . . the car's coming up the driveway.'

Janet yanks open the dryer door and submerges her body into its drum, grabbing the contents and throwing them on the floor. 'It's fine . . . it's fine, Lizzie,' she says, frantically dressing. 'Now you go and play in your Wendy house.' When Lizzie leaves as instructed, a squeaking noise trails behind. A certain precursor to crying. Then comes the rattle of keys opening the front door. 'Hello, we're back.' Mia's voice is subdued by the distance. Thankfully they sound as though they're still in the hall. 'Oh Colin, I think I've left my cardigan in the car.'

'No problem, I'll get it, love.'

'Would you be a darling, Col . . . Lizzie, Mummy's here.' Her drawl loudens. The clack of gladiator sandals approaches the kitchen. 'Janet?'

Janet yanks on her trousers, over her still slightly damp knickers, unpleasant against her skin.

'Lizzie . . . Mummy's back.' Mia's in the kitchen now. A mere wall between them. 'Janet . . . Lizzie,' she calls.

Janet slips on her shoes, grabs the mop and bucket resting against the washing machine, and leaves to face the situation.

'Oh, hey . . . I just thought I'd give the floor a mop. So, how did you get on?'

Mia smiles. 'Aren't you a darling. I didn't expect you to clean, silly. Though I suppose you can't help it.' Her nostrils dilate. 'It smells very bleachy, thank you . . . Look at me, Janet – two stitches and it's still throbbing like hell.'

'Oh, you poor thing. You go and see Lizzie in the garden, and I'll get you a cuppa before I go.'

Colin enters, clutching Mia's cashmere. 'Thanks, honey.' She slides the cardigan from his hand. 'You've got a good one there, Janet. He's been super kind.'

Janet smiles. 'I know.'

Mia heads off towards the patio, arm held aloft. Plastic-covered finger pointing upwards like a subtle version of those giant foam football match hands.

Colin's face relaxes into his normal, less polite expression. 'I need to get back and finish the strimming.'

'I'll just make the tea. You go out and wait with Mia, I won't be a minute.'

Reluctantly, he also leaves for the patio, and as soon as she's confident he won't look back she flicks on the kettle, darts into the utility room with the empty mop bucket, grabs the towel, and runs upstairs to press it into Lizzie's dirty linen basket.

Mia sips her tea, recounting her hospital experience. 'Honestly, I will never get over the fact you have the NHS. The triage nurse was a little stuck-up, but other than that the service was fantastic.'

Lizzie joins them. Without acknowledging Janet, she buries her head into her mother's lap. Janet reaches over and strokes the now only visible part of her baby-fine hair. 'Hey, Lizzie, thanks for a lovely day,' she says, knowing it will be the last time she sees her. That there's no way she can risk seeing any of them again.

On the journey home, Janet uses the silent rule to digest all that's happened, what she's done.

'Why do you smell of hospitals as well?' asks Colin at the traffic lights, winding down the window, breaking his own air conditioning rule.

Playing the scenario over and over, she summons justifications. What she did was terrible, but it wasn't only her own neck she saved. She did also save Elizabeth. And although the world doesn't know, God does. The cycle is complete. The signs understood. She needs to put it all in the past, move on. Be grateful. It all could have ended up so much worse.

They've entered the cul-de-sac. Mary is loitering, of course. Janet waves over, feeling an uncharacteristic lightness towards her neighbour.

They turn into the driveway. The engine is switched off, the handbrake wrenched upwards. Colin turns to her, smiles. 'By the way,' he says, 'we're going to the Pilkingtons' for Sunday lunch next week.'

43

Twists of the Metal Fence

She's unable to sleep. It's been the same every night since the pool incident.

Colin's snores seep through the walls, and for a moment she wishes she was back in there with him. The safety of human closeness.

'Claire,' she whispers. 'Are you there?'

She feels nothing of her presence in return.

Staring towards the ceiling, she waits for her vision to adjust. For blackness to lessen to grey. Avoiding closing her eyes, because each time she does, her mind is accosted by flickers of Molly, Nish, Lizzie, the impending Sunday lunch, imagined CCTV footage, Zofia.

She grabs a pillow and presses the soft cotton over her face. 'Rest in peace, Zofia,' she whispers beneath the down. 'I'm so sorry. Please forgive me.'

That sensation of near suffocation must have lulled her to sleep, as she's now stirring to a brain-grating noise coming from outside.

She extracts herself from the warm bed, shivering with the drop in temperature, and grabs her robe which is draped over the child-sized dressing table stool.

At the window, she pulls aside a small section of curtain, and spies. Colin is hacking at the brambles again. Another layer peeled away. She turns from the disquieting show, puts on her slippers and heads downstairs.

Her water-damaged watch now resides in the back of a drawer, but the kitchen clock shows it's coming up to nine. She never sleeps in this late. Even on weekends.

It appears Colin has made himself breakfast. Dishes left unwashed, of course. Perhaps she isn't awake, and this is a strange lucid dream. It would be wonderful if all of it was a dream. If she woke up on the bus, coming home from work on Claire's birthday. A *Wizard of Oz* ending.

His laptop sits on the island, and she flicks her eyes towards the window, wondering if she has time to peek at the fund. He hasn't opened it for a couple of days. And whenever he goes to tell her the amount, she insists she doesn't want to know. However, when alone, part of her feels she should witness the extent of her theft. But regardless of it being safe to look, she decides against. There's only so much her conscience can deal with before breakfast.

Making herself a tea, she stands in front of the sink, watches him. He's only a few feet from the end now. And she wonders which is the lesser of two evils – staying home tomorrow for Colin to continue with the garden and whatever he may uncover, or the danger of attending the Sunday lunch. She concludes the latter would be worse.

She heads out to the garden, Colin oblivious to her walking the stretch of lawn. The hedge trimmer is loud and abrasive against her recently woken brain. 'Do you want a tea?' she shouts. 'Colin, do you want a tea?' The power is cut, though the tool's blade continues to vibrate. 'I've just boiled the kettle. Do you want a tea?'

Once he's followed her back in the house, she's aware of the faint beefy odour arising from the pits of his T-shirt. 'Have you seen any foxes?' she asks, pouring the milk.

'Foxes? No, Janet, foxes aren't going to stick around with a bloody hedge trimmer hurtling towards them, are they?'

As she turns to place his cuppa on the island, he's opening the lid of the laptop. She'd hoped to create a pleasant interaction before attempting to wriggle out of the plans for tomorrow. But she can see now that the foxes weren't the best choice, and wishes she'd tried another tack instead. 'Toast?'

'I've already eaten, and we're out of butter.'

'Oh . . . right. Well, we've hardly got anything in, you know. We need to do a big shop this weekend really. I think we should cancel lunch tomorrow, otherwise we won't have the chance. And you can carry on with the garden.' The impromptu excuse sounds so mild and feeble once spoken. 'I could make us a roast dinner instead. Get a lovely big joint.'

He slurps on his tea. 'What are you talking about? We've got to go now . . . I've said we would. And I've told you, Mia said she'd tell Robbie he has to let me ride the Porsche again. For taking her to hospital.' That bloody car. 'And let's be realistic, love, your dinner wouldn't be a patch on his. You might be good at eggs, but your roasties are like bullets. Right, I need to crack on. Nearly there . . .' Contradicting himself, his fingers tap against the keyboard.

She walks past him, tea in hand. Hoping she'll feel able to deal with the stress after more caffeine and some morning TV.

'Janet,' he calls out as she reaches the door. 'We'd better start looking at cruises.'

'What do you mean?' she says, turning.

'The fund. It's nearly eight grand now.'

She runs the tap of the bathroom sink. Watches the mix of tea and stomach acid swill down the plug hole. When the porcelain returns to white, she splashes water on her face and dabs it with the towel. And after breathing slowly to ensure her insides are more settled, she runs back downstairs and opens the once again unsupervised laptop.

Pressing the back of her hand against her mouth, she suppresses the nausea rising again as she witnesses the numbers first-hand. £7,690. She can't live like this. She just can't. And her eyes peel away towards the cutlery drawer as she imagines extracting the rust-speckled knife and slashing it across her wrist.

A long blink stops the thought.

With racing heart, she searches for the website contact details. There doesn't seem to be a telephone number, only an option for online chat.

Hi, I'm Alan. What can I help you with today?

Hello, Alan, hope you're well. I'm trying to find out how to cancel a fundraiser?

No problem. Please go into My Account, then Settings. Highlight the one you wish to end, then click delete fundraiser.

I'm afraid I don't have an account.
Someone else set it up for me.

No problem. The person who set up the fundraiser can delete it on your behalf.

She stares at the screen. No, Alan. It's very much a problem.

Is there anything else I can help you with today?

No. Thank you.

Slow, trancelike, she pulls down the laptop lid and walks over to the window.

Observes as Colin hacks through the final layers of brambles. Twists of metal fence glinting through the gaps.

44

Ghost Chairs

This time Robbie greets them at the door. Open-armed, grinning. A glass of sloshing amber liquid in his hand. Large ice cubes clinking with each movement. 'Oh Jesus, it's when it rains like this that I wish we lived in California. Come on in, guys. Stay dry, stay dry.' He steps aside, sips on his whisky. The strong aroma competing with roasting meat.

'That smells delicious, Robbie lad.' Colin steps beyond the threshold while handing him a bottle of wine. Tesco this time. All the while, Janet fixes a smile. Words stuck like trapped flies within her dry mouth.

'Come on.' Robbie wafts them in. All actions larger than last time they met, and Janet wonders if that's not his first whisky of the day.

Mia appears now, summoning them through. The finger-protector replaced by a pink silk fabric wrapping. 'I know, I know, it's useless. But honestly, Janet, I couldn't stand that ugly plastic thing. It was doing something awful to my energies. And this is better than showing the boring bandage, don't you think?'

Stepping into the light of the kitchen area, Janet keeps focused on her hosts. Preventing her eyes from searching for Lizzie. Praying she's not there and at a children's party or something.

'Lizzie,' Mia shouts. 'Come and say hello to Janet and Colin.' She faces Janet and whispers, 'Honestly, she's been so funny the past few days. She saw the therapist this week and I'm worried it's made her worse. Hopefully you being here will bring her around.' She strokes Janet's arm then turns away, and in an upbeat voice says, 'Right, what can I get you both to drink?'

A chill trickles throughout Janet's body.

'Just some pop for me, thank you. I'm driving.' Colin emphasizes the word 'driving'. The hint about the Porsche goes unnoticed, however, as Robbie has left the cluster and is now shaking a sizzling pan in that chef's way. Colin bites on his bottom lip. An action Janet knows to mean, *damn it.*

'I'm jonesing for a gin and elderflower tonic – why don't you join me, Janet?' says Mia.

Janet catches Colin narrowing his eyes. 'Yes, that sounds lovely. Thank you,' she says.

Mia wanders towards the far end of the island and taps a small square metal panel on the nearby wall. Bowie's 'Space Oddity' bursts through seemingly invisible speakers, and she starts to sway, floral chiffon dress floating a beat behind.

Janet ensures she stays still. Terrified she'll be forced to dance again.

For a few moments they all remain separate. Doing their own thing. Which for Janet and Colin is standing rigid and stilted with fixed grins. Finally, Mia breaks the awkwardness by walking towards Janet, holding out a drink so carbonated, sparks are jumping from the glass. It looks mouth-wateringly refreshing, accessorized with bobbing lime, and she can't wait to take a sip, begin blotting out the horrors of the situation.

Mia joins her, their glasses tilting towards their mouths in unison. Mia licks her lips sensually. 'Is that not the best thing you've ever tasted?'

It isn't. That was the butter chicken curry she had at the Mandal in town a few years ago, but it's still very nice. The citrus stimulates her taste buds, and with each sharp swallow she prays it will ease her nerves, paranoia. A paranoia immediately assuaged by a waving Lizzie bounding down the stairs wearing a tutu. Lavender, huge, bouncy. In direct contrast to Claire's few frills of net on a bit of elastic, Lizzie's has copious layers of tulle and a luxurious velvet-beaded bodice which wouldn't look out of place at the Royal Ballet. She points her toes before each step, as though walking towards the stage to perform *Swan Lake*.

'Here's my girl . . . come on,' says Robbie, chopping pungent rosemary.

Janet feels her cheeks burn, hoping it will pass as the effects of gin. 'Hey, Lizzie, what a beautiful dress.'

'It's a tutu.'

'Sorry . . . tutu. It's beautiful.' The paranoia returns, sensing Lizzie's strangeness towards her, the avoidance of eye contact. Janet walks over to the island, casually leaning against the granite for support.

But the rollercoaster climbs the track once more, when Lizzie says, 'Janet, will you watch me do the dance I've learned?'

Janet can barely control her loud exhalation. Blowing with it the fear and tension she's been carrying around. It's fine. It's going to be fine. In fact, poor Lizzie has probably been worrying her little soul about her own secret. Innocent, yet thinking herself guilty. Children are loyal to pacts. A child has been harmed. She has harmed a child. The last thing in the entire world she'd ever want to do. The very opposite of what she believed she'd done in the first place.

Masking her self-loathing, she smiles. 'Of course, I'd love to.' And with that they both walk towards the lounge.

'We'll be putting out lunch in five minutes, you two,' calls Mia from behind.

You two. Spoken as if they're partners in crime. And they are now.

Lizzie performs her routine beneath the patio pergola as though on a stage, while Janet watches through the lashing rain from a single open panel of the bi-fold door.

The ballerina concentrates on her Bambi-like jetés, and after the final wobbly pirouette is executed, she stops and curtsies. 'That's brilliant, Lizzie.' Janet breaks into applause. 'You're a proper little ballerina, aren't you? I'm so proud of you.'

The child stares right at Janet. Then, without warning, darts through the downpour towards the house, pushing past her without a word.

Janet wonders if the effects of the gin had caused her to miss Mia calling them in for lunch. But when she turns, they're still cooking, preparing. Colin is shadowing Robbie, chattering. Presumably about cars. Even playing sous chef by passing him something from the fridge. He never does that at home.

And there's Lizzie, hugging her mother from behind. Head buried into the drapes of chiffon.

Janet drifts inside to join the pack. As she nears, Lizzie's face emerges from the folds and looks right at her again. Only for a moment, before hiding once more.

'Here she is. Do you want another gin?' Mia extends her hand, requesting the glass that Janet realizes is empty.

'Yes . . . yes, please.'

Janet and Colin have been seated in the dining room. The table and chairs are entirely see-through. 'We were so lucky Robbie managed to find this beauty to go with the Philippe Starck Ghost chairs.' Their legs are visible. Exposed. Because of this she doesn't quite know how to sit. Eventually opting for rigid, knees not too wide, not too close together. Colin appears to have copied her position.

Apparently they barely use the space to dine, but this is, as Robbie insists, 'The perfect opportunity.'

Apart from the furniture, the room is cosier than the rest of the downstairs. Or perhaps merely smaller. Claustrophobic. The window is about the same size as the one in Janet's lounge, but here the long, pale pink silk curtains, possibly the same material as Mia's bandage cover, slice away at the light. Janet now misses all the glass. The ability to see outside. Enabling her to maintain an eye on freedom, should she need to escape.

Lizzie pulls out the chair at the far end, while Mia lays knives and forks from a gripped cutlery bouquet. Injured finger extended, out of action. 'No, it's mainly used by Lizzie and Zofia for homework and painting and things.' Robbie darts widened eyes at his wife, then micro nods towards Lizzie who's now concentrating on rearranging her tutu to get comfortable. 'Sorry, I forgot,' Mia mouths back.

Both parents turn and glance at a framed photograph on a narrow console table at the far end of the room. 'Shall I . . .' Mia is still mouthing words. Robbie shakes his head.

Scrutinizing from a distance, Janet deciphers it's a picture of Lizzie, face painted as a tiger, and Zofia, who's sporting a glittery butterfly on the side of her face. Both are smiling, their cheeks touching.

Janet feels the au pair's empty eyes boring into her.

'Right, we're going to go and bring in the goods,' says Robbie, rubbing his hands together. 'Lizzie, honey, why don't you change into something else to eat lunch?'

The tutu is fanned behind her. 'No, Daddy, I'm fine.' She wiggles one more time in the chair then stops, though it's uncertain if she's settled or wishes to appear to be.

With Mia and Robbie gone, silence fills the room. Colin sips on his fizzy elderflower, then examines the glass. 'You know, I do actually like this.'

Janet turns to Lizzie. 'You look like a peacock.' She chuckles, re-establishing their friendship.

'Peacocks are green and blue and come up higher.' Lizzie gestures behind, her hand marking where the feathers would be if she were indeed a peacock.

'Who is that?' Colin nods towards the photograph. Janet knocks him with her knee, then realizes that the action could be seen.

'I think that's Zofia.' Her voice starts high-pitched, then reduces to a whisper. 'Lizzie's au pair who sadly died in the crash.'

'Oh, I'm sorry,' he says. 'She was very pretty.' Then, as if to lift the mood, follows with, 'Does your dad usually go for a spin in his cars on a Sunday?'

Lizzie shrugs. Gets down from her chair looking like she's about to cry. 'Oh sweetheart, are you OK?' Janet pushes back her own chair, standing to intercept Lizzie as she heads to the door. The attempt fails, and she watches as the plume of tulle exits the room.

'You've upset her now, Janet.' Colin picks up his fork and inspects it as though it were a piece of sculpture.

'You were the one who asked about the photograph.' The words barely escape through her gripped teeth.

He replaces the knife on the table. 'I didn't know who it was, did I? You were the one who said she was dead.'

'I think she already knew that, Colin.'

'Well, I didn't know it was her.'

She considers going to check Lizzie's OK, but is terrified at what may be encountered. Stepping towards the door, she gathers herself to leave, but instead slowly presses it shut, muttering, 'You're so oblivious, Colin.'

'I'm starving. This is late for lunch, isn't it?'

She returns to her seat. Stares over at poor, heroic, dead Zofia.

'I've excelled myself this time.' Robbie has burst through the door, lifting a large platter above his head, bringing with it delicious smells which hypnotize her away from disturbing thoughts. Mia is in tow, carrying a gold-spotted white dish in each hand. One filled with roast potatoes, distinctly un-bulletlike, and in the other an unidentifiable dark green leafy vegetable. Lizzie is attached to her mother's back as though partaking in a two-person conga.

'Elizabeth, you're going to make me drop them.' Janet leans over, takes the dishes from Mia and places them down on the table. 'Thanks, Janet . . . Now Lizzie, go and sit down.' Mia's voice is stern, her finger pointing towards the chair. Lizzie drops her head, does as she's told, tears once again teetering as she and her tutu squirm onto the seat. Daring to be the ally, Janet slides her hand across the glass towards hers. Clammy palm sticking and unsticking on its journey, until near enough to deliver a friendly tap. 'This looks lovely, doesn't it? Your daddy is very clever, isn't he?'

Lizzie places her elbow on the table, rests her chin in her hand and looks at Janet, eyelids descending into a squint. 'I'm not your friend,' she whispers.

'Janet, do you want a glass of this Bordeaux?' Mia is entering with a bottle of wine, though Janet hadn't realized she'd ever left. Fixing a smile to cover the effects of Lizzie's words, she nods in acceptance of the much-needed alcohol.

Mia pours. 'I'll get you some more elderflower, Colin . . . Oh jeez, yes, I forgot to say, Janet, I can't believe you never told us about the fundraiser for your daughter's headstone. I saw it on Twitter. We're obviously going to make a nice donation. Only I've been so busy, and—'

'No.' The sound of the word cuts sharp. Lowering her voice, she continues, 'No . . . honestly, please don't. It's exceeded the total now. The whole thing is making me uncomfortable.'

Mia moves on to fill her own glass, while Robbie stands at the head of the table, carving knife in hand, tea towel on his shoulder. 'Oh, but we must,' says Mia. 'We give to lots of charities, don't we, Robbie?'

Surging blood heats Janet's cheeks. 'Well, we're . . . we're not a charity, Mia.'

'No . . . no, of course not. I didn't mean—'

'Can I have some wine, Mummy?'

Mia forces a smile. Seemingly delighted at the change of subject. 'No, honey, it's grown-ups' juice.'

'Oh, come on,' Robbie pipes up. 'Give her a taste, it won't harm. We're so uptight about alcohol in this country, don't you think, Col? In France it's no big deal.'

Colin nods. 'Well, I—'

'Robbie, she's eight.' Mia shakes her head then turns to Janet with a pleading mother-to-mother look.

Janet smiles. 'I'm sure she'd hate it anyway, Robbie.'

Mia nods to her in appreciation.

'Well, let her try a sip then,' he says, picking up a piece of the lamb he's just carved and pushing it into his mouth.

'Just a sip, Mummy.'

After a pause, Mia reluctantly offers her wine. 'One teeny sip.' The child takes hold of the huge bulbous glass in both hands and lifts it to her lips. Mia extends her arm towards her, wiggles her fingers. 'Right, give it back now.' But Lizzie takes another much larger gulp, then cackles with laughter, her upper lip now wearing a red moustache. Mia snatches back the drink. 'Elizabeth . . . Robbie, she's had far too much now.'

With a delayed reaction to the bitter tannic aftertaste, Lizzie screws up her face and sticks out her purple-tinged tongue. 'Eurgh, it's horrible.'

'Well, exactly,' says Mia. 'Grown-ups have to practise liking it. I swear to goodness, Robbie, if she's sick—'

'She'll be fine. Come on, everyone, get stuck in before it gets cold.'

Janet serves Colin his roast potatoes, while he tells Robbie about his favourite meats. And the room suddenly feels so hot. Lacking oxygen. Why don't they open the windows? The windows are tiny compared to those in the rest of the house, so why don't they at least open them? She tugs at the collar of her blouse. Widening the gap between her throat and the fabric.

'Are you OK, Janet? You've gone very pale.' Mia stops pouring Robbie's glass of wine. One large final droplet breaking the liquid's surface.

'Yes, yes, I'm fine. I think it's just gone a bit to my head.' She hasn't so much as taken a sip.

'I'll get you some water . . . Colin, hold your wife's hand, she's gone a bit tipsy.'

'Tipsy? I'm pretty much sloshed now, to be honest,' says Robbie, carving more lamb.

'Well, I could take you for a spin later,' says Colin, face turning as red as the Bordeaux, finally getting it out there.

'Yes, Col mate . . . that sounds a plan.'

Unable to suppress his delight, Colin reaches over and taps his wife's hand three times.

'Come on,' Robbie calls out. 'Get stuck in. That's roasted asparagus and garlic-roasted kale . . . These are clementine-glazed carrots and they're the rosemary roasties of course . . . Oh, and that's the gravy. Mia, Lizzie, come on, sit down now please. Actually, you need to all give me your plates first for the lamb . . . Sorry, I told you I was a bit squiffy.'

Janet lowers her head on noticing the blood oozing from the sliced joint. Bile rising in her stomach, she turns, stops herself looking. 'Shall I pass yours to Daddy?' She rests her fingers on the rim of Lizzie's plate. But before she has a chance to lift it, Lizzie picks it up herself, and without making eye contact, slides off her chair, walks around the table and hands it to her father. Janet offers a wobbly smile. 'Little ones are so independent these days.'

'You can always get more, honey, but eat that first.' Mia takes the seat opposite Janet and winks. Woman to woman. 'Eyes bigger than her belly, that one.'

As Lizzie walks back to her chair, Mia follows her movement with a loving grin. But she doesn't acknowledge her mother. The only glance made is deadpan and directed at Janet.

With the food dished out, sounds of chewing and clinking cutlery commence. She looks at her plate. The bloodied meat turning her stomach. She's never eaten kale before. Or even knows what it is exactly. And she gets ever so embarrassed about how her wee smells after eating asparagus. However, she joins the rest, plays the part of tucking in. Swallowing is difficult with a mouth stripped of saliva. Experiencing what Mia may call bad energies, but to Janet it's common or garden dread.

The flesh breaks apart in her mouth. Iron blood seeping into her tongue. She controls a gag. 'It's delicious,' she says. Colin nods in agreement. Though she detects a wince as he chomps down on a huge forkful of kale. He never was one for his greens. Once describing broccoli as his nemesis.

'Sorry, y'all.' Mia gently puts down her cutlery. Pink-silk finger held elegantly above the rest. 'If it's OK with everyone, I think we should say grace.'

Janet nods. 'Of course.'

'You know what, even as an atheist, I think that's a great idea on this occasion,' says Robbie.

'Robbie, shush. Daddy isn't an atheist, honey . . . he just hasn't found his god yet.'

'Now, that's not true.' Robbie nods towards the wine, his hands pressed together as if in prayer.

'What's a theist, Daddy?'

'Take my hand, darling.' Mia holds on to her daughter's hand to her left and Robbie's to her right. Colin reaches for Janet's, and she in return clasps on to Lizzie's reluctant, rigid fingers.

Mia closes her eyes, as does Robbie. Colin manages to shove some lamb into his mouth, before joining them. Lizzie stares at Janet then lowers her lids. And after glancing towards Zofia's photograph, imagining the painful relief of blurting, confessing, before smashing her face into the glass table, Janet too plunges into darkness.

There's a moment of silence.

Then Mia begins.

'Dear Lord, I want to thank you for the gift of our daughter's life. For bringing us Janet. For creating such a beautiful person, so she would come to our darling Lizzie's aid, and now into our life as a dear friend. And thank you for bringing us Zofia, whose time on this earth was too short, but you obviously needed another angel in heaven.'

Janet remains frozen, eyes shut, unsure on everyone's status, waiting for the 'Amen'. But Mia has started talking again, so it can't be over. Although it doesn't sound like grace anymore. And there's another noise. From her right. From Lizzie.

Back in the room, the ceiling spotlights glare. Blinking, she turns to Lizzie, who's crying. Bawling, in fact. 'I told you she shouldn't have had the wine,' Mia throws towards Robbie. Who in turn nonchalantly lifts his glass to his mouth, eyelids hanging lower than usual, and says, 'What's up, my darling, do you feel sick?'

Janet takes some wine herself. Then more. Aided by the

alcohol, she dares to turn to her little friend, her pact person, and stretches a smile. 'What's wrong, Lizzie . . . ? Hey, do you have another dance to show me after lunch?' The volume of the sobs increases.

'Lizzie baby, tell Mummy what's wrong.' Mia pulls her daughter into a hug, pats her shoulder. 'Shhh, come on, tell Mummy. I can't help if I don't know.' She draws back and extracts the wet hair from Lizzie's face. Exactly as Janet would have done with Claire. 'Baba, please.' Mia's eyes add to the pleading, but the girl turns to look at Janet, and Mia looks at Janet, and the walls move inwards and the ceiling lowers and Colin chews and Robbie slurps. *Please don't*, Janet's eyes say. *We're friends. We made a pact. Please don't.*

And to her relief, the crying subsides. Reduces to a whimper. Lizzie rubs at her eyes. Mia kisses her cheek, then returns to her seat. 'That's better . . . Now have a bit more to eat then you can go and play.'

Disaster averted, Janet's heart rate slows, and she collects up her knife and fork, presses some lamb onto the prongs. While chewing, she dabs her forehead with her napkin, then takes a long, deserved swig of Bordeaux, her body gradually relaxing. But as she gulps, and the warm liquid coats her throat, Lizzie's crying resumes as she utters the same words over and over.

Red liquid trickles out from the side of Janet's mouth like she's been shot in the stomach.

She has.

'Janet lied, Mummy,' Lizzie is saying. 'And she made me lie too.'

45

The Last Surviving Brambles

'Janet?'

Her brain can't compute who's saying her name. Breaking the silence that's lasted seconds, minutes. She's unable to even distinguish between male or female, husband or near strangers. Somehow, she's by the door, hand hovering over the handle, with no recollection of moving there, or even standing. Her napkin is splayed beneath the table. Next to it, her knife.

'What's she talking about, Janet?' It's Mia who's speaking. She knows that now. Although her voice is different. Cold, flat.

It's over. And it's almost a relief. A peculiar calmness smooths over her.

'I did a bad thing, Mummy. I went in the pool when you were at the hospital and I couldn't breathe.' Lizzie's sobs intensify. Each word, petrol on a bonfire.

Mia looks over at Janet. 'I trusted you with her. I can't believe you'd keep such a huge thing like that from me.' Her speech, though softened, is tarnished with disappointment. Her eyes droop with hurt.

Such a huge thing.

Janet must say it. Pull off the plaster. Be brave.

But she's not brave. 'I . . . I just thought it was better you didn't know as you were poorly with your finger and . . . well, she was fine. She could breathe, she could . . . it was just that she panicked, and I got her out literally seconds after she jumped in. But she was so upset that you'd be angry, so I thought—'

'I see.' Mia flashes a look towards Robbie. 'I know my child can be very persuasive, Janet. But we don't encourage lies and secrets in this house.'

'I really am sorry.' She notices Lizzie steal a glance in her direction, igniting fears there's more to come. 'It was all my fault though, please don't be annoyed at Lizzie. I was in the wrong. It was my fault.'

Lizzie looks at Janet properly now, dries her eyes with a balled fist.

'I'm not annoyed at her.' Mia's tone snaps tight. 'You're a very good girl coming clean, Lizzie. Thank you. Is that everything? Are there any other secrets you've kept from Mummy?' Janet's sharp intake of air thankfully goes unnoticed. The child shakes her head and leans into her mother's beckoning arms, both now enveloped by netting. Janet's lungs deflate. Sensing Colin turning towards her, she dares to meet his gaze.

'What?' she whispers. He lingers on her eyes like he did in the Holmes Museum.

'I think maybe we should go,' he says, removing the napkin from his neck and placing it on the table.

'Don't be silly, Col . . . I thought we were going for a spin?'

Colin now clearly regrets his proposal, but Mia interjects. 'Actually . . . sorry, yeah. I think the energy around the lunch is too negative now. I think that may be best.'

'Mia, I'm really sorry, I didn't mean to—'

'No, it's fine, Janet.' Mia forces a smile. 'It's just one of those things, but I think Lizzie is tired and intoxicated—'

'For Christ's sake, Mia, she had a sip.'

'Shut up, Robbie. I knew it would end in tears . . . and what do you know?'

'We'll go.' Colin uncharacteristically bends to collect Janet's napkin and knife from the floor.

'You can leave that, it's OK.' Mia's laid-back LA vibe is now brittle, uptight. Robbie's head drops into his hands in a way that suggests his head has dropped into his hands many times before.

Janet looks over at Lizzie. Wanting to thank her somehow. But the face she's met with has a curled lip and angry eyes, so she turns, knowing they must get away from the place as quickly as possible, and never return.

She's grateful for the silent rule on the drive home. The rain has stopped, roads already sun-dried, but the atmosphere in the car is storm-heavy. Minus even the radio to temper the discomfort, she stares out of the window, fist pressed against her mouth, reliving the near miss. And as they travel the stretch of Worsley Road, leaving the situation, the Pilkingtons, further and further behind, it doesn't defuse the undetonated bomb that could still explode at any moment. Dependent on the whims of a little girl. Unless Molly gets there first, of course. Or the police with their CCTV.

'Have you got any other secrets that you're not telling me?' Colin yanks up the handbrake as they stop at traffic lights. Face ahead. Voice as flat as an automated answer machine.

'What? No . . . of course not.' She concentrates on keeping her tone light, free of guilt.

He maintains eye contact with the windscreen. The driving gloves he's taken to wearing since meeting Robbie make a sticking noise as he further grips the wheel and moves away.

'Colin, we've been together for twenty years. There's nothing you don't know about me.' In desperation, she places her hand atop his as it manoeuvres the gearstick. A new role in her repertoire. A wife with sudden sentimentality towards her marriage. Aware this is something he craves so dearly.

But he doesn't acknowledge the gesture. Instead, he pushes the stick with greater force into third, until they stop again at a zebra crossing. 'If someone had asked me up until today if you'd keep something like that from Mia, I'd have said no way.'

She doesn't respond. Not because she knows there's no point when he's in this mood, but because he's right.

They're at home now. She's upstairs, wearing her dressing gown and sitting on the bed. Tea and a chocolate éclair, intended to soothe her jitters, have lodged undigested in her stomach. The noise of the trimmer severs her nerves.

Once they were home, the silent rule had morphed into silent treatment.

After changing into his Bermuda shorts and an old polo shirt, he'd walked right past her and the tea she'd made for him, and headed out into the garden. And since, she's been sitting upstairs, fretting.

She's tempted to run downstairs and call Mia. Apologize again, test the waters. But she's a coward. Instead, she goes to the window, peeks beyond the curtains.

The job is almost complete. The few remaining knitted thick stems, fallen. Though still dangerous. Still able to cause damage despite having had their life source removed.

She observes as he butts the blade against the remaining thin layer. The last surviving brambles drop. The fence gradually being exposed. Sun twinkling against each metal picket. One by one. Until finally, that's all there is. A cold, tall, gaping fence.

The whirr stops.

The world is soundless.

In slow motion, he places the tool onto the ground. Walks towards what he's uncovered.

And all she can do is watch, breathless, as he lifts his hand. And, from the warped post, unhooks the string of sequins.

46

Terrible Things Happen

'Janet.' Her name thunders through the house.

She doesn't call back out to him, ask what he wants, but remains static, staring through the window. Unflinching as his stomps ascend the stairs.

Sensing his approach, she turns, impassive. A prisoner awaiting execution. And now the hangman has arrived.

'Janet. Oh my god, Janet,' he whispers. The sequins hang from his fingers like a captured snake. His face so perplexed, she wonders if he hasn't worked it out at all.

'What?' she says.

But her interpretation is wrong. So very wrong.

He leaves the room and all is silent, until a racket erupts next door. Drawers pulled from their carcasses. Wardrobes flung open. The scrapes of zips. Then quietness descends once more. A disconcerting yet luring quiet.

She follows him to the other bedroom. Legs numb, as though belonging to someone else. The door is ajar. There's a creak as she pushes it further open.

He's sitting on the bed. Bent forward. The jumper he'd bought her, the jumper she'd worn that night, a soiled, damaged bundle in his hands.

He appears to be oblivious to her presence. In his own

disconcerting world. But as she steps over the brass strip on the carpet, he mumbles into the cotton. 'Oh God, Janet.'

Her fingers feel the wall for balance. Still holding on to the lie, she says, 'What? What's wrong?'

Without words or acknowledgement, he stands and calmly lays the jumper on the bed. Spreading out the arms, ironing the creases of the trunk with the flat of his hand. Stepping back, he observes the evidence.

It's the first time she's looked at it since the hospital. Left to rot in the bottom of the holdall. The burning smell lingers, smears and snags that had once confirmed her being in the crash now mock the misconception.

He carefully places the string of sequins over the missing piece of the swallow. Puzzle complete. 'I knew something wasn't right. I went looking for you . . .' His fingers erase an escaped tear. 'I ran out down the cul-de-sac . . . but you were nowhere . . . and then I went back, got the car, and . . . Oh Janet, what were you doing? What have you done?'

She steps towards the bed, sits. Overtaken by a surrendered serenity. 'I swear I didn't know at first. I really had lost my memory.'

'Oh my god.' His hands slide downwards over his face. But once the action is complete, it reveals the same horrified expression.

'I couldn't remember, I promise. Not for a long while.' As she stands and moves towards him, he recoils. Exhibits a repulsion previously only reserved for Sean Kearney.

'So, you were going down there to—?'

'No.' Her response is involuntary. Shame intervening. 'No, nothing like that . . . I'd never do anything like that. I was distraught, and . . . well, I wanted to get away from you, the house. I had no money—'

'And no invented handsome soldier to pay for your fare.'

'I, I followed the foxes . . . I wanted to hide away. That's all.'

With a sigh, he paces like he did in the hospital when telling her about Claire. 'So why were you injured?'

'I slipped and smashed my head, and obviously the brambles were—'

'Yes, OK . . . OK, so you weren't on the train . . . then how did you get all that way?'

'I started walking beside the tracks.'

'Why go down there at all? Why not walk on the road like a normal person?'

'I told you . . . I only wanted to hide and—'

'What about Elizabeth . . . how did you find her, then?'

And so, the story ends. Weak, she lowers herself onto the edge of the bed. Allows the silence to inform him. Sherlock. And on cue, the pacing slows to a standstill. His face awash with dawning realization. 'So . . . so, it was all a lie? The whole thing?' His voice is low, lifeless. 'None of it was true.' This knowledge too burdensome for him to remain upright, he sits, joining her on the mattress.

They remain next to each other for some time. Immersed in acceptance. Until the stillness is eventually broken by Colin standing, walking over to the open wardrobe and pulling out the suitcase that Janet had refilled with winterwear and the cedarwood moth deterrents. With a guttural heave he throws it onto the bed, the hard corner knocking her arm. 'What are you doing?' she asks, over the sound of unzipping.

'I know what I *should* do. They should know . . . everyone should know what you are.' Case now open, he delves into the knitwear and throws it all out onto the floor.

'Colin, please, it's not like it sounds . . . I didn't know at first. I can explain.'

Opening drawers, he fishes out other clothes and flings them towards the plastic hollow. 'Can you? Go on then.'

She ignores the edge of sarcasm. 'As I said, I didn't know at first. I honestly thought I was on the train . . . thought I'd saved her. You all kept telling me I was in the crash and then the footage . . . and Molly . . . she told me I'd saved her, but . . . well, it was when we were leaving for London . . . I went into Claire's room and I remembered . . . remembered what you did, so I—'

'Went on TV?'

'I didn't know what to do, and—'

'So you went on fucking TV?'

She winces at the wrath not felt since Claire's death. When it was a struggle for him not to cause her physical harm. Seemingly scared of his own rage, he attempts to soften, lowers his voice. 'I stood by you after Claire, Janet. I stayed with you despite everything. I try so hard.' As he speaks, he walks back and forth from the wardrobe to the case, loading it with items. 'But how can I not constantly think it? That she'd be here now, alive and happy, and I'd . . . I'd be warning her off boyfriends, and she'd be borrowing money that she's got no intention of returning, asking for lifts . . . if you'd just let her sleep that night. If you'd loved me enough to let her sleep that night. I stuck by you . . . even though you killed her. I stuck by you, only to find out that you're a bloody lying sociopath or something.'

A punctured balloon, she slumps forward, lowers her head. The same words. Eleven years battered by the same words. 'I didn't kill her, Colin. You know, even Sean Kearney didn't kill her really. Not intentionally. Sometimes, terrible things happen. They just happen. Which makes it harder to come to terms with.'

After throwing his Simon Cowell shoes on top of the mound of clothes, he starts to close the case.

'Colin, please.' Despite her hand intercepting the zip, he continues to yank at it, catching the skin between her thumb and index finger. With a restrained yelp, she suckles the cut to soothe the pain.

When the case is fastened, he looks at her. 'Show me,' he says, pulling her wrist towards him, scrutinizing the wound. 'We should clean that up.' He takes her injured hand, guides her to the bathroom, turns on the tap, and places it under the cold stream. They both watch the pink swirls disappear down the plug hole. With a clean towel, he dabs it dry. 'Sometimes, I feel so angry that when you leave the house, I hope you die, so I can stop hating you for it. Then I'd feel the same about you as I do about Claire. Go back to just loving you.'

'Sometimes when I leave the house, I hope I die too.'

'Don't say that, you mustn't say that . . . My thoughts are terrible. You must never think that.' He retrieves a first aid kit from the cupboard. From it he removes a plaster, concentrates on peeling away the wrapper, then smooths it over the cut. 'You've done such a bad thing, Janet. To lie like that . . . continue the lie. I don't understand you.' He drops his head, their hands still touching. And they stay there for some moments, until he releases her fingers. 'Right . . . well, make sure you change the plaster if it gets wet. Keep it clean.' He returns the kit to the cupboard and goes to leave.

'Colin . . . are you going to tell on me?'

He turns back around, the look of disdain reappearing. 'We're not in bloody school, Janet. And I don't know . . . I don't know what to do about you.'

He leaves her in the bathroom and is soon out of sight. She listens to the deadened sound of him wheeling the case across the landing. The thud, thud, thud as he drags it downstairs. The squeak of the opening latch. The slam of the door.

She's made it to the kitchen and has put the kettle on. Gradually comprehending she can now do what she wants, eat what she wants, watch what she wants. She's dreamed of this moment for years. Except she'd be the one lugging the case down the stairs. But now it's here, it's nothing like she'd imagined. Only having happened because she's so bad, such a terrible person, even Colin can't bear to be near her.

The bubbling heightens, the switch flicks. But instead of making tea, she goes to the long cupboard. The home of the mop bucket and Christmas alcohol. And from there she extracts the dust-sticky bottle of Baileys.

Half filling a tumbler, the potent scent stings her eyes. From the freezer she grabs the ice cubes, drops them in, clink by clink, until the last emerges above the rim. An iceberg. Like her, so much hidden beneath the surface. She lifts the cool silky liquid to her lips. A cube knocks cold on her tooth. And as she leans back against the island, the hot iciness coursing through her body, the moment is severed by the ever-familiar sound of tyres on gravel.

She exchanges her previous small sips for gulp upon gulp. Throat stripped raw, she coughs. Smacking the near-empty glass onto the Formica, she stares towards the door, awaiting his appearance.

When it occurs, it's with a peculiar swagger. Proof he's been watching too many John Wayne westerns. As he stops at the doorway, she swallows hard to keep down the liquid. Arm stretched upwards, he rests against the frame, his left leg crossing over his right. 'OK,' he says. 'I won't tell on you, and I won't leave. We've got that money coming—'

'We can't take the money—'

'We've got that money coming and we'll book a cruise. Try and mend things.'

'We can't do that, Colin.'

Releasing his stance, he joins her at the opposing edge of the island. Presses his knuckles down on the worktop, pushing himself towards her. 'You've left us no choice, Janet. How weird would that look? Why would anyone give it back?' He grabs the bottle of Baileys, refills her glass and takes a gulp. 'Please tell me no one else knows about this.'

Her mouth forms to explain about Molly, the CCTV, Lizzie, but fearful of what he'll do, she says, 'No . . . no, of course not.'

He stares towards the ceiling, sighs. 'OK, OK, well, we can't look suspicious in any way.' He lowers his chin, scowls. 'You just can't be trusted, can you? With anything.' He moves closer to her, enough for his alcohol breath to induce her to cough again. 'And I'm telling you now, things are going to have to change.' And as she watches him, frozen, unable to summon the will to fight, the phone rings.

*

She remains in the kitchen. Listening. Colin's voice is faint, the clarity limited. 'Sorry . . . bless you . . . stupid sometimes . . .' Though the delivery is unquestionably sickly-sweet.

Slow, numb, drunk, she follows the conversation until she's standing in the doorway of the lounge. Colin's expression is incongruous with his speech. 'I know . . . I know . . . Of course we'd still love to come. She's been looking forward to the ball so much . . . Exactly . . . I know . . . And she'd be so upset if she didn't go, as well.' He stares at Janet. 'Oh, here she is . . . she's so embarrassed, Mia . . . Oh, hang on, she's going mad to talk to you. She wants to apologize herself.' He extends the phone towards her. Arm stiff, gripping fingers angry-white. As she slowly edges forward, he jerks the receiver, whispers, 'For fuck's sake, come on.'

With shaking hands, she takes it from him. 'Hey, Mia.' Colin mimes for her to smile. She complies, while concentrating on steadying her voice. 'I'm so glad you've called . . . I, I feel awful. It was all so stupid of me and . . . OK . . . OK . . . Well, thank you. I appreciate it . . . Of course . . . Yes, he's right . . . No . . . No, I wouldn't miss it for the world.'

The woman stands motionless in the hallway, as the husband walks around her, disappears. She stares upwards towards her daughter's room. If she ran up the stairs, pressed down the handle, opened the door, she might be there. On the bed. Lying on her stomach, watching The Little Mermaid.

Knowing that will not happen, will never happen, she turns towards the small mirror to her left, and imagines smashing her face into the glass.

Somehow, she's now in the lounge. She must learn how to be again. How to talk, walk, exist. How this house works.

The husband is sitting in his chair, head in hands. 'I'll never be able to forgive you, you know that. I want to, but I know I won't be able to. You should still leave. I'll only want to punish you. Make you suffer.'

She is now merely an effigy of herself, carved from marble. Her mouth the only part able to move. 'That's fine,' she says. 'That's fine.'

47

Lady of Leisure

'We're not half going to miss you, Janet.' Sam drops teabags into cups. Yellow nails bright against the grey gauze. 'Imagine not having your trolley as an example of what everyone should be aspiring to. It's going to be chaos.'

Janet smiles through the desire to cry. The girls echo Sam's sentiment as they take their seats at the staffroom table. Nish bends down and re-emerges with a glittery red bag which she hands to Janet.

'I hope you like it,' says Maria. 'It's from my sister-in-law's shop so if you don't, I can—'

'I'm sure I'll love it. You shouldn't have got me anything.' She digs inside, removing layers of tissue, until all that's left is a small blue velvet box. She stares at it for a moment, then takes it out.

'Go on then, open it,' says Nish, nudging Janet's arm.

She lifts the lid to reveal a pendant. Two silver angel wings, hanging from a fine chain. She pauses, head down, unable to speak.

'Do you not like it?' asks Maria. 'I know you usually wear sparkly jewellery, but I thought—'

'I love it . . . it's beautiful.' The faint words squeeze past the lump lodged in her throat. 'Thank you, everyone.'

Nish drapes herself around Janet's shoulders. 'It's going to be rubbish now.'

'Thanks a lot, Nish,' says Sam, carrying over mugs of tea.

Janet repacks the bag with the tissue to conceal her face, bury evidence of the aching sadness at yielding the final part of herself to Colin. 'I'm going to really miss you all.' Then with a forced smile, supernova bright, she raises her head and says, 'But who'd turn down the opportunity to be a lady of leisure, eh?'

Sam removes the lid from a large Tupperware box on the table and exposes a lemon drizzle cake. 'So, what are you planning to do with yourself?' she says, slicing off a piece of the sponge and sliding it to Janet on a paper plate.

Janet pops a morsel of the solidified drizzle into her mouth, bides her time. After an exaggerated swallow, she says, 'Well, I'm only here in the mornings, so it won't change much, but I'll look forward to having lie-ins.' She feigns a giggle. 'And I'll be able to spend more time with my dad. Colin's going to be increasing his hours to make up the wages, so I'll have to do his share of housework as well. I'm sure I'll be a right busy bee.' Of all the lies she's told, pretending Colin lifts a finger in the house makes her want to scream. She bites off a large piece of the sponge, while reaching in her pocket with her free hand to stroke Claire's dog. Both offer less comfort than she'd hoped.

'Is it because you've got all that GoFundMe money?' says Maria. 'You've got loads now . . . ten thousand or something, isn't it?'

'Maria, you can't ask things like that,' says Sam, looking towards Janet, clearly also desperate for an answer.

'No, no, I . . . I really don't want to accept all that money. It doesn't feel right.'

'Well, I bloody would.' Sam playfully slaps her on the arm. 'That's for you, that. These things don't happen every day, you know.'

'I'm so jealous,' says Nish. 'I wish I could just leave.'

Emma nods.

'And me,' says Maria, crumbs tumbling from her mouth. 'You're dead lucky your Colin will do that so you don't have to work.'

Nish drops her head, presses crumbs with her finger.

'Oi, you're all so cheeky. Little buggers, the lot of you. Go and get other jobs then. See how you like it out there.' Sam pats Janet's hand. 'You deserve it, love . . .OK, you lot, so I'm thinking that we meet tonight in the Dog and Duck at around seven, do a bit of a crawl . . . karaoke. Got to have a bit of karaoke on a leaving do, haven't we, girls?'

'Oh, no . . . I can't, Sam, sorry. Colin's booked a table for us tonight . . . at Nico's.' She's aware of Nish getting up, giving her a look. 'Sorry. I would, but you've got to book so far in advance . . . another time though, eh?' A rogue tear escapes, which is immediately swept away. The action disguised by twisting her hand as though she's looking at her watch. Feeling a further surge of guilt when faced with her bare wrist.

When it's all over, and she's been sent off with a smaller Tupperware box containing leftover cake, kissed the girls goodbye, made false promises to meet them at the pub next week, she takes the lift for the last time with Nish.

'Are you sure you want to do this, Janet?'

'Yes, of course. Don't be silly.' Her eyes fix on the doors.

'Why though? I don't understand.'

'You don't understand why I don't want to be a cleaner for the rest of my life?' She forces a laugh. It's not reciprocated.

'You love cleaning, though.'

Janet doesn't respond. Her stomach lurching as they drop down through the floors. 'Sam would have you back in a heartbeat and—'

'Nish, for goodness' sake.' Her near shout is punctuated by the lift jolting to a standstill. As the doors slide open, she turns to her well-meaning friend, feels for her hand. 'It's a good thing for me, Nish. Honestly, it is.'

She intends to take the bus the whole way to her dad's. No comfort to be gained from the cut-through today. Not from the scent of honeysuckle or fantasy holidays. The latter only a reminder of the cruise she'll be forced to go on with stolen money. But as they pass St Joseph's church on Worsley Road, she feels the urge to stand and ring the bell.

She's been inside St Joseph's once before. For the funeral of Angie Little, a drifted friend. They'd always been so close. Janet was even made godmother to her daughter, Constance. But then Colin came on the scene, gradually manipulating her away from all connections.

Seeing Constance at the service, all grown up, with that familiar glaze of grief and despair, Janet was too ashamed to introduce herself. An additional guilt she must carry. Though maybe she'll find her again. One day.

The church is small but pretty. The cemetery shabby and overgrown.

As she follows the row of weather-worn headstones the heavens open, spattering the slabs like a Jackson Pollock.

Bert Wilkins, beloved husband of Ethel Wilkins . . . Lorna Pickles, mother, sister, wife.

It's strange how the dead are not referred to as individuals, but merely by their relations to others. *Janet Brown, mother to Claire, beloved wife of Colin Brown.*

Standing on the worn-down steps, she looks beyond the arched doorway towards the beautiful stained-glass window and carved stone. A smiling vicar walks in her direction, but it dawns on her that she doesn't know what to ask anymore. What she even wants to know. So she turns her back on him and runs out into the pounding rain.

By the time the Oakland House entrance is in view, she's soaked and her teeth are chattering.

To her dismay, Helen appears again to let her in personally. 'Oh goodness, you poor sod.'

'I'm fine . . . I thought it was supposed to be sunny today.' She can't contemplate looking at her directly. Saturation an excuse to busy herself. All Helen now represents is the money, surging her anxiety.

'I swear the world is broken. One minute it's hot, the next you have to get a boat to the shops. Anyway, I'm finishing soon, I'll give you a lift home.'

Janet pushes her hair back from her face, shivers intensifying, aware of the wet patch of carpet forming below. 'No, I'm fine, honestly—'

'Hey, shush. Don't be silly. You can't go back out in this. It's no problem. You get yourself in there and dried off.'

*

In her dad's room, additionally burdened by the thought of enduring the lift with Helen, tears surface which she cannot allow to fully take hold. Thankfully, his mere existence makes her feel safer. 'Hey, Dad, I'm soaked. I'm going to dry myself off,' she says, addressing the back of his chair.

In the bathroom, she removes her uniform for the last time and drapes it on the warm pipe in the built-in cupboard. Swapping it for the biggest towel she can find and wrapping it around her goosebumped body. A smaller one turbaned over her hair. And she stands there, staring into the mirror. Red-faced. Hopeless. A person she no longer likes, nor understands.

Now dressed in a pair of her dad's trousers and an old shirt, she sits next to him on the little stool. His colour is good today. Cheeks pinch-pink, face relaxed. Concentrating on the old movie that's playing. She instantly recognizes it as one of his favourites, *The Cruel Sea*. And though he's unlikely to know this consciously, his smile indicates that somewhere inside, he's very much aware.

A puppeteer, she takes his hand, brushes his fingers against her cheek as he would when she was a child, making everything better. 'I'll be able to see you more from now on, Dad. I've stopped working.' Her applied grin gradually fades. She can't do it anymore. Even pretend to the person she loves the most. 'Oh Dad . . . I've done such a terrible thing . . . You and Mum, you brought me up right, but I'm a liar . . . I lied about Elizabeth . . . about the crash . . . and I know you hate lies, and . . . and I can't bear that.' The confession induces a wave of relief, immediately stopped dead by the sound of the door pushing open.

'I've brought you a tea.' It's Helen. Janet dabs her face,

re-plasters the grin. Panicked at how long she'd been behind the door. Helen comes further into the room. 'Thought you might need one. To warm you up.'

As Janet takes the cup, she's certain Helen's facial expressions aren't mirroring the kindness of the act. 'Thank you, Helen, that's exactly what I need.' She smiles. It's not returned. 'I'm going to stay with Dad a bit longer today. I wouldn't want to hold you up, so you head on.'

'No, it's fine, whenever you're ready. I'd like to have a chat, anyway.'

The effort to appear unruffled is Oscar-worthy. But she can think of no valid reason for which she can further refuse. 'Thanks, Helen,' she says. 'That's very kind.'

She slides into Helen's car, wrapped in her dad's old mackintosh, imagining it as a shield of paternal protection.

There's a stench of stale milk, and her feet rest upon a grease-seeped McDonald's bag. Helen puts on her seatbelt in silence, and Janet follows suit. 'It's very kind of you,' she says again, as if politeness can save her from ruination.

'Not a bother.' Helen starts the engine and distractedly watches the rear-view mirror, while reversing out of the parking space. After numerous heavy turns of the wheel, the vehicle drives away. Janet, a trapped animal, observing freedom through the half-fogged window, wipers rapidly swiping back and forth despite the easing rain. She could open the door. Old bangers don't have safety locks to interfere. She'd roll and roll on the tarmac until—

'I'm glad we've got the opportunity to talk, Janet.' The gearstick scrapes shrilly as it judders into third.

'Oh, yes?' She continues to stare towards the queue of rain-distorted cars ahead. Once again imagining her face smacking through the glass.

'Oh, nothing in particular . . . only how you're doing after the crash and things. Oi, get from up my bleedin' arse,' she shouts towards her own reflection. Janet's so relieved she appears to be safe regarding her earlier disclosure that she becomes light-headed, holding on to the grab handle to steady herself. 'There's always someone bloody tailgating around here,' Helen continues. 'What's the hurry with everyone? That's how sodding accidents are caused. Oh God, sorry, sorry . . . that was insensitive of me. I'm so sorry.'

'It's fine . . . I'm fine.' Janet moves her hand under the raincoat, presses on her heart. 'I'd rather put the whole train crash thing behind me now though, to be honest.'

'Oh Janet, love, you deserve the fuss. And you've got all that money coming to you. Which, actually, I did want to talk to you about as well. It's ending soon, only a couple of days left, so you really must remember to bring in your bank details when you next visit your dad. You should go on a lovely holiday or something . . . I had a quick look before we left and it's nearly at fourteen thousand now. Hey, Janet, I bet you never thought it would go that high. Can you believe it?'

Janet barely suppresses the urge to vomit into the McDonald's bag. 'No. No, that's too much, Helen. Honestly, I feel uncomfortable. I'd like it to go back to everyone. Can you do that? Can you send it back to everyone?'

Stopping at a set of traffic lights, Helen turns to her. 'Now what reason could there possibly be for you to return the money?'

The image of Colin hissing the exact same thing barges into her mind. 'I don't know.'

'Right, so enough of that nonsense now. People have pledged money because they want you to have it, OK?'

Nodding, she forces a smile. 'OK,' she says, tiny-voiced.

As they drive off again, her expression drops, brain working overtime. She'll have to perpetually forget the bank details. Avoid Helen until she can think of a way out.

For a while they settle into what could be perceived as a comfortable silence, but for Janet is about as comfortable as a bed of nails. Though when Helen launches into a rant about having a full evening ahead of laundry because her daughter's going on holiday in the morning, and she's old enough to go abroad but apparently not old enough to do all her washing, it feels even worse.

When they finally turn into the cul-de-sac, Janet's unable to hold in an audible sigh. 'Just here's fine. Thank you so much.'

'Not a bother, love.'

The car rolls to a standstill across the empty driveway, followed by the crank of the lifted handbrake and swish of Janet's eagerly released seatbelt. The rain having ceased, she climbs out, thankful it's over, desperate to inhale the newly cleansed air. But as she pushes the door shut, Helen shouts, 'Oh, hang on.' Janet pauses the action, bemused as Helen lets out a silly laugh, while comically slapping her forehead. 'Aren't we daft. I can get the bank details while I'm here.'

'What?' Janet's fingers tighten around the edge of the door.

'It'll save me having to keep asking you for them.'

The sound of the unclipped seatbelt, removal of keys from

the ignition, makes Janet light-headed. The sensation of blood draining from her brain. 'Yes . . . of course. Come in,' she says.

Helen enters her world. Even under the circumstances, she can't help but be embarrassed by the hall's sombreness. But perhaps it's only her warped perception, because Helen says with a genuine tone, 'Oh Janet, isn't it lovely?'

The comment doesn't lift Janet's spirits as it ordinarily would. 'Thank you,' she replies, the words sticking in her throat. Extending her arm, she gestures for the unwanted guest to enter the lounge. 'Can I get you a cup of tea?' Regardless of being about to commit potential fraud, crossing moral lines propelling her further away from her integrity, politeness remains important. The requirement to be a good host. Though she's confident the gesture will thankfully be refused with all that laundry to complete.

'That'll be lovely. One sugar, please.'

In the kitchen she flings open the back door, breathes deeply. The whoosh of restored blood loud in her ears. She makes the tea with uncooperative hands. Boiled water splashes over the sides of the cups as she pours, clipping the skin on her fingers. But she doesn't flinch. Doesn't run them under the cold tap. She can't feel the pain. She can't feel anything other than her twisted intestines working on the lemon drizzle cake.

Stirring in the sugar, she forces her composure. Reasons with herself that it will be OK. It will be OK.

'Here you go,' she says, reaching for a coaster before placing the cup on the side table. 'I won't keep you, I know you've got all that washing to do.'

Helen sinks back further into the sofa, steaming tea now in hand. 'No, I was just thinking, you know she's nineteen, Janet . . . It's about time she learned. I mean, I wish I was off galivanting to Greece tomorrow.'

'I do too . . . I really do.' Hovering in the middle of the room, unable to sit, she's unsure of what to do with herself, how to appear normal.

Helen, peculiarly comfortable in someone else's home, blows on her brew and sips. 'Hey, well, you'll be able to go anywhere once this money's transferred . . . Do you want to grab the details for me now, so we don't forget?'

'Oh – yes.' Janet smiles, turns robotically and walks towards the sideboard as if taking part in a funeral procession. As she pulls open the drawer, Helen's chattering warps into a slow drone. 'I love this carpet, though it must be a nightmare to keep clean . . . Is that your daughter? I'm so sorry, Janet, I can't imagine . . . We were going to buy one of the houses on Raymond Street but were put off by the school . . .' Janet responds with vague noises of implied listening while rooting through the laminated folder stuffed with paperwork. Shaking fingers lifting each page. 'Do you find all the mothers block the way with their cars?'

This time, from the gaping silence, she senses the requirement of a proper answer. 'No . . . no, it's not too bad.' She's gripping a bank statement now. Account name, Mr Colin A. Brown. Her eyes snagging on her wages, dutifully deposited every month. Though not anymore.

'Oh good, is that it?' Helen digs into her handbag, removes

a small diary, and extracts the tiny pencil concealed in its spine. 'Right, so first what's the name on the account?'

Janet presses it against her chest.

'Janet?'

'Sorry, I . . .' Swinging back towards the drawer, she returns the statement while gulping down the oesophagus-tickling cake. She selects a different sheet of paper and faces Helen once more. The page fluttering in her hand like a Victorian fan.

'Have you got the account name then?'

'Yes, sorry . . . it's Mrs Janet Amelia Brown.'

48

Jason Quartz

It's a week on and she's burrowed further down the rabbit hole. Deeper, darker. No possible way to scramble back up the muddied sides. The gnawing feeling that the only way out is coming full circle, back to how it all began.

At least Colin has burdened himself with some of the lying. When the Rail Accident Investigation Branch called to arrange a routine interview, he flew into his role with aplomb. 'I'm afraid my wife is suffering extreme trauma so it's out of the question at the moment. I'm sorry we can't be of more help . . . though I must say I'm appalled that a crash like this even happened in this day and age.'

£14,730 rests in her account.

It's done now.

Whenever Colin asks about the money, she plays ditzy. Tells him she's forgotten to give Helen the bank details again. Her being dumb is something he's always prepared to believe. Then she waffles on about the process taking at least another ten days to complete. Knowing there's only so long she can maintain the deception. That she'll have to transfer it eventually. But at least while it's in her own account, it feels less final. Less stolen. Less spent. Apart from the headstone she ordered yesterday from McIver's Memorials near to the cemetery. She's no idea how she'll explain away the transaction date. But with the strengthening notion that she may no longer be around, she had to get it done. It'll take months to be completed, but at least it's underway.

It will be marble. White. A mermaid carved into the face. The engraving – *Swim free, our Little Mermaid.*

Now unemployed, she's been mainly spring cleaning and has even tried making her own bread. 'That's the best thing I've ever tasted,' Colin had said when presented with her white country cob. 'Not just a face, eh?' She'd refused to laugh at his cruel joke. To be complicit. It's about time Colin realizes how unfunny he is.

The evenings have mainly been spent alone. Colin has already upped his shifts to accommodate this new arrangement. But his loss of home time is her gain. She can at least relax in her own company. Relax as much as anyone can with the constant threat of being outed. Waiting for *the* call from the Pilkingtons, Molly, the police. The ever-present hovering executioner's blade. But this evening is different. Worse. Her head is firmly placed on the chopping block. Because this evening is the charity ball.

Colin isn't home yet from his shift. On *North West Tonight* they'd reported a pile-up on the Mancunian Way. The traffic having only just started to move. For a moment her stomach had sunk, so she rang him. Uncharacteristically, he answered. 'I'm not talking but can you make sure my shirt is ironed. The traffic is hell and I'll have to run in, get dressed and go.'

So here she is, the ironing board set up in the lounge. Colin's shirt smoothed on top of the hummingbird-patterned cover. A cheese and Branston sandwich and cup of tea resting on the adjacent side table. Enough to line her tummy so she can ease her nerves with an alcoholic drink before the meal.

The Psychic Channel is on TV, but to her disappointment, it's that Hazel woman again, droning on. As soon as she's finished the shirt, she'll have to find something else to watch. In the meantime, she eats, sups, irons, in rotation. Experiencing only the slightest panic at the speck of pickle juice splashed onto the back of the collar. And it's after she's rubbed at the mark with her finger and is pressing it flat, the steam giving her a bit of what may very well be a Reiki facial, that she sees him.

Jason Quartz.

The iron's hiss snaps her out of the daze. Quickly, she lifts it from the sizzling polycotton. Watches.

He's walking onto the set, sitting on the psychic's sofa. Entranced, she's only just realized that Hazel is still speaking. '*So, do please call in, and Jason will try to answer the burning questions you want to ask your loved ones.*' The camera pans to his close-up. Smiling. Quiff shorter, blonder. A little less magician-looking than the last time she saw him.

The phone number scrolls across the bottom of the screen. Transfixed, her eyes follow its movement, left to right. And without much thought, she finds herself rushing towards the sideboard and extracting her address book from the drawer. Rooting in the cupboard, hands fumbling, she's unable to locate a pen, so rips away the lid of Colin's posh Parker. With the cold silver slipping between her fingers, she scribbles down the digits. Eyes flicking between screen and paper, screen and paper. Once she's ensured it's been copied correctly, she lifts the receiver, pauses for a huge inhalation, and dials.

A woman with a youthful sing-song tone answers the call.

Janet's breaths are so short, jagged, she can barely answer the posed questions. The poor researcher asking her to repeat herself numerous times. When their brief interaction is complete, she stretches the phone over to the sofa and places the base on the seat next to her. Giddy, she sits, steadies herself, and prepares for what she's about to do.

Talk to Claire.

She's next to be put through to Jason. There was a report on *Hello Britain* a few months back where Dr Paul was saying that the physical sensations of excitement and fear are closely related. And she can concur. Sitting there, stomach fluttering and churning, she's both excited about speaking to her baby and fearful at having to say goodbye.

'*We have a lady called Janet on the phone, is that correct?*' Jason is addressing the camera, gently patting his quiff.

Sitting upright, she grabs a cushion and places it on her knees. 'Yes . . . yes, that's right.' A lump the size of a gobstopper has developed in her throat. Swallowing, near impossible.

'*And you want to communicate with your daughter?*'

'Yes, please . . . Her name is Claire.'

Without acknowledgement, he closes his eyes. Extends his arm out straight, palm facing the camera.

Unblinking, she fixates on the screen, wills her to speak. Not one of their imagined conversations. But for her to really be there.

A soft smile washes over Jason's face as he nods, murmurs indecipherably. Then with clarity, he says, '*Yes, Janet . . . I have Claire right here.*'

There's a pause. Her brain, soul, absorbs what he's said.

And once it's reached every part of her being, it's not merely crying that occurs, but an expulsion of silent screams, soothed pain. All expressed into the cushion now lifted to her face.

She attempts to calm herself, mustn't miss a thing, a word. '*Janet . . . Claire wants you to know she's OK. That Grannie is looking after her.*'

Unable to contain her silence any longer, a guttural noise rises from her stomach and exits her lips before she is able to say, 'Can you . . . can you tell her that I love her?'

Jason laughs. '*Oh, she knows that already, my love . . . she keeps telling me how much you love her, and she says she loves you too, and you mustn't blame yourself.*'

The cushion drops to the floor as she stares at the screen, accumulated tears obscuring her vision.

'*Janet . . . Janet, are you there, my love?*'

'Yes . . . yes, I am.'

'*Claire has a message for you, but you've got to remember it's not like talking to someone in this dimension. It's not always entirely clear, so I may not make sense, or I may not be interpreting it correctly . . . OK, Janet?*'

She nods, slow, forgetting she cannot be seen. But maybe she can, because he says, '*OK . . . so Claire, she's telling me that you need to be brave . . . that's the word I keep hearing, brave . . . that she wants you to follow through with something. That's what you need to do to feel better, to feel at peace. She'll be there, she says . . . I think she's saying . . . except I can't quite . . . sorry . . . sorry, Janet, my love, she's getting fainter. Does any of that make sense?*'

Janet remains entirely still. Blinks towards the TV. 'Yes, Jason,' she says. 'That makes perfect sense.'

49

Closer to God

She sits at the dressing table in Colin's bedroom, now her bedroom once again, and stares into the mirror. Not at her reflection, but beyond. Mindlessly sliding a brush through her hair, going over and over what happened. She spoke to her. She really did speak to her. And she was OK. The message replays again in her mind, to which she whispers out loud, 'Tonight?'

Despite all the best efforts, her crown is lying awkwardly. She'd prefer to look nice, but questions whether it even matters. Opening her make-up palettes, her fingers swirl the colourful squares, and she smears and presses powders, creams, onto her face as competently as her capabilities permit. Not make-up artist standard, but sufficient.

Opening the wardrobe reveals all her clothes returned by Colin, and she retrieves the suit worn for *Hello Britain*. So preoccupied with not wanting to attend the ball, she'd neither requested money to buy something new nor bothered to check the suit beforehand. A brief sniff identifies the faint tinge of body odour. Particles of fear captured during its last outing. Ordinarily she'd be mortified, but tonight she's satisfied with layering each armpit with a spritz of Chanel No. 5.

She's dressed now. Ready. Or at least as ready as she'll ever be. And as she sits on the stool in acceptance, the sound of a key in the front-door lock echoes through the hallway. 'It's all ironed and up here,' she shouts. Then with a sharp intake of breath, practises her smile in the mirror to the sound of his footsteps ascending the stairs. 'It's all there on the hanger.' She nods towards the back of the door.

'I can't tell you what it's like out there. It's chaos. There's been a massive accident and some boy band is playing the Arena . . . And we're going to have to take the car.'

'I thought one of the—'

'Don't even ask . . . I've had murders with Mel. She reckons there's no one free to take or pick us up now. So much for perks of the job. Never mind getting there, it'll be a nightmare trying to get a cab home. It's so bloody annoying you can't drive – I can't have a drink now. Well, one. It's not fair I've got to play taxi all the time.'

But she can drive. She can. Though there's no point arguing. 'Well, we're OK for time. Just throw on your suit.'

Once dressed, apart from the bow tie with which he appears to be struggling, he looks unusually smart, handsome. She steps in front of him, feeling his eyes boring into her as she crosses and wraps the red paisley silk until it's perfectly knotted. 'You look nice,' he says. 'Like a bigger Grace Kelly.' He jigs his shoulders up and down, eases himself into wearing the suit. 'Right, come on then.'

She follows him out of the room, then stops, runs back to the dressing table mirror, removes the matching fascinator, and places it on her head.

*

'God's shining on us today.' He slides into a parking space on one of the coveted meters. 'It's free after eight, as well.'

Their brief walk from the car is carried out in silence. Her heart rate increasing with each step. Despite having been in Mia and Robbie's company numerous times now, Colin's knowledge of the lie changes everything. Deception is so much harder when someone else knows the truth. But it's only a couple of hours, he assured her. Then that's it. They'll ease off the connection. Friends naturally sliding apart as so often happens.

Manchester Cathedral puts the Daventry to shame. As they pause outside the enormous building, taking in its beauty, fascinator feathers tickling her face in the breeze, she can't believe she's never visited before.

'Look at that carving over the door . . . it's fantastic,' says Colin as they approach the entrance.

'The tympanum, you mean.'

He stops, looks at her. 'How do you know what it's called?'

'Just do.' She's amazed he can't remember. He'd mocked her long enough a few months back, when she'd thought the presenter of a documentary about religious architecture had called it a tampon. Funny how in the end she's retained the knowledge and not him.

The space described on the ticket as the Nave is breathtaking. Head tilting towards the soaring vaulted ceiling, she holds on to Colin's arm for steadiness. A central space is lined either side by pillars, like Moses's parting of the Red Sea. At the far end is a huge archway, before which sits a stage. Beyond that, a stained-glass window beaming luminous shafts of colour. It's the best of all the churches she's visited. Ruined only slightly by the low hum of pop music. She's suffused with a sense of spirituality. Closer to God than ever before. And being there immediately after her communication with Claire feels significant.

Round, white-clothed tables are dotted throughout. Lilies at their centres, along with half-drunk beverages, cutlery, and neatly folded napkins. She can't help but wonder if it would have financially benefitted the charity more if they'd instead donated the money spent on creating all this.

Guests are still pouring into the space like liquid. Smooth in their tuxedos and luxurious floor-length gowns. Strappy, elegant, fancy. She pats her fascinator, tugs at the bottom of her jacket, at her shame.

A waiter offers them both a glass of champagne, which they remove from the tray with awkward thanks. 'We can sip this for the duration,' says Colin. 'Hey, look, there's the actress from that weird programme . . . what's it called?'

'Oh yes, *Tenants of the Lake* . . . I didn't realize she was so tiny.' And for a moment Janet's caught up in the excitement of mingling in a world in which they don't belong.

'There they are.' Colin waves over at Mia and Robbie, sitting at the table directly in front of the staging area. They remain oblivious to Colin's attempt at capturing their attention. Robbie's arm reaches around the back of his wife's chair as she slaps the table, laughing. Mia looks exquisite in a white full-length gown, lithe tanned leg peeking from beyond a split, hair scraped back severely. Though nothing could ever make her appear severe. Robbie's black tux jacket is draped over her shoulders, worn with the effortlessness of a film star. They're both laughing now, talking to another rich-looking couple.

And the realization that she not only has to face Robbie and Mia, but will have to make conversation with strangers too, fills her stomach with acid.

Colin leads them through the tables. Janet imagining the looks on their posh friends' faces when introduced. Wonderment as to what people like Colin and her are doing hobnobbing with the likes of the Pilkingtons. Until Robbie will say, 'Janet's the lady who saved Elizabeth,' and their attitudes will immediately alter. She'll suddenly be worthy of a smidgen of respect.

Mia stands as they approach. 'Hello.' The word is elongated, her arms extended. Janet puts down her glass and slides into the gap as is expected, hugging into Mia's taut body. Praying the action is only releasing Chanel No. 5 and not body odour. 'Thank you so much for coming, you two.' Mia's tone is different. An actress playing a role. And Janet's uncertain if it's because Mia is also awkward in this environment, or she's attempting to conceal lingering resentment.

As the embrace ends, Janet sees Robbie slapping Colin's back, before moving over to her. 'Janet . . . you look smashing.' He kisses her cheeks. Once, twice, a third mistimed bump of noses.

'This is all incredible.' Janet stands stiff, unsure of what to do with herself. Without looking, she's certain Colin is doing the same.

Mia pats the adjacent chair, summoning her to sit. 'Isn't it drop-dead gorgeous. We usually hold it in the Midland Hotel but oh my, it is beautiful here. Though we've totally worked our hind legs off the past couple of days.' She pours herself a glass of wine, then lifts the bottle, a mimed enquiry as to whether Janet would also like some.

'I'm fine, thank you.' She raises the barely touched champagne.

As Janet and Colin take their seats, Robbie says, 'Guys, these are our good friends Antonia and Giles.' The couple's faces break into matching dazzling smiles. She's perhaps a model, though less editorial than Mia. More catalogue than *Vogue*. And he's much older, paunchy. Presumably monied.

'Well done you,' says Antonia, while stretching over to touch Janet's hand but not quite reaching.

Janet flicks a smile. 'Thank you.' Then a sheet of pained silence floats down over everyone. Giles fidgets with his keys resting on the table. Mercedes sign prominent. Colin slides his Toyota set from the linen cloth and drops them into the pocket of his jacket now resting on the back of his chair. 'So, tell me, Giles,' he says. 'What are your thoughts on these new resin driveways?'

Thankfully, the food is so delicious, conversation centres around the succulence of the salmon and its unusual flavours. 'I can't believe I'm the frigging chef and you're all arguing with me about it not being star anise.'

Colin is better at this than she is. Conversing with strangers. Desperate for it to all be over, she only manages to eat, listen, wait. Pushing the fact that she's a con artist to the back of her mind.

By the time the mains are gobbled, cutlery neatly rested on the marbled plates, her disquiet is escalating. So, when Mia dabs the corners of her mouth, Janet copies the action and pushes back her chair, declaring she's going to the ladies'.

*

The toilets are clad with the same sandstone as the Nave. A group of dolled-up women preen and cackle, their miniature glitzy handbags in a row upon the glass shelf. Thankfully, the cubicles are mainly empty, so she hurries through one of the oak doors, pulls down her knickers and plonks onto the seat, not caring that she didn't clean it beforehand. And bending forward, she attempts to control her speeding breaths.

By the time she re-emerges the women have gone, and she's grateful for the empty space. To be alone, even if only for a few moments. After washing her hands, she splashes the cool droplets against her ruddy cheeks while observing her reflection. Not yet a ghost, but not part of this world.

As she blots her face with stiff green paper towels from a dispenser, there's the sound of the door opening. She doesn't turn to acknowledge the intruder. Unable to deal with any more polite smiles or hellos. She remains in the same position, waiting for them to enter a cubicle.

'Mrs Brown? Janet Brown?'

She pauses mid-dab. Recognizing that voice. Confident, deadpan, cold. Defeated, she turns. 'Hi Molly, how are you?'

'I'm good, yeah. I'd prefer to be covering the city's crime rather than rich people eating free food, but . . . you know.' She's still in her uniform of suit and shirt. The addition of hair-clashing scarlet lipstick elevating the look to eveningwear. 'How are you doing anyway? So, you get invited to things like this now, eh? That must be nice.'

Janet throws the scrunched-up towel into the bin from a distance. Miraculously, it hits the target, bolstering her desperate act of cool, calm collection. 'I'm very well, thank you. As you know, Robbie and Mia Pilkington are the organizers.'

'Of course . . . lovely.' Silence lingers in the air along with her toxic perfume. 'Anyway, I'll let you get back to your meal.' She grins, exposing a lipstick-smeared front tooth. When she heads towards a cubicle, Janet prepares to make a quick exit. But as she reaches for the handle, she's once again the criminal in a *Columbo* episode. 'Oh, Mrs Brown, just one more thing.'

With reluctance, she turns back around.

'They've gone through all the CCTV, but they don't seem to have accounted for you yet.'

Janet wills her face not to redden, stands taller. 'Oh . . . well, it was very busy. I'm there somewhere.' She delivers an unwavering smile, possibly exposing the heart now firmly positioned in her mouth. Then yanking open the heavy door, she leaves.

Back at the table, palpitations worse than when she was perimenopausal, she fills a glass of water from an untouched jug, straining to keep her hands from trembling. After lowering herself into the chair, she sips, quelling the desire to gulp and gulp. 'Are you OK?' asks Mia, gently touching Janet's fist, resting next to a newly arrived plate of Eton mess.

'Yes, yes, I'm fine . . . got a bit of a headache, that's all.'

'Oh no, honey. I've got some paracetamol.' Mia digs around in her white butter-leather envelope bag before producing a blister pack of pills.

Janet complies, pops out two tablets, places them individually on her tongue and swallows. Aware of yet another act of Mia's kindness.

Tucking into his pudding, Colin seems to be having an in-depth conversation with the other couple. Oblivious as always to her state of distress. Although his serious face is somewhat undermined by a splodge of whipped cream balancing precariously on his chin.

Robbie stands, dips towards his wife, whispers in her ear. The mystery utterance ends with a kiss on her lips, before he turns and walks towards the stage.

Despite her appetite having evaporated, Janet collects up her spoon and slides in the sickly concoction. Appreciative for it at least eradicating the bitter tablet aftertaste.

Robbie is now standing at a wooden lectern. Mia gazing up at him, overflowing with pride, clapping. Initially alone, then Antonia joins in, then Giles, then Colin and finally Janet, along with the rest of the room.

The gentle soundtrack that's been humming in the background bursts into an ear-numbing two-second blast of Madonna's 'Crazy for You'. Robbie performs an exaggerated shocked jump, then bends towards the microphone as it fades back down to the previous level. 'Wow . . . thank you to whoever made that my theme tune. Obvious choice.' Hand on hip, he flicks his hair. The room titters. Janet joins in, dutifully, albeit a few moments behind like there's a satellite delay. 'Did you do that, Mia? I married you, for goodness' sake, what more do you want?' The chuckles intensify, while Mia plays the part of sulking wife. Pouted bottom lip, folded arms. *Look what a great sport I am, everyone. So down to earth and fun.*

'Shall we start again?' Robbie's eyes twinkle beneath the brash white spotlights. A stark contrast to the now dimmed room. 'I hope you've all enjoyed your meal. I know I did . . . mainly because I didn't have to cook it.' There's another wave of subdued laughter. And suddenly Janet's hit by how bizarre it is that she and Colin know these people. These charismatic famous individuals. If they didn't think she'd saved Elizabeth, they wouldn't give her the time of day. She turns to view the room, taking in the other well-known faces. Molly's unmissable hair catches her eye, making her quickly swivel back around.

'I want to thank everyone for putting on their glad rags and taking the time to be here tonight to support such an important cause.' He closes his eyes, gathers himself, then returns to the microphone with an enlarged smile and croaky voice. 'As you will probably know, our daughter, Elizabeth, was involved in the Manchester train crash which tragically killed six people, including our family friend Zofia. And without the NHS and the wonderful people at the Royal Manchester Children's Hospital, who knows what might have happened.'

Janet's meringue-laden stomach flips. Hoping she'll not be mentioned. That his speech ends there. While knowing she'll feel irrationally disgruntled if it does.

'And so, we want to pay them back. We've got some fantastic things up for auction tonight, generously donated from businesses all over the city . . . and we need you wonderful folks to dig deep.' The room fills with weak applause, and although Janet is washed over with relief, that twinge of disappointment cannot be denied.

'So, that's the cause. Now, I know you all want to get onto the fun bit, but first I must thank my beautiful partner in crime, my gorgeous wife, Mia.' Clapping rises, joined by whistles. He waits for it to subside, then says, 'And there's one more person I must thank.'

Colin grabs Janet's hand and squeezes it so tight his short

nails indent her skin. She's unsure of the message. Whether he doesn't want her name to be mentioned or is delighted that it's about to be.

'You're all probably aware of a wonderful woman – a special, selfless woman – who was also on that train, and despite suffering injuries herself, pulled our daughter from the wreckage and performed CPR on her before alerting the paramedics. And . . .' He drops his head, places a finger beneath his nose, pauses. Once able to look up again, he resumes. 'And I don't even want to think about what might have happened had she not been on that train, and not been the wonderful person that she is . . . So, will you please all put your hands together to thank Janet Brown. Thank you, Janet.'

Applause erupts. Louder than previously. Mia is pushing at Janet's arm, making her stand. Colin is on the other side of her, pulling on the jacket sleeve for her to sit back down.

Robbie bends into the microphone, smiles. 'Come on, Janet . . . come up and say hello.'

'Go on, Janet.' Mia is looking at her, earnest and doe-eyed.

Colin wins the tug of war and she drops to the seat. Feeling the warmth of his breath against her ear, spit landing in the canal, as he says, 'Say thank you, then get the fuck off.'

Weak-legged, she stands again. Chair scraping against the stone flags. Growing taller as she unfurls her long body. Colin had said it would be fine. That they'd eat and leave. But now the whole room is staring, clapping, waiting. A whistle comes from the far corner, joined by a percussion of cheers. Robbie the orchestral conductor of the symphony. Higher, higher, instruct his hands.

She walks towards the stage.

Blood pumping fiercely in her head. The fascinator's band vice-tight.

Reaching the steps, she carefully ascends.

One, two, three, four. She's up there now.

The actress treading the boards. Lights bright. Outwards, blackened. Robbie comes to her side. Pulls her inwards for a friendly – or is it patronizing? – hug, then guides her towards the lectern. The applause stutters to a halt, a hush permeates the room. Punctuated by a lone cough. She double taps the microphone's foam head. For no reason other than that's what she's seen people do. 'Hello . . . hi . . . thank you very much. That's very kind. Please do bid . . . help the poorly children.' She flicks a smile as Robbie kisses her cheek. Then she turns, makes her escape as the applause ripples once again. Head held downwards as she descends the steps, walks back towards the table. Only glimpsing up briefly to catch Colin nodding at her in approval.

'Let's give it up one last time for Janet Brown. What a brave lady.'

What a brave lady.

Brave.

She stops dead. The room still pelting her with unjust admiration.

You need to be brave, Mummy.

She's turning now. Gliding back towards the stage, towards Robbie's patter. 'Right, so let's get on with the fun stuff, shall we? I bloody love auctions. Always have done, ever since going once . . . going twice.' Giggles ripple through the audience. 'Sorry, people, sorry. I'll get better, I promise.' He's now aware of her return. Climbing the steps onto the stage. 'Oh, hello . . . are you the undercover joke police, Janet? Have you come to arrest me?' Although laughing, his face depicts confusion at her reappearance. His composure waning as she continues towards the front of the stage.

'Sorry, sorry, Robbie.' She gently manoeuvres herself to take possession of the lectern. 'I have something I need to say, please.' Microphone feedback pierces the air, silencing the room once more.

She stares outwards. Aware of them all. Molly, Mia, Colin, whose mouth is open as though catching flies. Robbie remains at her side, the only person still clapping. As though this was supposed to be happening. Was all part of a rehearsed act. 'Fantastic . . . we'd love for you to speak, Janet.'

Hands gripping the wood for support, she dips once again towards the microphone. 'Well, I . . . The thing is, the night of the train crash would have been my daughter's eighteenth birthday. Claire. She's called Claire.' She manages to swallow. 'And it hurts so much, you know . . . well, hopefully you don't know. I hope none of you know.'

Robbie puts his arm around her shoulders. 'Thank you, Janet, and we're so grateful for what you've done. Are you going to bid on me cooking a meal for you? I'd love—'

'Robbie here is a good man, and his wife, Mia . . . they've been so kind. Everyone has been so kind to me, and I hadn't experienced that in such a long time. It was my fault, you see. I was driving the car the night my daughter . . . Claire died. But saving Elizabeth . . . well, I . . . I thought it was some kind of atonement . . . that I'd been forgiven.'

'Janet, you don't have to do this, darling,' Robbie whispers into her ear.

She turns to him. 'I do . . . I do though, Robbie. I'm so

sorry.' Shielding her eyes with her hand, she looks out towards the crowd. 'I'm so sorry, Mia . . . And Colin, I'm sorry . . . Molly, I can see you at the back and, well, you're going to love this.'

A whispered yell from Colin reaches the stage. 'Janet, get down.'

'The thing is, I . . .' She pauses, slow blinks. 'The thing is, I . . . I didn't do it. I didn't save Elizabeth. And I wasn't on the train.'

Time stops. The cathedral, pin-drop silent. Until the murmurings begin. Initially small and unthreatening, escalating in waves.

'Janet . . . what are you talking about?' Robbie smiles towards the audience as though this is a joke in which he's willing to participate, if only she'd let him in on the punchline.

But she clears her throat. Stands taller. Talks louder. 'I'm so sorry. I went to the tracks that night to end my life, you see. I had nothing . . . and then afterwards, I thought I really had saved her. But when I realized I hadn't, I couldn't stop. I . . .' She lifts her head, looks up to the vaulted ceiling. 'I'm sorry, God. Please forgive me.' The volume of the music increases. The Beatles' 'All You Need Is Love' blasts from the speakers. This time remaining at the heightened level. She shouts over the song, over the ensuing commotion. 'And I want to pledge ten thousand pounds to the Children's Hospital.'

Mia stares up at her. Those kind eyes dancing with confused fury. Robbie is also down there now, comforting his wife. Antonia runs around the table, coming to her friend's aid, while Giles downs his wine. And Colin. Next to them all, head in hands.

Janet stands above the chaos. Looking out on what could

be a saloon bar scene in one of Colin's westerns. Then, neatening her jacket, adjusting her fascinator, she raises her chin, pushes back her shoulders and walks off stage, into the fire.

'I don't understand, Janet. Please tell me this is some kind of sick British joke.' Mia is standing, physically turning Janet around to face her.

'I'm so sorry.'

'What? But we invited you into our house . . . into our lives.'

'I know . . . I know you did, and I'm so sorry.'

Any remaining softness in her eyes hardens. 'Well . . . well you're a fucking psycho then, Janet.' Relaxed, bohemian Mia has transformed into a raging bobcat. 'I can't fucking believe you'd—'

'Come on, babe,' says Robbie, attempting to placate his wife. 'She's obviously not well in the . . .'

But Janet no longer hears. Insults cannot penetrate her newly built wall. The play is over. She's done it now. Bending slowly, she puts her arms around Colin, whose face remains hidden in his palms. 'You'll be fine, love,' she whispers in his ear. 'I spoke to Claire, and she's OK. She said she loves you very much.' And as she gently kisses his cheek, her fingers slide into his jacket pocket, wrapping around the cold metal of the keys, which she removes like a sleight-of-hand magician.

Upright once again, the moment breaks. Mia's screeches penetrate her brain. As do Robbie's pleas for his wife to calm. 'She obviously needs help, Mia.'

And with that, Janet turns, starts walking towards the exit. Intercepted by a gleeful Molly rushing towards her. 'Mrs Brown . . . Mrs Brown . . . Janet . . . we can give your side of the story, Mrs Brown.' But Janet continues beyond the requests, the comments, the furies.

Mrs Brown has left the building.

50

The End of the Cul-de-Sac

It's the first time she's sat in the driver's seat of a car in eleven years. Aftershock hitting, her hands shake as she inserts the ignition key, unsure if she can even remember what to do. She goes through the motions of how it used to work. Push back seat, put on seatbelt, adjust mirror, wiggle gearstick, check on Claire in the rear seat, turn over engine.

Are you going to go through with it this time, Mummy?

After counting to three, she engages first gear, turns the steering wheel, edges out of the parking space, and drives.

It's all coming back. Into second, third, fourth. Until eventually, she's pelting down the dual carriageway, Aretha Franklin's 'Think' blaring from the radio at what would ordinarily be a forbidden volume.

Once again, she is Thelma. Smiling at her first foray into bravery. Lost in the now. Unafraid at what she's done. What she's about to do.

Within the fifteen minutes it's taken to arrive at Oakland House, the torrential rain has reappeared. The brief run from car to entrance has caused the feathers of her fascinator to plaster against her forehead like an additional fringe. She presses the intercom with her wet hands, blotched red, and impatiently awaits a reply. While jigging on the spot, her mind returns to the cathedral. Imagining Colin talking to Molly. Or swearing to Mia and Robbie he had no idea. Or frantically searching for her. Or maybe he's already arrived at the parking space, initially believing the car's been stolen, before feeling inside his pocket and realizing. Whichever the scenario, even though it will take him a while to make his way home, she still needs to hurry.

'Hello.' The voice is unfriendly, unrecognizable. She's not that familiar with the night staff.

'Hi, sorry, this is Ernie Griffith's daughter. I think I dropped my keys here earlier and I'm locked out. Please can I just have a quick look?'

There's no response. For a while she's unsure if her request has been ignored, until a frown-faced woman trudges towards the door. Janet realizes they have encountered each other before, although she can't remember her name, having only referred to her as 'that miserable cow'.

'He'll be asleep,' says the woman, folding her arms.

'I know . . . I am so sorry. I'll be quick, I promise.'

After looking her up and down with an air of pity, the woman submits. Janet smiles, over-thanks, before scurrying beside the bluebells towards her dad's room for the very last time.

It's dark when she enters. The smell of human decrepitude somehow more prominent with the absence of light. Hand searching for the switch, she puts on the small lamp so as not to wake him fully with the glare of the main bulb. 'Hey, Dad, it's me, Janet.' She adopts the soft, low tone used to wake a sleeping child.

'Janet,' he repeats flatly.

Activating a button, she slowly raises the mattress so he's more upright, then reaches through the metal safety rails to hold his hand. Mirroring when she was a toddler in her cot. 'I can't stay long, Dad, but . . .' She digs in her bag, stopping the process to remove the irritating fascinator from her head and throwing it on the bedside cabinet. 'I've got something for you.' She pulls out the little Scottie dog, and after stroking its black tufted head, she threads her arm back through the gap. 'This is for you, Dad.' She presses it gently against his chest, guiding his hands to take hold of it himself. Smiling, tears track into the raised corners of her mouth. 'Hey, now listen . . . I've got to go, Dad. But I want you to keep this with you . . . against you. Imagine it's me. And I'll be with you. OK?'

He bends his head forward, attempting to kiss the dog but not quite managing. 'Would you like some cake?'

She laughs. Tastes salt as she swallows. 'I'd bloody love some cake, Dad. But I don't think there is any.' She stands. 'It won't be too long before you join me, and we'll be together again. So don't worry. I'll just be a bit ahead of you, that's all.' She bends over the rail, kisses his cheek. 'I love you. You're the best dad, you know that. See you soon, eh.'

Back at the house, she runs upstairs and quickly changes into a T-shirt, her cosy M&S cardigan, her softest trousers, and ballet pumps. It's important she feels comfortable.

She doesn't enter Claire's room. There's no need anymore. No time. Instead, she goes back downstairs, heads to the sideboard and pulls out an unused stationery pack, a small book of first-class stamps, and Colin's pen from its leatherette case. And as she's about to leave for the kitchen with the items, the phone rings.

She stands still.

Feels the shrill vibrations through her body.

Reaching out, fingers sliding over the shiny plastic, she picks it up, listens. 'Janet? Janet, what the fuck have you done? I swear to God, you fucking stupid cow . . . Come and get me right now. I can't get a cab and just missed a train . . . I'm outside Victoria Station and I'm telling you, Janet—' She drops the receiver back onto its cradle.

As she walks to the kitchen the phone rings again, lessening to a tinkle as she sits at the island, pushing Colin's laptop to the side. Despite her body shuddering with cold, she doesn't warm herself with a cup of tea. Merely tears the pages from the pad and makes her preparations.

Three sheets of paper lie side by side.

Edges must be neat, lined up. The contrast between their off-white and the black mock-granite of the worktop exposes any misalignments.

She's owned this stationery for years. A present from yet another drifted friend. Never retrieved it from the cupboard, never having noticed the delicate goldfinches printed in the right-hand corner. One perched on a branch, the other flying away.

The pen is heavy and cold. Initially nervous about him finding out that she's used it, her brain catches up. Of course, it doesn't matter now. These notes need to represent her properly, and nice ink is important. She'd hate to be remembered by the scrawls of a worn-out biro.

Shuffling further back into the tall stool, she blinks, slow, heavy, and proceeds to write. Though all three notes differ in their content, each one opens with the same words.

I am sorry.

Once finished, she folds the pages neatly into thirds and slides them into envelopes. Writing the corresponding names on the outside. Colin, Nish, and Mia, Robbie and Lizzie. An address and stamp applied to the last two.

She takes Colin's into the lounge and places it on his chair.

As the phone starts ringing once again, she leaves to post the others.

Although the pillar box is only at the end of the cul-de-sac, the downpour soaks her through. Cold bites at her bones, but her chest is no longer constricted by an imaginary whalebone corset. The lead weight she's dragged around for years has evaporated. All anxieties have gone. She is calm, peaceful.

The envelopes slip over the edge of the chipped red slot, followed by the faint sound of their cushioned fall. Pausing, she feels the effects. How she's really going to do it this time.

Running back to the house, she stops to take in Mary's hanging baskets. All the work she puts into them has paid off. They're full and vibrant. And she's sorry she never told her that.

The gravel seems different as she strides up the driveway. Nothing is familiar anymore. The same detachment is felt when she opens the front door, stands in that hallway. It's as if she's already gone.

Systematically, she drifts through the house, filling her bag with things she wants to take with her. And while doing so, she caves and enters Claire's room. Just to make sure. But she's right. Claire's no longer there.

At the dressing table, she picks up the shell necklace, puts it on. 'I'm coming, sweetheart,' she whispers. 'Mummy's coming.'

Back downstairs, she stops at the lounge. Stares into the space. Overwhelmed by hurtling memories, she moves on to the kitchen.

Sitting at the island once again, she pulls the laptop towards her, switches it on, and searches for the Manchester Children's Hospital charity page. From her bag she removes her debit card and makes the donation. Hoping that will at least help save a child.

Standing, she runs her hand across the island's surface. A crumb from the earlier cheese and Branston sandwich sticks to her finger. But it doesn't matter. It never really mattered.

At the back door, she turns the key, pushes it open, and looks out into the garden. It's longer now, barer. The fence, bejewelled with water droplets, glistening beneath the moon.

Outside, the rain has eased but the lawn is sodden. Grass scent bursts with each step. Beyond the fence, there's the rustle of a scurrying animal. She imagines the vixen playing with her cubs on the embankment.

She's at her roses now. Inhaling their lively raspberry perfume. Her nose tipped wet with accidental contact.

Her roses.

The only thing she will miss.

51

The Streets of Pwllheli

She is invisible.

Riding the number twenty-three bus through the streets of Pwllheli. Crisp cotton white top, like scrubs, creased at the shoulder, the XL label cut out because it itched. All humanized by the name badge *JAN.* And as always, a nod to her inner spark, sparkly earrings – stars, bought as a present to herself from the local craft market six weeks ago.

Resting her hot head against the cool window, she smiles while watching the daily rushes. Last days of summer sky poking through pink houses, blue houses, yellow houses. The abundance of colour contrasting with the white wings of seagulls, noisily planning their next swoop.

Sitting up straight, she remembers that in her handbag is the clotted cream fudge brought in by Loretta at the care home. Loretta keeps giving her dad naughty treats. He'd have been sick today if she hadn't confiscated them.

Extracting a small piece, she places it in her mouth. Eyes closing as she allows the delicious burnt sugar to melt on her tongue. She presses the bag shut to remove temptation. Wanting to save herself for ice cream.

The bus slows to a standstill. The pressurized sound of the

opening door echoes. A young hoop-earringed mother in a mini dress, barely an adult herself, struggles to board the bus with a buggy and toddler.

'Are you OK there, love?' Janet calls over.

The young woman nods, smiles. 'She's been playing up all morning.'

'Butter wouldn't melt though, hey? Are you being good for your mummy?'

The mother guides the little girl towards a seat. Dark spirals of hair bouncing over her eyes as she laughs, repeats, 'Mummy.'

Janet feels for the band on her wrist. Pulling it taut from her skin, she holds it there, then slips it over her hand and ties her hair into a ponytail.

As is usual with her new daily routine, she gets off at the earlier stop and walks the extra stretch to the beach. Occasionally stopping to sniff the salt air, eyes fixed on the ocean ahead.

When reaching Annie's Cafe, the loud bell above the door announces her arrival. She hasn't seen this assistant before. A lanky middle-aged man, looking quite uncomfortable in his white uniform and hat. Hesitating about which till key to press as two young boys with ice creams dripping onto their cones impatiently wait for their change. When the transaction is finally complete, she steps forward.

'Hi, can I get a pistachio brown cone with chocolate sauce, please?'

Lanky Man delves into the tub with a scoop and curls the green paste towards him. 'You off to the beach?' Mouth kinking into a smile, his crinkling eyes hold hers long enough to make her turn away.

'Yes, I . . . I'm meeting my daughter there.'

Once outside, she follows the scent of the ocean. Licking the ice cream fast enough to ensure it doesn't melt. Revelling in the sensation of the cold nuttiness tingling on her tongue. After all those years, it's still the best she's ever had.

Consuming the final mouthful over the bin at the edge of the beach, she sucks her fingers free of stickiness and walks over the grassy dunes, which fade into warm sand.

It's already quite busy for a Monday. People desperately grasping those last moments of summer. Though thankfully, they're scattered widely enough to not encroach. For her to have her own space. Unlike the weekends, which are so packed she prefers to stay in her studio flat or visit her dad. Still being able to glimpse the sea from his window.

The same spot is free again. Almost as though it's reserved for her each day. Not too near the water, but close enough to feel connected.

She drops her bags with a thud and kicks off her sandals. And she stands there. Hands on hips, torso rotating. Taking it all in. Never not astonished.

From the tote she pulls out a throw which she billows onto the sand. Sitting on it, she then removes the Tupperware filled with strawberries and chunks of wood-smoked cheddar bought from the farmer's market. Each visit, she leaves with a larger wedge. And as she pulls out the Ambre Solaire, that noise once again catches her by surprise. She removes the phone. Flipping up the spy-like top that will never lose its appeal.

Train tickets booked. You'd better get out your dancing gear. Nxx

Oh goodness. Why does everyone want to make her dance?

Slipping off her top and trousers reveals her swimming costume, swirled with pink roses. Unshackled, she's eager to get up and enter the water, but pauses. There's a bald man in the distance, heading her way. Stomach sinking, she can barely breathe as he nears, until he's close enough to see clearly, and she relaxes, exhales. It's just a man. Just a man.

And so she stands, the fresh air refilling her lungs, and ambles towards the ocean. The epitome of freedom.

The woman walks into the sea.

Foam shocks her toes, knees, stomach, as she pushes against the waves. Waterlogged costume sucked tight to her skin, firing goose-bumps across her arms, extending like wings. Her fingers, the feathers, tickling the water's surface.

Cold bites her chest and face and ears.

Her hair is the last to go under, absorbed like a jellyfish.

She is now submerged.

Cheeks puffed, skin tinged blue, bubbles escaping her nose.

And she waits. Eyes closed. Lungs emptying. Body desperate to rise.

Oh, here she is. Tiny fingers interlacing her own. Long blonde locks floating like seaweed. Tail of iridescent turquoise scales. Her tail tickles across the woman's legs.

'Are you coming, Mummy?'

The woman pulls the little mermaid's head towards hers and kisses it. 'Not today, sweetheart . . . not today.'

Acknowledgements

Firstly, thank you to Pan Macmillan for publishing this book. Especially Wayne Brookes for being such a champion of my work and the most supportive and fun editor a writer could wish for. Alex Saunders and Samantha Fletcher, for all their hard work and being delightful. And the entire team who have been involved in bringing this book into the world – Lucy Hale, Maria Rejt, Hannah Corbett, Rachel Vale, Rory O'Brien, and anyone who I may have missed, or as yet not been introduced to. Also, to the copy-editor Claire Gatzen, and proofreader Amber Burlinson.

Huge thanks of course to my lovely agent, Jo Williamson. For humouring my foibles and boosting my confidence when the well is dry, and always being so approachable and kind.

Immense gratitude to Gavin Towers for all his help and input with this book. Whose brilliant grasp of the English language and critique have made me a better writer. Although, I'm now fearful I can't write books without him. And his sidekick Victoria Towers, for providing such brilliant plot ideas throughout.

Thanks to Sara Naidine Cox for being an excellent plotting soundboard and offering fantastic feedback. And for reading the book almost as many times as I have.

A massive shout out to the D20s, a group created in 2020 for authors who published their debuts in the worst year possible to publish a debut. But a group which turned out to be made up of the most wonderful, generous and supportive people. I can't imagine being on this journey without them. A special thanks to Nikki Smith, Nicola Gill and Frances Quinn for kindly reading an early draft when I was freaking out about it, and for their helpful comments.

Another group that has been a lifeline – the West London Writers' Group. Thank you to Lisa Evans and all the members for allowing me to gatecrash from Manchester via Zoom and be privy to their excellent insight and critique.

Much appreciation to Ali Harper for all her guidance in the early draft stages, and for making me see the potential in the story. Caroline Hulse for being such an honest writing friend and helping me up my game. And Angela Feely for being a great friend and for reading an early draft.

Thank you to Martin Serene, for his unwavering belief in me and all his cheerleading, and Edward Knight, for allowing me freedom from the day job to create novels, and for being such a support during the writing of this book and throughout my life.

To all the Twitter folks who have endured all my book posts and liked and shared. Especially Paul (who didn't want to be fully named), for answering my excessive rail and train accident questions, and being so generous with his time and information, and Graham Bartlett for his help with police procedure queries.

Thank you to all the people who bought and/or read *If I Can't Have You* and/or this book. You are the most important of all.

And finally, a thank you to my cats, Mac (McFly) and Opal. The only company I had while writing this novel during the most difficult couple of years. Always by my side and offering me love and comfort. I miss you, Mac. You'll be forever in my heart.

If you loved *If I Let You Go*
you'll love

If I Can't Have You

BY CHARLOTTE LEVIN

'My name is Constance Little.
This is my love story.
But this isn't the way it was supposed to end.'

After fleeing Manchester for London, Constance attempts to put past tragedies behind her and make a fresh start. When she embarks on a relationship with the new doctor at the medical practice where she works, she's convinced she's finally found the love and security she craves.

Then he ends it.

But if life has taught her anything, it's that if you love someone, you should never let them go. That's why for Constance Little, her obsession is only just beginning . . .

'This is superb . . . and compulsive and disturbing and very well done indeed'
Harriet Tyce, author of *Blood Orange*

Read on for an extract . . .

*

They all stared.

The group of girls cooing over the fruits of their Christmas shopping trip stopped and slapped each other's arms. The Marrieds ceased to argue and held hands. The Reading Man lost his page.

I stood in the Tube carriage among them.

A young suity-booty City Prick and a Sloane Ranger with a leg-kicking infant on her lap parted ways to expose a seat for me. I don't believe out of politeness. Most likely out of fear, confusion. The fact my light-headed sways made it probable I'd fall their way.

Regardless of the reason, I was grateful, and squeezed my white taffeta-engulfed body between them, while attempting to keep the material under control, which proved impossible as the voluminous skirt overlapped onto them both.

The child, who I could now see was a girl, stroked my dress with her saliva-ridden fingers.

'Look at the princess, Mummy.'

The mother buried her spawn's head into her blazer, clearly wishing to God she'd just got a black cab as usual. However, her utter Englishness forced her to smile at me. I returned a semi-version, but was conscious of my front tooth, hanging by a minute thread of gum. It hurt. I closed my mouth and looked down at the blood covering my chest. It was odd how it had taken more to the embroidery than the taffeta.

Raising my head, I could see in the window's distorted reflection Sloaney and City Prick looking at each other behind me in wide-eyed horror. Though they appeared to be strangers, I'd bonded them. Beyond their ghostly images was the huge High Street Kensington sign. It was telling me goodbye. I remember thinking I'd write a book about it one day. *The Fucked Girl on the Train.*

As we pulled away from the station, eyes screwed and faces twisted with calculations as they tried to decipher what had happened. Was I the jilter or the jiltee? But as you know more than anyone, Dr Franco, people are rarely what they appear to be on the surface. The Marrieds may have in fact been illicit lovers, the shopping girls been out on the steal.

Sloaney pressed her Chanel silk scarf against her nose. It was my vomit-laced veil she could smell. I was tempted to turn and tell her everything. Ask for her help. But I couldn't, because I didn't know her. I didn't know anyone anymore.

She wouldn't have given a shit, anyway. Her only concern being I didn't scare Mini Sloane. I smiled at the kid. It cried.

I was already old news. People stopped gawking, or were doing so more subtly at least. They returned to their arguing, laughing, avoiding. Heads magnetically drawn down to phones. But then came the flashes. There was no doubt I'd feature heavily in conversations that day. Photo evidence was needed. I'd be trending on Twitter.

Reading Man glanced up from his book, *The Seven Habits of Highly Effective People.* Perhaps he was wondering which one my habit was. But then that's what I love about London. Rather than staring, why didn't they ask if I was OK? I was not fucking OK, people. In Manchester, I'd have been in someone's house by then, being handed a cup of tea with six sugars and a Blue Riband.

The Tube slowed to a halt. Earls Court. I could see them on the platform waiting for me.

My tooth dropped onto my lap.

*

My darling Samuel,

I've never written a letter before. Love or otherwise.

As much as I've been desperate to tell you how much I miss you, think about you until my head spins, my stomach constricts, it was Dr Franco's suggestion that I write.

You must know I intended to join you. I promise I did. But when it came to it, I couldn't. Not now I have something to stay here for. I'm sorry.

It'll be some time before I see you again and I can't stop fretting that I never got to explain myself fully. Aside from the brief, clumsy attempt you allowed me that day. That terrible day. I can't even steady the pen as I write these words.

Anyway, I've decided to take his advice. Tell you everything. From the beginning. My account of it all. My side. Moment by moment. Hurt by hurt. Though Dr Franco insists there are no such things as beginnings. Only the point from which someone is prepared to start telling their story. So I'll start from our beginning. And I promise it will be the entire truth. Something no one else shall know.

*

I often think about the first time I saw you: when they broke the news that Dr Williams had been killed at the weekend.

Dr Harris and Dr Short had gathered everyone into the surgery waiting room, even menials like myself, and Harris relayed the shocking details. 'You may as well hear it from me as there'll only be speculation.' Mrs Williams. An argument. The car that hit him as he ran across the road after her. How he was still alive when the ambulance arrived. How he was dead before they could get him into it. I heard it all. The terrible events. The intakes of breath. Linda blubbing next to me. I heard. But it was you who held my concentration.

You were the stranger among us. Kept your head down in respect. Or was it embarrassment? Your hair fell forward, draping your face in that way it does, and when you glanced up, your eyes, pale, unsettled, unsettled me.

Dr Harris hadn't been speaking long before Linda felt faint. With difficulty, her being built like a walrus, I eased her round the *Country Life*-covered coffee table and onto the nearest section of modular seating, before fetching her a glass of water as instructed.

You stood in the doorway. I could smell you. Lemons. My

hand brushed yours as I passed, but I didn't acknowledge you or smile, merely walked on as if you were a ghost. On my return, you'd moved further into the room, meaning there was no accidental touch.

As I'm sure you'll remember, Linda's reaction was stronger than everyone else's. Possibly even than that of Mrs Williams. It was always obvious she'd had a thing for him. We – Linda, myself and Alison – were responsible for all the doctors' admin, as you know. But Linda coveted Dr Williams's work. I could identify the glint through her cloggy eyelashes each time she had to go to his office. Poor Linda. The 'speculation' was that Mrs Williams was running away because she'd caught him with another woman. Another woman who wasn't Linda. It wasn't just his wife whom Dr Williams had betrayed.

I remember feeling conscious that I didn't look upset enough. Or shocked. Even the unfriendly agency nurses, or the Ratcheds, as I called them, looked emotional. But I was just as shaken and moved by Dr Williams's fate as everyone else. Only, I'd lost the ability to express. As you know, with me, it's all inside. Always inside.

With Linda now settled into a low-grade wail, Dr Harris brought the meeting to practical matters. As a private practice, there wasn't the option of telling people there was a three-week wait for an appointment. He wasn't prepared to lose money, dead partner or not. That was when he introduced you.

I never liked Dr Harris. Mainly because he was a wanker. But also, the way he'd always point – no, jab – with his party-sausage fingers, onto which he'd somehow managed to stuff a ring. I wondered about the woman who'd screw such a man for a nice house and car. I presumed that was her motive. But I couldn't imagine a house or car spectacular enough.

'Constance, I'll draft a letter for you to send out to all of Dr Williams's patients. You and Alison call anyone due to see him today and give them the choice of rearranging with me or Dr Short for later this week or keeping their appointment and seeing Dr Stevens instead. Please encourage the latter.' He summoned you further into the room. 'This is Dr Stevens from our Harley Street surgery.'

Grateful I could now look at you directly, I contemplated the intricacies of your face. Soaked you in. You were the epitome of posh. Everything I despised. Yet I was conflicted about how attractive I found you.

I observed as you pushed your fine-cotton white shirtsleeves further up your forearms, which you folded, unfolded, folded again before daring to draw the long breath that enabled you to speak. Before the words sounded, you broke into a smile, which forced me to momentarily lower my burning face.

'Hello . . . I'm so sorry about Dr W-Williams. I know he was very much loved by you all. Although it's in the saddest of circumstances I'm here, I look forward to working with everyone and getting to know you . . . and the patients.'

You delivered your stilted lines almost perfectly. Aside from that stutter with his name. Yes, I noticed. But I'm sure no one else did. You'd clearly been practising. I suspect out loud in your full-length bedroom mirror. And I could sense the relief once it had left your lips.

Your micro-speech triggered Linda's sobs to start up again

and gather momentum. Dr Harris instructed Alison to call her a cab, and for me to pack up Dr Williams's personal belongings in his office. I didn't want to. The idea scared me. His stuff. But I nodded subserviently, as I always did.

I remained in the waiting room, prolonging the task. Dr Harris had already left for his office. The Ratcheds had disappeared too. Alison was helping Linda on with her raincoat. You were shaking hands and talking in a low, respectful voice with Dr Short. I wonder, were you suppressing a smile at the contrast with his name and his practically being a giant at six foot seven? It always amused me. Stood next to him, I looked like a tiny child. He treated me like one as well.

Throughout all this you hadn't noticed me once.

To further delay going to Dr Williams's office, I headed to reception to pull up his appointments for the day. Alison was shuffling Linda out of the building, passing the responsibility on to a bemused taxi driver. The front door banged shut.

Minus the crying, all was quiet until Alison made her way to the desk.

'I can't believe he's dead.' She leant over the wooden ledge separating us to deliver her whisper.

I feel bad saying Alison was boring. It sounds cruel. But is something cruel if it's also true? Her boringness was a fact. And why do the boring ones talk the most? To be fair, I only listened to around forty per cent of what she had to say, so she may have been riveting for the other sixty. I even preferred the bitterness of Linda and her banging on about getting another thyroid test while tucking into her fourth KitKat Chunky of the day.

'Yes, it's terrible.' I stared at the computer screen.

'I just can't believe it. Dr Williams. Dead.'

'Yes. It's horrible. But . . . well, people die.' I knew it would show itself. My hands trembled over the keyboard, and I was overcome with queasiness.

'So what do you think happened? All sounds a bit fishy to me.'

'I think it was a terrible accident.'

I hoped she'd interpret my taut words as 'Shut the fuck up', yet she continued. 'Hmm . . . I'm not so sure . . . Isn't death weird, though? You're just not here anymore.'

'Don't you think you'd better call his patients? I'm worried you'll not catch them all in time.'

As she joined me behind the reception desk, I stood for her to sit in my chair, believing she'd finished, but no.

'That Dr Stevens is lovely, isn't he? I mean, I love my Kevin and wouldn't dream of looking at another man, but he's very handsome, isn't he?'

'I didn't notice.'

'So they say it was an accident, but Dr Williams's wife – Margaret, is it? – wasn't she—'

The door buzzed.

'That's Mrs Akeem. You'd better shush now,' I said, before escaping into the back in search of a cardboard box.

On entering Dr Williams's room, I'd expected you to be there, but it was pitch-dark. When I switched on the light, it wasn't only the space that was illuminated, it was death. The silence. His things. Just there. How he'd left them on the Friday.

No doubt you'd be aware of that phenomenon: when someone's belongings become both hugely profound and utterly useless at the same time.

The air, hot and clammy, made my nausea worse and I squeezed my stomach for relief. His Manchester United mug, half full with the tea I'd made him, looked lost. A large crumb – I'd guess from the stash of digestives he kept in his drawer – was stuck to the rim. During my interview, he'd picked up on my Mancunian accent. Presumed I was a Man United fan. I was by default, but I don't care much for football. He told me he went to uni there. Lived in Fallowfield. The opposite end to where I was. He was full of nostalgia, yearnings for my hometown, and I'm certain that's why he hired me. A link to his youth and happier times. Or maybe he just liked me. All I know is it wasn't my experience or qualifications. I'd already felt lucky that I'd managed to immediately land a job pulling pints in a dive pub. But I saw the vacancy for the surgery receptionist in a copy of the *Evening Standard* someone had left on the Tube and applied that night on a drunken whim. When he called to offer me the job, I felt for that moment like I was a real person. Worthy of something good. But I soon remembered that I wasn't at all.

I picked up the wooden-framed picture of him and his family, all smiles, and placed it face down in the box. Next, I reached over for the mug, but as I did, the nausea overwhelmed me, and before I'd had a chance to think, I'd run to the sink and thrown up. And again. And again. When it all seemed over, and I gripped the sides of the cold porcelain, breaths heavy, I felt a hand on my back and jumped.

'Oh God . . . I'm sorry. I didn't mean to frighten you. I was just . . . Are you OK? It's a terrible shock all this, I know.'

I faced you. Aware of how I must have looked, I turned back towards the sink and pulled paper towels from the dispenser to wipe the remnants of vomit from my chin before throwing them in the bin. 'Yes . . . yes, I'm fine. I . . . I don't know what happened. I must have eaten something.'

'Are you sick every morning?'

'No . . . God, no. I'm not pregnant, if that's what you're getting at.'

'No . . . I . . . Well, yes, I was getting at that, but I'm a doctor. That's kind of what I do.'

'Honestly, it's nothing. I've probably just got a bug or something. Dr Franco went home with one on Friday.'

'Dr Franco? I thought it was only Dr Harris and Dr Short?'

'Yes, yes, it is. Dr Franco just rents a room here. He's a psychiatrist or . . . psychologist. I always get confused. He's not here all the time, though. He also works with inpatients at some hospital in Ealing.' A strange look I was unable to interpret washed over your eyes. 'Anyway, Dr Stevens, I'd better . . .' I returned to the desk and picked up the mug.

'Alison, isn't it?'

You have no idea how much that stung. 'Constance.'

'Constance . . . of course, Constance. I'm sorry. I'm terrible with names.'

'Alison's in reception.' I took the mug to the sink and rinsed it along with the residue of my breakfast.

'And the office manager is Linda? Is that right? Is that it, then?'

'Yes. Yes, that's right. Apart from the R—' I stopped myself. 'Carol and Janet, the agency nurses. They're just part-time, covering maternity leave. For Rayowa, the proper nurse.'

'Well, thank you, Constance. For saving me from embarrassing myself again.'

I smiled, then turned back towards you, shaking the mug free of water. 'I'll leave all Dr Williams's medical things here, but let me know if you need anything ordering. Stationery or other supplies.'

'Are you feeling better?'

I dared to look at you properly, but your smile caught me off guard. 'Yes, Dr Stevens. I feel fine now. Thank you . . . I'm just embarrassed, that's all. Your first day as well.'

'Yes, I prefer at least a week to go by before the staff vomit in my presence.'

I would have smiled back had I not been so mortified. Instead, I quickly grabbed the box and said, 'I'll let you settle in, Dr Stevens, shall I? Get the rest later?'

You followed me to the door. Held it open like the gentleman I thought you were. It was then I caught your eyes directly for the first time. They were cold in the paleness of their grey. Unnervingly familiar. I turned my head, focused on a bald patch of carpet until you said, 'You couldn't possibly get me a coffee, could you? White, one sugar. Strong but milky.'